FOUND AND FORGED

IVY ASHER

For Jon Skelly.
All the fucks in this book are for you.
You are missed.

1

"That. Do you smell that rotten cauliflower mixed with sour milk scent?" Torrez asks me, his big hand moving to the small of my back and his chest just brushing against my shoulder as he leans down.

I shake away the distracting, dirty thoughts his proximity sends firing through my synapses, and focus on what he's asking. I take a deep pull and try not to crinkle my nose as the sharp, potent tang of rot filters in.

"Excellent," Torrez coaches as he lowers his voice. "That poker face is a must, especially around other shifters. You don't want to give away what scents you're picking up from them."

I nod and turn my attention back to the lamia we're questioning. His face is set like he can't hear anything we're saying and is simply waiting for the next question.

"Do you promise not to hunt another Sentinel down or assist anyone else who may want to?" I ask, ticking through the list of memorized questions we've been asking the lamia of this nest for the past week.

"I promise that all Sentinels will be safe from me," he replies casually, looking me in the eye as if it will override the new dose of rotten cauliflower and sour milk that's just permeated the air.

I shake my head at the lamia and try not to breathe too deeply of the lie he just tainted the room with. In a flash of movement, I magic a short sword into my palm, and remove his head. Torrez and I both jump back to try and avoid the spray of blood, but it does little to stop us from getting splattered as the lamia's body falls to the floor and then turns to ash.

"Looks like shower number three is in order," I grumble as Torrez pulls a handkerchief from his back pocket and hands it to me to wipe my face.

"Mmmm, I can think of worse ways I could spend my time," Torrez confesses, dropping his voice to that sexy rumble that he knows makes me wet.

The memory of the last shower we took together pops up in my mind, and I lick my lips at the thought of the sexy wrestle fight that occurred and the new cracks we left in the surrounding stone walls. Who knew fucking and fighting for dominance was so hot? Torrez's gaze dips to my mouth, and a knowing smile stretches across his face. I reach up with the handkerchief and clear his face of blood. He shaved this morning, and his face is smooth.

"I want these stubble free cheeks between my thighs," I tell him as I run my fingers over his strong jaw and up into his short black hair.

He steps into me and grabs my hips. "I can arrange that," he tells me.

The scent of warm pine swirls around me, and his brown eyes light up with heat and promises of pleasure.

"I can smell your want, Wolf," I purr seductively as I deactivate the runes of my mate mark. Color blooms around me as my wolf eyes give way to my Sentinel eyes. The smell of Torrez and his desire fades momentarily until he bends down and nips at my shoulder, and my senses are once again filled with the clean woodsy scent that he exudes.

"Mmmm, and I can smell yours, Witch."

A knock on the door pulls my focus away from the feel of Torrez's soft lips on my skin. The door opens, and Bastien walks in. He takes one look at the ash on the floor and nods.

"Another one?" he confirms.

"Yeah, what's that put us at?" I ask as I fight back the shiver that courses through me when Torrez nips at my earlobe.

"Fifty-three. Which is not bad considering how long Adriel was hunting Sentinels and mind-fucking this nest."

I nod in agreement, but I'm momentarily lost in thought. Fifty-three lamia who couldn't be trusted not to continue what Adriel had started. That's one-fifth of the 267 that were in the nest, but it seemed like a lot of them were coming out of the woodwork just in the past couple of days.

"How many are left?" I ask absently.

Torrez's hands drop from my hips, and he reaches back to cup my ass. He's purposely making it harder to focus on what Bastien's saying. I chuckle, amused with his efforts.

"That was the last. We only had twenty left for today, and you two flew through them. You're getting better," Bastien compliments me as he taps his nose.

I smile at the praise and release a tension-filled exhale. I'm glad to be done with trying to suss out who in this nest is still a threat.

"The sisters are ready whenever you are to go through what they're packing for you," Bastien adds and leans against the doorway, pushing his long dark brown waves away from his face.

I run my hungry gaze over his tall chiseled body. "I need to shower first, and then we can get all of that squared away."

"Dibs!" Bastien calls out, his hazel eyes eager and sparkling with humor.

Torrez's head snaps up, and he levels a glare at a now smirking Bastien.

"You snooze, you lose, Wolf," Bastien taunts, and Torrez throws his head back and releases an irritated growl.

I snicker at the exchange, and Bastien gives me a cocky wink that sends a zap of lust straight to my clit.

"Don't you start, Witch," Torrez jokes, and I throw up my hands, palms out, in a gesture of innocence.

"Hey, it beats roshambo," I declare.

"I liked that better. I keep forgetting we changed the rules," Torrez whines, and I laugh even harder.

"You liked that better because you won more," Bastien playfully accuses. "And I don't care what you say, I still think it's because you can somehow smell what we choose before we throw it."

Torrez grins and shakes his head. "Pshhh, I'm just that good," he announces cockily and then proceeds to pull his hand from my ass to make the universal sign for scissors and then blows on it.

I slap his chest on a laugh and move out of his personal space. I step over the pile of ash and reach for Bastien's outstretched hand.

"You've done me wrong, bro," Torrez jokes.

"Stop giving me those puppy dog eyes," Bastien scolds and then guffaws when Torrez pokes out his lower lip. "Fair is fair," Bastien defends.

"Heartless," Torrez calls out and grabs his chest dramatically. "At least let me watch if you won't let me play."

My head snaps to Torrez, shocked. His smile grows even wider.

"You know you'd like it," he teases and gives me a brow waggle.

I shrug because there's no way I could honestly deny that.

TGV strikes again.

Like they can hear that thought, Torrez and Bastien both laugh. Or maybe it's my lack of denial that they find so amusing. Bastien pulls me out of the ash-tainted room, and Torrez follows closely on our heels like the excited puppy he is. We pass a group of lamia in the hall, and they give us a wide berth.

It bothers me that a lot of the nest still acts like we're a threat and deserving of their fear. I suppose the ash dusting my clothes right now isn't exactly the most comforting sight to them, but we're not just killing all willy-nilly. We'll be leaving any day now, and we need to make sure this nest isn't a threat to us or the remaining lamia anymore before we go.

Surprisingly, the lamia have taken to the members of the Volkov shifter pack that fought with us like they're family. I don't know if it's a language thing or if their camaraderie finds its foundation in a mutual dislike for casters and paladin. Whatever the reason, they've welcomed each other with open arms, and the Volkov pack has pledged to protect the nest after the rest of us are gone.

It's one less thing I need to worry about or be responsible for, and I'm grateful for the alpha, Fedor—even though he hasn't let up with the Brun love. I swear, if I have to hear him gloat about how amazing Brun is one more time, I'm going to lose it. At first he was just talking her up to Torrez, but now he sings her praises to all my Chosen. *Fucking questionable taste, if you ask me.*

"Vinna," echoes up the hall from behind us, and I turn to find Becket and Enoch.

"Any luck?" I call out as they make their way closer.

They both slow and shake their heads. I let out a frustrated huff.

"We searched his quarters, the library, and anywhere else it would make sense for a crazy leech to keep books about Sentinels, but we can't find anything," Becket explains, and I look around the cave-hallway as if clues are written on the walls.

"He could have been lying, Vinna," Enoch offers with a shrug.

"Maybe," I finally admit. "I don't know why he would; he seemed to know so much."

"He was probably just fucking with you. His brother was Chosen, so he could have learned a lot from him. We don't know at what point Adriel went off the rails. He could have been getting the inside scoop for ages," Becket declares.

As much as I hate it, it's time I accept that he's probably right. There's no point stressing over what are probably non-existent books.

"This cave is massive. It would probably take a year to search every nook and cranny to be sure one way or the other. You'll be around Sentinels soon. I'm sure they can teach you more than any book Adriel might have had hidden somewhere in this place," Enoch tells me with a comforting smile.

Bastien rubs small circles on the back of my hand with his thumb, and nerves burst to life in my stomach at the thought of other Sentinels.

"Speaking of, when are we heading out?" Becket inquires.

Bastien's grip tightens on mine, but he thankfully keeps his mouth shut. If I have to dive back into the argument of why Enoch and his coven should come with us to Sentinel City, I'm going to punch him and then revoke his *dibs* for a month. Maybe not that last part, but definitely the punching will happen.

"We finished with the last of the interviews today, so as soon as everyone is packed and ready to go, we can head out. I'll check with Sorik and let you guys know."

Becket and Enoch both give me nods and head back in the direction they came from. Bastien tugs at my hand to get me moving, and I shove away my disappointment at not finding any Sentinel instruction manuals and remind myself of what Bastien and I were just headed off to do.

I wonder if Torrez really will just watch or if he'll join in on the fun?

"Wolf," Knox calls out as we turn down the hallway that leads to our room.

We all groan simultaneously and turn to find Knox jogging up the hallway.

Damn, he's gorgeous.

"Some Brun chick is asking for you. Something about needing help getting patrols organized," Knox explains, and I growl.

Torrez laughs, and I round on him. "Do I need to kick her ass again? What's her deal anyway?"

Torrez throws his hands up in a placating gesture. "She's who Fedor sent. The quicker we get her sorted, the faster we can all leave," he reminds me.

"Get *her* sorted? Should have let me rip off her head when I had the chance," I grumble and move my face away from Torrez when he tries to land an amused kiss on the tip of my nose.

"Let her know I'll be down to find her in an hour or..." He looks at me. "Make that two hours. I'll come track her down when I'm done," Torrez instructs, and my greedy vagina gives a greedy clench of excited anticipation.

"Will do," Knox replies. "Where are you guys off to?" he asks casually, but the glint in his eye gives him away.

"To fuck," Bastien announces and starts pulling me down the hallway again.

I laugh.

"Dibs on the next free moment she has," Knox shouts after us.

Bastien stops and rolls his eyes. "You can't call dibs on possible future opportunities; you have to be there in the moment to call it. Those are the rules," Bastien explains, exasperated.

"Don't know why we couldn't just stick to rock-paper-scissors," Knox grumbles. "No complicated rules for that one."

Torrez puts his fist out toward Knox. "Right! That's what I was just saying," he declares as Knox fist bumps him.

"Pretty sure you were cheating though," Knox tells Torrez, and now Bastien puts his fist out to Knox, ready for his fist bump.

I chuckle and shake my head at the bro-out that's happening right now. I squeak in surprise when Bastien slaps my ass suddenly and continues down the hallway. Knox follows us, and I laugh at the confused look Bastien gives him.

"What are you doing?" he asks Knox as he continues to follow us to our room.

"You said I had to be there in the moment to call dibs on the next opportunity. I'm coming so I can call dibs on the next opportunity."

Knox announces this like Bastien is an idiot for not making the connection.

"Well played," Bastien states with a head nod, and then we're all back to rushing down the hallway.

"Run faster," Torrez calls out. "Someone else will come

interrupt any second now, we need to mooove." Torrez vocalizes the last word like some SWAT team commander on TV, and we all pick up the pace.

Bastien throws the door to the room open and then stops suddenly, forcing the rest of us behind him to slam into his broad back.

"What the hell—" I start but stop when the sisters' smiling faces all look up from the backpacks they're currently packing.

"Perfect timing," Birdie beams, and she flits over and extracts me from the muscle sandwich I was just enjoying. "We need to steal you for a bit, Vinna, so we can pick out the items you think will work best for this trip, and then we'll get your pack finished and loaded up."

I look back longingly over my shoulder at the guys, and Lila giggles.

"There will be plenty of time for ravaging later, Love. The sooner we get this done, the better," she consoles me, and thank fuck I don't blush, because the way she says *ravaging* would have done the trick otherwise.

"You three are as bad as the Captain," Knox accuses and then dives out the door to avoid the hiking boot Adelaide throws at him with a laugh.

"These packs are ready to go," Birdie announces, pointing to four packs lined up against the wall by the door. "Would you boys use those strong muscles Vinna is always going on about, and carry those up to the vehicles?" Birdie bats her eyelashes at Torrez and Bastien, and they fold like cardboard.

"The *dibs* still counts!" Bastien declares as he picks up two packs and walks over to me. He kisses me soundly and then bends down a little to look me in the eyes. "Paused only," he imparts as he turns and heads for the door.

"Just paused," I shout at his back as he disappears out of the room.

Torrez chuckles and shakes his head. "Greedy, greedy, greedy," he heckles as he grabs the two other packs and turns to follow Bastien out the door.

"TGV forevaaaahhh," I call behind him and then laugh when I hear his guffaw echo back down the hallway and into the room.

"You have excellent taste, I must say," Adelaide tells me and then snaps a shirt at my butt. I squeak in protest and scramble away from her when it looks like she's going to do it again. "That Torrez and Siah are just the sweetest, and you know how we feel about *the boys*," she tells me as she adds her shirt weapon into the kind of pack hard-core back-packers wear.

"Is it their sweet personalities that you're a fan of or their sweet heinies that have been catching your eye?" I tease and chuck a sock at Adelaide. "Don't think I haven't seen that dreamy look in your eye as you ogle Siah."

She gasps in faux outrage.

"Oh yes, I know the one, it's that look that's normally only reserved for a delicious cinnamon roll and a cup of creamy chai," Lila calls her sister out, and I crack up.

"Like I said, I was simply admiring Vinna's *excellent* taste," Adelaide defends, her giggle ruining the innocent look she's going for. "And it wasn't me making goo-goo eyes at that shifter fellow who carried supplies into the kitchen the other day, was it?" Adelaide casually throws out there, knowing I'll embrace my inner Mave and pounce on it like a piranha.

"Ooohhh, who was it?" I press, taking the bait with not an ounce of shame.

"I believe his name is Artemi," Birdie offers, getting in on the action.

Lila full on blushes, and I have to fight to keep from cracking up. "Hold on," I order as I dive onto the bed and get myself situated comfortably. I lean back against the headboard and then adjust the pillow at the small of my back. "Okay, ready," I announce and fix my excited smile on Lila. "Tell me everything!"

2

I knock on the door lightly, a heaviness in my chest doing its best to chase off the light and happy the sisters just deposited there. I know the circumstances suck behind their arrival, but I'm so glad the sisters are here. They ground and lighten everyone in a way that only they are capable of doing. I listen for an answer and then knock harder when one doesn't come.

"Come in," Sorik finally calls from the other side of the closed door.

I turn the knob and attempt to calm the whirling of my insides as I walk in to find Sorik sitting next to Vaughn.

"Am I interrupting?" I ask hesitantly, taking in the book Sorik has in his hands and then studying Sorik himself. His long blond hair is pulled back, and he has a hint of stubble on his face. He's still rocking that Viking vibe, but I can tell things are weighing heavily on him.

"Not at all," Sorik reassures me as he closes the novel and offers me a warm smile.

I give him one back and pull up a seat next to Vaughn.

"No chaperones today?" Sorik teases, and I chuckle. "I'm aghast that they've let you out of their sight."

"The sisters chased them all away so we could pack and girl talk," I offer.

"Ah yes, the sisters are formidable opponents," Sorik proclaims, his eyes filled with respect and humor.

"That they are," I agree with a laugh. "What are you guys reading today?"

"We were just diving into *Intensity* by Dean Koontz," Sorik tells me as he holds up the book so I can examine the cover.

"I haven't read that one yet, is it good?" I ask awkwardly, avoiding the deeper topics that are sitting in my throat as though I've taken too big of a bite of them and I now need water to help me swallow everything down.

"It's excellent, one of my favorite reads and one I come back to time and time again," Sorik declares, as he looks down at the book in his lap fondly. "I'll lend it to you as soon as we're done with it."

I widen my eyes in exaggerated surprise. "I'm honored you would trust me with such a treasure."

He grins. "Obviously, if anything happens to it, I'll come for you."

"Obviously," I agree with an amused smile.

I wasn't sure about Sorik before, but in the past week, I've gotten the chance to know him better. He's kind and funny, and he has this way about him that I find soothing. If I'd grown up the way some of the guys have, Sorik would be a father to me. At first I didn't know how I felt about that, but the more I interact with him and observe him, the more I see how incredible it would have been to have him growing up. We both fall into a comfortable silence as I take in the quiet third party to our banter, Vaughn.

He sits statue-still in the chair, just waiting to be instructed. He's frozen, in some state of limbo, action and inaction radiating from every cell. I've gotten past my hope that at some point he'll just turn to me, make eye contact and see the world again...see me. I'm familiar with this version of him now. It's simultaneously a strange comfort and a fucked up thing that all of this now feels normal.

I don't bother asking if anything has changed; it's clear that it hasn't, or we wouldn't be sitting here.

"The sisters just finished packing, and Torrez is meeting with Brun to get whatever she needs squared away before we leave," I tell Sorik in an effort to chase my sudden sadness away. I try—and fail—at not sounding like a petulant child.

Fucking Brun.

Sorik gives me a knowing smile, and then his eyes move from me to my dad, his amusement evaporating.

"Have you decided what you think we should do with your father?" Sorik asks me, like somehow I'm the deciding factor in all of this.

I appreciate his efforts to include me and to help me feel like I have a say, but Sorik knows Vaughn better than I do. He should really just consult himself.

"I already told you, I don't think I'm the best person to make decisions for him..."

"Who better to make decisions than his child?" Sorik once again lovingly argues.

I release a frustrated huff and run my fingers through my hair. "Sorik, stop doing that...please," I beg. "It just makes me feel like shit. I know he's my dad, but I don't know him. I don't know how to feel about any of this. One minute I'm happy he's even here, and the next I feel like I'm in fucking mourning. The only person in this room who knew him well enough to decide what he'd want, is you, and you know it. Stop putting the weight of his future on my shoulders, it's too much."

Sorik's gaze fills with understanding and sympathy, but it's also wrapped up in resolve.

"You will get to know him, Vinna—"

"You don't know that," I sigh. "He might never wake up; this could be all there is for him...for me...despite your hope otherwise."

"Even if this is all there is, I will help you get to know him," he counters, and I push out of my seat and start to pace, my troubles nipping at my heels relentlessly with each step. We're quiet for a long time as I try to work things out, and Sorik silently lends his support as I move restlessly around the room.

"It doesn't feel right to leave him with Aydin and Evrin," I finally admit after I've circulated around the space several times. "I know the sisters said they'd take care of him, but I just don't like the idea of him..." I trail off, not sure what I'm trying to say.

"Being so far away?" Sorik provides.

I shrug.

"I just don't know how he's going to come with us or what we'll even be walking into," I confess.

"But we'd be there to watch his back, to make sure he was okay," Sorik supplies.

"We would," I agree. "But if things go bad?"

"Vinna, you're a Sentinel requesting access to a city of Sentinels. What exactly do you think is going to go wrong?"

I give Sorik my best *come the fuck on* look and make another rotation around the room. "I honestly have no idea. The Sentinels have stayed in hiding all this time for a reason. Who's to say how they'll feel about me knocking on the door and asking *what's for dinner*."

Sorik gives an amused snort and rubs a hand over his face. He's been like a rock of positivity and support over the past week, but I don't miss the exhaustion and worry in that simple gesture.

"I'm sure it will be fine," I offer dismissively, beating Sorik to the positive comment I can sense sitting on the tip of his tongue.

He smiles, but it doesn't quite meet his eyes.

"Then it's settled," Sorik agrees, thankfully changing the subject. "Vaughn stays with us." His eyes fill with pride, but I turn away from it, not wanting it to find purchase in me.

If he only knew how fucking conflicted I am about all of this, he'd probably think I'm the shittiest daughter ever.

"So, walk me through the plan again," I ask so I don't have to look too hard at my feelings of inadequacy or at just how overwhelmed I am by all of this.

"We'll drive as far as we can, which should take a couple of days, and then we have maybe a couple week's worth of camping and hiking ahead of us. I turned back when I felt the barrier, but it seemed that the heart of the settlement was in a valley surrounded by mountains."

I nod and catalogue everything he tells me. I try to picture what he's describing, but I can't quite wrap my mind around it. I run my gaze over Vaughn's face. His eyes are distant and fixed but the same color as mine. Sorik must have trimmed his dark hair, because it's shoulder-length now and looks healthy and shiny again.

"What do you think...dad?"

The word *dad* still feels foreign in my mouth, but I'm trying to say it more often so it doesn't sound so stiff and weird. I know he's not going to answer. I'm not sure why I even ask, but it feels important to me not to treat him like he isn't here, like he doesn't have an opinion. I nod my head as if he just voiced his agreement and clap my hands together once.

"Okay, let's do this."

* * *

Evrin pulls me in for a tight hug, and it makes me laugh.

"You're getting good at that," I tease and crack up even more at the blush that sneaks up his neck as I pull away. "Looks like you're finally ready for that *I love hugs* t-shirt I've been saving for you."

Evrin narrows his eyes at me. "Give me that shirt and I'll burn it," he threatens, the corners of his lips fighting not to break into a smile.

"Pshhh," I say, waving the threat off. "You know you'll wear it; cuddle it when you miss me and all that shit."

Evrin cracks up and shakes his head at me. It's nice to hear his laugh again. Everyone has been grieving the loss of Keegan and Lachlan, but it's been especially hard on Aydin and Evrin. It's nice to see some lightness and cheer in his eyes.

"See, that wasn't a denial," I point out as I move down the line of goodbyes.

Aydin is standing there waiting his turn as the guys and I all work our way down the line of loved ones, hugging and saying reassuring shit that none of us knows if it's true.

"You sure we shouldn't come with you?" Aydin asks me for the fiftieth time as he pulls me in for a bone crushing hug that lifts me off the ground and helps fortify my soul.

"Pretty sure you're going to have your hands full with Silva and the Elders Council," I remind him, and he cringes at my words.

Everyone, including the twins, has agreed that Silva needs to be turned in for torturing lamia. No one is really sure what the elders will do, but it'll be up to them to decide. Silva is notably absent from the hug assembly line. He's been confined to a room with twenty-four-hour guards. The

17

twins said their goodbyes earlier, but I haven't had a chance to ask them how it went.

"We'll call as soon as we can, let you know what's going on," I tell Aydin in an effort to reassure him.

"You better, Little Badass. We'll be nervous wrecks until we know all of you are okay," Aydin warns me as he sets me gently back on my feet.

"Love you, big guy," I tell him, and we both get a little choked up.

I remind myself that this is not goodbye forever, just for now. I shake off the cloak of melancholy that just fitted itself to my shoulders and move down the line to the sisters.

"You will call us if you need anything," Birdie orders, and I nod and pull her tightly against me.

I want to tell her thank you for seeing me and loving me just as I am, but it feels too much like a permanent goodbye, and I don't want that. I'm passed on to Lila who cups my face and looks into my eyes with such adoration and affection that I start to well up. "We are proud of you, and we can't wait to have you back home where you will never be allowed out of our sight ever again."

I laugh and thank her with my eyes for lightening the heavy emotions floating through me. Adelaide is last in line and pulls me down to her and wraps me up in a fierce hug.

"You take care of them, okay?" she tells me and nods toward everyone loading up in the SUVs.

"With my life," I vow to her, and she squeezes me even tighter.

"We love you, sweet Vinna. You come home to us, you hear me?"

I nod and wipe at a tear that's making a run for it down my cheek. I look back down the line filled with people who mean more to me than I have words for. I never thought that this would be my life, that these people would feel like the lifeline that they are. But as I look at them, lined up, radiating love and support, I can't comprehend how I got so lucky. I didn't realize how much I was missing before Lachlan and the paladin threw me into this world. I now know what the word *family* should look like, and it looks like them.

Adelaide lets go, and I step back, my heart full to almost bursting. I've been nervous about what will happen with the Sentinels, but it suddenly seems like no big deal. Whatever goes down in the next couple of weeks, I have a family to come home to, and love and friendship guarding me every step of the way. In this moment I know, without any shadow of doubt, that it will all be okay.

Peace sweeps through my body, and I give one last wave before climbing into the back seat of the SUV and closing the door behind me. Ryker looks back at me from the driver's seat.

"Ready?" he asks me, his gaze filled with excitement and strength.

"I am now," I reassure him, and he turns to start the car.

Valen snakes an arm around my back and pulls me into his side.

"Sentinel City, here we come," Knox shouts out, and the rest of us hoot and holler our agreement as we pull away and our journey begins.

3

S abin turns down the volume to Fivefold's "Lost Within." The brakes squeak as we slow down, the sound amplified by the quiet in the car.

"Looks like this is the end of the road," he announces, and I open my eyes and sit up from where I was dozing on Siah's shoulder. Knox sits up from where he was lying in my lap, and I already start to miss the calm that's been floating around the car until now.

Dust from the dirt road we've been traveling on for most of the day plumes around us as we come to a stop next to the other vehicle. We all sit there for a minute looking around at the short yellowing wild grass and the small hills in the distance that flow into baby mountains.

"Looks a bit like home, only drier and a little flatter maybe," Valen offers, and a couple of the guys nod their agreement.

Knox opens the door, and crisp air sneaks in to chase away the heat. It's not insanely cold, but I can imagine the temperatures will drop the higher we hike. We climb out of the SUV we've been crammed into for the past couple of days. Moans and groans sound off all around as we all stretch out our limbs and revel in the feel of room to move around. Heat sinks into my core as the guys' groans start sounding way too close to some of the noises they make when they come, and I smile and look up to the sky as I stretch my back.

I straighten up, and my gaze lands on Torrez and the knowing grin he's now wearing. I shrug shamelessly, and he chuckles.

"Dibs," Sabin shouts out, and we all turn to him.

"What are you calling dibs on?" Siah asks, voicing the confusion that I'm also feeling.

Sabin looks around. "Um, shit, I don't know. Whenever Torrez chuckles like that, I've just been calling dibs. It's his *I smell my horny mate* laugh."

I crack the fuck up. "You've been capitalizing on his chuckle," I ask as I lean over and laugh my ass off.

Torrez shakes his head, his features filled with surprise. "Sneaky Wizard."

Knox turns to Ryker, his gaze almost offended. "Fuck, why didn't we think of that?"

The question sends me into a whole new fit of laughter that has me wiping away tears. "You guys are out of control," I chide with a smile and then squeal when someone slaps my ass.

I turn to find Valen and the cheeky smile he has plastered onto his face. "We can't help it if we all just want to spend more time with you."

"Hey, I'm not complaining," I explain and rub at my stinging ass cheek. "But that doesn't make any of you less ridiculous," I finish.

"Eh, you know you love it," Knox announces as he approaches me. He pulls lightly on the end of my hair until I tilt my head back far enough that he can lean down and kiss me.

"True," I admit happily against his lips and then smile as a groan fills the air.

"Can you all keep the PDA on lock? Not everyone wants to live that porn life as much as you all seem to want to," Kallan gripes as he climbs out of the other SUV and stretches.

Knox's response is to start making loud obscene noises which makes me laugh more and has Kallan rolling his eyes.

"I'll remember you feel that way when you find a girl that you want to be all over all of the time," Becket taunts his coven mate, and Kallan shakes his head.

"At this rate, that might never happen," Kallan confesses on a grumble and then heads to open the back of the car and pull his pack out.

I leave his words hanging in the air like something fragile I know I shouldn't touch, at least not yet. I need to talk to him and Enoch, clear things up, but I don't know how to approach it with them. Hiking to Sentinel City is probably not the best place to do it, especially not with all the other guys around. There's a lot of unfinished shit just hanging in the air for everyone to try and avoid. We're all distracted by this new goal, this new mission, but I wonder how long the distraction will last. Reality is bound to come crashing down at any minute, and it's leaving me antsy and unsure of how things will land and survive the fall.

I give Knox one last peck and then grab my bag out of the back of the car. We all gear up and wait for Sorik to do the same. Nash moves to stand next to me, and Bastien who's standing on my other side stiffens. I side eye Nash for a second. I suspect that he does this just to get a rise out of my Chosen. I've never quite known where I stand with him, and that's certainly not changed, but he's becoming an interesting puzzle to try and piece together.

"We'll hike until we find a good spot to stop for the

night. It isn't too steep, but if any of you need to stop for any reason, just let the people at the front know," Sorik announces, and we all nod and voice our agreement. "I didn't run into any scouts or anything before, but that doesn't mean we might not now. Our traveling party is a bit more conspicuous, so if you see anything or *feel* anything out of the ordinary, call it out."

With that, Sorik turns and starts to make his way away from the cars and out into the hills. Siah moves to walk with him but suddenly stops and looks back at me like he's confused.

"I think he just remembered he has a mate who might want him by her side instead of by his friend's side," Nash informs me, clearly having watched the same reaction I just saw.

I smile warmly at Siah and try to communicate silently that it's fine if he hangs with Sorik. I know their friendship goes way back, and I'm not bothered by it. Fact is, I don't always know how to manage this pack of Chosen. I worry a lot about whether they are all getting what they need. Nurturing relationships with each of them is no joke, and we're all working hard at this. I'm lucky that they are all figuring each other out and building those bonds as well. They all get along, which means things are *so far, so good,* on the mate front.

Enoch makes his way over to Nash, and I find myself watching my Chosen to see if his proximity to me is going to be a problem. Knox and a few others are watching him, but they're keeping their mouths closed. They've been doing this since I put my foot down about them coming with us. It's obvious that they still aren't a fan of Enoch or his coven being here, but they aren't being vocal about it, and they aren't starting shit.

I'm not sure if it was the way the magic reacted when

Siah joined our bond, and Enoch and his crew were unaffected other than a little glowing, or if they've just had more time to process and deal with the other coven's presence and can bite their tongues better. Either way, I'll take it, regardless of how much I'm expecting the ceasefire to crumble and the bullshit to start again.

"So how are you holding up?" Nash asks me as we all fall into place behind Sorik, Siah, and Vaughn.

I shrug and tuck my thumbs into the pack straps on my shoulders. "Good," I answer casually.

Nash snorts, and I turn to watch his face, my eyebrows dipping down in question.

"What? You've decided I'm not good?" I challenge as he shakes his head and runs his gaze over my face.

"I'm not deciding anything. I just don't see how you're good with anything that's going on."

"What would you prefer I be then?" I snark.

Nash releases a sigh. "I don't know. It's just that you thought you were the last of your kind, and yet we're hiking to a city full of Sentinels. Your uncle died. Your mates' uncle hates you. He's also headed back to Solace to stand trial for crimes he committed to find his sister and your father, one of who happens to be traveling with us on this quest that just might get us all killed. And you're just...good."

I give a humorless snort at his wrap up of things. "I've felt cautious, unsure, sad, relieved, hesitant, excited and a ton of other shit. Right now, this is an adventure, and I'm surrounded by people I love and care about, so I'm...good."

I take a moment to study Nash. I've been busy with the sisters, the logistics of this mission, my dad, my mates, the lamia. I haven't made time to check in with Nash and his coven. I take in the tightness around his eyes and the flattening of his lips and realize that his question about how I'm feeling is more about him than it is about me.

"How are *you*?" I ask, and I watch his brow furrow in confusion.

"I'm fucking nervous," he admits.

I give him a reassuring smile and a soft shoulder bump with my shoulder. We step around an old log sitting in the middle of the path we're on.

"Anything I can do to help you feel less nervous?" I offer and then give him the space to think about it.

"What do you do when you feel fucked up and restless?" he asks me.

I think about it for a minute. "I usually need to do something physical: run, fight, get stabby with something."

Nash laughs, and a few other chuckles sound off around the group.

"We're all unsure of what's going to go down," Bastien surprises me by saying. "But you're not alone. We'll all deal with whatever happens together."

I don't fight the smile that creeps over my face as I watch Bastien comfort someone he doesn't even like. Nash nods his head at Bastien's declaration, and I can see his shoulders relax a little. I'm pretty sure I hear Becket mumble something about "afterschool special bullshit," but I ignore it and instead bask in my mate's awesomeness.

"I'm sure we'll all run the gamut of feels as we get closer to Sentinel City. Just know we're here if you need to get the nerves or whatever out of your system," I offer. "Fuck knows, I'll probably need the same."

Nash studies my face as my words sit in the air between us.

"I mean, I'm good now, but that could turn into *freaking the fuck out* at any minute," I admit, and Nash snorts out a laugh.

He gives me a small smile, the *thanks* clear in his eyes. Nash looks away, his expression contemplative, and I leave him to his thoughts. I reach out and lace my fingers with Bastien's. He's so hot when he's being all sensitive and shit.

Torrez's chuckle fills the silence, and Sabin, Knox, Ryker and Bastien all suddenly shout *dibs* at the same time.

"You pricks can't steal my thing!" Sabin exclaims.

"Our thing now, bro," Knox teases and dodges the punch Sabin aims for his arm.

"Never telling you fools anything again," Sabin declares, but the amused smile fighting to take over his face sells him out. "First one to the top of the hill sleeps in Vinna's tent tonight!" he suddenly declares and then books it.

Two seconds later I'm left in a cloud of dust and man grunts, laughing my ass off. Maybe my vagina *is* more magical than I thought it was. Who knew?

4

"This is bullshit," Knox announces once again as I throw my pack in my tent.

I remind myself to take a deep breath and not tackle him and put him in a choke hold until he stops sulking.

"Technically, Sabin never specified who could or couldn't win, so it's fair play regardless of whether or not you think it's bullshit," Kallan retorts while zipping up the door to his and Becket's tent after throwing his bag in it.

Enoch sets his bag next to mine, and I can feel the eye daggers being chucked at him from all angles.

"A tie is a tie," Enoch once again voices as he watches Knox add his bag to the tent too. "We both won, so we both sleep in here tonight," Enoch declares, zipping up the closure to my tent, one of his eyebrows rising in challenge.

"As much fun as it is listening to the nonstop bickering about shit I just don't give a fuck about, I'm getting hangry," I announce and then go in search of the pack that has snacks and other provisions stuffed in it.

My legs feel a little jelly like, and my exhaustion is playing a key role in my pissy emotions. Well, that and the drama that started when Enoch and Knox reached what was considered the *top of the hill* at exactly the same time. The fragile acceptance between my Chosen and my Shields crumbled to dust, and every old wound that ever existed between these two groups broke open.

The problem is that I understand both sides of the arguments, but we need to figure out how to work together and get over all this bullshit. I just wish I had some idea how to make that happen.

"Anything I can help you with, mate?" Siah asks me with a cheeky smile and understanding in his eyes as I growl at a granola bar that's refusing to let me open it.

I release a hollow chuckle. "Tell me more about how compulsion works," I joke. "Because I could really go for some *forcing them to get along and work together* until all of this is over."

He chuckles and shakes his head as he looks over his shoulder at a new argument that's just started between Nash and Ryker. "Yeah, unfortunately I'm not that good," he admits, taking the bastard unopened granola bar from my hands and opening it in one try.

He hands the stubborn sustenance back to me, but before I can take a bite, the argument going on behind me gets even louder. I sigh and blink through the eye twitch I can feel starting up.

"I don't think any lamia is that good," Siah observes, and I cringe as the name calling and posturing starts.

The short brittle grass and tall trees surrounding our camp site for the night suddenly feel like they're closing in, and the yelling is not fucking helping.

"Enough!" I bellow, the frustrated declaration bouncing around the trees and surging back at me.

Enoch and Knox are squaring off with each other at this point, oblivious to how *over* all of this I am. I send a pulse of

Sentinel magic out and watch as it slams violently into both of them, forcing them to stumble back away from each other. That finally does the job of catching their attention, and they both turn to me, anger and confusion in their gazes.

"Follow me," I command and then turn and trudge away from camp before anyone can say anything.

I can tell by the sound of crunching brush behind me that more than Enoch and Knox are following, which is good. It's time for everyone to get this shit out of their system. I find a clearing big enough for what I need and stop in the middle of it. I turn around and catch frustrated looks from both my Chosen and Shields, along with a healthy dose of curiosity staring back at me.

"We have no idea what we're walking into, but even if we're greeted by a bunch of tree hugging Sentinel hippies, all of you have to cut this shit out," I demand as frustration boils over inside of me and stains everything. "I have tried to give you time and understanding in hopes that, as grown ass males, you could work this bullshit out. But obviously that is not going to happen. So it's time to switch shit up." I gesture at the space around me. "Fight," I declare and then step back to give them the space to do just that.

"What?" Valen asks me at the same time Torrez gives an amused holler of approval and rubs his hands together eagerly.

I turn back to Valen. "Fight it out. Beat the shit out of each other. Fuck shit up. I honestly don't care anymore, but whatever it is that's fueling the hate and mistrust, get it the fuck out so we can move the fuck on."

Valen raises his eyebrows.

"Don't give me that look. You all have been itching to do this since our first training session. So go for it. I refuse to be the referee between you anymore." I look at each of my

Chosen. "They are my Shields. Like it or not, we're all connected. You can see that as a bad thing if you want, there's nothing I can do about that. But I'm tired of you trying to make *me* see it as a bad thing."

I shake my head and look at Becket, Kallan, Nash and Enoch in turn. "I think everything happens for a reason. I trust my magic and each of you. So beat each other bloody if that will make you feel better, but when the fighting stops, so does the bickering and the petty bullshit."

"I don't have a dog in this fight, I'll just be over here egging them all on though," Torrez announces as he steps away from the group.

Siah follows him, and they both get comfortable and lean back on the trunk of a surrounding tree, ready for whatever happens next. The guys are all looking at each other and then back at me like they're not sure what to do. I cross my arms over my chest and wait. Maybe they'll finally see how ridiculous all of this is and we can just fucking move forward already.

No sooner does that thought cross my mind than Knox walks up to Enoch and gets in his face.

"No magic, just me beating the shit out of you the ol' fashioned way," Knox challenges.

Enoch snorts. "We both know who ranked higher when it comes to hand-to-hand combat. I'm happy to remind you of that fact though, since you clearly need it."

Enoch unzips his jacket and hands it to Nash. He starts to stretch out and limber up, and the rest of the guys all back up to give them space. Knox pulls off his jacket and his t-shirt. He bends over to remove his shoes, and I take my time studying the muscles in his back. They flex as he straightens up and hands everything to Bastien.

Nerves flutter through me. I worry that letting them do this could just make it worse. Instead of working this anger out of their systems, it could just give them a taste for each other's blood and make them even more hungry for it. Well, fuck it. It's a risk I'm willing to take because I'm at a loss at this point for what else to do. Talking doesn't seem to work. Rationalizing doesn't seem to work. The competition and anger is too deeply rooted.

"No permanently disfiguring each other in any way. No biting, no junk punches, no eye gouges, no hair pulling. If your opponent taps out, you will back the fuck off. When the fighting is over, you will move on and stop living in the past. Understood?" I bark at them.

Knox and Enoch both nod as they stare angrily at one another.

"Begin," I announce.

Knox and Enoch both just stand there for a minute, sizing each other up. Knox is half a head taller and bulkier than Enoch, but Enoch doesn't look fazed by that at all. They both start simultaneously circling one another. They look like predators trying to convince the other one that they're the prey. I can practically feel the hate and anger wafting off of them. It feels heavy and oppressive, and I just hope to fuck they can both purge it.

They charge each other at the same time, their movements a blur. It's brutal and beautiful, the way they hit and dodge and look for an opening all while setting a punishing pace with their fists. Enoch gets a hold of Knox. He picks him up and body slams him to the ground. The other guys wince and *ooh*, but I watch Knox's calculating face as he yanks Enoch's legs out from under him. They grapple, both pressing for the upper hand.

Enoch tries to push Knox off of him with his legs. It forces Knox back, but then he dives over Enoch's outstretched legs and nails him in the face with a right hook. It's such a graceful move I didn't expect from my big beefy Knox, and I smile and file it away to try out in the future. The hit opens a cut on Enoch's cheek, but the two continue to go at it like the blood doesn't matter.

Enoch lands a few knees amidst the flurry of punches, and I'm surprised that all of the guys on the sidelines aren't shouting their support or guidance. Everyone is just watching tensely. Taking this seriously. Waiting for the outcome. Knox bellows out in pain and grabs his side. The sound of him hurting sparks something in me that I have to hold back. It makes it way fucking harder for me to see the violence in a disconnected, analytical way. I find myself glaring at Enoch for a second before I shake it off and remind myself why we're here. Why things have come to this.

Enoch tries for another shot at Knox's ribs, but Knox spins and nails him with an elbow to the head. Enoch stumbles, the hit making him unsteady on his feet. Knox sees the opening and pounces. He charges Enoch, tackling him to the ground, both of them landing hits to each other's faces. A cut opens up above Knox's eye, but he has the upper hand and clearly won't be distracted by the blood now dripping into his socket. I step in when Enoch stops throwing hits and instead attempts to shield his head from Knox's onslaught.

The fight is over. Knox won.

I tap on Knox, but he doesn't stop his attack. The guys rush over and help to pull him off of Enoch. But what I see in Knox's face drops a heavy weight in the pit of my stomach. I check on Enoch, hoping that maybe Knox just needs a minute to snap out of battle mode. To let the hate and rage go.

Enoch sits up and swears. He's pissed off, but he stands up, brushes himself off and looks at me. His gaze is filled with frustration, but there's resignation and acceptance there too. I nod at him, and he wipes blood from his face and turns around and heads in the direction of the tents. Relief bubbles up inside of me as I watch him go.

This bullshit can finally be over now.

That thought turns to stone and sinks into oblivion inside of me as I turn back to Knox. He's watching Enoch walk away like he's still hunting him. This fight changed things for Enoch; it clearly did *not* change things for Knox. Anger and frustration flare inside of me. I approach my Chosen and watch them congratulate Knox and pump him up over what just went down.

"Anyone else want to fight?" I ask tersely.

Kallan, Becket, and Nash are still standing off to the side, and I look from them to my Chosen. They all shake their heads.

"Sure?" I press. "Because this will be your last chance to air any grievances with each other using your fists," I inform them all again.

No one steps forward.

"Good," I declare. "My turn then."

5

"What?" Bastien and some of the others ask as I strip out of my coat and shirt revealing the sports bra I'm wearing underneath.

"What are you doing?" Becket asks me as I kick off my shoes and push my jeans down my hips. I flex my toes against the frosty grass and start hopping in place to get my blood flowing and my body warmed up.

My movement pulls Knox's focus back to me, and he gives me a confused look. "What do you mean *your* turn?" Bastien demands again, but my gaze is locked on Knox.

"What? You think you guys are the only ones with issues? The only ones so pissed off that you need to fight it out?" I ask.

I square off toward Knox, welcoming all the rage and fight I still see in his face.

"Vinna, don't do this," Sabin starts, and my glare snaps to him.

"This is between me and Knox. Stay the fuck out of it."

Sabin jerks back like I've just slapped him across the face, but it's not my words that hit him so hard, it's the pain I know he can see in my eyes. His forest green gaze bounces back and forth between my seafoam green stare. Then he takes a conciliatory step back. Sabin backing off seems to confuse the others. I wait to see who else's objections will need to be dealt with, but everyone stays quiet, unease floating in the air.

"I'm not going to fight you, Killer. You already know how I feel about that." I roll my eyes at Knox's declaration and step into a fighting stance.

"You're my mate, and I'm not going to hurt you," he declares more urgently as I move toward him.

"You're not going to hurt me?" I ask sweetly. "I think we're way past that, Knox, you've been gutting me since Enoch and his coven showed up at our door with runes."

Shock flashes through Knox's gray eyes, and he searches my face like he doesn't quite understand what I mean. I stomp down the flood of pain that surges through me as I think back to all the accusations and mistrust that Knox has flung my way since then, and let my fists purge the hurt. I strike out at Knox, and he steps back, alarmed, and blocks it. My hit is halfhearted, not because I don't want to beat the shit out of him, but because I won't really go for him until I know he's going to fight back.

I swing at him again and let him dodge it.

"What the hell, Killer?" he asks as he continues to weave away from the easy pace I'm setting.

"From the minute they showed up at the door, you've made it clear that it was either you or them. You know I can't draw the line like that, and yet you keep pushing for it," I growl at him.

I execute a low spin and kick his legs out from underneath him. Knox goes down and then immediately kips back up angry.

"We are your Chosen. We are enough. All they do is

create problems and fuck with the good that *we've* got going on," he growls back at me.

"No, that's all *you've* been doing, Knox." I punctuate my statement with an open-handed hit to his chest. Knox steps back a few feet and glares at me.

"Becket helped save my life. I don't know what I would have done if he hadn't been with me during my time in Adriel's dungeons. He was there for me, pushed me, trained with me despite what I did to his father."

I stop holding back as much, and Knox and I become a flurry of swings and blocks.

"His father betrayed his people and deserved what he got," Knox counters, and I increase the tempo of my attack even more.

"Doesn't make Becket's loss any less painful. Doesn't remove the scars that will be left because of what I did." I move to roundhouse Knox, and he barely dodges it. "Kallan trains me in a way that I understand. I've come so far in such a short amount of time because of him and his coven's help with my magic."

Knox grunts irritably and jumps back to avoid a low jab I throw at him.

"Nash irritates the fuck out of me, but he forces me to see things in a different way. He forces me to think and strategize and puzzle things out because of the weird shit he does and says."

Knox catches my fist and pulls, trying to throw me off balance. I spin in toward him like a tornado, elbow ready to clock him. He leans back like he's an award winning limbo competitor, and I'm not able to connect. I'm not sure if Knox will actually press back the more I attack him, but from the way he's so expertly dodging my hits, I know it would be a good fight. He's lithe and quick. His instincts are spot on, and he can read his opponent well.

"Enoch wants to protect me. He wants to keep me safe, and he's not afraid to teach me and train with me to make that happen."

Knox growls. "Enoch wants to use you, that's who he is. He wants what you have because of what it can do for him!" he snaps at me.

"So did you!" I yell back, stopping my attack and stepping into his face. "The night I marked all of you, what did you say to me? *Thanks for the upgrade.* You pointed out more than once that you and your coven would be better off with my marks, that it would make you the best paladin out there."

"That is *not* the same thing, and you know it!" he shouts back.

"How is it any different? You think you're the only one that can see the advantages of what I can do and can also still care about me? They are my friends, Knox!"

"And I am your mate!" he counters.

"Exactly! You are my mate. You are my Chosen. I fucking love you, but you still don't trust me." My voice breaks as the accusation flies out of my mouth, and I slam a fist to my chest to help knock my heart back together.

Knox reels back like I've punched him. "I do trust you."

"No, you don't. If you did, you wouldn't dismiss what I say so easily," I tell him, parroting something he once said to me. "I tell you that I trust them, that my magic chose them for a reason, and I stand by that. But you decide that you know better. That your past impressions are more worthy of your trust than I am."

Knox glares at me but doesn't say anything. I still feel the need to fight in the twitch of my muscles, but we just stand there, staring at each other.

"You once said to me that nothing hurt worse than when I doubted you, doubted my place with you. Knox, do you not see that you've been doing the same thing to me?" I pull my eyes from Knox and turn to the others. "I know you all have history, but you *have* to get the fuck over it. You are my Chosen, and they are my Shields. We are all connected. So stop trying to rip me in half or prove that my magic is wrong for marking them. Just fucking trust me...please," I beg, frustration and defeat welling up inside of me and forcing the word *please* to come out on a whisper.

I turn back to Knox, but he's staring at the ground, wrestling with his thoughts. I go quiet, giving him time to process. The cold air nips at my exposed skin, but I don't dare move. This moment feels too fragile, like the slightest movement or noise could break it beyond repair. Knox releases a deep sigh and looks up at me. He doesn't say anything, just studies my face for a couple of minutes before his gray eyes settle back on mine.

We both just stare at each other, silently communicating our hurt, doubt, insecurity. His stormy gaze morphs into sorrow, and tears well up in my eyes.

"Are you in or out?" I ask him on a whisper.

The last time these words were spoken between Knox and me, he was placing a challenge at my feet. A challenge to trust my Chosen, to love them, to be a team with them no matter what. I watch his gray-cloudy gaze absorb all of that, and then I wait.

"In, Vinna, always in."

A relieved breath rushes out of me as his words burrow into my soul. The next thing I know, his lips are on mine. His fingers are in my hair, his body is pressed against me as he consumes all my sadness and replaces it with heat and love, understanding and apology. I can taste his *sorry* as he teases my tongue with his own. I can feel his claim and his promises in the way he holds me. He lifts me up, and I immediately wrap my legs around his waist, never pulling my lips from his.

I don't pay attention to the fact that he walks us away from the others. I just kiss him, needing him to erase the cracks and the hurt with his lips and his body. He sets me down on my feet when it's just the two of us surrounded by trees and rocks and plants.

"I love you, Vinna," he whispers reverently against my lips as he pulls back to lift my sports bra over my head.

His mouth is back on mine, consuming me. Fusing us. Pouring all of his need and declarations into my soul and filling me up.

"I love you, Vinna," he whispers into my ear, and then he sucks on my neck and presses traveling kisses down my body. He pushes my underwear down and pulls a hard nipple into his mouth at the same time.

I moan his name like a prayer, reveling in the heat that trails through me with his touch. He runs his fingers through my folds, moaning when he feels how wet I am for him. He moves to my other nipple and circles my clit. He spreads my arousal through my lips and whispers his declarations of love against my breasts and throat as he returns to my mouth, his kisses filled with worship.

I come with his mouth on mine and his fingers playing with me. He pinches my clit and sucks on my bottom lip, both of us groaning at how good it feels. Knox lifts me back up and positions his big arms under my thighs.

"I love you, Vinna," he declares as he thrusts inside of me, guiding my body down his length until he's deep inside of me and we're both panting. He lifts me up his length and then back down, setting the pace, and I roll my hips in a way that helps him hit all the right places.

"I love you, Knox," I whisper against his mouth as I suck on his tongue and fuck him out in the middle of nowhere.

Frost-kissed air caresses our naked bodies and tries to steal the heat that we're creating.

Knox presses me back against a smooth tree, pinning me with his hips as he works in and out of me faster. I gasp and mewl encouragement. Our *I love yous* battle back and forth between our pants and moans. Knox pulls a hand forward and plays with my clit as his lips drop to the line of runes on my shoulder. He traces them with his tongue and sucks on them, and I have no choice but to splinter into a trillion pieces.

His name rides my shout, and his thrusts become urgent and deeper. He fucks me hard into another orgasm, and then it's my name being shouted to the setting sun as Knox presses deeply into me and comes. He moves inside of me shallowly as he rides his orgasm. We both work to catch our breath, our foreheads pressed together.

"I'm sorry, Vinna. I couldn't see past how I was feeling, and I'm sorry."

"Thank you," I tell him, cutting off more of his apology with a soft kiss against his full lips. "I know all of this isn't easy. I know I ask a lot. Just know I love you and I don't want a future that doesn't have you in it."

Knox kisses me again, his mouth and tongue all passion and apology.

"I'll make it work with your Shields. We all will. We'll do better," he promises, and I have to blink back the tears that well up in my eyes.

Knox kisses my cheek where one manifestation of sorrow escapes, and repeats his promise until I can blink back my emotions and nod.

"I'm always in, Killer, always," he reminds me.

I smile at him and breathe out the last vestiges of hurt.

"Samesies," I whisper and then nip at his ear lobe.

Knox growls at me playfully and rolls his hips,

reminding me that he's still deep inside of me at the moment.

"How long do you think we have until one of the guys walks through the trees, calling dibs?" I ask on a chuckle, suddenly feeling lighter than I have in weeks.

Knox's deep laugh vibrates through me, and he runs his nose over the runes on my shoulder. "Enough time for me to show you how sorry I really am for a second time. You game, Killer?"

I laugh and then moan when he grinds into my still spread thighs. "Do you even have to ask? TGV forevaaaah-hh," I shout into the sky. "Let's just see how sorry you really are," I declare on a groan-infused giggle as Knox flicks his tongue against my hard nipple.

"Challenge accepted, Killer. Challenge fucking accepted!"

6

"My money's on fangs," Bastien announces.

Nash, Kallan and Torrez all nod and voice their agreement. I roll my eyes.

"I hope not," I huff.

"Now, now, now, what's wrong with fangs?" Siah exclaims, giving me a playfully indignant look. "I mean you had no complaints about them just the other night," he teases, and I rush to cover his mouth to stop him from talking. He bolts, and the other guys all start blocking me so I can't get to him.

"Don't be shy, Vinna. None of us are confused about what you and Siah are doing when you sneak off *for a snack*," Valen tells me, putting air quotes over the last part of his statement.

I slap his arm and laugh, giving up my efforts to tackle Siah and purple nurple him.

"Oh, so you'd have no issue if we were making out and I went all fangy on you?" I challenge, my tone amused.

"Fuck, if your fangs can do for us what Siah's fangs do for you, then I'm game," Ryker states. I laugh even harder and release a pleased sigh just thinking about Siah's bite.

The guys crack up and trade fist bumps with Ryker and then with Siah.

"I don't think it will be fangs, it'll probably be speed or something like that," Nash announces. Sabin and Valen both man grunt in agreement.

"No way, she already has those through her old runes. New runes should do something different, shouldn't they?" Knox asks, and the group turns to me like somehow I know whether that's true or not.

"Well, let me just dust off the instruction manual I've been keeping from all of you and find out," I snark as I mime opening a book and turning the pages. "Oh, here it is," I chirp as I slowly flip them the bird.

Snorts of amusement sound off all around me, mixing with the sound of heavy footfall as we hike through the hills, Sorik leading the way.

"Just activate the runes already, and then we'll know who won," Enoch encourages. The smile on his face grows when all the others start agreeing with him.

"Dibs on the first bite if she does go all fangy," Torrez shouts out, and I laugh at the groans that start up and the high fives he gets from Siah and Knox. "Gotta think on your feet, compeers," he teases, and they all start razzing each other.

I can't help but smile at the camaraderie that's floating around the group today. It's been almost two weeks since the Enoch and Knox showdown happened. It hasn't all been smooth sailing, but everyone is really trying to make things better. I'm starting to get used to the banter and teasing that's been happening more and more freely between my Chosen and my Shields.

"Fine, but don't blame me if I get all bite happy, and you all orgasm so much you can't hike anymore today."

"There are worse ways to go," Valen states.

"We were going to be stopping soon anyway," Ryker adds.

"Do we all get bite orgasms, or is that offer exclusive?" Kallan questions, his hand partially raised like he's waiting to be called on.

I laugh, and before anyone can say anything else, I activate the new runes on my shoulder that showed up after Siah became part of my Chosen. Nothing happens. I run my tongue over my teeth, but my canines don't feel any different. I work to mask my surprise that the runes don't give me what I suspected they would. The guys all look at me expectantly. I shrug and give them a big toothy smile so they can see for themselves.

"No fangs," Valen confirms as he leans in and studies my teeth just to be sure.

Disappointed groans and sighs sound off all around me, and I join in. I thought it would be fangs too.

"So what is it then?" Sabin asks, and I shrug my shoulders again.

"I don't feel any different."

I start to jog so I can check to see if somehow I have new lamia speed, but I don't flash anywhere. I activate my runes down my legs and go full cheetah mode, but it was the same speed I had before. I run back to the guys and try not to feel disappointed. They look just as puzzled as I do.

"Maybe it was compulsion—try to make us do something," Bastien encourages.

I stare deeply into his eyes. "You will never steal my food again," I command and then wait.

Siah hands me an apple, the look in his eyes eager to see if my command worked. I take a bite and slurp up the juice that tries to escape the side of my mouth. Bastien leans over and licks the side of my hand where more juice dripped down. He then grabs my hand and takes a big ass bite of my apple. He winks at me as his full lips close around the crunchy fruit, and I have to stop myself from leaning over and licking a hint of juice from his lip. Fuck, he's hot, even when he *is* stealing my food.

"Maybe I did it wrong?" I say, looking to Siah for answers.

"Maybe. Did you feel any power in your command when you gave it?"

"Nope," I admit.

"Then it's probably not compulsion."

"Well, what is it then? I don't feel different, but the runes have to do something, don't they?"

"Maybe not in this case," Ryker offers. "Maybe they're more a mate mark than an ability enhancer."

I deflate a little. Siah wraps an arm around me and pulls me into his side. "You really wanted fangs, didn't you?" he teases me quietly. I chuckle and wrap my arm around his waist.

"Fuck yeah, I did, who doesn't want to induce orgasms with their bite?"

Siah cracks up and then gives me a quick peck. I lean into him wanting more. "Don't worry, mate, we can get into a bite war later, really test our limits this time."

My smile goes from hungry to beaming to predatory. Siah laughs even harder.

"TGV strikes again," Torrez teases.

I chuckle. "You know it, Wolf."

I release the magic in the runes Siah's bite gave me and shoo away the letdown I feel over the fact that they don't seem to do anything.

"Should we try the new rune on all of our palms?" Ryker asks, and a new surge of excitement rushes through me.

"Let's stop here for tonight," Sorik announces as he comes to a stop and takes off his pack. "I think a storm is moving in, and I want to track ahead and see if there's a faster way to the mountain than the way I went last time."

I look past Sorik at the mountain in the distance he must be talking about.

"Siah, Nash, Teo, and Enoch, you're with me. Teo, can you shift into your wolf? We're getting close, and I just want to be sure we're not going to cross paths with something we're not expecting," Sorik orders.

Torrez nods and starts stripping down. This results in my immediate drooling from all lips, and some of the guys groaning in playful disapproval.

"The rest of you put up tents and build a big fire. It's going to get very cold tonight."

"On it," Bastien and Valen say at the same time.

"Vinna, I'm going to leave Vaughn with you, okay?" I nod and step up to my dad's side. I've been in charge of him a couple times so far on this trip, so I shouldn't feel awkward doing this, and yet for some reason, I still do.

Everyone sets their packs down, and the group going with Sorik moves out. The others quickly fall into a familiar rhythm of getting tents and camp set up. I spot some large boulders off to the right and decide it's a good place for Vaughn and me to take a load off and stay out of the way of the guys as they set things up.

"Vaughn, walk with me," I instruct, and we both make our way toward the rocks. I dismiss my uneasiness over his dead eyes and his ability to do as he's told. It's weird that I'm not bothered by it when Sorik is in command of my father. But when I am the one who has to direct him, reality sucker punches me every time, without fail.

"Vaughn, sit here on this rock," I tell him, pointing to exactly where I want him to be.

He sits, and I take a seat on the rock next to him. I'm quiet for a while as I watch the guys work. They move like well-oiled camping machines these days, and it's captivating to watch.

"So how was today?" I ask Vaughn.

Unsurprisingly, he doesn't answer.

"Sorik says we're getting close, which is awesome and equally fucking terrifying," I admit. "Any of this look familiar to you? I know my mom talked to Sorik about this place, so you probably knew about it too. I wonder what landmarks she used to explain how to get here?"

I look around at the surrounding trees. The landscape has seemed the same for the past week or so. No major signs that we're headed anywhere other than a wandering trek out in the middle of nowhere, but Sorik says this is the way. I probably look like an idiot out here, talking to a man who we don't even know if he's in there anymore. Maybe the Sentinels will have some way to help him.

It's a hope I try not to look at too closely, but an ember of it glows in the center of my chest, nonetheless. But just in case that never happens, and this version of my dad is all I will ever have, I'm trying to get to know him and help him to get to know me. I figure if the roles were reversed, I'd want someone to be tender and kind to me that way.

I slip off my rock and kneel at Vaughn's feet. "Dad, lift your left leg and set your foot in my lap." He does as he's told, and I begin to unlace his hiking boot and pull it off. His thick sock is next, and then I check his feet for blisters or areas that look like they could break down soon because of rubbing. Sorik showed me how to do this our first night camping. I hadn't given any thought to the fact that if Vaughn were hurting from a blister or pressure sore from his pack, he wouldn't be able to tell us, so a nightly routine of checking him over started.

I rub the bottom of his foot for a minute and then send

some Healing magic to fix a spot on his heel that's a little too red from today's walk.

"So where did we leave off?" I ask and tilt my head in thought. "Oh that's right, Beth had just decided it was time to leave New Mexico. Laiken and I didn't know that Beth had already decided that Nevada was our next stop, so we would take turns spinning this ratty old globe that she had found at a garage sale. I mean, the thing was barely hanging on, but that didn't stop us from giving it a spin, closing our eyes, and sticking our finger on a spot. Wherever our finger landed was where we decided we were moving next. The rule was that the chooser had to tell the other person a story about how life would be in our new home."

I put my dad's sock and shoe back on and switch to his other foot.

"Laiken landed in the middle of the ocean one time. I was sure she was going to tell a story about mermaids or something, but I should have known that Little Laik would never go the predictable route. She spun a story about an underwater city that felt so real, I swear I could smell salt in the air. She spent a week telling me all about it, and I was riveted."

I chuckle at the memory and fist bump the melancholy that accompanies it.

"The story ended up taking a weird turn when the city broke down and we had to become cannibals to survive, but I'm telling you even *that* didn't make me not want to crawl into that fantasy world she created and live there. That was when I knew Laiken had a gift. She could make you see things in a way you never thought about. She had been doing that for me her whole life, but in that moment, I realized just what a powerful gift it was."

I smile wistfully up at my dad as I continue to catch him up on my life.

48

"I'll probably always wonder what she would have done with that gift; the possibilities were endless." I go quiet for a bit, thinking about her. "I hear her in my dreams still," I admit. "It's not often, but I catch her from time to time. Does mom still talk to you?" I ask, and I find myself searching his face despite its blankness. "Sometimes I get the urge to ask Sorik about her, but I don't want to make him sad, so I don't."

Silence stretches between us as all the questions I have about my mother and him and Sorik go unvoiced. I watch as the last of the tents go up and the sun dips lower toward the earth. The gray clouds that have been hovering all day take on a purple hue as the night slinks its way in to replace the day.

"Dad, are you cold?"

I stand up to go track down a jacket but freeze when his head swivels over to me. The blank look is still in place, but I've never seen him move without specifically being told to do it. I watch him for several minutes, my heart slowly settling down into its normal rhythm. Nothing else happens. I move to his other side to see if he'll do it again.

"Dad, are you cold?"

He doesn't move this time. Just stares off into the trees like he's caught in their clutches somehow. It's as though his consciousness is tangled in the branches so badly that if he just stares at it long enough, he can figure out a way to separate it all. I don't know how long I watch him sitting on the rocks like a statue.

"Bruiser!" Bastien calls, pulling me from my uneasy observation. "Dinner time."

I give him a wave and watch my dad for another beat. "Dad, stand up and follow me," I instruct.

He follows, and I try not to sneak wary glances at him over my shoulder as we both head back toward the camp in silence. I'm not sure what happened, but I need to pay closer attention to him. Maybe this is normal and I've just never noticed before. I make a mental note to ask Sorik when he comes back.

I push back against the guilt that starts to steep in my center. I've wanted to keep Vaughn at arm's length. I have no idea how to deal with this situation, and keeping him close while not getting too close has been working for me. But there are obviously things I'm missing in trying to keep my distance.

I throw an apologetic smile at Vaughn over my shoulder. It bounces off his stone-like features and falls to the ground. I let out a resigned exhale and silently vow to do more for him, to do better. I lead Vaughn to the warm fire that's already bright and blazing in the middle of the tents. I order him to sit down and watch him for another beat. I turn around, guilt and disquiet settling in my bones. My eyes land on Ryker's, and he opens his arms in welcome.

I step into him, and as soon as his arms wrap around me, I can feel some of my anxiety melt away. Ryker presses his lips to the top of my head, and I hold onto him like the lifeline he is.

"You okay?" he asks, running his hands up and down my back in soothing gestures.

I breathe out a sigh and nuzzle his chest. "Yeah, my eyes and wishful thinking are just playing tricks on me."

"Here." Ryker directs me to sit in a fold out camping chair.

He kneels at my feet and pulls a booted foot into his lap. He tugs at the laces, and I smile, recognizing exactly what he's doing.

"Ryker," I protest and attempt to reclaim my foot.

"Squeaks," he mocks. "Let me take care of you. Don't be

stubborn. Besides, we both know you love it when I work my magic."

He winks at me, and I chuckle, unable to help myself. I lean back in the chair and run a hungry gaze all over his face and body. His blond hair is longer than it was the first time we met, and I reach out and run my fingers through it. Ryker smiles at me, his full lips and happy blue eyes doing all the right things for the butterflies in my stomach. He pulls my shoe and sock off and then starts rubbing my foot. I moan when he digs into a sore spot with his magic hands. Ryker grins.

"Love that noise," he teases and then massages another sore spot.

"Love you," I counter, and I lean forward with pursed lips demanding a kiss.

Ryker happily obliges and then leans back and gets to work rubbing my aches and pains away. We don't talk. We just soak in each other's presence and let it work as a balm for all the apprehension and strain this adventure is causing. I let out a relieved breath as he silently does his thing. His answering grin is filled with tenderness and raw affection.

"Don't worry, Squeaks, I got you."

My smile mirrors his. "Ditto."

Ryker starts on my other foot, and I chase away any emotion or thought that doesn't allow me to just appreciate my mate and focus on how much I love him. I'm one lucky girl, that's for fucking sure.

7

I wake up with a start. My heart is hammering in my chest with alarm, and my breath is cloudy from the cold air. I rest a hand on Valen's chest next to me, but he's sound asleep, his breaths deep and even. I sit still, activating the runes on the helix of my ears, and listen. The night is quiet other than the normal noises made by sleeping males in their tents. I deactivate my runes and slip out of Valen's arms. I tuck the sleeping bag around him, careful not to wake him up.

I press my wool sock covered feet into my untied shoes and quietly unzip the front of my tent. I step out and gasp. Everything is coated in a soft blanket of snow. There's a wet ring around the stones that surround the still burning fire, and I move toward it, putting my unprotected hands out toward the heat. It's not snowing still, but the unmarred white covering twinkles up at me like it's hinting at buried treasure. I've never seen snow other than in pictures. I take in the soft white landscape with wide-eyed awe.

"Couldn't sleep?" Torrez's deep voice wraps around me like a warm Snuggie, and I turn to find him stepping up to the fire next to me.

"Something woke me up. What time is it?"

"Just past three in the morning. Was that *something* Valen?" Torrez asks me with a teasing smile.

I chuckle, white steam billowing from my mouth as I do. "No, he's passed out in the tent, but something had me sitting up in bed with my heart racing."

"Bad dream?" Torrez asks, his warm brown eyes studying my face.

"Don't think so." I shrug. "You on watch right now?"

"No, just got off it. Ryker is checking the perimeter."

I rub my hands together, hoping the movement and the fire work to warm them up a bit faster. *Fuck, it's cold.* Torrez throws an arm around me and pulls me into his side.

"Here, I'll help with that," he announces as he tucks me tightly against him.

"Why, thank you, kind sir. Nothing like getting felt up before everything freezes off," I tease.

Torrez chuckles and runs his hands up and down my arms. "I'll have you know that I'm hot."

"Oh, I'm aware of how hot you are," I tell him as I press in against him and roll my eyes.

"Why are you out here without a coat?" he asks me as his hands continue to trace warm paths up and down my arms and across my back.

"I was just going to stretch out and see if I can shake off this restlessness. Besides"—I slap his chest with the back of my hand—"where's your coat?"

"I'm practically a walking, talking space heater, and I was just about to work off some of my restlessness," he counters.

"Ahh, does Sabin know you're jacking off in the tent when he's asleep?" I joke and then squeak when Torrez slaps my ass in mock punishment and faux outrage.

"I was going for a run, you dirty Witch. But feel free to add me jerking off to *your* spank bank."

"I will, thank you," I tell him with over-the-top appreciation.

"You want to come?" he asks.

"Well, with visions of you masturbating, how could I not?"

Torrez slaps my ass again and nips at my neck. "Come on a *run*, not come on my dick, Witch. I mean, maybe you can have that too if you play your cards right."

He steps away from me and wags his eyebrows, his eyes sparkling playfully. The cold air immediately presses against me where he used to be, and a shiver skates up my spine.

"But it's cold," I whine.

"Once you get moving, it won't be, but I understand if you'd rather cuddle up under the protection of your tent and another mate. You Witches do have such *delicate* sensibilities. We wouldn't want you to break a nail now, would we?"

Torrez smiles at me playfully, his challenge hanging in the air. He steps back and starts to take off his shirt. I appreciate the view for a couple beats, excitement and adrenaline starting to bubble up inside of me.

"Fine, but last one to the trees has to be on the bottom," I call out, and then I take off in the direction of the distant tree line.

Snow crunches under my boots, and I realize too late that I never tied them. Fuck, I hope they stay on, because I do not want to run barefoot.

"Cheater!" Torrez shouts at my back, and I *shhhh* him over my shoulder.

"You'll wake everyone up," I whisper shout back to him.

I laugh quietly as I face forward and run harder. He's

cursing quietly as he struggles to get his boots and pants off, so I press my lead. I shove magic into the runes on the back of my legs and haul ass. I suck the cold air into my lungs, and I'm pretty sure they're going to have a solid layer of freezer burn by the time I kick Torrez's ass to the tree line. I want to check behind me and see if he's shifting yet, but I squash the need to perv on his nakedness and focus on the smooth snow at my feet and the trees that are quickly getting closer.

I'm at a full Sentinel magic enhanced run as I break through the tree line first. I whoop my victory in my head. I activate the runes Torrez's mate bite gave me while simultaneously activating the runes for my advanced hearing too. The night explodes into a feast for my new senses. My vision sharpens, and my nose fills with all kinds of new smells. The sounds of small animals skittering away is alluring, but I ignore it and race through the trees.

I know Torrez is full wolf now, and his four paws are a hell of a lot faster than my two feet. I push myself harder and hope my untied boots don't try anything funny. The night is quiet, and the blanket of snow absorbs sound in an interesting way. Everything sounds softer, and there's a magical peace that radiates out because of that. There's a crunch that sounds off as my running feet leave their mark in the pristine white floor, but the noise doesn't disrupt the peaceful feeling out among the trees tonight, it complements it.

My lungs stop protesting the cold air and start to appreciate it. Wind whips past me, the icy touch becoming a balm to my warming body. My hair trails behind me like a cloak, and I smile as the restless nagging that's been growing in my gut the closer we get to Sentinel City, is forgotten in all the fresh air and freedom. I fucking love to run in the woods at night. I can just picture Torrez somewhere behind me, stalking and planning his next move. All while his tongue hangs out of his open mouth as he drinks in the same happiness that a good run gives us both.

My breaths no longer puff out like smoke in the air. My skin is no longer offended by the cold. My boots are thankfully still on my feet, and soon I'll have my mate inside of me, moaning my name and worshipping my body. And in this moment, that's all that matters. The stress of Sentinel City and what it might drop at our feet sluffs off my shoulders, and I'm suddenly just a girl playing cat and mouse with a man who she loves.

That thought flits through my mind just as I hear paws leap from the snowy ground. The crunch is distinct, and something in my instincts knows exactly what that means. I stop, drop and roll. Torrez's big gray wolf goes soaring over me, flying through the air where just a second ago my body should have been. I somersault back onto my feet and tackle him. He growls at me, and I growl back.

"Try harder, Two Socks," I tease, and then we both slam into the ground.

We're a spinning ball of fur, teeth, claws, skin, hair and muscle. We both try to wrestle the other into a submissive position, neither one gaining the upper hand for long. The massive gray wolf nips at my shoulder, and I bite down on his ear. We both back off just to clash back again, the dance repeating itself over and over.

Torrez almost pins me, but when he tackles me, my boot goes flying off my foot. It arcs high up and then comes falling back down to smash him hard in the back of the head. He gives a dazed shake, flinging snow, slush, and mud from his fur. The sheer oddity that my boot just did that sends me into a fit of laughter, the likes of which make the big wolf give an unamused huff.

One second I have a behemoth gray wolf above me, and the next thing I know, a naked Torrez is now in its place.

"Fuck, you have enough weapons on that body of yours, you don't need to make your shoes do your dirty work too," he grumbles and rubs at the back of his head.

I laugh even harder. "It just flew up and then kapow." I giggle hysterically, unable to get a hold of myself as the image keeps replaying over and over again in my mind.

"Oh, it's funny, is it? Getting brained by a hiking boot is *that* amusing?" he demands, laughter dancing in his brown eyes.

"Don't worry, I'd never let anyone know that the great Mateo Torrez was taken out by a shoe," I offer as I fight off another round of giggles and wipe laugh tears from my eyes.

"Oh, and what would you say then?" he asks, his fingers roaming over my torso in search of ticklish spots.

"I'd say you never saw the Chihuahua coming!"

I squeal when his fingers dig into my stomach, activating the tickle giggles and forcing me to squirm.

"You wouldn't! Take it back!" he demands as he plays my body like a well-known instrument, wringing out all the laughs he can from it.

"What? They're very vicious dogs; people would sympathize!" I insist on a squeal before I get a hold of Torrez's only ticklish spot on his neck.

He squees like an Avengers nerd who just walked into a restaurant filled with the whole cast, and I completely lose my shit. The high-pitched tickle-scream he just released is about as far from manly and wolf shifter as one can get. Torrez succeeds in pinning me to the ground, which can't be helped in my laugh-weakened state. I'm laughing so hard it sounds like I'm honking like a goose, which just makes me laugh even harder.

"Fuck, you're beautiful when you're laughing and happy and lying underneath me," Torrez observes.

Heat pools low in my stomach, and I try to tame my giggles. "Only then?" I jibe, fishing shamelessly for more compliments.

Torrez leans down and nips at my exposed neck, his wolf growling deeply with approval. The growl vibrates through his chest, and I revel in the feel of it against my breasts. I deactivate all of my runes, making Torrez and the surrounding forest brighten with color.

"Fine, gorgeous all the time. Stunning when you're laughing, and radiant when you're screaming my name."

He grinds into me, and I giggle and then flip him onto his back. "Pretty sure I won the race and therefore get to be on top."

Torrez muscles me on to my back again. "Pretty sure you cheated and therefore were disqualified from winning."

"Now, now, Wolf, it wasn't my fault you couldn't get your shoes off. You did invite me to come."

He gives an amused huff. "Only if you played your cards right, remember?"

"Well then, royal flush," I shout out, naming the highest hand I can think of in poker. "Does that count?" I ask, leaning forward and sucking Torrez's bottom lip into my mouth.

He claims my mouth in return and deepens the kiss. "Yeah, that'll do," he pants between kisses as he hurries to undress me. I reach down and stroke his length, pumping him slowly up and down as I kick off my other shoe and hope it rolls off to join its sole-mate. My clothes are wet and somewhat muddy from our wrestling, but I don't even feel the cold as Torrez peels them off of me. He wedges the fabric underneath me and presses against my now naked body.

He really is like a walking, talking space heater, and I cling to him as he kisses down my neck and focuses on my breasts.

"Mmmmm, Go Fish," I call out as he sucks on my nipple and plays with the other one between his thumb and forefinger. Torrez pulls away and locks eyes with me, his gaze filled with laughter.

"Um...I beg your pardon?"

"Oh, I thought I'd call out card game wins, just in case I still needed to play my cards right," I say, a cheeky smile on my face.

My lips spread wide over a smile, but my mouth O's as he chuckles and then quickly moves down my body to suck on my clit. He wastes no time owning my pussy, licking, sucking and teasing until I'm a mewling mess. The turned on growl he gives every time he spreads me wide and licks me sends delicious vibrations through me, and I'm on the verge of orgasming in no time. Like the sexiest fucking rollercoaster ever, Torrez takes me right up to the peak, pauses to build anticipation and then hurtles me over the edge, breathless, panting, and screaming out.

"Old Maid!" I shout out as I float languidly through my orgasm, and I can feel the laugh that's vibrating through him as *Old Maid* becomes a fervent prayer of appreciation on my lips.

Torrez moves back up my body, worshipping with his kisses as he goes. He locks eyes with me and nuzzles my nose with his own.

"Winner, winner, chicken dinner," he calls out, and then he lines himself up and thrusts deeply inside of me.

I'm caught in between a laugh and a moan as Torrez starts to work rhythmically in and out of me. The sound of our bodies separating and slamming back together dances in the air all around us. A snowflake lands on the tip of my nose, and I open my eyes to find that it's started snowing again. The big fat flakes drop down to the ground lazily like they have all the time in the world. They take the slow scenic route as they fall from the sky and twirl and sway until they rest on the forest floor all around us.

"Gin!" I shout out when Torrez hits that specific sweet spot inside of me. We both crack up and once again easily get lost in the feel of each other.

"You were made for me, you cheeky Witch," he declares, punctuating each word with deep thrusts.

"Well duh, Lobo Gris."

"Lobo Gris? Really?"

"I've run out of good wolf slurs," I admit and then reach up to pinch my nipples as he speeds up. "Two Socks and Spanish were my Hail Marys."

"Who the fuck is Two Socks?" Torrez grunts out, close but holding back his orgasm.

"You know, *Dances with Wolves*," I encourage, but he just looks confused. "Google said it was a movie."

"Sounds fake," he teases, batting my hand away so he can suck a nipple into his mouth.

I moan and run my fingers through his damp black hair. He starts to fuck me even harder. "I guess I could call you, like, derogatory pet names now that I've used up all the wolf ones. How would you feel about Fifi?"

Torrez growls and looks up at me, never missing a beat as he pumps in and out of my pussy. "I feel about the same as you would feel if I stopped fucking you right now. I can feel you already starting to pulse around me. Call me Fifi and watch that orgasm float away," he threatens playfully, and I glare at him.

I keep my mouth shut and throw my head back so I can get lost in the sensations of his body on top of mine. Moving in me, feeling so right and *sooo* fucking good. Another orgasm sweeps over me like a blizzard, and I scream out, "Uno!"

Torrez presses in even deeper and goes still, his orgasm a mix of my name and laughter.

"I love you, Fifi," I tease as we both just lie there in orgasmic bliss.

I crack up when he pulls out and then flips me on all fours.

"Oh, I'll show you Fifi," he declares, and then he thrusts back inside and fucks the Fifi right out of me.

8

I'm buzzing with restlessness which, at this point in our adventure, is my new normal. We're close, and we can all feel it. We've been hiking for just a couple hours, and it's lacked the joking and ragging that normally goes on. We're all quiet. Observant. Anticipation sits heavy on each of our backs as we get closer to our destination with each step.

None of us are sure what will happen. Sorik said he turned back when he saw the barrier the first time he traveled this path. He wasn't stopped by anyone or followed. His discovery seemed to go unnoticed. I keep thinking Sentinels are going to pop out at any moment with a "halt who goes there," but as we close the distance, nothing happens.

That should make me feel relieved or help calm my nerves, but it's setting me on edge instead. We crest yet another hill in what seems to be a hike of never-ending hills and mountains, and then there it is. A luminescent barrier that stretches as far as I can see to the left and right. It's bookended by large mountains on each side, and from what Sorik said, Sentinel City sits somewhere in the middle of a valley. We all knew we'd been getting closer to our destination, but from the way everyone sort of freezes, I don't think any of us expected that today would be the day.

I feel the pull of the barrier like a siren's song. I don't know what the fuck it means, but there's an undeniable call to do something. I take in the faces of my Chosen, my Shields, and Sorik. I can tell that the call is singing in each of them as well. Slowly, we start down the hill toward the barrier, and I trace the familiar features of my dad's face as we go. I once again find myself wondering if he's in there. If this barrier tempts him to some unknown action too.

I scan our surroundings for any movement, while also taking in the barrier. We stop about ten feet away, and all anyone can do is just stare.

"Everyone feeling—" Valen voices.

The resounding yeses cut him off before he can even finish the question.

"Anyone else just want to touch it?" Becket asks, and the confusion and fascination in his tone makes me want to laugh.

"I've never been so attracted to a magical phenomenon...well, aside from Vinna, that is," Siah utters with awe, and I simultaneously swoon and agree with his assessment of the barrier.

I too feel like Dory when she finds a squishy and declares that it's hers. I just want to rub myself all over this shimmering barrier, call it my shiny, and announce that it's now mine for forever.

"I wonder what it is about it that has that pull?" Ryker queries, and we all grow silent again as we stare at the myriad of colors that are shimmering in front of us.

"It almost feels like it's...I don't know...missing something maybe," Bastien observes.

"What do you mean?" Valen asks.

"I don't know how to explain it, but it feels like it's

63

reaching out for something, and it desperately wants whatever that something is. Like it's crying out for it."

"Like it's the lock in search of a key," I whisper.

Bastien's words take a moment to soak in, but as they do, I can pick out exactly what he means. The barrier isn't calling out in this cheerful "let's all frolic together in happiness and bliss." It feels more like something that's wounded and is begging for relief.

"It's giving me the fucking heebie jeebies the more I stare at it. So whatever we're going to do to get through this thing, let's do it already," Enoch declares.

I blink a couple times and then pull my focus from the call of the barrier. I don't see anyone on the other side of it or sense any kind of threat.

"So, anyone feeling like we should stray from the plan?" I ask.

No one answers right away as they study the barrier, each other, and then me.

"You're the strongest individual source of magic, so that still makes the most sense to me," Sabin offers, finally breaking the silence.

"I still think it's risky," Knox starts. "But we'll all be ready to lend a hand if you need it," he adds, and the trusting smile he gives me warms me to the core.

I take a deep breath and turn to the barrier again. I can't lie, there's a part of me that worries this thing might act like a giant bug zapper and just fry my ass on contact. But I argued that I was the best option for figuring out how to get through it, and now I have to Sentinel the fuck up and hope it doesn't cook me until I'm golden brown and crispy.

I slowly release the air I just pulled into my lungs and give myself a solid pep talk of *here goes fucking nothing.* I reach out and do my best to keep my poker face intact, which exudes an air of *I got this* and thoroughly hides the face people make when they're about to touch something super icky. I walk the ten feet that separate the group from the barrier and then just stare at it.

I suddenly feel so unprepared, which makes no sense.

We've been hiking for weeks, knowing this was the destination. We've gone over plans upon plans for what to do when we get here. We're finally here, and yet this all feels surreal, like a dream I'm going to wake up from at any moment. I pull in a deep breath and shake the uncertainty from my limbs. I lift my hand and pause.

What the fuck is my problem?

I roll my shoulders twice and banish any hesitation from my body. I touch the barrier with a tip of my finger and then quickly pull my hand away with a squeak of terror and excitement. I wait for my body to spontaneously combust, but when it doesn't, I turn to the others and give them a wide smile.

"Yay for not dying!" I shout out, unable to help myself.

Bastien and Torrez both shake their heads at me, but I don't miss the smile in their eyes. I wasn't just incinerated, which means I'm walking on cloud nine. I blame *that* for why I don't stick with the *test the barrier with magic* plan that we all agreed to, but instead step into the shimmering rainbow coated magic instead.

Shouted protests bounce off my back as I'm suddenly enveloped by the Defensive magic of the barrier. I know that my Chosen are going to rip me a new one, but I'll have to deal with that on the other side. I continue to walk through the barrier, and it feels like I'm surrounded by jello. I'm engulfed by a cool dense sensation, and I move like I'm making my way underwater. I look over my shoulder to see that the guys are all arguing, but the sound is lost to me.

I see Knox mouth the words *fuck it* before he also steps into the barrier. I watch him cringe, like he wasn't sure what to expect when he touched the magic, but just like with me, there's no issue. The other guys all enter the magic force-field one by one, and we all start making our way through to the inside of what the barrier is protecting.

We've all had different theories about the barrier and how to navigate it. The original plan was to make contact and then go from there. We figured contact would help determine if the barrier was hostile and defensive. Was it simple protection or something else entirely? Looks like Sorik's theory won. He thought that maybe the barrier could recognize Sentinel magic and would respond accordingly. He figured that would be the only way other Sentinels could go in and out. I wondered if they *did* come and go though, since supposedly everyone thought they died off.

Maybe my mom ran away?

I come out on the inside of the barrier and step into the shadow of a mountain that's directly in front of us. I pause for a moment, disoriented because when I was on the outside of the barrier, it looked like this was sparse trees and flat land.

"Are you fucking kidding me?" Torrez rages at me when he makes it through the barrier too. I turn, ready to reassure him that it's all fine, but the angry look on everyone's faces has me shutting the fuck up.

Shit.

"My bad," I offer weakly, knowing if one of them had gone off script like I just did, I'd be just as pissed.

"I'm going to try really hard to not sound like some fucking caveman right now, but, Vinna, you can't just pull shit like that!" Torrez growls at me. "Your actions and choices don't just affect you anymore, and the lack of consideration you just showed all of us is not fucking cool."

"Fuck, I know. I went all raccoon, I saw the shiny and

just went for it. I'm fucking sorry," I offer, looking each of them in turn.

Torrez pauses, suddenly not sure what to say. "You should be sorry," he adds, floundering.

"I am. Seriously, I get it. I won't pull that shit again," I vow, and more than one of them gives me a questioning look.

Torrez runs his fingers through his hair and huffs out a frustrated breath. "Real talk, I thought she was going to defend herself. I'm not sure what to do now," he leans over and mumbles out of the side of his mouth to Sabin.

I chuckle, as do a couple of the other guys.

"You can punish her in all the best ways later," Sabin tells Torrez conspiratorially, and my vagina makes it known that she really likes the sound of that.

Torrez releases an amused snort and shakes his head at me. "No more solo vigilante shit, Witch," he scolds again.

I run a finger over my heart in the shape of an *X*. "No more solo vigilante shit," I agree.

Everyone seems appeased by my declaration, and the focus goes quickly from me to our surroundings.

"Looks like we have more hiking in our near future," Ryker observes, his head tilted back to take in the big mountain eclipsing our presence on this side of the barrier.

"Yeah, I kind of thought there'd just be a big city waiting here for us, and maybe we'd get, like, a parade and shit," Becket voices, and I shake my head at him while fighting an amused smile.

"What if there isn't anyone here?" Knox asks, the question promptly wiping the amusement from my face. "I mean, we all just thought there'd be others on this side of the barrier, but what if there isn't? What if the barrier protects nothing now and just...is?"

That thought flaps around the group like a pest no one

wants to land on them. I run my gaze over the shadowed trees, grass and shrubs surrounding us.

"Yeah, that thought never really crossed my mind," I confess.

"Me neither," Bastien and Valen both say at the same time.

"Well, the only way we're going to find out is to either go up this mountain or around it," Enoch observes, and we all tilt our heads back to take in the high peak above us.

We all let out groans and growls of annoyance. None of us had any idea what kind of welcome we would receive, but we were all thinking that getting to the other side of the barrier would mean no more walking.

"All those in favor of going around?" Sorik asks, raising his hand to cast his vote.

Everyone else follows suit. Without another word, he heads off to the right, and we begin our trek to skirt around the base of the rocky mound that's now in our way.

"If there is anyone here, how long do you think it will take before we're on their radar?" Kallan asks.

And it's right at that moment that heat runs through me. It's like Kallan's question alone has activated my runes in some way. They start to glow, and I heat up. At first I'm confused by the sensation, because there's something oddly familiar about it, which makes it even more strange.

"Um...something's happening," I voice at the same time that several of them ask, "Do you feel that?"

It's that question that triggers the memory of the last time this happened. Magic builds inside of me like I'm a pressure cooker, and I know that any second now, it's going to explode out of me and do something to the barrier we just walked through. The last time this happened was when I first crossed the magical barrier onto Lachlan's property. My magic sort of just... highjacked it. I suspect that the same thing is about to happen, but the magic that's rushing into me now is a hell of a lot more intense than anything I experienced the last time.

I wince at the force of magic building in me, and my eyes land on Siah's worried gaze. He opens his mouth to say something to me, but my head fills with a rushing sound, and I can't make out what he's trying to communicate. All of sudden, his runes light up, and it's as if someone just flipped the on switch for all of my Chosen.

Their glow is blinding, and I try to turn away from it and shield my eyes, but I can't move. I strain against the magic filling me, and just when things are bordering on painful, the magic explodes in a brutal flash like a bomb just went off. My scream is lost to the thundering sound of magic pouring out of everything that I am. It doesn't ripple out like it did at Lachlan's barrier, but blasts straight up until it slams into the dome of the barrier above us and then umbrellas out.

I feel like I'm watching my soul, my essence, drain out with it, but I don't have enough time to be scared by that when magic simultaneously blazes out of each of my Chosen. Their magic doesn't join mine to feed the barrier surrounding us, but slams directly into me instead. I can't see what's happened to Sorik, my dad, or my Shields. I'm blinded by the light that my Chosen are feeding into me and that *I'm* subsequently feeding into the barrier.

The wrongness, the missing piece, I felt before when it came to the magic in the barrier slowly changes, and what felt incomplete and off, now feels healed and right. Contentment settles in my chest, and just like that, my magic blinks out.

I take a moment to catch my breath. I'm just about to internally start high-fiving myself for not feeling like I'm going to pass out—which is how I felt last time this happened—when my Chosen crumble to the dirt. Panic zaps through me. Reality violently yanks me away from the pride and peace I was just fist bumping. I scramble to Sabin who was the closest to me when he fell, and pull his limp body into my lap.

Fear hammers in my chest when I realize that I can't get to all of them at once. Sabin's chest moves slowly against mine. That feeling is the only thing that holds me to the here and now and keeps me from completely losing my shit.

They're okay, Vinna. They're just unconscious. They're alive.

I repeat this over and over again to myself, wrapping the words around me like the tether they are. I ass-scoot with Sabin in my arms, slowly moving so that I can pull them all to me. I notice absently that the circle of diamonds that recently showed up on my palm is still glowing, but I ignore it as the need to touch each of my guys and physically make sure they are okay overpowers everything else in my mind.

"What in the name of *Close Encounters of the Third Kind* just fucking happened?" Kallan asks, his eyes trained on the ceiling of the barrier. Light pulses and flickers through it, punctuating his question.

"Well, if there is anyone here, they know they have company now thanks to that light show," Becket announces, and I don't miss the irritation in his tone.

"Everyone okay?" Nash asks as he rushes over to check on each of my Chosen.

He methodically checks each of them, while the rest of his coven and Sorik sound off with their yeses, and I try to stop freaking the fuck out. I welcome the numbness that starts to take over as I chant *they'll wake up, they're fine* over and over to myself. I work to compartmentalize my worry and panic, because Becket is right. I just fucking light showed a *honey, I'm home* to anyone who does live within these magical walls.

Fucking annoying unpredictable magic!

"We need to move. If anyone is here, it's possible Becket might get the parade he's been dreaming about, but there's also a chance that they may want to fuck us up too," I tell them.

"Kallan, you see any good defensible positions?" Enoch asks.

Kallan immediately starts scanning everything around us with a more critical eye. "We can move higher, see if there's anything good up there that makes us less sitting duck-ish."

I nod in agreement and arrange Sabin flat on his back. "Each of us needs to carry one of my Chosen. Let's go!" I shout out, and then I grab Sabin's leg, roll on top of him and use the momentum to get him up on my shoulders into a fireman carry.

"Dad, we're placing Ryker on your shoulders. You will carry him and make sure no harm comes to him," I order.

There's no reaction to my direction, but when Enoch and Kallan place Ryker on Vaughn's shoulders, he holds him there. At this point, I'll take it. I call on my runes and shove magic into all of my limbs to help support Sabin's weight. He's taller than me and has more muscle, but I didn't realize he would feel this heavy. Maybe it's the weeks of walking or the drain on my magic, but I feel shaky as I hold him.

Enoch and Kallan get Siah on Sorik's shoulders, Bastien on Nash's shoulders, and Valen on Becket's shoulders. Then they both execute the same roll I just used. Kallan picks up Torrez, and Enoch picks up Knox.

"On me," Kallan directs, and we all follow him, single file, toward the densely packed trees. Adrenaline and panic fortify my tired muscles, and I focus on keeping Sabin safe on my shoulders. I debate if I should use any of my other runes to try and ensure nothing can sneak up on us, but I worry what will happen if I burn myself out from trying to do too much.

Fuck it.

I'm not sure what we're walking into, and we're seven people down. We need all the help we can get. I activate every rune on my body that isn't a weapon, feeding magic into every mark on me that could give us the tactical advantage. My hearing increases. Color fades away and everything becomes more detailed as my eyesight changes. I breathe deeply, the familiar scent of trees, dirt, foliage, and the people I'm with filling my nose.

It's as if threads from my body sink into the mountain with each step, helping me identify movement in and on the soil and navigate the terrain. *Well, that's new.* With each step I take, I feel better, stronger, more rejuvenated. I file that away to be looked at later; I don't know what it is, but I'll take it.

We hike for about twenty minutes, burrowing deeper into the thick forest, when I feel it. We're being watched.

9

I feel eyes on me. But regardless of every magic fueled ability that I have activated right now, I can't tell where. I stop midstep, goosebumps rising on my arms. I open my mouth to say something to the others, when something drops from the sky and slams into the earth fifteen feet away. Dirt, rocks, and other forest floor debris go flying up all around us. Alarmed shouts are about all we can get out as more mystery things start dropping from the sky. I spot limbs and feathers on one projectile before my vision is blurred by the dirt cloud that forms as it slams into the ground.

My Shields, Sorik, and I all work quickly, dropping my Chosen to the ground and forming a protective circle around them. I try to scream for Vaughn to get in the middle too, but he can't hear me above all the chaos that's going on around us. Sorik darts for him though and yells a command in his ear. Relief fills me when Vaughn sets Ryker down gently and then lies on top of him.

My throat tightens at the sight of my father protecting one of my Chosen with his life. I don't know what I would do if anything happened to any of them, and a part of me wants to lie on my dad to protect him too. I drop kick all concern and worry away, and armor myself instead with the vicious need to protect them all. Once again I tap into my baser self, the one that screams for blood and demands that *you don't fuck with what's mine.*

I call on my long sword and clap the hilt to force it to replicate. I can feel Enoch doing the same behind me. Becket calls on his maces. Kallan palms his throwing knives, and Nash twirls both of his short swords in his hands. Short swords materialize in Sorik's hands, and I summon a bright yellow-orange defensive barrier around where my Chosen lie unconscious. I chase away the fleeting thought that they're going to be pissed they missed the action. I call on an offensive barrier, the magenta protection strengthening the yellow-orange barrier protecting them.

People step through the thick dirt-clouded air, and we all realize quickly that we're surrounded. A couple of them have wings, but the rest look just like us. From what I can make out through the clouds of debris now slowly floating back to the floor of the mountain, I catch various shades of men, with a couple of women interspersed. They all wear a type of black armor, but it looks leather-like as opposed to metal. They appear to be slowly closing in on us, and I can make out through the hazy air, glowing orbs floating in the hands of some and weapons clutched in the hands of others.

Sentinels.

I spot black markings like mine on some of them, and I can't help the awe that surges through me.

I really am not the last.

I scour every inch of them that I can see, hungry to know more, but painfully aware that this situation does not feel friendly.

They can motherfucking fly.

I fangirl to myself and then work to calm the fuck down. Excitement tries to fuck up my game face, but I hammer it into submission.

Not the fucking time or place, Vinna.

They don't say a word as they slowly move to close around us. There's an unmistakable arrogance wafting out with their presence and the way they carry themselves. These people know they are the top of the food chain. They saunter through the cloud of dirt their landings created, like gods expecting worship. Warning pulses up my spine, and I know I can't let my awe get the better of me. I quickly glance at my Shields and Sorik; *we* are all that stands between them and my Chosen.

"By order of Sovereign Finella, you are trespassing and have a dispatch order on your heads. Speak of your origins, or you will be destroyed," a man directly in front of me announces, his grip tightening on the spear in his hands.

I scan the surrounding Sentinels. "Did your *Sovereign* order you not to kill us if we tell you where we're from?" I ask, unclear as to why they'd want to know where we're from if they've been ordered to *dispatch* us.

"Who are you and how did you get in here?" a female voice demands, ignoring my question. I can't make out who said it, but it seems to come from my right.

We stay quiet, assessing the situation.

"We will not ask you again. Who are you, and how did you get in here?" the same female voice demands, a hard edge working to counteract the youth that rings in her tone.

"We walked," Sorik answers calmly and vaguely.

Another Sentinel shouts out, "Impossible," at the same time a humorless laugh fills the air. The laugher steps out of the dirt haze, and my eyes go wide despite my efforts to be calm, cool, and collected.

He has fucking wings!

The dude prowls forward looking like some *GQ* angel of death. I take in his flawless alabaster skin, black hair as long as mine, bright aubergine colored eyes, and a smirk that looks like it's this dude's favorite accessory. Well, aside from all the muscles that is. Massive gray and tan wings sit on his back, and I try not to stare at them as his amused gaze passes judgment on me.

"You'd really like us to believe that you just walked through an impenetrable barrier?" he mocks, running his eyes over Sorik and my Shields dismissively.

"Couldn't have been that impenetrable, as we're having this discussion right now," I challenge. "It seemed pretty Sentinel friendly, so if that's not what you wanted, you should really have it looked at," I add.

"There are no Sentinels outside of our borders," another woman states snidely, and I turn to her.

"Well, what the fuck do you call us then? If it's marked like a Sentinel and fights like a Sentinel..." I trail off, giving my swords a little twirl to emphasize my point.

Unease ripples through both sides as I finish speaking. That humorless laugh starts up again, and the male with the wings steps closer, the others with him mirroring his actions. "I see only one Sentinel surrounded by too much unworthy magic. What did you let them do to you, Kitten?"

I bristle at his implication and the sneer his grin becomes. Titters pepper the Sentinels opposite me. I glare at them, my *we come in peace* attitude quickly morphing into a whole lot of *fuck you.* I tilt my head at him appraisingly and twirl both swords in my hands. "Now now, oh winged and douchey one. You should worry less about what they've done to me and more about what I'm going to do to you."

"We're not going to ask again, how did you get in here?" a dirty blond male Sentinel demands again, and I'm officially done playing this game.

"How the fuck do you think we got in here?" I snap at him. "You know how your barrier works and who it will and will not let through. Cut the bullshit. You can see what we are. If that doesn't matter to you, and I suspect that it doesn't, then shut the fuck up and make a move."

There's a good chance I'm not the magical top dog amongst these Sentinels, but I'm ready to find out.

The dirty blond male feeds magic into the white orb in his hand. "I can only imagine how quickly you'd spread your legs for pure light, given all that you've done to mark the *filth* you stand with. Don't worry though, I'll take care of them, and then I'll take real good care of you," he declares.

Disgust, fury, and disappointment thunder through me.

"Well, I'm about talked out, how about you, Vinna?" Becket asks me.

I quickly take in the number of Sentinels surrounding us, the barriers over my Chosen and my dad, and nod my agreement with Becket. We charge without a word of warning, and for a quick second, I see surprise on their faces before it's replaced with arrogant outrage. I run right for the winged asshole.

Orbs of every color are lobbed at me as I attack. They seem to think if they can take me down first, the others will be easy pickings. I have no idea what we're up against, but I know none of us will go down easy. My runes flash out shields that send the Sentinel's attacking magic bouncing away from me. Panic flares in a few of my opponents' eyes, and it spurs me on even more. I have no idea what any of these Sentinels can do, but the unknown is a two-way street that works in our favor too.

I clash with another Sentinel that steps in my way with an axe. He swings at me, and I lean back just in time to avoid having my head split open. My blade slices up his side. Pivoting around a downward slash, I slam a sword into his upper back. I release the magic for that sword and call another, but I'm intercepted by two more Sentinels before I finally reach the guy with the wings. Surprisingly, he's just standing there waiting for me, excited anticipation radiating off of every inch of him.

A battle soundtrack sounds off all around me; weapons clang and smash together, shouts and war cries rent the air. Bloodlust bubbles up in my chest, and I feel in every fiber of my being that it's not just my life riding on the outcome of all of this, but the lives of everyone who is now connected to me.

It's Bastien's face that flashes in my mind as I bring my sword down to clash with the claymore now gripped in the angel of death's hands. Valen's smile that lights up my insides as I spin and land an elbow in the winged man's side. It's Knox's touch that fortifies me as I swing another blade down and draw first blood along the winged Sentinel's thigh. I shake off a bone rattling hit to my right shoulder and focus on the acceptance that's always waiting for me in Ryker's blue eyes. I let go of the magic of my long sword and step in closer to my winged opponent.

I force myself inside the reach of his sword and call on my throwing knives. Sabin's voice as he speaks the words *I love you* plays over and over in my head as I become a tornado of movement, slashing, defending, and marking up the arrogant Sentinel I'm fighting. I get a blade up under his wing, and his pained cry is drowned out by the phantom feel of Torrez when he holds me and whispers *mine* in my ear.

Pain flares in my stomach, and I look down to see the hilt of a long dagger sitting dead center in my stomach. I look up into the satisfied aubergine eyes of the winged asshole who just stabbed me, and I smile. He thinks he has me.

"You'll have to do better than that," I challenge as I call on a short sword and slice up the front of his arm. I can feel the ghost of Siah's fingers in my hair, and it's as if he's pushing it to the side so he can kiss his mark on my shoulder. Each of them have put their trust and faith in me. They've accepted me for what I am and have worn my marks with honor, love, and devotion. I am theirs, and they are mine. And I will not fucking lose against this prick.

The dagger is ripped from my stomach, and I bite back my cry of pain. I won't give this fucker the satisfaction. I lift my leg to kick him away from me, but a shout behind me has my blood running cold.

"Enoch, behind you!"

Nash's panicked warning goes off like a cannon shot behind me. I try to turn to see what's going on, but I'm stopped when a flash of purple magic pulses through the fighting and I'm thrown backward. I fly through the air and slam hard to the ground. I land on something large and giving, but I'm too dazed to focus on what. I'm muddled from the hit and slow to get up. I try to shake the fogginess out of my mind and figure out what the fuck just happened. I blink sluggishly, trying to bring things into focus.

Bodies litter the ground. No one is left standing. Terrified, I look to where my Chosen are. The barrier around them is still intact, and I let out a relieved breath. A groan sounds beneath me, and I look to see I'm wrapped up in wings and long black hair. I roll off of the guy I was just doing my best to kill and push up onto my feet.

Dread starts to takeover, and I search for Enoch and the others frantically, fear whirlpooling inside of me. Sorik gets to his feet close to where my dad and my Chosen are. He runs a concerned gaze over me and seems to relax a little until his eyes land on my stomach. I look down to find blood soaking my shirt. I whip my shirt over my head and press it hard against my stomach. I ignore the pain as I scramble through the bodies still on the ground, looking for my Shields.

I spot Enoch and run toward him. He groans and pushes onto his back, coughing as he does.

"Fuck, are you okay?" I ask, skidding to my knees next to him.

"Fine," he croaks out, but my relieved sigh catches in my throat.

"Enoch...what the hell?" I whisper, shocked.

I lean forward to study the new marks that he has on his throat. Four of the marks I recognize. Enoch, Kallan, Nash and Becket have them lining their middle fingers, but the top rune is unfamiliar. It's a crescent moon on its back with a smaller one directly underneath it. There's a black vertical line through the middle of both the crescents and three dots at the bottom end. All of the runes run up the front of Enoch's throat. He covers them with a hand as if he's trying to protect them.

"Where the fuck did those come from?" I ask, not sure what the hell is going on.

"They're mine," a female announces from somewhere behind me.

I rise and spin around quickly. Sure enough, the owner of that statement has the same marks on her throat.

"Who the fuck are you?" I ask, taking in her armor and her long tangled red hair. She looks like she's my age, but I can't be sure.

"No, the question is who the fuck are you? What have you done, bringing filth within the barriers?"

Enoch gets to his feet, and her loathsome stare moves from me to him. Her hazel eyes trace the runes on his throat, and I can practically see the fury boiling up and scalding her from the inside out. The reality of what the fuck just happened goes off like a bomb in my mind, and I stare at the woman in shock. The tic in her jaw pulses with fury. I scan the now slowly moving bodies for Kallan, Nash and Becket to be sure. I only spot Nash as he slowly gets to his feet, but the five runes running down his throat confirm everything.

Whoever the fuck this chick is, she marked my Shields as her Chosen. Judging by the virulence in her eyes, she's not fucking happy about it either. Well, fuck her, that makes two of us.

10

Eople shake off the shock from the hit of magic and start to get up. The more others shake it off and stand, the more threatened I once again feel. The wild looking redheaded Sentinel across from me just stares angrily like she's waiting for something. I realize slowly that it's backup.

We were unsure of what would happen once we found Sentinel City. Would we find acceptance and answers or something else? I watch the other Sentinels rise and ready themselves for another fight. Well, I guess we have our fucking answer.

I unlock the vault in my soul that houses all my hate and rejection. I invite all my outrage and hurt feelings to come out and play. I well up with anger and pain, well past my limit for all of this bullshit. The runes on my body light up in response, and I feed their glow with my frustration and malice. This bitch thinks she's pissed? That she can call my friends and family filth and attack us with no consequences? Think again.

I take a step forward, magic storming through me. Power demanding punishment. The other female's vicious stare flicks to me when I move, and shock immediately replaces her outrage. The winged asshole Sentinel that I was fighting steps up behind her, and a thunderous roar of building magic starts in my chest. I pull on my endless cavern of magic, ready to cut everything and everyone who stands against us to the ground. The female lights up as well, but I'm fresh out of fucks for this Sentinel bitch and her vitriol.

"I came here looking for answers, looking for others like me," I snarl, my voice filled to the brim with power and disgust. "But I can see there's no decency or honor among you, and I won't find what I'm looking for here. We'll leave, and you can go back to whatever fucked up ways guide your addled minds. If you try to stop us, then I'll slaughter each and every one of you, and then we'll leave. I'm good with either option."

The winged Sentinel I was fighting smiles like my threat is funny to him, but it doesn't mask the worry in his eyes. The redheaded female who marked my Shields looks around like she's working out just how much damage I could do before they could stop me. Her eyes land on mine, and we take each other in for a beat. I see the calculation in her gaze and give her a ruthless smile.

"You have no idea who you're fucking with," I warn her.

Like my words are the magic key needed to unlock all of my Chosen from unconsciousness, one by one they wake up. Relief slams through me as each of them gets to their feet. Ryker is the last to pop up, having to order Vaughn off of him before he can join his compeers in assessing what the fuck is going on around them. The guys don't say a word. They look around for a couple blinks and then light up just like I am.

I try not to look shocked as each of their runes explodes with purple light. I had no idea they could do that. I shove away my shock and questions, and embrace the power that washes over me as each of them readies himself for whatever is about to go down. The other Sentinels look more and more unsure and nervous with each passing second. They dart glances at the redheaded female and the winged male. These two must be in charge, and I quickly put together a game plan of priority targets if this all goes to shit.

The red haired female Sentinel studies my newly conscious Chosen and deflates infinitesimally.

"You can leave if you'll swear an oath to keep any knowledge of this place to yourselves," she proposes.

"Suryn, no!" the winged asshole protests, but she silences him with a slash of her hand.

She turns back to me. "As for them"—she gestures to Nash, Kallan, Enoch, and Becket—"they need to be dealt with and will not be allowed to leave."

Each of my Shields sounds off, outraged by that statement, but I just watch her. "You have no say in where they will or will not go," I counter simply.

"My magic would say otherwise, or do you not see *my* marks on them," she snaps back.

"Then your magic and my magic are going to have a problem. I marked them first."

I reach out and hold up Enoch's hand, the runes on his finger punctuating my statement. This all feels a little too elementary school *finders keepers, losers weepers*, but if this chick thinks I'm leaving them behind, then she's got another thing coming.

I watch this Suryn chick closely as I lay out my challenge. I see shock, anger, and worry quickly flash through her hazel gaze. She stares at Enoch's hand, tracing my marks there when suddenly her shoulders relax. Her eyes move from Enoch's hand to mine.

Shit.

"Shields...not Chosen," she points out, the arrogant

disgust back in her tone. "Not even full Shields, you've not accepted them."

Her statement teaches me several things at once, the first being that Adriel didn't lie when he flung the *Shield* kernel of wisdom at me. Second, there *is* a reason why I don't have any of my Shields' marks. And lastly, we're fucked. Can I kill the Sentinel that just marked Enoch and the others? Will that hurt them? I've never asked Sorik what happened to him when Grier died. It felt wrong to ask him to dig through what he experienced for my own curiosity. Obviously, Enoch and the others wouldn't die, but would it do anything else? They're not full Chosen yet, but still.

"Looks like we'll fight for 'em then. Winner claims them all, and the loser fucks off," I state simply.

"Nice try," the winged Sentinel spits out as he steps toward me. "This issue will be decided by the Sovereign. Only she has the authority to make this decision," he declares, shooting the Suryn chick a glare like he's daring her to say otherwise.

"Is this the same Sovereign that ordered you to kill us?" I ask with mock sweetness, sending a flare through my magic and forcing it to pulse out like the threat it is.

Suryn and the winged wanker don't say anything, but I take their silence as confirmation.

"Nah, I'm cool, tell her thanks but no thanks on the attempted hit." I turn my back on the other Sentinels and stride over to my guys. I'm trying not to freak out and to make sure they're all okay, but I don't want to be so far away from them anymore. I expect Kallan, Becket, Nash and Enoch to follow, but only Becket, Kallan, and Nash do. Enoch hesitates like he's unsure of what the right move is here.

The Sentinel with the wings gives me another of his patent smirks. "It seems we got off on the wrong foot. You see, no one has ever breached the barrier before, let alone signaled their arrival the way that you all did. I'm sure you can understand our jumping to the defensive."

He pauses for a second like he's expecting us to agree with him. I stay quiet.

"There's clearly more going on here than we initially realized," he states, gesturing to Enoch and Nash and backpedaling from his previous superior attitude. "You mentioned you were looking for answers. I can safely say that *now* so are we. Let's put this unfortunate first meeting behind us. That way we can all find the answers that we need here."

"Unfortunate first meeting?" I ask, scoffing at his word choice. "You mean the one where you showed up and tried to kill us?"

The arrogant prick smiles like he thinks that's funny. "Technically, you attacked first," he throws out there smugly.

I don't say anything as my face morphs into a look that says *come the fuck on.*

"My name is Ory," he offers after a moment of awkward silence. "This is Suryn," he announces, gesturing to the redhead with the new marks down her throat. "And you are?" he asks, dazzling me with a smile that I'm sure usually gets him what he wants.

I'm not surprised that he doesn't introduce anyone else. I doubt the self-importance that's radiating off of him would allow him to see too far past his own nose. I run my gaze up his black armored body to his ebony hair, fair complexion, and dark purple eyes. I then dismiss him with an unimpressed glance away. I study Suryn and the other armored Sentinels all standing at attention, well, except for the wounded and a couple who are missing heads. I wonder who went full Queen of Hearts, but I'll swap battle stories with all the guys when we're safe and alone.

Ory grins, like my silence is exactly what he wants. Maybe it's the bad experiences I've had in the past where giving my full name has clued someone else into things about me while leaving *me* in the dark, but I'm hesitant to give them any info about me.

"I'm a Sentinel. These are my Chosen, and the rest are *my* Shields," I offer vaguely. I wrap Sorik and Vaughn in *whatever title these people want to see*, not wanting to explain any further who they are to me.

"Come now, Sentinel, don't be like that," Ory teases with a mock pout.

"Next time, maybe start with all that polite shit instead of an attack, see if it gets you pleasantries and introductions," I snap, tired of this back and forth.

I want to leave, but the Chosen marks on my Shields have put a wrench in that plan. If they don't want to let all of us go, we could fight our way out. But even if we did manage to get out of here uninjured, would they leave their barrier to come after us? There are a lot of unknowns floating around, whether we stay or go.

I look back the way we came and catch Suryn's grip on her katana tighten. I tense, not sure what the best plan is here. Fight and risk someone getting hurt or maybe worse? Go with them and risk probably the same thing? I activate the runes behind my ear.

"*What should we do guys? We can bail and probably fight our way out of here, or we can go with them and hope for the best.*"

"*If we try to leave and they call reinforcements, we could be in trouble,*" Sabin states.

"*If we go with them, then we'll definitely get outnumbered, and we could be in trouble,*" Valen counters.

"*Maybe doing what they want will buy us some good will*"

though. I mean, if we're potentially fucked with both options, then let's catch more flies with honey," Ryker points out.

"Fuck, I'm sorry guys," I tell them.

"This isn't on you, Bruiser. We were all hoping this would work out better than it is," Bastien reassures me.

"I mean, I hate to be that guy who's all optimistic right up until he gets killed, but maybe the feathered fucker is right and we all just got off on the wrong foot," Valen adds, and I smile at his nickname for that Ory dude.

"Okay, so we go with them?" I ask, making sure we're on the same page.

Unanimous yeses fill my mind. I disengage my runes and turn to Sorik and my Shields. "You guys good with us extending some unearned cooperation?"

They're quiet for a moment.

"I'm cool with whatever keeps us from being dead," Becket adds, and the others all shrug their agreement.

"Your mother was levelheaded and compassionate. I think we might find more of that amongst her people than what our current company is showing," Sorik adds.

I keep my *let's fucking hope so* to myself and turn back to the feathered fucker and the grumpy redhead.

"So take us to your Sovereign then," I capitulate.

I just fucking hope we can withstand whatever shit they may throw at us.

"Right, then..." Ory agrees, clapping his hands together and spreading his massive gray and tan wings.

One other Sentinel in his group who also has wings does the same thing.

Are there runes that can give you those?

I chase away my curiosity about it like an old lady chases cats out of her house with a broom. I will not envy this douche. Fuck his wings. I pull my internal broom out again when my thoughts conjure up this old show about immortals Beth used to watch. No, brain, we cannot just cut off his head and hope we grow wings.

Sentinels just start taking off into the sky like fireworks. I watch in awe as even the ones without wings just take off like it's nothing.

How the hell do they do that?

Ory must notice that we're not suddenly levitating and following their lead. He looks confused. "Do you not fly?" he asks suddenly, like the thought just occurred to him.

The image of all of these Sentinels dropping like missiles out of the sky flashes through my mind.

"Nope," I respond with a shrug. "You go on ahead and announce our imminent arrival to the Sovereign. We'll meet you there," I offer. I doubt they're that dumb, but it's worth a shot.

Suryn rolls her eyes at me. "Looks like we'll be taking the long way," she announces to the Sentinels that are still on the ground. She looks offended by the fact that she'll have to walk.

"Go inform the Quorum of what's happened and that we're on our way," she tells the female next to her.

The Sentinel nods and shoots up into the sky. I watch her trajectory, itching to know how she's doing that.

"It's Elemental magic," Sabin announces in my head, like he can read my mind.

I whirl around to face him. *"What the fuck? How the hell are they doing that with Elemental magic?"* I demand.

"They're manipulating the air. It's very difficult and taxing, and it's a surefire way to drain a caster quicker than a lamia," Sabin explains. *"I honestly don't know how they're doing it and are still able to stand, let alone fight."*

I stare up at the sky, no longer able to see the Sentinels that just took off. Ory is saying something, but I don't pay it any attention.

"You've been holding out on me?" I accuse, and his answering snort echoes in my mind. *"I'm going to kick Kallan's ass too for not cluing me in. Are you telling me I could have been flying my happy ass around this whole time?"*

"Like I said, it's not common practice among casters; it requires too much magic. I didn't think about the fact that, as a Sentinel, you have more magic and therefore could fly your happy ass around without killing yourself."

I smile and shake my head at him. *"As soon as we get home, we're going to flight school,"* I declare, and a stunning smile appears on Sabin's face.

"Let's go," Suryn snaps at us.

The order pulls my attention away from Sabin, and I watch as she runs her gaze over me and then my group. Her face scrunches up with obvious disgust. I do the same back to her. Fuck this snooty bitch.

"Well, get a move on, we're going to be walking the rest of the day," she snidely informs me, gesturing away from her body like she thinks I'm going to go first.

I bite back a groan at the announcement of more walking. At this rate, I'm never going to have to do cardio again.

"If you think I'm going to put you psychos at my back, then you're an idiot. Lead the way," I tell her, mimicking the same arm sweep she just gave me.

Her eyes narrow, but she takes a step and then another. "Fine with me, *Sentinel*, you'll find we don't scare so easily."

I scoff at the implication that they're tougher than we are, but stay quiet. I don't give a fuck what these people think of me. I just want to get this shit sorted with my Shields and get the fuck out of here.

We fall in line behind the eleven other Sentinels. No one talks. I activate my mental link with all my Chosen when it's clear we're only going to get the cold shoulder from them.

"Are you guys okay?" I check in, worried once again about what happened earlier with the barrier.

"We're good, just trying to figure out what the hell happened," Ryker explains.

"What happened was we all lit up like fucking spotlights, did something to their barrier, and then you guys went down like a wall of bricks. Did I hurt you somehow?" I fill them in, tension radiating from every cell in my body.

"No, you didn't hurt us, but I could feel you tugging at my magic when you went all nuclear with the barrier," Valen tells me, and the other guys sound off their agreement.

The other Sentinels take turns peeking over their shoulders to watch us. *Tougher my ass.* Enoch and his coven are whispering quietly back and forth, and I know I need to find out if they're okay too. I look back, and Sorik gives me a smile and a thumbs up, like he can read the worry in my face. I smile back and then tap back into my conversation with my guys.

"It must be a barrier thing. I did it before at Lachlan's house. It didn't make anyone pass out, but I wasn't connected to them like I am with you. It did put them on their ass though," I tell them, recalling Lachlan and his coven going flying when my magic pulsed out into their barrier.

"So how long had you guys been fighting before we woke up?" Knox asks, and I can hear the anger and frustration in his mental tone.

"Not long. They showed up about twenty minutes after we decided moving targets were better than sitting ducks. We only went at it for less than ten minutes before that Suryn chick's magic went all claimy with the other guys." I don't do anything to temper the irritation I feel at recounting that information, and Ryker reaches out and rubs comforting circles at the small of my back.

"What's with Wings McGee, over there?" Torrez asks, and I

look up to find Ory the winged douche staring at us.

"No fucking clue," I tell him.

"I want wings," Knox admits, and I crack up.

"Dude," I tell him in agreement.

"Why do the assholes always get the best toys?" Knox adds, and I reach out and pull him into a hug.

"I wonder which rune does that? Think you can magicjack him like you did with Elder Kowka?" Bastien encourages.

I chuckle and then go quiet contemplating his question. Can I do that?

"Might not be a rune," Sabin observes. *"He could be mixed with something that has wings."*

"I don't know," I answer. *"That was my first thought, but they kept calling us filth and unworthy magic. I'm not getting the impression that they think very highly of other supernatural species or magic users. They went straight for the slut shaming for being with you guys, so I doubt these Sentinels are getting it on with other supes, even if it does give them wings,"* I explain.

Sabin nods, but he looks lost in thought.

"It's probably the opposite really," I add. *"Wouldn't surprise me if a bunch of fucked up Lannister inbreeding shit is going down in these parts. That dude clearly has a screw loose."*

I jerk my chin in the direction of Ory, and a growl rumbles up from Torrez's chest. Several Sentinels stop and trace the sound back to Torrez with alarmed expressions.

"Tell your mutt to keep his threats to himself," Suryn orders.

"Call him a mutt one more time, and I'll cut your fucking tongue out," I retort.

She rounds on me, a katana appearing in her hands. I flash short swords into my palms and step toward her. My Chosen and Shields all move to block my way, annoyingly boxing me in. They call on their own various weapons and take up defensive positions around me.

Fucking hell, I could really use that rocket rune right about now.

"Suryn!" Ory yells. "Stand down!"

She points her katana at him. "I don't take orders from you," she grinds out between clenched teeth.

"Not normally, but I am the Voice chosen by the Sovereign herself, so in circumstances like these, I outrank you. You will stand down and keep your mouth shut until the Sovereign states otherwise!"

They glare at each other, and I try not to judge myself too much by the enjoyment it gives me to see the power struggle going on between them. Suryn stomps off, and Ory watches her go with a resigned huff.

"I don't think your girlfriend likes you very much," Bastien tells him.

Ory shoots him a glare and then storms off in the same direction as Suryn.

"I think we're growing on them," Valen deadpans.

I slam a hand over my mouth to keep the laughter inside, but it doesn't work. I lose it. I try really fucking hard to get a hold of myself, but the harder I try to shut the fuck up, the harder I laugh. A couple of the other Sentinels eye me, judgment clear in their gazes. I'm sure I look like a fucking nutter. Good. Maybe they'll be less likely to fuck with us if they think we're bat shit.

My giggle fest slowly becomes contagious, and the other guys start to guffaw. The more they laugh, the more I laugh. It makes no sense that I'm suffering from a giggle attack in the middle of the shit that's going down, but I have no fucks to give.

Ory watches us over his shoulder, and I can't read the expression on his face.

Oh yeah, definitely growing on them.

11

Torrez growls at me as I dart out of the protective circle he and the others have formed. I blow a kiss at him over my shoulder and drop back so I can talk to Kallan and the others. We've been walking for hours, all of us silent and contemplative. It's like the giggle-off drained us of the last dregs of our energy. I've hit my limit with the quiet. I was planning on talking to Enoch and his coven when we were alone, but the need to talk about their new marks is making me itchy, and I just can't put it off anymore.

Becket looks up as I fall in line with them and gives me a small smile. I return it, dismissing any reservations it stirs up. I'm still waiting for him to go back to hating me, and I'm not sure what to do about the fact that he hasn't yet. We need to talk, but for that kind of chat, I need to wait until it's just the two of us.

"You guys okay?" I ask quietly.

Ory and another winged Sentinel take notice of our chatting, and I wonder if they have the ability to increase their hearing and eavesdrop like I can.

"I don't think any of us are close to any kind of version of okay," Kallan tells me, and I rub my shoulder against his. Enoch snorts his agreement with Kallan's assessment.

"Yeah, I'm not sure what to think about any of this," Enoch admits.

"How can she just mark us? I thought there had to be sex and shit as a catalyst?" Becket asks.

I shrug. "Sentinels can mark Chosen without sex, but I thought it had to be a conscious choice that they made, like when I marked Torrez and Siah. She looks as confused by her magic as I did when I unknowingly first marked Valen, Bastien, Sabin, Ryker and Knox. So I don't know."

"Could have warned us that it hurt that bad," Nash razzes, but I don't miss the wince that sneaks over his features.

I bark out a humorless chuckle and roll my eyes. "They're just Chosen marks for now, just wait until you become a full Sentinel," I rib back and then quickly go silent.

Will they become full Sentinels? Would they bond with that nightmare of a female? I can't bring myself to ask any of that though, and the unasked questions seem to loom heavy in the air all around us.

"So how the hell do we get rid of these?" Becket finally voices, pointing at his throat. Enoch and Nash exchange a look, but I don't try to interpret it.

Frustration starts to simmer inside of me yet again, and I wonder if I will ever reach a point in my life where I'm not holding hands with this emotion. I was hoping for answers here. That I'd be able to piece things together and better understand who and what I was. My irritated gaze hops to our guides. I watch these beings, so much like me but not, as they silently lead us who the fuck knows where.

I can feel the tiny amount of hope I had get snuffed out with each muffled footstep toward where they live. I didn't want to look at that ember of hope in my chest too hard, because acknowledging it was just inviting more disappointment. But as I feel it die, I can finally admit how much I was hoping I would find my people here. That they would welcome me with open arms and become everything I have always wanted. I should have fucking known better.

We all dive back into brooding silence, robotically setting one foot in front of the other. We walk like that for who knows how long when suddenly the terrain around us starts to change. The trees thin, and the ground starts to even out. The other Sentinels grow more tense the closer we get to our destination. And then, like with the barrier protecting this place, we crest a hill, and the city is... just there.

It's something out of some fantasy fairy tale. The large castle—that looks like it's made of some kind of decadent cream colored stone—sits proudly in the middle of it all, like it alone rules everything around it. The massive structure dwarfs the large houses that circle it. There are more and more houses and buildings that flare out in a ringed pattern, growing smaller the further they are from the proud castle. The structures are all different tones of cream with gray roofs, and it all looks clean and organized.

Fields, growing crops and supporting livestock, lie far in the distance on the complete opposite side from where we're standing. I'm distracted by the occasional body that arcs in the air as Sentinels fly to and from their various destinations. I tamp down the envy that once again surges in me.

We're led out of the tree line toward the outermost ring of the city. For a people that says no one has ever breached the barrier, they sure as fuck have a lot of guards. Males and females sporting the telltale black armor walk the perimeter, and I can spot black specks moving on every level the castle has and wandering around the ringed streets between rows of houses.

I had zero expectations about what Sentinel City would actually look like, but I'm stunned to find something that looks like a CGI special effect that belongs in some epic fantasy movie. It all looks so calm and peaceful, which is in direct contrast to the unwelcoming assholes I've met up to this point.

"Welcome to Tierit," a Sentinel that hasn't spoken until now offers as he passes by.

I'm too stunned to respond, which is probably good since I don't know if he actually means that we're welcome, or is saying it like it's a threat.

"By the moon," Bastien exclaims, and someone snorts in agreement.

"Why did I picture log cabins as far as the eye can see?" Valen whispers with awe.

"Because you're a weirdo," Ryker responds, not missing a beat.

"I had a dream it was some castle built into a mountain," Torrez throws out there.

"Probably shouldn't have watched *Lord of the Rings* right before we left," Sabin teases. "Although this is pretty damn close to something you'd see in one of those movies," he adds.

I shake my head and then jump, shocked, when someone snarls at us to keep moving. I turn to glare at the bearded asshole, but it's exactly what I needed to snap out of my stupor. I don't care how mesmerizing this place looks, it's important to remember that they don't really want us here. I take a step forward, shaking off my dazed awe and slamming myself back down to reality.

"We stay together no matter what. If they try to separate us, we fuck them up," I declare as we move closer to the small houses bordering this place.

Everyone nods and sounds off their agreement, but an uneasy pit opens up in my stomach. We're all pretty tough individually and even more so as a group, but I'm staring at a massive city full of Sentinels. The odds of us fighting our way out of here are zero. I know we were in a lose-lose situation before when we agreed to cooperate, but the reality of what we could be up against just bitch slapped me across the face.

Every cell in my body goes on alert, and uncertainty wells up inside of me. I've always been able to trust myself and my abilities, but staring at this place has me faltering. We make it several rings in before we run into a large concentration of Sentinels. There have been guards and people dotted here and there, but nothing like the bustling crowds we walk into as we get closer to the castle. People go silent as soon as they spot us, and several of them immediately call on a weapon or some other magical defense.

I take in the light gray fabric they're all wearing in a myriad of different styles and the markings that everyone carries on their bodies. Some of them have markings on their faces, others you can catch a hint of runes leading into a sleeve or collar. I have the weird urge to ask all of them to strip down so I can see the runes that mark their bodies.

I want to compare what I have against theirs and learn about the differences. But the threat that floats around the atmosphere as soon as others see us tells me that curiosity would fucking annihilate the cat...the Sentinel, the Chosen, the Shields and anything else with these people.

Eyes track us warily, some of them filled with unfiltered

anger. I make a point to meet each of the angry gazes head on. They radiate a certain *I am not to be fucked with* vibe, so I do all that I can to ensure they get that same clear message from me. I almost wish we had *we come in peace* tattooed over every inch of my body, but maybe even that wouldn't make much of a difference with these people. These Sentinels have secluded themselves for a reason, and it's clear in their response to us that they want to keep it that way.

The sun is setting, and the bright colors are reflected all throughout the walls of the city; it's beautiful and feels like a trap. It's like the city itself is trying to lull me into a false sense of security and appreciation. The cream colored stone all around us is smooth enough to be marble, but it appears to be softer somehow. I want to touch things as we make our way through rings of houses, but I don't want to lose a hand or have any of my actions taken as an attack.

We approach a massive iron and wood gate that blocks the way to the castle. The gate opens up on its own accord as we get closer. We step through and have to fight our instincts to call on weapons and protect ourselves as we're surrounded by more black armored Sentinels as soon as we're through the gate. They say nothing and do nothing, just fall in line around us as we're led further in.

I trace the features of my Chosen and Shields. Tics in jaws, tight features, vigilant eyes are what I find. I meet Sorik's gaze and see the concern and worry in the tight lines around his eyes.

"If this goes bad, you get Vaughn out of here," I tell him, reminding him that this is what we agreed to before, and nothing has changed.

He's in charge of Vaughn, and I'm responsible for the rest. Sorik nods, and I take a deep breath and turn forward. I have no fucking clue why I think the plans we made before still apply here. There may be no getting out of this shit. I shove that thought away and attempt to refortify my faith in who I am and what I can do. I've always been able to rely on myself and my abilities. I'm smart, I'm capable, and I love these guys.

They are my family, and I will find a way to keep them safe, no matter what.

We're escorted down several halls, but I'm too on edge to pay attention to the details of this place beyond the directions. Our steps echo through the cavernous spaces that make up this castle. It's an ominous sound that sends a rush of adrenaline through me. I do my best to catalog the lefts and rights we take. I can tell by the looks on the faces of others in my group that I'm not the only one.

Large black lacquered doors swing open, and we're led into a very long empty room. At the far end of the massive space, there's a large throne with three smaller thrones positioned on each side of it. A boom echoes around the vast space as the doors are closed behind us, and the black clad guards immediately separate to line the outside walls of the room. I recognize one of the guards as a guy I stabbed in the fight earlier.

Everyone is silent. Suryn looks pissed off, and Ory just looks bored as he cleans dirt out from under his nails with a dagger.

"All hail Sovereign Finella, Leader of the Marked, Ruler of Tierit, Blood Savior, Walker of Realms and Gate Keeper," a voice bellows out in the room, his announcement bouncing off the cream stone walls and ramping up my unease.

I hear the telltale sound of synchronized marching first, and then I spot the guards as they perform some synchronized stepping bullshit either meant to impress or intimidate. It does neither for me. They part to reveal an older woman, maybe late fifties, who is so fair she almost looks albino.

Her white hair is sleek and straight, the gold ornate crown on her head reflected in the sheen of her tresses. She doesn't look our way as she strolls up to the biggest throne. I'm shocked that the Sovereign is a female. I don't know why that sends a spark of hope through me, and I try to dismiss the irrational relief.

Beth was a woman, I remind myself as I take in the Sovereign as she seats herself. Her sleeveless gown is red and more revealing than I'd think a queen would be down for. Slits up the side of the gauzy fabric reveal milky white, toned legs. A plunging neckline reveals cleavage that's not as perky as it probably once was.

I spot four runes on her shoulder, four runes running horizontal over her left breast, and one between her eyebrows. I'm surprised by the lack of markings other than those. I figured the leader would be even more decked out than I am. More figures are led in behind her, but they're hidden by the guards as they do their synchronized entrance thing. The guards eventually part, revealing a man.

His dark skin is a surprising contrast to his unusual eyes and pure white hair. His pupils are the lightest shade of purple I've ever seen, and I'm mesmerized by the one of a kind color. He watches me curiously as he moves toward the thrones. I look from him to the entrance and catch sight of the other person behind him. Acrid rage burns through me. How is this possible? Golden red eyes meet mine, and everything inside of me screams with blistering fury.

How the fuck did Adriel get here?

I claw at my neck needing to make sure there's nothing there. But I don't feel any relief when I just feel my skin under my nails. I watched that piece of shit turn to ash in front of my eyes. This doesn't make any sense. I call on my long sword and take a step forward before I even know what I'm doing. Growls and statements of shock ring out around me from all of my guys, and Becket quickly falls into step next to me as we both begin to sprint toward Adriel. I'll fucking make sure the piece of shit stays dead this time.

12

"Vinna, no!" ricochets off of me, but I don't care. All I see is red. All I feel is the need to fucking end him once and for all. Shouting fills up the chamber, and the shields from my runes activate to keep orbs from touching me.

Adriel's eyes widen with surprise. Satisfaction percolates through my acrimony and bloodlust.

"You better fucking be afraid," I shout at him as I close the distance.

Someone tackles me from behind, and I thrash to get out of their hold. I need to fucking kill him. I scream as I fail to break away from whoever has me. Chaos erupts all around me, and the sounds of fighting hit my ears. Fangs sink into my shoulder, and pleasure courses through me, battling for control with the need for vengeance raging through my veins.

"Vinna, focus," Siah demands, and then he bites me again. I groan from the sensations his bite sends flooding through my system and whimper because I don't want to be feeling them right now. I want to be feeling Adriel's body turning to ash in my hands.

Siah licks at my neck, and I try to buck him off of me.

"Vinna, listen to me," he orders and then flips me onto my back. I release the long sword in my grip, not wanting to hurt him, but I'm fucking pissed.

"Get. The. Fuck. Off. Me," I snarl, ignoring the clanging of weapons now sounding off all around me.

"Vinna, think it through! How did Adriel survive?"

"I don't know!" I scream at him, panic and anger bleeding out of my tone.

"You watched him die, Vinna. He turned to ash right in front of you. What else would make more sense here?" Siah demands, his eyes pleading with me to get something, but I have no fucking clue what it is.

"Siah, if you love me, you will get the fuck off of me right now!" I shout into his face, my demand cracking with frenzied emotion. It's like everything I've been feeling and battling inside is leaking out of me in this moment.

"It is because I love you that I can't let you up, not until you understand, my mate," he whispers softly into my ear, and I can hear the grief in his voice. "That is not Adriel."

Siah's declaration and the hurt that I know he's feeling by doing what he's doing to me right now smash through my need to kill. I blink, stunned, as I try to wrap my brain around what he's saying.

Adriel's voice fills my head as I think back on the things he told me while holding me prisoner.

"He shouldn't have been Chosen; it should have been me!"

"Who shouldn't have been Chosen?" my voice demands as the memory echoes in my mind.

"Sauriel, my brother."

Adriel's voice fades away, and I make the connection that Siah is so desperate for me to make.

Fuck.

I stare up into Siah's light blue eyes and shake my head, instantly pissed off at myself. I fucked up.

"How bad is it?" I ask, knowing shit is hitting the fan all around us based off the noise I hear going on. I can't bring myself to look yet. I need another minute to let the truth soak in. Adriel is dead. I killed him.

"Eh," Siah states casually, punctuating it with a shrug. "Pretty sure Adriel's brother just shit his pants. All of your mates are guarding you and your Shields. Your Shields are trying to get Becket to see what you now see. It's a battle, but I think we can take 'em." Siah gives me a playful wink, and I can't help the tired chuckle it evokes in me. "You good, mate?" he asks sweetly. "Sorry about the biting."

"No, it was good thinking," I tell him as I push up. He rocks back onto his feet and offers me a hand to help me up.

Sure enough, Enoch, Kallan, and Nash are furiously arguing with Becket. My Chosen surround us, each of them engaged in a fight. We're surrounded by armed and angry Sentinels. The Quorum—which apparently includes Adriel's brother Sauriel—are all standing in front of their thrones, exuding outrage over what just happened.

Shit, shit, shit.

Wasn't I just fucking vowing to keep everyone safe? But I go and lose my shit, pretty much guaranteeing that no one is safe now. I try to think through what I can do to stop all of this. I'm pretty sure me raising my hand and announcing *my bad* isn't going to cut it. Where's a damn white flag when you need one?

Someone hurls magic at Ryker, but his shield flares up to protect him. Another orb is lobbed our way, but I'm distracted by the Sovereign as she sits in her throne, an annoyed look on her face. "I want them cut to pieces!" she declares with a bored tone, like it's already a foregone conclusion for her.

The guards press in against us, and we all respond. I get kicked in the gut and shoved back inside the circle that my Chosen and Shields have inadvertently created while they defend against the attacking Sentinels. Instead of immediately rushing back in, swords up, I call on my Offensive magic and start hurling orbs filled with a whole lot of *fuck off* at the guards.

I'm surprised, even though I really shouldn't be, when some of them have shields that pop up and protect them just like I do. My orbs still knock them over like bowling pins but don't do more than that. I keep at my *bowling for Sentinels* plan, throwing barriers around the ones I knock down so they can't get up.

I fling another barrier out, and then my heart stops when a pain filled cry reaches out and grips my soul in a stranglehold. Terror seizes me as I turn to see a raised sword arcing down toward Sabin. He's fighting another guard, and there's no way he can stop the other sword's progression. Moments with Sabin flash in my mind. His smile. The wrinkle he gets between his eyebrows when he's concerned or perplexed. His lips against mine, and the way it feels to be loved by him, treasured by him.

"I am the wrong bitch!" I bellow as I flare purple.

I open the source of my magic completely and demand everything it's got. The pressure builds inside of me in a flash, and I grit my teeth against the pain as I watch the blade inch closer to Sabin like it's in slow motion. I wait until my magic intensifies to an *I can't take this* level, and then I shove it out of me. The pulse passes through my guys and doesn't even make them sway—which is exactly what I wanted—but as soon as it slams into the other Sentinels, it flattens them. They slam to the ground with such force that the sound reverberates around the room.

My purple magic rages like a tsunami toward the Sovereign. It smashes against a barrier and shatters it like glass. My magic slams into the leaders of this city. It blows the royals back into their thrones and then flips those thrones on their backs. I'm pretty sure my magic just made it clear what it thinks of their monarchy.

I stand there, a little shocked by what I just did. I've used this ability before, both on purpose and on accident, but never on this level. The room goes from a battlefield to eerily quiet. We stand there, trying to take in what just happened and catch our breath. I run my gaze over all of them but don't see anything I should be concerned about.

"Should we run?" Bastien asks after a minute as his eyes skate over all the people on the ground in the room.

"I don't even know if we can," I admit. "Will we make it out of the city?"

"You'd have to leave us behind. They might be able to track us through that chick's Chosen marks," Kallan announces, and once again I have no clue if they can, or even would, come after us. I know I can alert my Chosen as to where I am and that I need them; can it work the other way around?

"Fuck," I shout out and run my fingers through my matted and tangled hair. "I've fucked this all up."

"No, *they* fucked this all up when they attacked us in the forest," Valen states calmly.

"Definitely not the most welcoming lot," Sorik agrees.

I look around the room at the unmoving figures. I can still see that the guards are breathing, so they're not dead, but at this point, I don't know if this is a good thing or a bad thing. I trace a path toward the thrones and move off in that direction.

"What're you up to, Killer?"

"I'm going to fix the thrones and put the royal assholes back in them. Maybe if they come to upright instead of ass-up, they'll be more understanding."

"Oh...oh...better idea," Knox announces, raising his hand like an eager student. "What if they wake up and find us sitting on their thrones? You know, let 'em know they fucked with the wrong coven from the get go."

I chuckle and then start fixing chairs like I'm cleaning up from an epic party.

"You good, Becket?" I ask as he eyes Sauriel warily.

"Yeah, talk about a mindfuck though. Think I can kick the asshole a couple times before he wakes up? You just know this fucker knew his brother was operating with a few screws loose."

"I won't tell if you don't," I offer on a grunt as I get the big black royal with the almost white eyes settled in his now upright throne.

Snickers bounce around the room.

"I love when she goes all ruthless," Bastien sighs dreamily.

I roll my eyes at him and hide my smile.

"Yeah, she had my heart from the minute I saw her beating the shit out of you," Valen agrees, giving his brother a cheeky grin.

"Anyone need healing?" Ryker asks.

The guys all answer no or shake their heads. I look down at my stomach, just now remembering that I got stabbed earlier.

What the fuck does that say about this day that I forgot about taking a dagger to the gut?

I run my hands over where the wound should be. Dried blood and dirt flake off, but it doesn't hurt, and I can't for the life of me find a wound.

That's fucking weird.

I twist and try to look at my back, like somehow the stab wound is going to show up there when it's not showing up on my abdomen, but there's nothing aside from proof that I could really use a shower.

"What's wrong, Vinna?" Sabin asks me when I start turning around like a dog chasing its tail.

"I got stabbed earlier," I tell him as I make another revolution.

"What?" multiple voices demand all at once, and the next thing I know, I'm surrounded by worried and upset Chosen and Shields. Hands search my body for a wound that's no longer there, while Ryker and Nash both start firing out instructions and questions.

"Fucking hell, you guys. Back off for a second. I can't find a wound. Nothing hurts. I'm fine!" I insist.

Ryker looks at me confused. "What do you mean you can't find a wound?" he asks at the same time Nash insists, "You are not fine! Getting stabbed does not equal fine!"

I ignore Nash and answer Ryker. "Just like I said, I don't have a wound anymore."

"Are you sure you were actually cut?" Kallan questions, his gaze tracing my body like he's double-checking that everything is okay.

"No, she was bleeding earlier. I remember," Enoch states.

"You saw her bleeding earlier and didn't say anything?" I expect a comment like this to come from Knox or maybe Bastien, so I'm surprised when it's Becket who rounds on his coven mate.

"It all happened fast, I only caught a glimpse, and then all that Chosen mark shit happened with the other girl," Enoch defends, and I step in between them when it's clear Becket doesn't think that's a good enough answer.

"It's fine, seriously. We have bigger problems to deal with right now. We can solve the disappearing stab wound later."

I throw my hands up silencing any further argument, and everyone gets back to work positioning Sentinels around the room in a way we hope will make them less murdery when they wake up.

"How long do you think they'll be out?" Sabin asks as he sits a guard up against a wall. All eyes turn to me.

"Pshhh, you know I'm just winging this shit, right? I know fuck all about anything."

"Maybe we can track an archive room or a library down and see if we can find some answers before everyone wakes up," Sorik suggests.

"I'd be game, except so far no one is pounding on the doors, demanding to know what's going on. I worry the minute we stick our head out unescorted, we won't get very far," Sabin tells us, and we all nod in agreement.

"Where's an invisibility cloak when you need one?" Knox jokes, and we all laugh.

"What if she knocked out the whole city?" Becket questions, and once again everyone turns to me.

"Don't know fuck all about anything," I repeat, pointing a finger at myself and repeatedly jabbing it down above my head.

"By the moon, this sucks," Ryker states, shaking his head with frustration.

"Tell me about it, bro. Story of my damn life," I agree.

"These fuckers have all the answers," Enoch points out, toeing the leg of a guard.

"Yep, and I doubt after all of this they'll be in a hurry to share any of them with us. Not that they seemed like a helpful bunch before that," I add.

A groan fills the room, and we all freeze. I scan the

unconscious bodies, looking for one that looks less unconscious.

"Shit, looks like girlfriend is waking up," Torrez points out, and I follow his outstretched arm to find Suryn the surly Sentinel trying to sit up.

Well, this should be fucking fun.

13

W e all watch her slowly come to, not sure what the fuck else we're supposed to do. Enoch looks pained, watching her struggle to sit up. Suryn slowly blinks her eyes open, and her confused gaze lands on me. I give her my best *if you don't kill me, we can be friends* smile and throw in a little wave to drive the point home. She seems out of it for a couple beats, and then I watch as what happened registers in her gaze and she scrambles to her feet.

"What the hell did you do?" she demands. She looks frantically around the room and cries out when she finds The Quorum passed out in their thrones.

A katana appears in her hands again, and she charges toward the thrones. I'm surprised when she doesn't go straight for the Sovereign, but instead dives to check on Sauriel. We all watch relief flood her pained features when she realizes for herself that he's still alive, and for a moment, I feel bad. Suryn points her katana at me and glares.

"I'll gut you for this," she growls at me between clenched teeth.

And just like that, my sympathy evaporates. "He's asleep,

not dead, calm the fuck down. I could have slit everyone's throats while you were out if I'd wanted to. Fuck it, I still could. But I'm not here to hurt anyone. Keep your threats to yourself unless you want me to start making some of my own."

Valen leans over to me. "Ix-nay on the slit everyone's throats-ay," he tells me, using the worst pig Latin ever.

I give him a look that says *what? I could have*. He smiles and shakes his head.

"Might want to lead with more of an apology when the others wake up," he teases me.

"You think the leaders of the strongest magical race in existence are going to thank you for not slitting their throats after you attacked them?" Suryn asks incredulously, pulling my attention back to her.

A couple more moans fill the room. One is coming from Sauriel and the other from the ebony skinned royal with the freaky eyes.

"Well, I guess we're about to find out," Torrez observes.

I cringe, wound tight as fuck with tension.

I start chanting a positive mantra to myself of *please don't execute us* as I watch the Quorum males come too.

"Dad, are you okay?" Suryn asks Sauriel, and my mouth flies open in shock.

"Damn, my money was on lover, not father," Siah quips, and Bastien grunts in agreement and fist bumps him.

"What happened?" Sauriel croaks out, sitting up straighter.

"You were attacked," Suryn accuses, and they both look over at me.

I plaster that same *I didn't kill you, so let's be cool* smile on my face and once again wave, because apparently I can't fucking help myself.

Like daughter like father, he glares at me.

"Now before you go and decree something you'll regret, like 'Off with their heads,' allow me to explain," I tell him.

Sauriel doesn't say anything, and I'm not sure if this means *yes, please explain* or maybe he's imagining all the ways to make us suffer for my insolence. I jerk in surprise when the creepy eyed male rasps, "Go on." I totally forgot he was waking up too after the whole father bomb was dropped.

"I had a run in with your brother Adriel that's going to leave some intense scars on my soul. I thought you were him. I didn't realize he was a twin. Your face threw me off."

I internally facepalm. *Your face threw me off? Really, Vinna?*

"Um...I know it looks like I'm here to start some shit, but I swear that couldn't be further from the truth. I was just hoping for some answers, that's all."

"Where is my brother now?" Sauriel demands, and from the looks of things, he looks like he's ready to fly out of his throne and hunt his twin down himself.

"He was in the Belarus area when I found him," I offer vaguely, my eyes darting over to Becket and back again.

I don't know if telling Sauriel that I ashed his twin is going to work *for* us or *against* us. Right now, I'm oh for one in the *hey, by the way, I killed someone in your family* department, and this could go either way.

"Was?" Sauriel demands. "As in he's gone underground again?" Sauriel bashes his fist on the arm of his throne and shouts something that sounds like a curse but in a language I don't know.

"No...I killed him," I state casually, hoping the fist bashing is a sign that he might be open to his brother's death being a good thing.

Sauriel's shocked gaze flicks up to me.

"That's why it was such a shock to see you waltz through

those doors. I'm sorry for that whole trying to kill you thing, but I promise it was just a case of mistaken identity."

I cross my toes in my boots, hoping somehow Sauriel and the creepy eyed guy will be somewhat understanding. It's not lost on me that neither of them have checked on the Sovereign. I'm not sure why Suryn and these two are awake when no one else seems to be coming to, but by the stars, I hope they're in a forgiving mood.

"You killed Adriel?" Sauriel asks, his voice a disbelieving whisper.

"I did."

"You said you breached our protections to get some answers, what did you mean by that?" Creepy Eyes asks me, his features contemplative.

I debate for a moment where to begin with my story. "I've been told that I'm a Sentinel, but no one seems to know exactly what that means...including me. I thought for the longest time that somehow I was the last to exist, and then I found out that I wasn't. I'm trying to figure out what all of this means. Who I am, and why I can do what I can do."

I pause for a moment, not sure what else to say.

"We've all been making the best of a difficult and confusing situation, but I'd hoped in coming here, that we could stop navigating in the dark. If I had known you would just try to kill us, I wouldn't have come."

Another groan pulls everyone's attention away, and Ory's wings flex slightly as he fights to regain consciousness.

"The dispatch for death was not unanimous. In fact, it was only supposed to be executed if you posed a threat," Creepy Eyes states, and then he turns his weighted gaze to Suryn.

"Tawv, did you not see what she did here? She clearly is a threat," Suryn offers in response to Creepy Eye's scrutinizing gaze.

I growl at Suryn and take a threatening step forward. I'm probably not helping myself here, but her casual disregard for the lives of the people I love is clouding my good sense.

"Bullshit. My Chosen were unconscious when you dropped from the sky. It was six of us against more than two dozen of you."

"Seven of you," Ory corrects, pushing his long black hair out of his face as he shakily gets on his feet, like somehow my count being off by one really makes any difference.

I don't correct him, not wanting to point out that Vaughn is basically a catatonic puppet that couldn't raise a hand to defend himself on his own, let alone attack them.

"It doesn't matter anyway, they sustained no casualties and the fighting stopped when Suryn marked some of them as Chosen," Ory states while dusting himself off.

He misses the subtle shaking of Suryn's head and the death glare she shoots him when he doesn't zip his lips the way she's silently communicating she wants him to do.

"What?" Sauriel yelps and turns on his daughter, his eyes demanding an explanation.

I wonder why she called my Marked posse *filth* when her own dad is a lamia Chosen. You'd think she'd be more understanding of Sentinels that were created and not born.

"How?" Sauriel demands when she doesn't immediately explain.

"I don't know, I moved to slice one of their throats. As soon as I touched him, my light sparked. I couldn't control it." She pauses, dropping her eyes away from Sauriel's like she's ashamed. "Do you think Wekun would remove—"

Creepy Eyes, or I guess his name is Tawv, hisses and looks at Suryn like she's said something horrible. "You would betray your light so easily?" he demands harshly cutting her off mid question.

But any response is cut off by a twitch of the Sovereign's

hand. I watch as all the other Sentinels that are awake look at the movement like it's a snake that's going to strike and bite at any second.

"We will discuss this later," Sauriel growls at his daughter. "But the Chosen Marks change how all of this must be dealt with." He turns to me. "If you want to live, then I suggest you bow, keep your head down, and don't speak unless directly spoken to."

I'm taken aback by the instructions, and I look to the guys for a moment, asking with my eyes if this guy is for real. Bastien and Sabin both shrug at the same time.

I turn back to Sauriel, but something about the tension that's now making his spine straight and his shoulders tight has me bending to get on the ground. My soul rebels against the vulnerable position this puts me and all the guys in, but I did just knock the queen bee of this hive on her ass, so maybe a little groveling will get us past that. I drop my head but keep my weight on the balls of my feet and on my palms, just in case.

I can feel the unease rise in the room and settle on the back of my neck. Everyone is utterly silent like they're afraid to take a breath, let alone speak.

"What is the meaning of this?" a feminine voice demands, her tone even, the pitch not nearly as shrill as what I thought it would be based on what she looked like.

I'm tempted to lift my head so I can read her expression, but I keep it down like I was warned to do.

"There's been a development with our guests," a voice I recognize as Tawv's states flatly.

"I assumed as much simply from the fact that their heads were still attached to their bodies after attacking your Sovereign," she states casually.

I can tell she's going for flippant, but I hear the bite deep in her statement.

"The female is light born, the others are all Chosen," Sauriel provides as if the information bores him.

"Why should I care if one mutt wants to claim so many unworthy? Do you not see the state of your people, unconscious, on the ground all because of the temper tantrum of one little back dweller?"

I bristle at her statements and fight not to fist my hands in anger. *Fucking bitch.*

"Yes, your views on this are clear, but according to Original Law, she is a light born nonetheless. And not all of the Chosen are hers. It seems that Suryn's light has marked several of them."

"You lie," the Sovereign growls out, and it's everything I can do not to look up to see what the hell is going on.

"It's the truth, Sovereign. My light responded and could not be stopped," Suryn butts in.

"Then you'll need to be purged with them," the Sovereign declares coldly, and I hear several shocked gasps.

Oh, it's fine when she wants to slaughter us, but threaten little Suryn and they're nothing but outraged.

"Have you no mercy for even your own blood?" Sauriel demands at the same time Tawv supplies calmly, "You may be the Leader of the Marked, but you don't have that authority. An independent tribunal must be called to rule on the death of a Tierit born, and you know it. It's Original Law and cannot be deviated from. You recall the Original Laws, do you not? You only vowed to uphold them upon your ascension."

I want to high-five Tawv. *Own that hoity bitch, Creepy Eyes.*

The room goes quiet, and we all hold our breath, waiting to see what will happen.

"Fine. Call a tribunal," the Sovereign seethes. The rancor in her tone makes the hair on my arms stand up. "I have no doubt they'll see things the way I do. Until then, keep this filth out of my sight! If they so much as look my way, Original Law won't save them again," she hisses, and the scrape of a chair shrieks through the quiet room.

Soft angry footsteps move away from the throne area and become fainter and fainter as they march away. Unease and resentment filter through my worry. I once again find myself either wanting to run from this place and never look back or to burn it all to the ground. What the fuck is wrong with these people?

I sit up. I'm done being on my knees for people like this. Sauriel is whispering something to his daughter, and she nods as he grabs her shoulders and pulls her in for a hug. I look away, feeling like I'm spying on something that's none of my business. My eyes land on Tawv's, and we just watch each other for a beat, neither of us eager to break the silence.

"A tribunal will be called tomorrow. They will hear your case and decide your fate. Until then, you are protected guests. Suryn will show you to your rooms and serve as host for the duration of your stay. You are free to travel where you'd like, with the exception of the Royal wing. And just like with any citizen of Tierit, you are not permitted to leave the boundary. Do you understand?" Tawv asks, his gaze leaving mine and flitting over everyone else in my group.

None of us say anything. He takes that as some kind of agreement and rises from his throne. Without another look or word, he exits out of the same side door he entered through.

Sauriel hugs Suryn one more time and then steps away from her. "You should rest. I will speak with you more tomorrow," he tells her. He hesitates for a second, like he wants to say something more, but seems to decide against it and leaves instead.

Suryn watches his back until it disappears through a door. She turns her fiery gaze to Enoch, and they stare at each other. I'm waiting for her to say whatever nasty thing that's obviously sitting on her tongue and then lead us to wherever we're supposed to sleep tonight. I don't even care if it's in the royal kennels at this point, which really wouldn't be shocking with the way these fuckers talk about us. Suryn shakes her head instead and then looks at Ory. He's busy staring at me, which seems to piss Suryn off, and she proceeds to do her own stomping act out of the room.

I forgot Ory was even there, he's been so quiet. His wings flex behind him once, and then he blinks, losing our staring contest.

"Well, that was interesting," Ory states as he turns to look in the direction that Suryn just stormed off in. "Looks like host duties now fall on me."

Ory doesn't look nearly as bothered by this fact as Suryn was. That should probably concern me, but at this point I'm done. I just want out of this room, away from these people and hopefully somewhere I can pee.

"Follow me," he announces, turning swiftly and almost taking out Becket with a wing.

I take one more look around the room and wonder when these guards will wake up. I trace the now empty thrones and spot the starlit night sky through a window on the far back wall. We need to figure out how the hell to get out of here, and the first order of business...is getting those fucking Chosen marks off of my Shields.

14

I'm dead on my feet by the time Ory shows us to where we'll be staying. He led us through what had to be a hundred hallways and several different floors. I'm pretty sure it was done to confuse us, in which case he succeeded, because I have no fucking clue where we are in relation to where we came in. Luckily for me, I just don't fucking care.

Ory is standing in the doorway of the suite of rooms we'll be occupying for our *hopefully* short stay in this hell hole, informing us that food and drinks will be brought up promptly and going through some kind of itinerary he's set for us tomorrow. He must have come up with these activities on the hour long walk it took to get to these rooms. I'm pretty sure the Sovereign just stated that she wanted us kept away from her; I didn't hear anything about all these tours and interviews and shit that the winged windbag is going on about.

I rub at my tired eyes and promise my bladder for the thousandth time that I'll empty it soon. Ory is still droning on with no hint that he's going to leave us alone anytime in the near future, so I decide I need to take matters into my own hands. I walk right up to Ory. He seems confused by my approach but doesn't stop jabbering about whatever the fuck he's going on about.

"Sentinel," he greets mockingly as I move until I'm chest to chest with him.

I don't say anything, and he smiles over my head like he thinks I'm trying to intimidate him but he's just too tough for that. I run my hand slowly up the frame of the door and wait until he looks down at me. His aubergine eyes flicker with suspicion and then interest as I look up at him and smile sweetly. Ory presses against me slightly, reading what's happening all wrong. I lift my other hand and place it gently on his chest, and then I shove him out of the doorway and promptly slam the heavy black door in his face.

I lean against it and sigh. I can just make out Ory snickering on the other side, and I shake my head. *That dude is a fucking weirdo.* I sag against the black lacquered wood door and take in the room. We're finally alone. There's so much to talk about, and yet I don't feel ready to dissect it all in this moment. So instead, I take in the details of this suite they've exiled us to.

I push off the door and join the others in the large room that's the nucleus of the suite. Its walls and floor are made of that same soft cream stone. There's carved vines and blooms in the corners that rise up to a high ceiling. Rugs and sofas sit in the middle, and a large dining table is pushed against a back wall that looks like nothing but windows from the top of the table to the very high ceiling.

I walk over to it and try to get my bearings with what I can see outside. It's near impossible. I don't know this place well enough to pick out any landmarks in the city or around it. It doesn't help either that they don't have electricity. Apparently, everything is lit up with fairy light. I'm not sure if that's a spell or if there are Sentinels out there responsible for the little white orbs that dot the hallways, the streets of the city, and the ceilings in this room. It's definitely not actual fairies like I first thought when Ory announced what the light was. He was quick to make fun of me when I tried to talk to an orb, hoping the little tinker bell would show his or herself.

Several open doors lead off of the main area, and I can see four large room options. At least we'll all be together within hearing and fighting distance if push comes to shove around here. No one's really saying anything. We're all just looking around and doing our best to fight off the exhaustion that's clear in everyone's features.

"Well, I don't know about you guys, but I'm about to pee my fucking pants. Now, we all obviously need to talk and come up with a game plan, but can we sort out our bodily functions first?"

I don't really wait for an answer before I dash through the closest door on my right in a desperate hunt for something that resembles a toilet...or a vase...fuck it, I'd take a bowl at this point. I'm doing the pee dance by the time I track down the somewhat hidden entryway to the massive bathroom, and I make it, just barely.

My bladder now blissfully empty, I wash up and quickly exit so someone else who's in desperate need can manage their shit. I plop down on one of the soft red sofas. I'm so dirty that I feel bad sitting down on the plush furniture, but then I remember where I am and proceed to rub my nasty self all over the cushions. A little something to remember the *filthy mutt* by.

"So what the fuck are we going to do?" I ask when everyone is headed back into the room and settling comfortably on some piece of fancy looking furniture. Bastien and Valen saunter in and proceed to pick me up, plop their asses on the couch I was just lying on, and then set me down across their laps. I'm too tired to object, and even if I did, it would be empty. They all know that I like the manhandling.

"Well, we need to get the hell out of here, but I'm not sure how," Sabin states, and several of us grunt in agreement.

"The issue is the Chosen marks. If we could get rid of them, then we could at least try to make a run for it," I state on a massive yawn.

I have to make a concentrated effort to keep my eyes open. Bastien is running his fingers through my hair and slowly working the tangles out while Valen is tracing patterns on my leg that I'm finding very soothing right now.

"Is there a way to get rid of them?" Becket asks as he looks down at his hands. "These are just the beginning ones, right? We don't get any more unless we..." He trails off, apparently not wanting to talk about the *fucking* that leads to the whole shebang of Sentinel markings.

"I don't know," I once again admit. "I'm seriously starting to hate those fucking words," I add on a growl.

"Do you think if you marked them, it would trump the other Sentinel's claim?" Ryker asks, his gaze contemplative.

"I did mark them. That sure as fuck didn't keep what she did from happening," I point out.

Ryker shakes his head. "No, I don't mean mark them as your Shields, I mean mark them as your Chosen?"

Bastien stiffens underneath me, and Valen's soothing patterns suddenly stop. I stare at Ryker for a moment just to be sure I heard him right.

"I don't know if it works like that," I offer hesitantly, trying to think through the ramifications.

If it got us out of here, it could be worth it. But then what?

Ryker sighs. "It might be our only option. They can't stay here linked to that female. You heard what the Sovereign said, she's going to kill all of them."

"Can we force Suryn to come with us?" Nash asks, and all heads snap to him. He tenses a little. "I mean, if she's going to be murdered for marking us, maybe she'd be interested in escaping too, that's all I'm saying."

I try to picture the redheaded arrogant ass of a Sentinel voluntarily fleeing with us. "Yeah, I just don't see that happening. She doesn't seem like she'll ever be our biggest fan."

"But we don't even know her, so can we really say for sure at this point?" Enoch defends, and I bristle.

"Are you defending her?" Knox asks, voicing the question that's on the tip of my tongue.

"I'm not..." Enoch trails off. "I don't...maybe...yeah, I guess I am defending her. I don't think we can just write her off based on what happened today."

I give an incredulous snort. "Why the fuck not? She called you filth. I don't know what kind of rose colored Chosen glasses you're viewing this chick through, but there is no part of her that is okay with the fact that she marked you."

"But didn't you guys say you were all freaked out in the beginning too?" Nash counters.

"Dude, that was not the same thing," Sabin tells him. "We didn't know what the marks were all about, but we were all on board with Vinna."

I don't point out that Sabin wasn't exactly on board until a little bit later. Technically, he's right though. He was worried about how fast things were progressing, but he didn't actually hate me—which is not the case with Suryn.

"But you guys *did* say that you were all okay being on board because you trusted the magic. Shouldn't we be trusting the magic in their case too?" Siah asks, gesturing to Enoch and the others.

"Not when the magic is tied to a ruthless psychopath," I counter.

"You could have been a ruthless psychopath for all I knew when we sealed our bond," Siah counters.

I open my mouth to dispute what he's saying and quickly close it.

Fuck, he has a point.

"Trusting the magic becomes a moot point if they decide all of us need to die. If sticking with her equals death, then we need to find a way to either sever the tie, or like Ryker said, trump her claim," Kallan states, his features pensive as he stares blankly out of the back window.

Something about the look on his face has me pausing. I'm clearly not a fan of the Sentinel who marked them or this situation, but I realize in this moment that this can't be easy for any of them. They're now tied to someone they don't know, with an uncertain fate that's not looking so good, no matter what angle it's viewed from.

"I know we're all feeling antsy and very eager to get away from here, but the reality is we don't have to decide tonight. This whole tribunal thing buys us some time. Tawv said they will call one tomorrow, but I don't know if they decide in one day or if it takes time," Sorik states.

"Yeah, I have the feeling it could go either way. The Sovereign seemed pretty convinced they'd just do what she wants," Siah points out.

"So if they decide pretty quickly against us, then we have our answer on trying to trump the marks and fighting our way out of here. However, if we get time, then we can try to learn as much as we can about this place and our options. We can see if *their* Sentinel was just having a bad day," Sorik tells us as he gestures to Enoch and his coven. "And gauge if we think there's any hope that she could be swayed to our side. They said we can go where we want, so let's try to find some answers if we can," he concludes.

The rest of us go quiet as we consider that plan.

"That works for me," I state at the same time the others voice their agreement.

"Let's fucking hope the tribunal consists of a bunch of people the Sovereign pissed off," Torrez adds, and we all sound our agreement.

"If we do get a chance to do some reconnaissance, I want the covens to stay together. We can find more if we're looking in different places, but we need to be smart about it. Enoch and the Shields, you guys stick with each other and watch each other's backs. Same goes for us. We can split up to cover more ground but still be somewhat safe in numbers. If anything even remotely feels off, signal, and the other group will come running."

Everyone nods their understanding.

"I think it would be best if I stay close to our rooms with Vaughn," Sorik adds. "No one has paid him too much attention with everything going on, but that could change the more they see all of us. If they learn that he does whatever he's commanded to do, that could be used against us."

I release a tired exhale. "Good point," I agree. "We can take turns watching him here; that way you're not cooped up all the time."

Sorik gives me a kind smile. "I wouldn't be bothered by the down time, so don't worry about me. It will give me time to see if there's any hope of reversing or completing what went wrong when Adriel tried to make him a lamia."

I turn to look at Vaughn. Sorik's words swirl around in my mind. A spark of hope settles in my chest. I don't want to acknowledge it, but as I stare up at the fairy lights above our head, I can't help it. Who knows what abilities lie in the marks of the people of Tierit? If there was ever a place where Vaughn could get help, this place is probably it. I work to keep the newfound hope under my boot though. I don't want that hope to get too high, or think of what things could be like if Vaughn were to get better. Getting excited over possibilities, maybes, and long shots has not really turned out well for me, and I worry somehow that just my hope alone could jinx all of it.

"Okay, let's all get some rest then," Ryker calls out. "Enoch, you guys can take this room," he instructs, pointing to the room on the right. "Sorik, you and Vaughn can have the back room, and we'll take the two on the other side. Everyone cool with that?"

Shrugs and nods answer Ryker's direction, and slowly everyone disperses to their designated room. I watch as my Shields tiredly break away, and I'm once again struck with how fucked up all of this must feel for them. Sabin steps into my line of sight and offers me a hand up from the twins' laps. I get up with a groan and wonder if I've ever been this tired before.

I feel physically drained in ways that I didn't even know were possible—it's a struggle just to blink at this point. But aside from the physical exhaustion, I feel wiped out on an emotional level too. I sigh, and Sabin gives me a half smile that makes me feel like he can see right to the heart of me.

He leads me to the room with the bathroom I claimed earlier. I take in the red bedding on the large gothic looking bed, the headboard a whole wall of draped fabric. It looks like Royals R Us did the interior decoration, it has a similar vibe to every bedroom I've ever seen in a period flick. There's a fireplace on the other side of the room with intricate flowers and vines carved into the mantel and sides.

I follow a carved vine in the corner of the room up to the ceiling, and in the dim fairy light, I can just make out what appears to be a scene from Fantasia carved into the stone all above us. Correction—an X-rated version of a scene from Fantasia.

"Sweet, we got the centaur porn room," I observe, my head tilted back so I can take in all the many positions that I wouldn't have thought half-horse people could accomplish. Guess that whole four legs thing isn't as much of a hindrance as one would think—not that I've ever thought about centaur sex or really even centaurs in general—but I sure as hell will now.

"Huh, how are they sixty-nining?" Knox asks, tilting his head to the left like it will help him somehow make more sense of what he's seeing. "Are horse legs that bendy?"

I snort out a laugh and shake my head at him.

"I don't know if this is going to scar me or help me," Ryker states in confused awe.

He stops next to me, his head craned all the way back as he takes the ceiling in.

My focus is pulled away from the graphic art when Valen, Bastien, and Torrez show up in the doorway with a large mattress and bedding I can only assume was recently pulled off the bed in the other room. Knox, Sabin and Siah move to lift the mattress off the bed in this room, and they set it down next to the other one in the middle of the floor.

I kick off my shoes and push my nasty, mud crusted pants down my legs. I lost my shirt in the fight earlier when I yanked it off and pressed it to my stab wound before it disappeared. I pull my sports bra over my head and smile at Siah when he pulls off his shirt and hands it to me. We're all dirty and should probably clean up, but it's clear everyone is too tired to give any fucks. I crawl to the middle of the mattresses and snake in under the covers.

None of us managed to keep our packs amidst all the craziness, but we'll have to worry about that tomorrow. My Chosen crawl into bed around me, but I'm on the verge of passing out before they can even settle. I feel arms around my waist, and they pull my back into a warm muscled chest. Someone else's fingers interlace themselves with mine as another set of feet cradle my own. I'm out seconds later, exhausted, warm, protected.

15

Knox announces that food just arrived and that he's going to spell the platters of food to check for anything that could fuck us up. His call to breakfast reaches me in the bathroom, and I use my magic to quickly dry my hair. I eye the black clothing that I pulled from a pile that was delivered for all of us. It seems we get to dress the part of Tierit Sentinel Guard, and something about that is doing funny things to my chest.

I tighten my thin towel under my arms and run a hand over the black leather armored vest that ties over a black shirt. I can't figure out what fabric the shirt or pants are made out of. It's softer than cotton but stretchy. The pants have armored leather patches sewn onto the vulnerable parts of the leg. And the arms of the shirt sport the same protection.

I'm in awe and pissed off at the same time. The craftsmanship is incredible. I've probably never seen a more badass set of clothing than the armored clothes the guards wear here, but it makes me feel like a fucking outcast at the same time. I wanted, more than I could admit before, to belong here. But they don't want me. They don't want us.

I look into the mirror and run my eyes over my features. Maybe someday rejection won't sting as much. Fuck knows I should really be used to it, but despite my efforts to not care, I do. I just can't seem to help it. I look away, not wanting to see the dispirited girl that's staring back at me.

I unfold the clothes and try to shake away the images they immediately conjure. We could be good at this: guarding, missions, the general badassery that clothing like this brings out in you. If only these people didn't want to hide away from the world, they could do so much with their abilities. Slowly I pull on the clothes and try not to hate myself for liking how they feel. I can't tell if we were given these things from some thoughtful intention someone had, or if they're trying to rub it in even more just how out of reach all that they have is always going to be for me. They could have given us the gray clothing that I saw the other citizens of Tierit wearing, but they gave us this instead, and it's fucking with me.

A knock on the door forces me to push my thoughts away. I force myself not to look in the mirror before I answer. I don't want to like this, to like how I look in it. I don't want to miss it when it's inevitably taken away. The door swings open to reveal Sabin. Like me, he's dressed head-to-toe in black, and I have to remind myself to breathe.

He looks like a warrior wet dream.

"Hey, I brought you boots. I don't know if I feel freaked out or impressed that they got all of our sizes right. Or maybe their magic has something to do with it. I thought the armor looked too big, but as soon as I pulled it on over my head, it fit like a glove."

I force my eyes to stay locked on his, not letting them hungrily roam all over his body the way they want to. Sabin is looking down at his arms, clearly in awe of how the clothing fits. He misses the hardening of my eyes as I mask the pain a bunch of useless clothing is causing me.

I need to get a fucking grip.

"Thanks," I offer as I grab the boots and slip past him to find somewhere to perch so I can put them on.

A couple wolf whistles fill the air, but I don't look to see who's giving them. "Don't!" I shout and sit on the arm of a chair and start lacing up my boots. I ignore the crack of emotion in my voice, and the room goes silent at my outburst.

What the hell is wrong with me?

I try to shake away my funk as I pull on my other boot. I look up and don't stare at anyone long enough to discern their expression. I don't want to see the pity or attraction or whatever else they're feeling; I have too much warring inside of me to take on any more.

Someone pounds on the door outside in the main room. Torrez watches me for a moment more and then leaves to answer it.

"You have been summoned for the selection of the tribunal."

Irritation dribbles through me when I hear Suryn's voice filter in. I walk out from our separate quarters and into the main room, and Suryn's equally irritated gaze runs over me. She dismisses my presence with a purse of her lips and turns around to march away. We all quickly fall into step behind her. It's annoying that we have to follow her temperamental ass around or risk never finding anything. This place is massive though and, so far, confusing as fuck. Note to self, if they don't try to kill us today, getting the lay of this castle might be wise.

Kallan, Enoch, Becket, and Nash have to rush to catch up with us. I can feel eyes on the back of my head as we wind through the never-ending hallways and stairs. I know one or more of my Chosen are trying to figure out why their mate has gone full ice queen, but they'll have to wait to get those answers until we're out of here and I can say them aloud without fracturing.

Suryn leads us into the same room with the thrones we were taken to yesterday. We arrive a hell of a lot faster than I thought we would, and it confirms my suspicion that the winged asshole, Ory, *was* fucking with us last night.

The throne room feels a little less intimidating in the bright light of a new day. It's lacking the presence of a shit ton of guards and the Sovereign, which I'm taking as a good sign. I wonder how long it took for all of the guards to wake up. I'm not sure if any of the Sentinels we knocked out last night will be itching for retaliation, but we should be careful just in case. Not that any of us were going to be frolicking all willy-nilly around here in the first place, but still.

Suryn makes her way up the stairs at the front of the room. She walks casually to one of the smaller thrones positioned on the side of the Sovereign's larger chair and sits down. I can tell that she likes how it lets her lord over us. I can also tell that she's purposely not looking at Enoch or any of his coven.

Tawv, Sauriel, and three other mystery Sentinels walk into the room from the side door. The two Sentinels that were standing guard at each of the doors stand a little straighter and watch the Quorum closely as they move toward the seven thrones at the front of the room.

"Good morning," Tawv greets us as he gets himself comfortable in the same throne he sat in last night to the left of where the Sovereign was seated. "I hope you all were able to get some rest," he continues, and a couple of us nod while the rest are quiet.

"Today we will be selecting members of the tribunal," Tawv announces formally. "Once selected, they will convene and go about coming to a decision on the Sovereign's dispatch order for Suryn of the Second, her Marked, and for the Sentinel of unknown origin and her Marked."

With that, the three mystery Sentinels who Tawv and Sauriel left by the side door bring in something that looks to me like the Stanley Cup's older brother. I've never seen the hockey trophy in person, but this version of it is just shy of the size of Tawv. It looks tarnished though, and I notice there are symbols etched into the metal instead of names like the hockey trophy has.

Tawv, Sauriel, and Suryn watch while the other Sentinels set the giant metal cup in the middle of the room. No one says anything. I wonder if maybe Tawv will explain what the hell these three guys in gray monk robes are going to do, but the Quorum seems keen to just pretend like we're not here now.

One of the robed guys calls on a gilded dagger. It appears in his hand and catches the sun and sparkles in a fascinating way. *Maybe I am part raccoon; I sure do seem to be distracted by shiny things*, I observe, and then I start when the robed guy slashes his palm with the blade.

"Did not see *that* coming," Knox whispers, quietly commentating on what the Sentinels in the middle of the room are doing.

"It kind of looks like a more elaborate version of a beacon spell," he observes, and that has me thinking back to the night that I found out Lachlan was my uncle. The blood I put into the brownie bowl and Keegan doing his thing over it until all hell broke loose. I try to blink away the images of Keegan and Lachlan with their heads pressed together, comforting each other after Lachlan had attacked me.

Another robed Sentinel slashes his hand and places it above the chalice portion of the hockey trophy looking cup.

"What team do you think they're trying to summon?" Torrez asks quietly, and I snicker.

"Thank fuck I'm not the only one who thinks they stole the Stanley Cup," Bastien states, and he fist bumps Torrez and then Knox.

The last robed guy cuts his hand and, like the two Sentinels before him, holds it above the bowl of the cup. Oddly, I can hear the blood drip into the mouth of whatever that overgrown chalice thing is, and Siah shifts his weight on his feet next to me. I turn and look at him. His features are tight, and he's staring at the wall across the room like it has all the answers.

Fuck, he's probably hungry and needs to feed. I mentally berate myself for not thinking about Siah's hunger and needs before we left this morning. My other Chosen consumed every spec of food on the five platters that were brought up to us. They ordered more and were just digging into it when Suryn showed up. We all slept like the dead last night and woke up ravenous. Whatever happened at the barrier, the fighting, and everything else, had the whole crew running on empty.

I couldn't eat, my stomach was in knots, but I'm a fucking dick for not thinking of Sorik and Siah. I look away from whatever the trio of Sentinels is doing to the cup now and eye Sauriel. *I wonder what he does for blood?* Like Sauriel can feel my eyes on him, he turns to me. I don't look away. I study his face, searching for the same madness in his eyes that were in his brother's. I'm taken aback when his lips lift into a kind smile. My eyebrows drop in confusion, and I try to decipher just what the hell he means by smiling at me. His red-gold eyes go from warm to a little sad, and I struggle to understand why.

Chanting starts up in the room, and I pull my perplexed gaze from Sauriel back to the Sentinels and the cup. They murmur something together that I can't make out.

"Which one of us do you think will get selected for the Triwizard Tournament?" Ryker teases, and more snickers sound off from the guys.

"Not it," Sabin calls out on a whisper. "I can't fly a broom or fight a dragon," he confesses straight faced, but his forest green eyes sparkle with amusement.

"Can't fly a broom?" Torrez asks with faux shock. "Even I can do that. You just got your wizard card revoked," he announces like it's a thing.

I shake my head at them and don't fight the smile that their back and forth is coaxing out of me.

The inside of the cup lights up, and an orb goes hurtling out of it. The pink light streaks up and disappears through the ceiling.

"I'm thinking, based on the lack of panic or screams *that it escaped*, that the light is supposed to do that?" Valen comments, voicing all of our concern and subsequent deduction.

The chanting continues, and another pink orb goes streaking out, this one flies up toward the thrones and goes dive bombing through the window. Tawv and Suryn look bored, not at all impressed by the light show. Two more orbs streak out, exiting through opposite walls, and the chanting never ceases.

Another pink orb rises out of the cup, and I wonder where this one will go. We all try to track it as it shoots like lightning toward us. Several of us shout out a warning, but it's too late. The pink light slams into Sabin before any of us can so much as dive out of the way. He gasps like he can't breathe and grabs at his chest. I panic and reach for him, terrified of what the fuck just happened.

I call on my Healing magic and shove it into him. I

search him for a wound or something that needs to be fixed, but I don't feel anything. Sabin pulls in a deep breath of air and looks down at me, wide-eyed with the same shock and fear that must be on my face.

"I'm okay. I think I'm okay," he reassures all of us as he rubs at his chest.

My frantic panic is slowly replaced by a whole lot of pissed off. I call on a short sword and step toward the gray robed Sentinels. Clearly, the word isn't out about what happens when you fuck with someone I love. Time to fix that.

"Sentinel, no!" Tawv yells at me, and a barrier flashes up to protect the robed males in the middle of the room.

I turn my *pissed off* on him. "What the fuck was that?" I demand, each word punctuated by a step toward him.

He holds his hands up in a *please hear me out* gesture. "This is how the tribunal is selected. There was no way to know who the source would call. Your Chosen has been selected, that's all that was."

I pause, baffled by what the hell he just said. "What?" I snap.

Tawv's gaze softens. "The source selects the Sentinels it decides are best suited for the task. That's what the light does. It finds the person that's right and calls them to duty. I am surprised that it selected one not of our kind, but the source has spoken, and it cannot be undone."

I glare at him.

"You have my word, Sentinel, that until the tribunal makes a decision, you and yours will not be harmed here."

"Well, that would have been nice to fucking know before you shot a fluorescent snow globe at my Chosen," I thunder at him. "Next time give us the respect of telling us what's going on. Or I won't give you the respect of not retaliating when you touch what's mine!" I threaten, pointing at him with my short sword.

"You have our apologies, Sentinel," Sauriel offers, and I glare at him, Suryn, and Tawv for a moment longer before I let my sword disappear and step back to my guys.

I meet Sabin's gaze, and he gives me a small smile and a reassuring nod.

"So Sabin now decides our fate?" Ryker asks clearly, as confused by this turn of events as the rest of us are.

"No, Sabin is one of *five* that will make a ruling on what is to happen with Suryn, her Marked, and with you," Tawv corrects.

"And how does that work?" Sabin questions, stepping forward and rubbing at the place in his chest the orb thingy just flew through.

"The five tribunal members will partake in a fact finding mission. You will interview others, take the laws of Tierit into account and then decide whether the Sovereign's order should be upheld or a new order decreed."

"And I'm just allowed to be a part of this even though I'm also on trial here?" Sabin asks.

"It is unorthodox, I will agree, but as I stated before, the source chooses, and that is that. You have been selected, and therefore you will work with four others to come to a decision about what's best for Tierit and the Sentinels and Marked in question."

"So it's like a trial?" I query, making sure I understand all of this correctly.

"In a way," Sauriel answers. "There will be five tribunal members that make the ultimate decision. But you are also allowed a representative for each party in question in attendance. The representative is permitted to ask questions and present information to the tribunal to help them reach a decision."

"The other tribunal members will arrive shortly," Tawv declares. "They will be set up in a room and begin doing their duty immediately. Do you have a representative you would like to also be included in the proceedings?"

My first response is to shout out *me*, but I pause and turn to the other guys to see what they think.

"So any of you moonlight as a lawyer in your past?" I ask, the question light and flippant, which is the exact opposite of what I feel right now.

Hollow laughter sounds off around me, and then everyone goes quiet in contemplation.

"I can do it," Torrez offers. "I can smell emotions, which might come in handy somehow. I've also participated in interrogations as pack Beta, so there's that."

The way Torrez says *interrogations* immediately makes me curious. I make a note to find out more about that later. The other guys all voice their agreement.

"So do we also get a representative?" Kallan asks Tawv.

We all look up at the Quorum member, waiting for his response.

"Suryn of the Second has selected Sauriel of the Second to serve as her representative. As her Marked, her representative automatically covers you as well," Tawv states.

"Oh good, we've been allocated as property," Kallan snarks.

"There are worse things than being claimed," Sabin reassures him.

"Yeah, like being executed," Knox adds jovially.

I snort out a laugh.

"I guess it's good we'll have eyes in on the tribunal and will get a peek at what's going on," Ryker states.

"Yeah, we have one vote for *do not kill*, at any rate," Enoch agrees.

I give Torrez a nod and Sabin's chest a pat before stepping away from our little huddle. I turn back toward the thrones, and Torrez steps forward.

"I volunteer to be the representative of my pack for the tribunal," he announces.

Sabin steps forward and fist bumps him. Suryn snorts when Torrez uses the word *pack*, and I shoot a glare her way.

"Excellent," Sauriel announces and nods his head at Torrez.

The back doors open up, and I turn to find a female Sentinel that looks to be in her fifties. She has unusual ash toned hair and eyes that match her cinder locks. She steps into the room with a resolute air about her. Another woman, this one younger looking, walks in behind the first. Her long white blonde hair is down to her waist, and her eyes are a surprising black. Aside from Suryn's hazel eyes, this woman's eyes are as dark as I've seen on all the Sentinels we've come across. She eyes me and then my group, but try as I might, I can't read any emotion in her features either for or against us.

A male strolls in that looks like a teenager. He's tall and gangly and aims a sneer in my direction before passing me and joining the two other women who are now standing at the base of the stairs that lead up to the thrones. I suddenly feel way less comfortable with my life being in the hands of other people with this guy on the judging committee.

Lastly an elderly woman hobbles in with the use of a cane. Her eyes are a milky white, and every inch of her skin has a line or wrinkle to it. She's grumbling irritably as she makes her way to the others, and I imagine getting selected for this is a lot like jury duty. You have to just drop every-thing whether you like it or not. I wonder for a moment what the daily lives of these Sentinels are like. What do they do with their time? Do they have families, jobs?

"Excellent!" Tawv claps, yanking me from my thoughts.

"Tribunal, do you know who you would like to speak to first?"

"We will question Suryn and her Marked," the gray haired female states, and Tawv nods.

I look at Sabin, confused. How does this chick know what's going on? Did news of what happened yesterday get out to every Sentinel within the barrier already?

"That light, when it hit me, seemed to upload all the information about what's going on and what was expected of me at the same time," Sabin explains, and my eyebrows shoot up with surprise.

"They can fly *and* upload information using fluorescent flying snow globes?" I question, well aware of the whine in my tone.

"Seems like it," Sabin confirms, a grin on his face.

"Well, that's just great," I exclaim petulantly.

Sabin pulls me in for a peck and then boops my nose.

"Guards, escort the tribunal, representatives, and those who have been selected for questioning to their designated room. Sentinel, you and the remainder of your Chosen are dismissed until you are either called for questioning or the tribunal has made a decision," Tawv decrees, rising from his throne.

A guard rushes forward at Tawv's command and leads Sabin and the others out. Torrez winks at me before he exits the throne room, and I smile at him even though I don't feel good about watching him, Sabin, and all of my Shields leave. The large wood doors shut behind them, and the room grows bleak and quiet.

Tawv clears his throat, and I jump when the sound of it is closer than I expected him to be. I whirl around, and he gives me a thorough once over.

"Come with me, I have something for you," he states,

and with that, he calmly walks to the side exit of the throne room.

I turn and look at my remaining Chosen. I'm not sure what to think of that cryptic statement. The guys shrug, unsure what to make of it also.

"Fuck it," I announce and move to follow the creepy eyed Quorum member. We officially have time for some reconnaissance while the tribunal meets, whether that's for an hour or a week. Tawv is as good a place to start as any for information.

Bastien chuckles as he, Valen, Ryker, Knox, and Siah all fall into step with me.

Tawv reaches the side door and turns to me expectantly. "Well now, lost Sentinel, let's see if we can't get you found."

16

W e move steadily through the streets of the city. The deep purple robe Tawv put over his deep purple armored clothing sways ominously behind him as he walks. I don't dare ask where we're going. I'm too fucking worried that if I say anything, he'll suddenly remember that I'm a hated stranger and that he isn't supposed to be helping me. I suppose that's assuming he is in fact helping me and not leading me into an ambush of some sort.

Another passerby puts the fist of one hand over the bicep of the other, and Tawv nods his head in greeting. I didn't notice anyone doing this hand gesture to Ory or Suryn when they were bringing us into the city, so I'm assuming this is something reserved for the Quorum members, or maybe it's a Tawv thing. I'm buzzing with questions, but I keep my mouth shut and attempt to keep track of what ring of the city we're on and what direction we're heading in.

I follow Tawv down another street that spits us out into some kind of a market. All kinds of things are displayed for sale on wooden carts. Turquoise fruit, or maybe it's a vegetable of some sort, is stacked on one cart next to someone selling jewelry that's infused with Light—or so the sign says. Clothing in tones of gray and black are on display on several carts, and I wonder why there aren't options in other colors. Maybe the lack of color has a purpose? I've only seen Tawv and the Sovereign in colored clothing, but the bedding and furniture in our rooms were various shades of red, gold and blue. The gray and black seems like a conscious choice and not the result of not having the dyes to make other options possible.

Some stalls consist of people selling some magical ability or another. I'm surprised when I see several stalls that focus on fertility. I realize in that moment that I haven't really seen any children. I suppose it's possible parents are keeping their precious kids away from the big scary strangers, or maybe Sentinels have a hard time having kids. Judging by the lines at the fertility stalls, I suspect it's the latter issue.

"So, Sentinel, may I ask your name?" Tawv asks me out of nowhere, and it takes me a minute to pull my attention away from the hustle and bustle of the market and realize he's talking to me.

"Vinna," I answer after a beat of hesitation. "This is Valen and Bastien," I continue, pointing to the twins. Tawv gives them a nod. "Siah and Knox," I offer, gesturing to them. "And this is Ryker. My other two Chosen, Sabin and Teo, are with the tribunal."

Tawv nods again and goes quiet. He winds us through a couple stalls selling pots and pans and other housewares.

"Do you know who your parents are?" Tawv inquires.

"My father was...is," I correct, "Vaughn Aylin. He was a paladin with the casters before he met my mother."

"Ah, so the line is from your mother's side then," Tawv

inserts, but he seems like he's saying that more to himself than posing a question to me.

"Um...yeah. Her name was Grier."

Tawv stops suddenly. If the dude had brakes, they'd be screeching right now. He studies me intensely and then tilts his head to the sky in contemplation. "Grier of the First House?" he asks on a reverent whisper.

"I don't know. I never met her?"

Tawv's almost white eyes fill with sadness. "So she *is* gone then," he states quietly, his shoulders sagging with resignation. "The Bond Weavers suspected as much, but her House was still holding out hope when they couldn't be sure." He looks at me speculatively. "It all makes more sense now that you are here. Her magic in *you* must have been what was throwing them off," he states, like he expects me to understand what he's talking about.

"Wait, what?" I stop him mid step and ask, abandoning my *keep quiet and go with the flow* plan.

"Your mother left us almost four hundred years ago. She was part of a group of Sentinels who were assigned to do a Chosen search outside of our boundaries. The Sovereign at the time was responding to a push from the people for new Chosen bloodlines. You see, many of the lights of the Tierit Sentinels weren't marking other Sentinels of the city. We had done a search once before and had success," Tawv explains.

"Grier and two others were the only ones not to make it back. The Bond Weavers could feel that they were alive, so all we could do was wait. Then, one by one, their light went out. Grier's light, however, only dimmed some twenty-odd years ago, and then it was reported that it was brighter than ever. So the First House believed that maybe she was injured and healing. But alas, it was *you*. They will mourn and rejoice all at once," he states matter-of-factly and then turns and begins to lead the way again.

I reel with all this new information. I've wondered for so long where my mom came from and what she was doing out in the world all alone. How did Adriel find her? *She was out looking for mates.* I cling to these new puzzle pieces of information and put them in place in the story of my existence. He said something about a First House? Does that mean I have relatives that are still here? My heart hammers in my chest at the thought, but I furiously stomp out the flicker of excitement that flares in my soul.

Fuck off, hope, we've been down this road before.

"So if you guys knew there was a possibility she was still out there, why didn't you go looking for her?" I ask, biting back the other part of that question that I can't bring myself to put a voice to. *Then maybe you could have found me.* I swallow down the vulnerability and frustration that's sitting in my throat.

"That is not our way, Vinna. Your mother knew the risks when she left."

I grab Tawv by the arm, stopping him. Talon's dying words ring in my head, and I wince at the memory of what he told me about how he met my mom and helped her escape.

"She knew that she could be captured by a psycho lamia and tortured for hundreds of years?" I state, my tone and eyes bleeding frustration and indignation. They knew she was out there, and they just left her. Tawv closes his eyes as if this information pains him.

"Not those circumstances exactly," he croaks out after silently absorbing the sting of my words for several seconds. "But she was aware that there have always been others that hunt and covet our kind."

I shake my head at him, not satisfied with that answer, but what else is there to say? Enoch told me about how the Sentinels up and left the casters without a backward glance. The Forsaking he called it. Why would I expect any different from these people? I may not know exactly what the First House is, but I can tell it means *something*. My mother was something to these people, and they left her to suffer. I let resentment build a wall around my hurt, burying the loss, pain, and abandonment deep inside where I can ignore it for a time.

"Maybe you're right," Tawv tells me, agreeing with something I haven't voiced. "Maybe we should have shaken off these walls and taken our place like many of us wanted to do. But the Sovereign died, and with that came change and fear. Only time can tell what the future holds for the Light Marked." Tawv pats me on the arm twice and then whirls back around and nimbly steps away.

Bastien reaches out and twines his fingers with mine. I know he's probably picking up on all the turmoil that's frothing inside of me, but I don't have it in me to turn around and reassure him. I don't want to wear a happy-mask to cover up all the fucked up shit I'm processing right now. I squeeze his hand once and then move to follow Tawv again.

"Here we are," he announces as he leads us through two more rings of the city streets.

We stop in front of a house that's bordering a fair amount of what looks like farmland. The house itself looks like a quaint cottage that's in the process of undergoing some repairs. Before we can open the rickety gate and walk up the path to knock on the front door, it opens, and out walks a giant of a man.

I thought Aydin was massive, but this guy has to be almost eight feet. His hair is long and black as shadows. His skin darker than Torrez's and Knox's. His eyes are like black holes, threatening to suck us all into oblivion with one wrong move. There isn't an ounce of fat on his shredded body, and I can vouch for this because the dude is sans shirt. He sports a brutal scar across the front of his neck. As he turns to pull the door shut behind him, I catch two more gnarly looking round scars where it looks like wings might have once been.

Before seeing Ory and the other mysteriously winged Sentinels, I probably wouldn't have made that connection with the placement of his scars, but now it feels undeniable. This is a male that's experienced some seriously fucked up shit. When he turns back around, he's carrying what at first appears to be a pile of gray rags.

"Getta, I'm grateful for you agreeing to do this," Tawv states, his tone oozing respect and admiration.

I watch the shadow soaked giant, waiting for him to respond. So when a frail female voice finally answers, I find myself surprised and searching for the source. It takes me a minute to realize that the pile of gray rags that the giant is carrying is actually the feeblest looking woman I've ever seen. Her hair is white, and her paper-thin skin has clearly been loved by the sun. Her eyes are a milky white, the pupil a light blue. I'd wager that she's blind, and based on the fact that she's being carried, very fragile.

"Now, I didn't agree to anything. I only said I would see if she's worthy. So don't go twisting my words like your kind is prone to do." The old woman glares at Tawv. If I didn't know better, I'd think Tawv cowered slightly at her reprimand.

"Of course, Getta, I apologize for misspeaking," Tawv offers as he bows in supplication. I watch the two of them, a little confused.

"Is this the lost one?" Getta asks, and the giant carrying her dips her down so she can get a good look at me.

Her cloudy gaze runs all over my face. She studies me in a way that feels both intriguing and unsettling simultaneously. She reaches out a twig thin arm, her bony hand palm up and expectant. I stare at it for a moment before placing my hand in hers. I think that's what she wants anyway. She gives a satisfied hum and closes her eyes. She flips my hand over and strokes it with skeletal fingers I'm afraid might break and turn to dust at any moment.

She traces the rune on my palm and sighs. "Hello, old friend," she greets shakily, nodding her head like my rune is suddenly talking to her.

I look to the guys, my eyes asking *what the fuck*. Knox smiles and shrugs. Valen makes the universal sign for crazy by circling his pointer finger at his temple. Getta slaps the palm of my hand with more strength than I expect, and I snap my head back in her direction.

"You carry all the right signs, girl. Ones lost to time and greed bloom like a flower on you. Your glow rivals that of the sun, but none of that tells me if you're worthy."

With that, Getta slaps the massive protruding pec of the male carrying her, and he pulls her away from me. He moves toward the back of the house, and I once again take in the two scars on his back.

"Don't just stand there, girl. Follow his fine ass and come with me."

My eyebrows shoot up to my hairline in shock. Knox and Bastien both bark out laughs that they promptly turn into coughs. I look at Tawv, wondering if this lady is for real, but he just does as Getta says and walks toward the back of the house. I fall into step behind him, not sure exactly what's going on or who the hell this lady even is.

The back of the house is packed dirt and a single water trough set just to the side. I don't see any animals hanging about, so I'm not sure what the trough is for. The stoic, scarred giant sets Getta down in the middle of the round packed dirt yard, and she looks even more slight and decrepit than she did in the massive male's arms. She pinches his ass as he walks away, and I see the male roll his eyes and his chest vibrate with laughter even though no sound accompanies it.

"Come here, girl, and stop staring at Issak; he's taken."

I immediately avert my eyes and scramble to join Skeletor granny on the hard packed ground. "Sorry, I didn't mean to stare at your...Chosen." My apology comes out more like a question because I'm not sure how this match worked out, and I don't see runes on either one of them.

"Oh, he's not mine. I'm just keeping him warm until the right one chooses her path and comes to claim him."

The massive male snorts, and she narrows her eyes at him. "You know I'm right, and you better start doing what needs to be done so you can be worthy of her," Getta snarls at him.

"I see," I reply simply, trying really hard not to picture exactly what she could mean by keeping him warm.

"Now, girl, answer my question," Getta demands, and I look at her, confused.

She doesn't say anything else, and I have no idea what question she's talking about. I turn to the guys hoping somehow they caught it, but they all shrug uselessly. Something raps me hard on the shoulder, and I yelp and turn. There's nothing there, and I search for whatever the fuck just tried to give me a dead arm.

"Are you going to answer me or not?" Getta asks again, her fragile shaky voice laced with irritation.

"I'm sorry, what was the question?"

"Are you worthy?"

"Worthy of what?" I ask even more perplexed.

"Wrong answer," she replies, and then a staff appears in her hand, and she whacks me with it. She hits the exact same spot she just hit on my arm, and I jump back away from her with a squeak.

"What the fuck?" I ask incredulously as I rub my arm.

Knox is laughing so hard I think he's crying, which is no fucking help to me.

"Wrong answer," she parrots again, and faster than this old bag of bones should be able to move, she whacks me hard on the thigh.

Motherfucker!

"Listen, I don't know what you're asking. A little context would be super helpful," I tell her, and the sneaky bitch whacks me again.

"Are you worthy, girl?" she demands again, and I'm starting to get really fucking frustrated with all this cryptic shit.

"I don't know, lady, you tell me," I snap at her, and this time when she tries to hit me, I block it with my own staff.

Getta giggles, and interest sparks in her cloudy gaze. "Now you're talking," she tells me, and she goes in for another hit.

I block it again and stumble back away from her. She advances, and I'm floored at how quickly she moves. She can't seriously want me to fight her, can she? I mean, she clearly has some tricks up those cobwebbed sleeves, but Getta the granny wouldn't stand a chance in a real brawl. Fuck, I'm worried if I breathe too hard on her, it'll break something.

She swings for me again and misses.

"Getta, I don't know what your deal is, but if you keep swinging at me, I'm going to defend myself. I don't want to hurt you," I explain, looking at the others in hopes that they'll help me convince this senile old bat to activate her chill. One minute she's being carried around like a baby, and the next she's going full *Kung Fu Panda* on me.

The giant black haired male leans back against the house like none of this is a big deal. Tawv watches what's going on with rapt attention. Ryker and Bastien have joined Knox's giggle fest, and Valen just gives me a thumbs up like the worst soccer mom ever, just chilling on the sidelines.

"What's the matter, girl, afraid I'm going to kick your ass?" Getta taunts me, and I let loose an involuntary laugh.

I reel back just in time, barely dodging a swing aimed for my head. I glare at Getta, my patience with her bullshit starting to run real fucking thin.

"Fine. You want a fight? I'll give you a fight. Don't accuse me of elder abuse or say I didn't warn you," I growl between clenched teeth when Getta jabs at my stomach with her staff and nails me once.

I feel awkward as fuck wanting to beat the shit out of this little old woman, but it's clearly what she's aiming for. I stop running around the packed dirt yard on the defensive and swing a couple offensive strikes out at Getta. She blocks them with an excited hoot that convinces me she really and truly has lost her damn mind and wants to fight.

Is this going to be me when I'm a billion years old? Just taunting anyone who walks by because I'm itching for a good match?

I'm equally amused and horrified by that thought. I can just picture my Chosen shouting at me from the house, telling me to bring my wrinkled ass back in and stop taunting the neighborhood kids.

Fuck it. Let's go, Wrinkle in Time.

I stop pulling my hits and go balls to the wall at Getta. She screams with delight and meets me move for move. I'm not sure what to think about the fact that this woman, who is clearly older than time itself, is keeping up with *me*. I call on my runes and pick up the speed. I'm a blur as I spin, twirl, flip, slash, jab, and whack at Getta.

And holy motherfucking shit, she's also a blur as she dodges, parries, blocks, loops, and redirects my hits. I spin, punching out with one hand at the same time I bring my staff down toward her with another. She dodges my fist, but I just clip her with my weapon.

I keep from celebrating my hit with an excited shout and feel kind of bad. I'm about to ask her if she's okay, when she looks up and smiles at me. And then in a flash, Getta stops fucking around and shows me what she's *really* made of.

17

In a haze of movement, Getta and I attack and defend like we're in some epic fight scene in a martial arts movie. I'm all Crouching Tiger to her Hidden Dragon as we race all over the back yard, trying to beat the shit out of each other. I block a hit so hard that my arms vibrate from the force. I call on my runes for strength and deliver my own bone jarring hits, blow for blow. I don't know how long we go at each other, streaks of movement in the morning light as the sound of our staffs smash together in a rhythmic soundtrack that accompanies our grunts and whoops and shit talking.

I hear my guys cheering and commenting on the action, and it spurs me on. I gotta give it to the old coot, her game is on point. But I know she'll start to lag and tire at any moment, and that's when I'm going to fuck the old bitch up. Sweat trickles down the back of my neck as I bend, rotate, retreat, and then press forward.

And just when I think I'm about to gain the upper hand, Getta shows me that she's got more in the tank than I thought.

We're creating a dust tornado as we speedily circle each

other and look for an opening. Getta leaps at me like a fucking spring chicken, and then suddenly it feels like I'm Neo in *Matrix Reloaded* when he's fighting a fuck-ton of Mr. Smiths. Getta is fucking *everywhere*. I haul ass to keep her from connecting a hit anywhere on my body, but it's a pace I know I can't keep up forever. Getta uses her staff to pole vault over me, and I swing for where her trajectory says she should be landing. In a move that defies gravity, she changes direction and kicks me square in the chest so hard I see stars.

I'm thrown back and land hard in the trough, the cold water coating me in even more humiliation. The guys go silent, like the shock of what just happened has struck them completely mute. I stare at Getta, dumbfounded. How in the fuck did she do that? Mr. Smith is not supposed to kick Neo's ass. She walks slowly over to me, as if each of her bones are suddenly feeling her age. I don't blush, but I feel my body heat with embarrassment. I can't believe that I just lost a fight to the Crypt Keeper. I haven't fucking lost a fight in...I can't even remember.

My humiliation goes beyond my underestimation of Getta though. I needed to win in order to be worthy of whatever the fuck she could tell me. I'm once again so fucking close to the answers, but this time, I only have myself to blame for losing them. Getta stops just in front of me and leans on her staff. Her cloudy white eyes land on mine, and she stares at me like she can see right into my soul.

"Are you worthy?" she asks me again.

My eyes sting as I look away. "I guess not," I admit, and I feel something in me crack at that admission.

"As you say," Getta agrees, and then she jerks her chin at Issak.

He lumbers over and scoops her up like something that's precious to him. Her staff disappears in her hands, and she rests her head back and closes her eyes. I watch Issak's back as he carries Getta away, and I feel like the last of my hope goes with them.

I pull myself out of the trough, ignoring the hand Valen steps forward and holds out for me to take. I can't even look at him or any of the guys. I don't even want to know what's written on Tawv's face right now. I had a shot to get myself and my Chosen some real answers, and I blew it. I wasn't good enough. Water drips off my skin in rivulets, and I wish it could take my shame with it.

Siah steps toward me, opening his mouth to say something, but Knox stops him and shakes his head. For a moment, all I want is to be wrapped up in a hug, but I shove that shit away. I fucked up. I don't get to be coddled and ask for lies about how this is all going to be fine. None of this is fine.

Tawv turns his back on me and moves away from the tiny cottage. I follow him. Maybe if I train harder, I can come back and try again. I can't bring myself to ask him if that's possible though. I just shutter everything up as Tawv leads us silently away. I don't look back over my shoulder as we widen the distance between us and Getta's house. That place will forever be burned in my brain, the mortification seared into my soul. There's a good chance I might never be good enough to beat her, and then where does that leave us?

My Chosen are all silent as we make our way back, and I'm simultaneously sad and grateful for that. The castle comes into view, and the restless itch just underneath my skin is almost overwhelming. I need to move. To run. To train. To beat this humiliation and loss out of me, and I need to do it right now. I hope these fuckers have a gym. I need to not feel less than, and that's the only place I can do it.

* * *

"Kings and Queens" by Thirty Seconds to Mars blares in my ears as I finish another round of the obstacle course and immediately drop to do one hundred push-ups. Thankfully, I had my phone on me when our little welcome party attacked us. I do the thing Enoch taught me on our hike here and send a zap of Elemental magic into my phone to keep the music going.

They don't have a traditional gym here, but they do have a training facility just outside the castle. The place cleared out when I showed up. There were a couple Sentinel stragglers here and there who wanted to see what I was about, but they're long gone.

I've been at this for hours.

Ryker went back to the castle with Tawv to check on Sorik. And Bastien, Valen, Knox and Siah are all endeavoring to give me as much space as they can. They're guarding the doors, but they're out of sight, and I'm doing all I can to put them out of mind for a while.

My heart beats steadily in my chest, the thump off beat from the drums of the song. It's like it's telling me there's no running from it or what happened. Internally, I put my middle fingers up at it and run anyway, hoping if I can just be fast enough, all these emotions won't catch up and drown me.

I finish my push-ups and run to the padded poles that seem designed to take hits. It doesn't move or sound like a punching bag, but the feel is close enough. I whale on one of them, one hit flowing seamlessly into another as I try to go numb and not picture everything that's wrong in my world. Talon, Lachlan, Keegan, my dad, my mom, Laiken... There's just so much loss, and I don't know how to cope with any of it.

I don't fit with the humans. I don't fit with the casters.

And now I don't fit with the fucking Sentinels either. There are too many secrets, too many unknowns, too many wrongs and injustices, and I just want to know why.

I'm not normally that needy bitch who needs to point out how unfair it all is and figure out my place in it. Bad shit happens all the time, and life can *always* be worse. But for some reason, the mysterious *why* of it all is hammering at me. No matter how hard I push myself, I can't escape what broke open when Getta broke what I thought I knew about myself.

A booming crack fills the training facility, but I ignore it and continue to pummel the pads. One more hit. Two more hits. Three. Four. Five. Six. Wood splinters under the pad, and dagger-like slivers fly out from the now broken wood of the beam. I turn and shield my face, but I feel a few of them pierce the skin of my arm and back.

When the wood chips and dust settle, I huff out an annoyed breath and turn to survey the damage. The thick pad covered pole is split in half, the top part angled down like it's bowing to the ground. There are at least a dozen more poles like this one lined up, and just over an hour later, I look back down the line at each and every shattered one of them. I swipe sweat from my face and hope they'll take a credit card for the damages.

I don't feel better.

I jog back to the beginning of the obstacle course, gearing up to run it again, when Siah steps in front of me.

"You've been going at this for five hours," he states simply. He looks over to the destroyed combat poles and raises an eyebrow at me. "And you're bleeding..." Siah's nostrils flare slightly. "A lot," he finishes.

I'm surprised the others let him in here. They're usually good about giving me space when I need it. So either they're worried too, or he snuck past them. I shrug and move to step around Siah, but he just blocks my path again. A frustrated growl starts in my throat, and I look at him and silently scream for him to move. His bright blue eyes study me. Desperation and overwhelming sadness are all I feel slamming through me right now. They must be pouring out of me like I'm a sieve, because his eyes soften and he steps into me.

"What can I do?" he asks softly, his knowing gaze reading me like I'm his favorite book.

I don't know how to respond to his question. I take stock of how I'm feeling, frustrated that I'm not able to run my problems down like I usually can. This is not working the way I need it to. My eyes flit back and forth between his, and I hold in the vulnerability that wants to spew out of my mouth.

Siah lifts his hand and places it softly on the front of my neck. Something about his touch, the possessive yet supportive way he's gripping me, shatters the walls I'm desperately trying to mortar together.

"Just get me out of my head. I can't fucking escape it," I finally plea. Every cell in my body is begging for relief from the disappointment, pain, rejection, and loss pumping through my veins.

Siah dips down until we're at eye level, and he just watches me for a beat and then nods. I want his mouth to crash down to mine, for his touch and kisses to become as frenzied as I feel inside, but he just turns me slowly and pulls me back against him.

Confusion bubbles up inside of me, and then I hiss in pain as Siah pulls a five inch long sliver from my back. He drops the fragmented wood piece to the ground unceremoniously and bends over and licks the wound. A shiver of pleasure rakes up my spine, and goose bumps crawl down my arms and legs.

I bite back the hiss as Siah pulls another sliver and another from my body, and I ride the moan when his tongue and lips brand my back. He takes his time inflicting pain and then pleasure as he clears my skin of debris. His fangs scrape against the top of my shoulder, and I can feel his erection pressing at my ass as he brings his hand around to my front and grips my neck once more.

His mouth moves up to my ear, and he just stands there breathing against the shell of my ear as he nuzzles me and pulls me back against him.

"There, that's better," he finally whispers in my ear, his voice dripping with want and need. His other hand dips to the ties of my pants and slowly begins to unlace them.

My deep aroused breaths morph into short pants as delicious anticipation battles my pain-laced desperation.

"Shhhh," Siah whispers in my ear when I give an impatient huff. "I've got you, mate," he reassures me, and when he finally has my pants unlaced and loose, he shoves his hand inside and strokes my folds.

I whimper and move to grind against his palm, but Siah tightens his hold on my throat. He nuzzles my hair, his lips skimming the side of my neck and my ear. The feel of him is driving me fucking crazy. I need more, more to drown it all out. Can't he see that? Feel it radiating out of my every pore?

He spreads my lips and puts two fingers deep inside of me as he shushes me again. I gasp and lean back against him, tilting my hips forward so he has even deeper access. He circles inside of me slowly, the base of his palm firm against my clit as he does. Wetness pools at my core, and he spreads it around as he teases me and works me until my desperation for emotional oblivion morphs into desperation for him.

I relax against him, relinquishing any desire for control,

and Siah nips at my ear and starts to move his fingers in and out of me at a gradually faster rhythm.

"There you go," he huskily encourages in my ear when I melt against him. "Let your mate help make it better. I've got you," he tells me as his other hand moves from my throat and dips into the top of my sports bra. He squeezes my breast and pulls his other fingers out of me to rub slow circles around my clit. "Your mates are here for you, standing guard, protecting you. Listen closely and you can hear their hearts, each beat in sync with yours at all times."

Siah pinches my nipple and then slips his fingers back inside of me. "We hurt when you hurt, laugh when you laugh, back off when you need it, and challenge and guide when you feel alone and lost. We will always find you, always bring you back. And we all know you'll do the exact same thing for each and every one of us."

Siah kisses my neck with just a hint of fang, and I mewl.

"So let go, my mate. Pass the burden on your shoulders to the rest of us, because we're all here to help you carry it."

With that, he rubs my clit harder, and I explode into a haze of pleasure and gratification. Siah's words hook themselves inside of me as he wrings every ounce of ecstasy from the orgasm wracking my body. Brick by brick I watch my walls crumble, and I stare at them, wondering why I felt like I still needed them. What he's saying isn't new. I know this about my Chosen. I wonder all the time how I could have gotten so lucky, but at the same time, I'm just so fucking sad.

Siah rips off one of my boots to free my leg from my armored pants. He pulls my sports bra over my head and spins me until I'm facing him. He brings his stunning blue eyes level with mine and whispers, "I've got you," against my lips before he leans in and tastes me. I close my eyes and do all I can to get lost in him, the feel of his tongue against mine, his hand in my hair as the other grips my ass and then dips down to my thigh to pull my leg up to his waist.

I open for Siah in every possible way. He skillfully unlaces his pants and then positions his freed cock between my thighs. He presses into me slowly as I deepen the kiss and the connection between our souls. I let every fucked up emotion I'm feeling pour out of me in my kiss, in the way my pussy grips his length, and my hard nipples press against the armor of his shirt. It's in the plea of my voice when I moan his name, the desperation in my fingers as I hold onto him while he fucks me vulnerable.

He slams into me, each thrust timed with his words, "I've got you. We've got you," whispered in my ear and dripping with the vow he's making in this moment.

In this moment, I'm not unworthy. I'm just his.

Siah's hands are tender and worshipping, while his cock is fast and punishing. It's like his hands are reminding me of love and devotion, while he's fucking me in a way that reminds me to never doubt the declarations of either him or my other Chosen. I throw my head back and focus on the sensation of him moving in and out of me. Playing with me. Sucking on me. My orgasm builds again. Siah backs up until he's sitting on something, and control of his thrusts falls squarely in my hands. I ride him without missing a beat, grinding against his base when he's deep inside of me, and then lifting myself up just to slam back down and repeat it all.

He grabs the front of my neck with one hand and tangles the other in my hair. I hold onto him for leverage as I bury him deep inside of me over and over again.

"Look at me when you come, Vinna," Siah demands, and my eyes spring open until I'm drowning in his intense ice-blue gaze. I can tell he's close, and I'm on the verge of shattering into another orgasm, when he leans forward and nips at my bottom lip.

"We've got you," he says one last time, and I burst into a million sensation-filled pieces as I come. Siah watches me, his gaze drinking me up, and then he lifts his hips off the bench we're on and growls my name as he comes. His thrusts turn shallow, and I watch rapture streak through his gaze as his orgasm flares through his every cell. And then he bites me.

I scream and melt into a puddle on top of him as his fangs punch euphoria into me. He pulls my blood into his mouth and swallows. I writhe on his dick and under his mouth, my body begging for more. He reaches up and slices open a spot on the top of his corded shoulder, and I attack the welling blood like I was born a creature of the fucking night.

Siah and I feed until we're full and drunk on each other's sex laced blood, and then we both bite each other again at the exact same time. We tighten around each other and spiral into a new orgasm that leaves us both panting and pliant. He comes back down first, and when I open my mouth to fix that, he chortles and cradles my face in his hands so my teeth can't get to him.

"Talk to me," he encourages. "And then I'll let you bite me as many times as you want."

I laugh and then sigh. I run my thumb across his kiss-swollen lips and trace his features slowly with my fingertips as I sort through my thoughts, with Siah's "I've got you" ringing in my head. I dig through all of my feelings to find the most overwhelming one. Maybe if I speak it, it won't hold so much power over me anymore.

My gaze is intense yet hesitant as I look from one ice-blue iris to the other.

Here goes nothing.

"I feel...fucked up," I admit, and I'm surprised by the flood of sadness and emotion that pours into my eyes and my voice as I own those words.

"I'm just so fucking lost," I repeat again, and then I spill into a million tears on his lap.

18

All the frustration, sadness and loss that's been building over the past couple months streams steadily out of my eyes. I feel like I've opened the floodgates and now there's no hope to get them shut again. Siah steadily wipes away my purged emotions. He silently dries my cheeks and rubs my back until I feel spent and empty. I take a shuddering breath and chuckle hollowly at myself.

I'm a fucking mess.

"Sorry," I offer him as I sit back and try to pull my shit together.

"For what? Being a complex person with emotions and needs? We're all like that. We all feel *lost* at some point."

I study Siah's face as he dismisses my apology. "When have you felt lost?" I ask quietly.

"Many times."

His gaze grows distant, and I can practically see the memories rise in his gaze.

"I was seventeen when my whole family died from a plague that swept our town. I never got sick, but I was forced to stand by helplessly and watch as it first claimed my baby sister, then my little brother, my mother, my two older brothers, and lastly my father. We were a farming family, and there was no way I could plant the fields, tend to them, and bring in the crop all on my own. So the lord that owned the land put me out so that a new family could have the house and manage the crops.

"I went from happy carefree son of a farmer to a beggar in less than a handful of months. That was my first taste of *lost*."

Siah's eyes suddenly match how I've been feeling on the inside, and I run my palm down his cheek in an effort to soothe some of the pain I've asked him to dig up.

"I met *lost* again half a dozen years later. I had managed to get hired on as a farm hand in another town, and I had worked my way up into the good graces of another lord. I managed several grain houses for him, and he invited me to accompany him to see about more land and a mill he was wanting to purchase. I was in a strange city, and I enjoyed the food and drink a little too much. I went outside to relieve myself, and that's when a creature attacked me. It felt like it was tearing my throat open. I was choking on my own blood and couldn't even shout an alarm. When I woke up, I couldn't understand how I was still alive, but then I quickly realized that I wasn't, or at least not in the same way as before.

"I felt lost for years until I met Sorik, and then it slowly began to recede. Sorik felt lost until he found your mother, and then he felt lost again after he lost her and his compeer. You see, we all go through it at different stages and in different ways. It doesn't make us weak, and it's nothing to apologize for. It just is."

"Do you feel lost now?" I ask, realizing that Tierit and everything that's happening here isn't just overwhelming for me. My Chosen are all here hoping for answers too.

Shame ripples inside of me as I once again recall that *I'm* the reason we don't have the answers we're all looking for.

"Right now, with you in my arms while I'm still buried inside of you? No, I don't feel lost. But that night with Sorik in wolf territory, when you first walked through the trees and the moon lit up your face? I felt lost in that moment. Like somehow I was connected to you, but I couldn't understand how. When our eyes met for the first time, you felt inevitable to me, but that made no sense."

Siah brushes hair back from my face and cradles my neck, his intense gaze locked onto mine. "When Sorik explained who you were to him, I thought that my purpose was finally clear. I would help him protect you. That felt right to me in a way I had been missing since my life was stolen from me in a piss covered alley.

"But then you walked through the door after that caster had been working on me and offered me your wrist...your blood. Right then and there, I felt lost again, because I couldn't just protect you from afar like I thought, I needed more. But you were mated, and I didn't see how I could fit into any of that."

Siah looks away, and I can feel the pain radiating off of him.

"I've been alone for so long. I've had Sorik, and his friendship has been a lifeline for me more times than I can count, but I've felt homeless and adrift since I was seventeen. I'm terrified I always will."

His confession wraps around me like a familiar blanket, because he's just spoken into existence feelings I've been trying not to look at.

"Every time I settle into something good in my life, it's taken away. I've fought my *whole* life to be safe, to be strong, to be secure...to be worthy. And yet I feel like it all slips through my fingers like sand just when I think I have a hold of it. You would think, after everything, I would learn not to hope or think that maybe *this time* if I can just hold on tight enough, then I can keep the safety and the love and the belonging in my grip...but I never can," I confess.

My eyes sting with emotion, and I lean into Siah's palm when he moves it to cradle my face. "I get so close, but it's never enough. Beth got Laiken killed. Talon lied to me. My uncle was too broken to love me. The elders fucked with me. Adriel...he killed my mother. He shattered my father. And now, here I am surrounded by Sentinels. I'm not the last. I don't have to be alone. But they don't want me. I'm filth. I'm unworthy."

Tears stream down my face, and sobs bubble up in my throat.

"I've tried so hard to be the best, to be the strongest, to find my place, but I never can. I'm everything to these people that Beth always told me I was, nothing, and it fucking kills me."

Siah lets me sob. He holds me as I fracture, and hugs me until I'm ready to figure out how the fuck I move forward now. He pulls my lips to his and kisses me softly, and then he kisses each of my cheeks and once again dries them with his thumbs.

"I don't know about the why of things, but I do know this... You are *everything* to me and your other mates. I have no doubt about that."

I try to shake my head, to remind him of all the times in my life that prove I'm unworthy of safety and love and goodness, but Siah cuts me off.

"Can I make you a deal?" he asks, his eyes searching mine. I hesitate for a minute and then nod.

"I'll be your home if you'll be mine," he tells me, and the simple request makes me swallow any argument I held waiting on my tongue.

He's not force-feeding me lies about who I am and what I can be. He's just asking for something he should have always had and that I could never deny him. I stare at Siah for a beat, overwhelmed by his quiet and steadfast offer. *I'll be your home if you'll be mine.*

"Okay," I answer simply, and just like that, I see a ray of light in all this darkness.

I may not have been good enough for Beth not to torture or for Talon to be honest with. Lachlan couldn't love me, and neither the casters nor the Sentinels could accept me. But despite all of that, somehow, I fit with Siah, Sabin, Valen and Bastien. I fit with Ryker, Knox, and Torrez. Maybe I'm not worthy, but they want me all the same.

And it's not just them. The sisters are waiting for me back home, so are Aydin and Evrin. Mave and Cyndol were blowing up my phone before we lost service on the hike here. And I've found Sorik, Enoch, Kallan, Nash and Becket. I have more than I've been acknowledging, worthy or not, and it's time for me to see that and Sentinel the fuck up.

"You're pretty good at this mate shit," I tell him with a smile.

"I am, aren't I," he teases, and I grin.

I release a deep breath and lean in to kiss Siah softly. "Thank you," I whisper against his lips.

He smiles and runs a hand down my spine. "Like I said, I've got you."

My grin is blinding, and I move my lips to his ear. "Now fuck me again, mate, and then let's go relieve the others from guard duty."

Siah growls and then palms my ass. "Don't have to tell me twice. Let's see how many times I make you scream my name."

And with that, the fucker bites me.

* * *

Knox hollers triumphantly when he finally wins the epic thumb-war we've been having for twenty minutes. He puffs up about it like he's just done something amazing, but my hands are a fuck-ton smaller than his, so really, can he be *that* proud of a win?

"Gentlemen, I've finally found something that Vinna Aylin isn't good at," he announces jovially.

Given the fact that I just fucked us all over by losing a battle with Mother Time, Knox's innocent statement stings more than it probably should.

"Too soon, Knox," I tell him shaking my head. "Way too fucking soon."

"What? I thought ol' blue eyes got you fixed up right as rain. You know, with his cock and his fangs?" he tells me, wagging his eyebrows at me. "Siah, we were counting on you, what happened?" Knox shouts, his booming voice filling the main room we're sitting in.

Siah peeks his head out of our room. "What are you shouting about?"

I slap Knox in the chest. "Nothing," I tell him and shoot a glare at Knox.

"Killer is still feeling all fucked up about the old lady. I thought you got that sorted," Knox tells him, ignoring my irritated eye roll.

The front door opens, and in walks Enoch, Kallan, Nash, Becket, Sabin, and Torrez.

"Thank fuck," I mumble under my breath, their presence saving me from having to talk about the source of my eternal shame.

"They're back!" Knox calls out, and all the other guys join us in the main room.

171

Torrez heads right for the leftover platters of food that are on the back table and starts stacking his plate with meat.

"They not feed you?" Valen asks him, eyeing the mountain slowly forming on Torrez's plate.

"No, they fed us," Torrez replies, looking over at Valen like he doesn't understand why he's asking the question.

I laugh softly and watch as Kallan plops down on the couch to the left of the one I'm sitting on. He runs a tired hand over his face.

"Well, second impressions of our Sentinel, Suryn, are not really any more favorable than the first," he announces.

Becket gives an agreeing grunt and drops down on the other end of the couch.

"I dunno, I kind of like it," Nash argues, and he laughs when Kallan gives him a disgusted look.

"You always like the bitchy ones, so no surprise there. You'll probably jerk off to the way she looks at us like we're shit on her shoes," Becket flings at Nash.

I choke on a cough when Nash just shrugs and admits, "Probably." Enoch shakes his head and leans against the arm of the couch, a small smile playing at his lips. I try to decipher the look I see in his grey-blue gaze, but I can't suss it out.

"So what happened?" Ryker asks as he comes out of Sorik and Vaughn's room.

He walks over to where I'm sitting on the couch and wedges himself between Knox and me. I laugh, and Knox grumbles as Ryker makes himself at home and drapes an arm over the back of the couch behind me.

"That's better," he sighs and relaxes against me.

He starts playing with the ends of my hair and ignores Knox's *cockblock* accusation.

"They took us to this room that had a big round table in it," Sabin starts.

"It was very King Arthur Chic," Torrez throws in before he begins to devour what I think is a pig's leg.

"We all sat down, and then Sauriel started asking questions. We were allowed to interject any questions that we also had, so it was just a back and forth until everyone had all the answers they were looking for," Sabin finishes.

"So what did they ask?" Valen queries.

"They asked Suryn if she was born here. What her role was. They asked if she had ever marked anyone else, how it happened," Sabin pauses and tries to remember if there was anything else.

"Don't forget when Port asked her if she would strip her marks rather than die with her Marked if that's what the tribunal ruled," Kallan grumbles.

"What did she say?" Knox asks.

"She said she would strip her marks."

"Can you even do that?" I ask, leaning forward.

"I mean, they must have a way; otherwise, why ask that question?" Sabin responds.

"So Port is the guy who was all glarey?" I ask, recalling the younger looking Sentinel from the throne room who didn't look too happy to be there. He was the only other male on the tribunal aside from Sabin.

"That'd be the one," Becket confirms as he leans over and tries to steal a piece of cheese from Torrez's plate. Torrez growls at him and slaps his hand away.

"So what's your Sentinel's deal?" Bastien asks.

I ignore the itchy dislike that crawls up the back of my neck when Suryn is referred to as my Shield's Sentinel...again. I don't like her, but Siah was right when he reminded us that trusting the magic is what's most important. Her magic marked them, and like it or not, there's fuck all I can do about that right now.

"She's twenty-three. Her dad, as we all know, is Sauriel,

Adriel's brother. But her mother used to be Sovereign over the Sentinels. She died when Suryn was nine. What's interesting is that Suryn is supposed to be the Sovereign. I guess Sentinels are matriarchal. Leadership passes from mother to daughter unless there isn't a daughter, in which case the people elect a new line for leadership."

"Huh," I comment and lean back into Ryker, raptly listening as Enoch goes on.

"Well, they thought Suryn was too young, so her *aunt* is filling in until Suryn comes of age after her awakening."

"So the current Sovereign is her aunt?" Siah asks, and Enoch nods.

I shake my head and can't fight the smile that breaks across my face. I put a hand over my mouth to hide it, but it doesn't stop the giggle that leaks out.

Enoch turns to me. "What?"

His question makes me laugh a little harder, and I try to stop. "Nothing really, it's just your dad is going to slip into a happiness-coma when he finds out you were marked by the next leader of the Sentinels. I can just picture his face now," I tell him as I try to swallow down another giggle. "How many times do you think she'll stab him the first time he tries to make her do something she doesn't want to do?" I ask no one in particular, and then I completely lose it.

Elder Cleary is a manipulative ass, and I can't wait for him to meet his son's new mate. Well, that's if her people don't sentence all of us to death first.

Everyone bursts into laughter, including Enoch. He tries to hide it, but I catch the smile and shake of his shoulders before he gets a hand over his face and shakes his head. The fact that not even Enoch can deny his father's thirsty ways amuses me to no end. As much as I dislike Suryn, I almost want to start rooting for her and them to work out just so I can sit back with a bowl of popcorn and watch the shit go down between her and the elders.

"Well, I guess that explains Sauriel's comment about the Sovereign condemning her own blood," Ryker observes, and Enoch nods, still working to pull his features into a more stoic mien.

"After the tribunal established her history, they asked to see her runes, and that was about it," Enoch finishes.

"What did they ask you guys?" Valen calls over his shoulder as he follows Torrez's lead and fills up another plate of food.

"Pretty much the same stuff," Becket shrugs. "Where we were born, how we met, how we ended up here. They were more interested in you than they were in us really."

"How so?" I ask.

"They asked all of us what we knew about you. How we met. How you met your Chosen and us. How you marked everyone. What your abilities were...shit like that."

"Did you tell them what she can do?" Bastien asks, the accusation in his tone clear.

Becket and the others bristle.

"What do you think?" he challenges.

"I don't know, that's why I'm asking," Bastien grinds back.

"We kept everything as basic as possible," Enoch defends. "We didn't make her vulnerable, Bastien. The truth is *we* don't know everything Vinna can do. We stuck with what we know."

"Meaning?" Knox presses, and Enoch rolls his eyes and gives a frustrated huff.

"Meaning we told them she has multiple branches of magic, but not how proficient she is in any of them. We told them about the weapons we have—and therefore know she has—but nothing about her runes beyond that. Like Enoch said, we didn't leave her vulnerable," Kallan snaps, and then he gets up and storms off into his room.

We all watch him leave. No one speaks for a couple beats as the tension in the room settles a bit.

"So what did you all end up doing today? Find any answers?" Nash asks innocently.

And now it's my time to get up and storm off into my room.

"What happened?" I hear Torrez ask as I shut the door on that question and on this day. I stare at the mattresses on the ground for a minute, longing for the oblivion of sleep, but I'm too wired. A bath it is.

19

The steam soaks into my pores, the heat both cleansing and just on the cusp of overwhelming. I rest my hands on the lip of the tub that is built into the floor of the bathroom and let the coolness of the stone soak into my limbs to combat the heat of the water.

I rest my head back and close my eyes. I try to settle into the relaxation I know I should feel, but my fight with Getta keeps playing on the inside of my closed eyelids like they're a movie screen. Her question of whether I'm worthy is like some fucked up soundtrack to the whole thing, and no matter how hard I try, I can't find an off or a mute button.

I slip under the hot water and sit at the bottom of the deep tub, hoping it will somehow drown my memories of Getta and being bested. It doesn't. The day still plays on a loop, like my mind is going all *Groundhog Day* until I see whatever the fuck it's trying to show me.

I focus on my brief conversation with Tawv, ruminating on what I learned about my mother instead of honing in on my epic fuck up. Enoch said that Suryn's mom was the Sovereign before her sister stepped in. So was she who was in charge when my mom was sent out on a mission for new blood? Or did she rule after?

Something about that feels important to me. Maybe it's just that this place wasn't always so anti-stranger or maybe it's something else, but I file that away in my mind as something worth taking note of. A part of me chimes in with the thought that I must still have family here. Tawv said the people from where Grier came from were still holding out hope that she was alive. So someone here obviously still cared for her.

My lungs burn, and reluctantly I push up from the bottom of the tub. I break the surface and gasp to pull air into my angry lungs. I roundhouse all thoughts of Sentinel family away, because even if it's true they exist, it doesn't mean shit for me. They cared about Grier, but I'm not her. I wipe water from my face and jump when Valen's deep voice fills the bathroom.

"I wondered for a second if I was going to have to pull you out," he tells me, and I track his voice to where he's leaning against a far wall.

"Well, you'll look for any excuse to give me mouth to mouth, so I'm sure you wouldn't have been too put out," I joke, but it sounds hollow.

The corner of Valen's full lips turns up slightly, but if I want one of his mind numbing smiles, I'll need to do better than that.

"May I join you, or were you hoping to continue waterboarding yourself alone?" he asks with a cheeky grin, and I snort.

I don't say anything, but I gesture toward the water in clear invitation. I sit back on the bench seat that circles the entire interior of the tub. Valen watches me for a second like he's gauging what's the right move here, then he pulls his shirt up over his head. He unwraps the hair tie from his hair, the thick waves falling around his shoulders as he brushes his fingers through them.

"Your striptease game is on point," I observe as I lean back and enjoy the show.

"Thank you, I've been practicing," Valen deadpans, and I chuckle.

"Like in the mirror? Or are you and the guys starting an all-male review and just haven't told me?" I ask amused.

"We were waiting for the routine to be perfect," he tells me casually as he slowly unlaces his black armored pants. "Well, that and for the bedazzled thongs we ordered to come in."

Valen gives me a roll of his hips, and I snort out a laugh.

"Do you guys do spirit fingers, because nothing gets me going like well executed spirit fingers."

"Well then, you're in luck, my love, because we give really *gooood* spirit fingers, and our shimmies will have you screaming for more."

Valen slips into the water, and I watch greedily as, inch-by-inch, his incredible body is swallowed up by the bath.

My nipples go hard as he dips all the way under, wetting his hair. He comes back up dripping of water and sex, and I lick my lips and drink him in with my eyes.

"Shimmies, you say?" I ask him, humor and lust dripping from every word.

"And just wait until we get to the hair flips, Vinna, you are going to soak your panties."

I give an overexaggerated moan. "You *do* know how to get me all hot and bothered."

Valen chortles and gives me a wink, but his playful gaze suddenly turns a little sad. "I've noticed a lot of bothered lately, and I hate that. Need to talk it out, fuck it out, fight it out...all of the above?" he asks, his hazel gaze studying mine.

I wipe my hands down my face and sigh. "I'll be okay. It's

just all been a lot," I confess. "From the minute I met Lachlan and the others until now, it's just been one crazy thing after another. I don't really even get time to process what the fuck just happened before the next thing is breathing down my neck."

Valen gives me a knowing nod.

"I think that's all this is," I tell him, gesturing to myself. "Maybe all the emotion is catching up to me now. Or maybe I'm finally seeing that my future isn't going to be the Sentinel sunshine and rainbows I secretly hoped it might be. Or maybe it's all the above, but I'm figuring it out," I reassure him.

I sag back against the wall of the tub, as if my admission sapped all of my energy.

"Anything the rest of us can do to help?" Valen asks as he sits down on the opposite side of the massive inground bath.

I trace water droplets with my eyes as they move slowly down his cheeks and drip off his chin. Some of them dart sideways, daring to skim his full lips before tumbling from his face and dripping back into the tub of water.

"Do you think a lot about the future?" I ask randomly, and I can tell the question takes him a little off guard.

"Yeah, I guess. I mean, Bastien and I have known we were going to be paladin since we were young. So when I think of the future, I think of that mostly; the next test we have to take or physical training we have to do at the academy. Sometimes I wonder about the assignments we might go on, things like that."

I nod and contemplate his words.

"But what do you see now?" I ask, fidgeting with the ends of my wet hair.

"Now that we won't be paladin?" Valen clarifies.

I nod again.

"I'm not sure. Like you said, everything has happened

pretty fast with Adriel and now this," he tells me, gesturing to the castle walls surrounding us. "I know we'll be together," he offers, his tone radiating certainty. "I guess that's all I really need to know right now."

I give Valen a small smile, but the question of *now what* seems to burrow deeper into my brain until it feels more demanding.

"What do you think will happen with Silva?" Valen asks me, his gaze equally as contemplative as mine is now.

I offer my patent shrug. "I honestly have no idea. You would know better than I would how the elders deal with shit like that."

"Yeah, that's true. I just wish I understood what was happening with him," Valen admits, and my heart aches for him. "Bas and I thought he had come to terms with what happened to our parents. I mean, Silva is a good guy, but to do the shit he was doing... It's just hard to reconcile the uncle who raised me with the crazed man who attacked my mate."

Valen stares at the water, and I hate the haunted ring in his voice.

"Hope is a bitch," I admit after a couple beats.

Valen looks up at me, confused.

"I'm not saying what Silva did was okay, it fucking wasn't, and he should face consequences for it. But I don't think that it automatically tallies Silva in the bad guy column. I think finding me stoked hope in him. Maybe it was hope he didn't even realize he had, but add a little *Vinna exists* kindling to it, and that flicker could be a bonfire in no time. He got hopeful, and then he got desperate."

"Yeah, I could see that," Valen admits on a sad nod.

"Some casters put themselves above the other supes," I scoff humorlessly, realizing that Sentinels clearly do it too. "It's easier to hurt others when you think of them as *lesser*.

It's not like the lamia, shifters and other supes exactly have their own paladin to protect them and call foul when shit goes down. Silva and the others looked at lamia like they were the enemy instead of looking at the enemy and realizing that some of them just so happened to be lamia. Aydin and Evrin will probably have consequences to face too, from the first lamia they tortured for information," I state.

"Actually, I don't think they will," Valen disagrees. "They were ordered to purge those lamia, they just worked them over for information beforehand. That technically doesn't violate any of the rules. What Silva, Lachlan, and Keegan were doing was unsanctioned, and *that* is the big no-no."

I snort at the logic of it all. From what the guys have said, Silva will probably only get his title stripped, maybe not even that. He'll probably just get reassigned to a different paladin coven, but with the deaths in his current coven, that was inevitable anyway.

"Do you hate him?" Valen asks me, and I pause not sure how to answer that question.

Do I hate him?

"No," I answer after a moment. "I don't hate him, but I don't respect him or like him all that much."

I worry that admitting that could create some kind of issue. Silva is the twins' family, their *only* family.

"I don't expect you to feel the same way about him though," I quickly explain. "My experience with Silva, Lachlan, and Keegan was obviously very different from your experience with them."

"Does it bug you when we talk about them?" he asks, and my worried gaze softens.

"No. They're your family. They raised you. I like hearing there are other sides to them than the ones I saw."

Valen nods simply, but I can see his shoulders rise like a weight was just lifted from them.

"Did you think I'd be mad if you still cared about them?" I ask curious. It had never really dawned on me before that any of the guys could be worrying about this.

"No, I didn't think you'd be mad. *I* felt like I was betraying you somehow. We all did. We saw the way they treated you. That's not who any of us thought they were."

"Valen, just because they didn't want me doesn't mean they didn't want you," I reassure him.

Valen stares at me for a moment, his gaze tracing my face. I'm not sure what he's looking for.

"Come here," he eventually says, his warm voice wrapping around me like a tether.

"Why?" I ask, suddenly eyeing him warily.

Valen chuckles. "Just come here, I want you to sit on my dick while I tell you a story."

I laugh, and butterflies flutter to life in my stomach. "Well, how could I resist such a flowery offer?" I snark, but I get up anyway and inch closer.

When I'm within reaching distance of Valen's long corded arms, he snags me by the waist and pulls me toward him. I squeak at the manhandling, but spread my legs to straddle him as he pulls me chest to chest. Valen runs his hand down the runes on my spine, and I shiver, very aware of the erection nestled between my thighs. My breasts press against Valen's wet muscled pecs. I *love* the feel of his naked body against mine.

"I've wanted you from the moment you woke up in my arms, sitting on me just like this," he tells me, rolling his hips up just like he did that first movie night when we woke up alone all twined together. "I realized how hard I was falling for you when you disappeared after we went dancing. I saw you in the back of that SUV, covered in ash and blood, tenderly and carefully taking care of your friend's ashes, and I knew I was a goner. You were it."

Valen kisses me softly, and I try to swallow past the tightness in my throat.

"Bastien wanted you from the first punch, Sabin from the first 'fuck you.' Ryker fell the day you came back after cliff diving and told us about what happened with the shifters. Knox wanted you from the first time he ever saw you. Siah knew you were it when you offered your blood like it wasn't a big deal; you saw him for him and not the monster others had spent his whole life seeing. You had Torrez from the minute you broke his jaw. Do you see a pattern here?" Valen asks me, leaning back so he can stare intensely into my eyes.

"That I kick a lot of your asses?" I joke, and Valen laughs.

"No, that you have all of us. Hook, line and sinker, you have us. *We* want you. We *love* you, and we're going to keep on doing that forever. I know you didn't find what you were wanting to here or with Lachlan. But you *do* have it with us. You know that, right?"

Valen's eyes are beseeching. I run the tip of my nose against his and run my fingers through his wet hair. I lift up on my knees and position myself until I feel Valen's hard length line up with my opening, and then I slowly sink down on top of it. Valen moans and grips my hips tighter.

"Should I take that as a yes?" he teases, and his cock twitches inside of me.

"Yes," I tell him. "Now let me sit on your dick and tell *you* a story," I parrot, grinding against the black curls at his base.

Valen chuckles and nuzzles my neck, nipping at Siah's runes on my shoulder. I pull his head back so I can stare in his eyes.

"I love you," I tell him, pausing dramatically. Valen stares at me, waiting patiently for more, but for me, that's it. That's the whole beginning, middle, and end to this story. I love him, and I always will. I smile sweetly at him and lean in for a kiss.

"The end," I tell him, and then I lift up on his shaft and drop back down.

Valen laughs as he deepens the kiss, and I begin to ride him faster. Water sloshes up the sides of the tub as Valen and I let our bodies shout *I love you* to the other over and over again. Valen leans down and sucks on my nipples, supporting my back with one hand and playing with my clit with the other. I revel in the feel of him everywhere and drive harder, pushing for both of our release.

I can feel Valen is close, and just before he can come, I lean in and whisper, "Now show me those spirit fingers."

He bellows out a laugh that twines with a moan as he comes. He rubs at my clit harder, and I fall off the edge right behind him, screaming, "These are spirit fingers!"

20

I stare at the old school parchment invitation announcing that my presence is requested by the tribunal. It looks so ancient and out of place in my hands that I expect it to crumble to pieces at any moment. Or maybe it will go full Harry Potter and become a mouth that yells at me to get my ass down to the tribunal room. It does neither of those things. I fold it back up and drop it on the table.

"Do you think that you and Siah combined could *both* push magic into him, and that would complete the transition into a lamia?" Ryker asks Sorik, who nods absently in thought.

I've been listening to all of the guys speculate on what they think is going on with Vaughn and how it could be fixed. The consensus is that when Adriel's magic wasn't enough to complete Vaughn's transition into a lamia, it left him in this weird stasis. Adriel's magic was enough to keep Vaughn from dying, but not enough to turn him all the way, and now he's stuck being what he is now.

"Maybe," Sorik tells Ryker. "I don't know if either of us have enough magic though. Vaughn was a Sentinel, so if he *can* be turned into a lamia, I imagine it would take a massive amount of magic to complete the transition. If we try and fail, I worry it could make Vaughn worse off than he is now. I'm hesitant to attempt anything until we know more."

"Was Sabin right?" Knox asks, pulling my focus from the Vaughn talk.

He gestures to the parchment on the table. "Did they summon you today like he thought they would?"

"Yep, looks like there's guards waiting outside to escort me down," I confirm.

Bastien gets up from the couch he's chilling on, and Knox follows.

"Did it finally come?" Ryker asks as I flash him a goodbye wave and head for the door.

"Sure did," I chirp.

"Call if you need anything," Siah shouts after me.

"Will do," I tell him.

I open the door and pause when my escort is none other than the gray and tan winged Sentinel, Ory. His grin lights up when my face falls at the sight of him.

"Why, good afternoon, Sentinel," he greets me with an exaggerated bow. I roll my eyes, not able to help it.

Knox and Bastien are silent sentries behind me, their *I will fuck you up* game strong. I step out of the room, and Ory and another nondescript Sentinel fall into step on each side of me. Bastien and Knox take their place at my back. We make our way down the corridor, my surroundings becoming more and more familiar with each passing day.

Ory's wing brushes against my shoulder as we walk. I ignore it. I'm pretty sure he's doing it on purpose. It's fucking killing me to not ask how he has them. Are they a rune? Something else? The questions itch in my throat, but I keep quiet. I'm pretty sure he knows I'm dying to know, which is why he keeps practically shoving the appendages in my face, but the last thing I'm going to give this guy is any amount of satisfaction.

"Nervous?" Ory asks me when we make our way four floors down the wide twisting steps.

I don't respond.

"It's okay to feel worried. You should be," he offers unhelpfully.

I can't figure out this dude's angle. He's antagonistic, but I'm not sure if that's just who he is or if there's a purpose for it. Maybe I should have Nash try to spend some time with him, I could never figure that kid out either.

In no time, we're in front of the doors that Sabin described earlier as leading into the room the tribunal was holding court in. They open of their own accord, and I enter. Bastien and Knox move to follow me, but Ory stops them.

"Were you summoned also?" Ory asks them smugly. "Didn't think so. Which means you can scurry off back to the room, as you're not wanted here."

I growl at Ory, irritated, at the same time Bastien takes a menacing step toward him. I catch a glint of excitement in Ory's eyes that sends worry fluttering through me.

"We'll be right here until you're done," Bastien tells me, never taking his eyes off the winged Sentinel.

They stare at each other for a couple more seconds before Bastien moves in front of me and kisses me. I can feel the claim in it, and it makes me smile. Bastien steps back, his own grin reflected in his eyes, and then Knox's lips are on mine. Knox nips and teases both of my lips in a thorough kiss. Then he and Bastien step back and position themselves to guard the door.

I activate Knox and Bastien's runes behind my ear as I walk through the doors and they shut behind me. *"Love you guys,"* I tell them, a wide grin spread across my face, and both of their chuckles bounce around my head in response.

"That little winged fucker is into you, I can feel it," Bastien tells me, and I give him an incredulous snort.

"I think he just likes fucking with all of us, and he knows that's the quickest way to rile you up," I respond, and Knox and Bastien's own incredulous snorts fill my mind.

"Whatever it is, the prick better watch himself before I pluck him," Knox informs me, and I can't help the smile that breaks open on my face. I'm led to a large round table where Sabin, Torrez, Sauriel and the four other tribunal members are already seated.

"Gotta go," I announce and then recall the magic in the runes behind my ear.

Sabin smiles at me and nods to a chair. I pull one out and sit in it, not sure exactly how this is going to go down. Sabin said everyone simply asks questions, but this all feels stuffier and more formal than the conversational way he and Torrez described it. I notice that Ory and the other guard stand in opposite corners of the room, and I'm irritated that they're in here, but Knox and Bastien aren't.

"Offer your name, please," the female Sentinel with the gray pixie cut and the gray eyes asks me, her request sounding neither friendly nor abrasive.

"Vinna Aylin," I tell her, and she gives me a nod.

"My name is Naree," she tells me.

"I am Mote," the younger looking female with the long white blonde hair and the dark eyes says.

"I am Port," the male Sentinel on the tribunal introduces. He looks less angry today, but I'm not going to read too much into that.

"And I am Wella," the eldest female offers.

I nod at all of them and lace my fingers together on the table. Wella and Port both eye the marks on my hands and arms.

"I believe you know the others seated at the table," Naree announces, and I give her a nod.

"Excellent. Then we will begin," she decrees.

"Do you know why you are here, Vinna?" Wella asks me.

"I breached your barrier," I answer, my tone making it seem like more of a question than a definitive answer.

"That, and you attacked the Sovereign," Port snidely adds.

"I didn't attack the Sovereign," I defend. "I attacked *him*," I explain, pointing to Sauriel. "I mean, I didn't actually get to him, my Chosen stopped me, but I *tried* to attack him."

Port sneers at me and shares a look with Mote.

Well, shit.

"So you admit that you attacked a Quorum member?" Naree asks me.

"Yes, but it's not that simple," I counter.

"And why is it not that simple?" she presses.

"I thought he was his brother, Adriel. I came in search of Sentinel City...I mean...Tierit right after I fought Adriel. When I saw Sauriel, I thought somehow he was still alive," I explain, but it doesn't seem to be impacting the narrowed eyes everyone on the tribunal, except for Sabin, is giving me.

"Did you have a plan to attack the Sovereign when you breached our barriers?" Naree asks me, dismissing the Adriel topic.

Why do I get the impression that these people don't care that he was hunting and torturing Sentinels?

"What?" I ask, surprised by her question. "No. I didn't even know there was a Sovereign until Sentinel guards were dropping out of the sky and announcing that the Sovereign had ordered that we be dispatched," I declare.

"How did you get through the barrier?" Mote demands, leaning forward with interest.

"We just walked through." I'm struggling not to fidget in

the chair as they rapid fire questions at me. This is way more hostile and formal than I was expecting. The way Enoch and the others described their questioning and Suryn's questioning did not involve weighted glares of judgment and a shit ton of accusations.

"We are the tribunal that has been called to decide whether or not you and your Chosen pose a threat to our community and leaders. Lying to us will not help your cause," Port states with a sneer.

"I haven't lied," I defend, looking from Port to Sabin and Torrez, my gaze screaming *Mayday*.

"Vinna, after you realized that Sauriel was not in fact his identical twin brother, Adriel, did you stop your advances on him?" Sabin asks me.

"Yes," I answer simply and try not to sigh with relief that not everyone here is filled to the brim with prejudgment.

"When the Sovereign issued a dispatch order against you, what did you think of that?" Sauriel asks me.

"I didn't understand why. We were hoping to get some answers in coming here. I didn't know that I would be ordered to death for that. I would have never come and put my Chosen and Shields in harm's way if I had known we wouldn't be welcome here," I add.

The room grows quiet for a moment, and I sit there awkwardly wondering what they'll hammer me about next.

"We know, from your Shields and your two Chosen here, a great deal about you," Naree states matter-of-factly. "Sabin has explained how you came to the casters and has detailed the events leading up to your discovery of us here in Tierit. Your Shields discussed your abilities and your training, and all of them have confirmed you're... How did you put it, Sabin? Ah yes, you're *winging this whole Sentinel thing*."

I try not to shake my head with frustrated humor at that

description of it. I don't hear a question yet though, so I keep my mouth shut and don't respond past a nod.

"You were raised by a human, is that correct?" Naree asks me.

"Yes."

"When that human cast you out, you began to rely on a lamia, is that also correct?"

"I didn't know he was a lamia at the time, but yes," I tell her, and I push down at the grief that wells inside of me at the thought of Talon.

"Are you what the casters call a mimic?" Naree fires at me, and I start to wonder if she's the only one who has questions now or just wants to confirm my back story.

"Yes."

"How many total markings do you have on your body?"

"Um..." I pause, thinking through her question. "I don't actually know, I've never counted them."

"Would you be comfortable showing them to us?" Port asks, and I don't like the glint in his eye as he does.

I pause again and look to Sabin for guidance. He gives an imperceptible shrug.

"Is this somehow going to be used against me?" I ask no one in particular.

"It would give us an idea of your importance, which would factor into our decision. Beyond that, I don't see how they could be used against you," Wella tells me.

I study her cloudy eyes for a second, and then I look to Torrez. He gives me a nod, confirming she's telling the truth.

I push out of my chair.

"Commander, would you please invite the cleric in so he can assist us with identifying any unknown marks?" Naree orders Ory, and he nods and leaves the room.

I stand there, unsure if I'm supposed to strip down now or wait to give this cleric a show too. I'm not necessarily shy or overly modest when it comes to my body. Enoch did mention that they looked at Suryn's runes too, so this request isn't completely out of left field, but it's very clinical, and I feel uneasy about it.

A gray robed man is led into the room. I'm not sure if he's one of the guys that helped blast an orb through Sabin, but I glare at him all the same. He sits at the round table next to Sauriel and looks up at me expectantly.

I guess I'll take that as an invitation to *show me what you got.*

I begin to undress, unlacing my armored vest and pulling it off. My shirt goes up and over my head, and then I pull my boots off. I untie my pants and push them down my hips and off my feet. When I'm in my sports bra and underwear, I step back from the table and hold my hands out.

I'm not sure what I thought they were going to do once my runes were visible, but I didn't expect them all to get out of their chairs and come inspect me. I look over at Sabin and Torrez and notice that they look tense, which isn't helping me as I try to activate my chill.

The cleric brings his old book with him as he comes to look me over, and he immediately starts flipping through the pages as he scans my shoulder and arm.

"Fascinating," he whispers.

"Explain," Port demands, his patience clearly running thin with anything and everything.

"Her patterns are fascinating. The runes trade off from defensive and protective forms to offensive and weapons forms. They're layered in a way that makes her very powerful and very protected," he observes.

The cleric steps closer to me, and I bristle at his proximity.

Don't threaten him. Don't stab him. We need to convince

these assholes I'm not a threat, not give them more fuel for my death pyre.

I repeat that fact over and over again as the robed Sentinel closely looks me over.

"Huh," he comments, and once again starts frantically searching through his book again.

"What is it?" Naree asks, and I also look at him, ready for the answer.

"These runes on her shoulders and some on her hands are unusual. They look like runes that have been documented, but they're just slightly altered. It's a more evolved magic than we've seen in, well...I don't know. I'd need to consult to be sure."

"Well, can you tell us what you *do* know?" Mote asks, her tone taking a page from Port's annoyed book.

"Yes. She's quite the arsenal. She has several swords and some smaller blades, maces, a staff, bow and arrows, axes, whips, spears..."

"I have spears?" I ask the cleric in surprise.

He startles at my question and then gives me a nod. "Yes, here." He points to a rune on my wrist. "And here is a shorter set," he informs me, pointing to another rune close to the back of my heel. I study the rune on my arm and have to fight not to call on it so I can see for myself. Don't want these people thinking I'm trying to attack them.

"She also has several runes for speed, strength, enhanced senses, shields for offensive and defensive purposes, and her light *called* Shields, which in its own right hasn't happened since the time of the gates."

He circles around me and points to my chest. "Her connection with her Chosen is intricate and reinforced in several different ways, which is very unusual. She has mental, emotional, *and* proximity connections."

"So what does all of this mean?" Sabin questions, and I look to the cleric, eager for the cliff notes version too.

"She's more marked than anyone has been since the crossing. It's advanced and evolved in a way that I haven't seen here in Tierit. She has seven Chosen, but I suspect she could call more if she wanted to. But the most intriguing thing to me at this point is that her Chosen runes"—he picks up my palm and points to the runes down my ring finger and hand, and I don't even try to punch him for touching me, I'm so caught up in what he's going to say—"her Chosen marks are also incorporated in some of her other marks. Portions of them have altered some of her other runes. I think that's the source for the evolution in some of her markings and I suspect her abilities also."

"I don't understand," Port snaps, and I start to feel bad for the cleric. Looks like I'm not the only one this group isn't a fan of.

"We've operated under the understanding that born Light Marked pairings would result in the strongest magic and markings. But her markings would say otherwise. None of her Chosen are born Light Marked, and yet their abilities still enhanced hers when she marked them. She was strong before but became even more so with each pairing," the cleric concludes, and the room once again goes silent.

Well, shit. Try to call my kickass magic enhancing mates filth now, motherfuckers!

I smile at Sabin and Torrez and snicker silently at the smug grin Torrez is wearing.

"I'd love to study your markings and abilities more, if you would be open to that?" the cleric asks me with excitement in his eyes and a kind smile on his face. "I would need to do a thorough analysis to confirm what I've stated today, but it would really help us to understand your light and abilities."

Okay, maybe not all the robed Sentinels are orb firing assholes.

"I would say that's cool with me, but really that depends on these guys," I tell him, gesturing toward the tribunal.

The cleric looks at me, confused.

"They may vote that I need to die," I explain, and the guy suddenly looks like I just slapped an ice cream cone out of his hand.

He whirls on the tribunal. "You cannot do that," he orders them, looking a little surprised by his own vehemence.

"You will not presume to tell us what we can and cannot do, *cleric*," Port snarls at him, and the cleric takes a step back and tucks his book into his side.

"You would be making a tremendous mistake," the cleric states, and he flashes a glare at each one of the members of the tribunal in turn and storms out.

The room goes quiet for a minute.

"I agree with him," I offer unsolicited, my thumb pointing toward the door the cleric just stormed out of.

Torrez barks out a laugh that morphs into a cover-up cough. No one says anything still, but Naree's narrowed eyes tell me all I need to know about her thoughts on my opinion. *Fuck.* I think we need to come up with a plan for getting the fuck out of here *before* the Tribunal comes to a decision. The way they are looking at me right now does not bode well for me and the guys at all.

I move to get dressed when a pounding on the door starts up. I jump in surprise as the insistent booming sound invades the quiet room. Ory rushes to see what it is, a sword suddenly in his hand and his feathers bristling at his back. He flings the door open, and a stout man comes stomping in.

"What is the meaning of this?" Wella demands.

The new guy unrolls a parchment and takes a deep breath. "Vinna of the First, you have been summoned by the First. You are to be immediately escorted to the First House, where you will be reunited with your people and claim your rightful place. Anyone causing a deviation from this order will be seen as committing an act of war against the First House and will be dealt with accordingly."

The stout man stops, rolls the parchment back up, and then just waits like none of this is a big deal and he didn't just come in here saying shit like *claim my rightful place* or *it'll be an act of war.* Dude just fucked with all the *I'm not a threat, don't kill me* vibes I've been putting out this whole time.

Who is this guy, and what the hell is going on?

21

"This is not done," Port bellows, and for a guy that looks like he just finished puberty, he sure can go purple with outrage. "How dare the First interrupt this tribunal and make such ludicrous threats!"

The stout guys responds by opening the parchment again and reading it word for word.

Nope, definitely didn't imagine that whole claim my rightful place *part.*

"You tell the First—"

"Port, sit down before you say something that your whole House will come to regret," Wella commands, and I'm surprised when Port actually listens.

He looks like he's chewing glass as he sits his grumpy ass in the chair, but he does it nonetheless. Wella turns to the others.

"Are there any other pressing questions that need to be addressed?" she asks.

The stout dude unrolls his parchment again and reads it. Naree rolls her eyes, and Mote gives an outraged huff. Port gets even more purple but stays quiet. I look to Sabin and find the same confused expression that I know I'm wearing too.

"Fine, we are done with this Sentinel for today," Wella announces, but the acid in her tone as she does—and the looks on the other tribunal members' faces—scream that she's not fucking happy about it.

I glare at the stout invader. If this guy, or whoever sent him, causes the tribunal to hate us even more than it seems they already do, there's going to be a reckoning.

"Come with me, Vinna of the First," the guy commands.

"Sure, just give me a minute to get dressed, oh, and figure out who the fuck you are and where you're trying to take me," I tell him with a glare and a look that says *come the fuck on.*

What does he do? He opens the damn parchment up and reads it again.

"Is there someone else here who doesn't have a broken record for a brain that can tell me what the hell is going on?" I ask, turning to the angry tribunal members.

"Your family and House want to meet you," Sauriel explains, like it's all just as simple as that.

The answer feels like a punch to the chest. I turn to Sauriel as the last word leaves his mouth. Sabin's and Torrez's heads both snap in his direction, and we all just stare at him in shock.

"Tawv told us who your mother is. Clearly, they have found out too, and..." He gestures to the Sentinel stuck on repeat. "Would you like to meet them?" he asks me.

Panic and excitement flash flood through my veins, and I'm not sure what to say. *Yes, I'll meet them if you promise they'll be nice to me? No, they can fuck off for leaving my mom to rot with Adriel instead of looking for her?* My mouth is dry, and my chest feels heavy. I know I need to say something, but all I can think is...how much is this going to hurt? Can I withstand another cut or another blow from people who should give a fuck, but probably won't?

My eyes move from Sauriel's red-gold gaze to Sabin's forest green one. I'm trying to be strong and not show how rattled I feel, but I feel fucking rattled.

"I don't know if this is a good idea," I admit to him, and a knowing and comforting smile spreads across his face.

"Are they good people?" Torrez asks.

"They are," Sauriel responds.

I snort at the same time Port does. "By whose standards?" I ask as I give Port the side eye.

"The First, I'm sure you could guess from the name alone, is the oldest House of our people. They are powerful," he supplies, pointing to the parchment-holding guy and toward the tribunal.

Yeah, I get that they might be the kind of people that say jump and everyone around them asks how high. I look from Sabin to Torrez, still unsure of what to do.

"It's your call, Witch," he tells me unhelpfully.

I chuckle when Ory and Naree both give a little gasp at Torrez's pet name for me.

"If they hurt you, we'll fuck them up," Sabin states simply.

Sauriel turns to him, a hint of outrage in his eyes, and then turns to Torrez like he thinks he'll find more reason there. Torrez shrugs, brushing off Sauriel's obvious displeasure with Sabin's statement.

"We will," he backs his compeer up, and my heart swells with gratitude and appreciation.

I swallow down my nerves and apprehension and take a deep calming breath. "Okay. I'll meet them...not that I really have much choice in the matter," I grumble, looking over at the parchment-holding messenger.

Sauriel turns to me, and it seems to take him a minute to

process my acquiescence. I can see him practically shake off Sabin and Torrez's threat and collect himself. He pushes out of his chair. "If it is okay with the tribunal, I will escort you," he announces.

Wella gives him a slight dip of her chin, and he steps away from the round table.

"It's okay, I have some of my Chosen outside; they can take me," I tell Sauriel, ignoring the panic in my voice.

"I think it would be best if I accompany you, Vinna," Sauriel states cryptically.

Sabin and Torrez move to stand up too, but Naree shakes her head. "Sabin, you have to stay until the tribunal ends questioning for the day. Teo, it's your choice if you want to stay or go, but another representative cannot be called in your place," she tells them.

I look over at my guys. "It's fine," I reassure them, even though I couldn't feel further from it. "Bastien and Knox are just outside. They'll make sure I'm good," I tell them.

Distractedly, I wonder if I should change? *Get it together, Vinna, you don't have any clothes other than the black armored shit the Sentinels handed over.* I run my fingers through my hair and then roll my eyes at myself. *It's just your mystery family that probably won't like you anyway, not a first date. Calm the fuck down, crazy.*

"Thank you for your time, Vinna of the First," Mote tells me, but her sneer and the way she says *of the First* makes it clear her thank you is really more of a *fuck you.*

I nod absently, dismissing the jab. All I can focus on right now is all that could possibly go wrong meeting this so called *family* I apparently have. Ory and the other guard again move to each of my sides, and the doors to the room open on their own to let us out.

Knox and Bastien snap up from where they were leaning against the wall, bored.

"That was fast," Knox observes, elbowing the other Sentinel out of the way so he can stand next to me.

"Yeah, we're going on a field trip," I state cheerily, but even I can hear the worry in my tone.

"Where?" Bastien asks me, looking at Ory and Sauriel like he's assessing which is the threat that needs to be dealt with first.

"Oh you know, just your everyday run of the mill family reunion," I chirp like a sick bird.

"Family reunion?" Knox repeats, confused.

"Well, shit," Bastien mutters.

"Yep, that about sums up what's happening inside," I confess.

"We'll fuck them up, Bruiser. You say the word, and you're out of there," Bastien reassures me, and I laugh.

"Sabin and Torrez said the same thing," I admit on a laugh. I link my fingers with Bastien and Knox and take a deep breath. I immediately feel better with them here.

"Safe word is *pineapple*," Knox announces, and I choke on another laugh.

"Where the hell did you get *pineapple*?"

The tips of Knox's ears go red, and the sight immediately piques my interest. "Uh...read it in a book once."

"What the fuck kind of book were you reading with safe words in it?" Bastien questions.

"It was about a cupid and these genfins which are like fairies or something. You should read it; you'd laugh your ass off," Knox informs him, and Bastien shakes his head. "Don't knock it before you try it. Sabin is the one who gave it to me."

"Well, if it's Captain approved, it can't be that out of control," I joke, and Knox snickers. He brings my hand up to his mouth and kisses my palm. "You know he's not nearly as prudish as you tease him for," Knox razzes me.

My mind immediately goes to the intensely hot and deliciously dirty shit Sabin whispered in my ear as we fucked early this morning while everyone was still asleep. I smile at the memory and release a contented sigh. Knox and Bastien both laugh and give me a knowing smile.

"Ready?" Knox asks me as Sauriel and the messenger guides us out of the castle.

"As I'm ever going to fucking be. Here's to hoping no one needs an ass kicking."

"Spoil sport," Bastien teases, and I laugh.

We don't go far from the gates of the castle. It appears that the home of the First is just down the street. It's massive, which is no surprise, and guarded as much as the palace of the Sovereign is. *That* does surprise me though. It's a pretty strong indication that not all is right in the land of Tierit. Which is further supported by what went down in the tribunal room just to summon me here. What are these Sentinels guarding against? Knox's and Bastien's gazes skim the sentries, and I can tell they're wondering the exact same thing.

We make it through the gates and up the pathway that leads to the mini palace the First occupy. There is a small orchard of some sort within the walls, and I notice that peculiar football shaped fruit growing that caught my eye when they first brought food to us in the castle.

Sauriel stops suddenly, and I almost slam into him. Knox pulls me back just in time, and I flash him a thankful smile and turn forward to see what has Sauriel stopping in his tracks. We stand at the bottom of the steps that lead to the front door. At the top stand two white haired Sentinels. The man and woman watch us like they're spellbound.

Sauriel and the messenger bow to them, and then the messenger scampers off. The woman gasps as her eyes land on mine. A hand flies to her mouth, and she shakes her head slightly. Her white-hued pixie cut is stark against her deep olive-toned skin. Her lilac eyes well up, and I watch as the grip she has on the man's hand tightens to what looks like the point of pain.

The man stares at me, his lips parted in shock. He doesn't seem to notice the death grip his companion is giving him as his teal eyes trace over me.

"You really are hers," he states gently. "I know they told us you were, but I couldn't hope..."

"Until now," the woman whispers, quickly wiping at a tear that's escaped her vibrant purple eyes.

I stand tall, not sure what to do or say. My heart hammers in my chest. It's clear they know Grier, but I have no idea who these people are to me. I have no clue how to feel about the way they're looking at me right now. Knox and Bastien tense and step forward when the man takes a step down toward me. He freezes.

"We would not hurt her," he defends, looking at my Chosen like he's affronted by what they just did.

"With all due respect, we don't know you, and that has not been our experience here," Bastien states simply.

The white haired man sort of reels at Bas's statement and looks around like he's not sure how to respond. His teal eyes land on Ory and light up.

"Ory, you know them, please reassure them that they're safe here," he commands.

I snort and step forward, Bastien and Knox moving aside for me. "He was one of the first to attack us. His reassurances will fall on deaf ears," I inform them, stepping around Sauriel and up the steps.

"Hi, I'm Vinna," I offer, and I hold a hand out in greeting.

The woman is too overcome with emotion to say anything, but the man eyes my outstretched hand and then places his fist over his bicep and bows to me. I'm stunned by his actions. I've only seen other Sentinels give this gesture in the presence of Tawv and Sauriel. Why the fuck would this dude be giving it to me? Ory hisses, and I turn to find him staring at what's happening in shock.

The woman suddenly bows too, and I watch, confused as tears drip from her eyes to the cream stone of the stairs. Her emotion reaches out to me on some visceral level, and my throat tightens. They both straighten at the same time, and I'm suddenly wishing I hadn't come up here to stand with them. This is fucking weird, and I don't know what to do.

"Good greetings to you, Vinna. I am your Tok, and this is your Marn," the man informs me, and his voice fills with emotion.

They think these words should mean something to me, I can see that in their eyes, but I don't know what the hell they're saying. I look to Sauriel, my eyes pleading for him to help me make sense of what this means.

"This is your mother's mother and her father," he tells me kindly, and the light bulb goes off.

"Ahhh, I got it," I announce, and I turn back to my maternal grandmother and grandfather. I've never had grandparents before, so I have no idea what the fuck to do. I clear my throat and shift my weight a little. "I'm sorry about your daughter," I tell them. "I never got to know her, but I've been told she was incredible."

"She was," Marn agrees, and her eyes are so fucking sad that I ache for her. "You look like her," she tells me on a whisper, and Tok wraps an arm around her and pulls her into his side. He kisses the top of her head sweetly, and the loving gesture warms me.

The two of them take a moment and just lean on each other. Their grief is palpable, and I feel like I'm intruding on what has to be a very painful and difficult moment. They lost their daughter. I know she's my mother, and I grieve that loss in a way, but it's different. They knew her. I miss what I picture a mom would have been like, but they know the sound of her laugh, the things that made her smile. They saw her first steps in this world and probably watched her leave the barrier, holding onto hope that she would come back to them. Their loss, in a weird way, feels greater in this moment than mine could ever be. I mourn the idea of what she could have been to me; they mourn who she was.

"I'm so sorry," I tell them again, struggling to know what else to say.

Marn looks up at me and shakes her head. "Don't be sorry, you are here and *that's* what matters. We're sorry, we're making this very uncomfortable for you, and we'll stop. It was just...seeing you...it made it all so real. I wasn't prepared for it to hit me like that."

I give her an understanding smile, and her eyes fill with loss and gratitude.

"May I..." she trails off.

I wait, giving her the room she clearly needs to move forward with whatever she wants to ask.

"May I embrace you?" she asks me hesitantly, and I'm taken aback for a second by her request.

"Sure," I tell her and try to mask the uncertainty in my answer.

She steps forward like she's just as unsure about all of this and wraps her strong arms around my waist. She's about a head shorter than me, and her ear rests over my chest as she holds me tightly. I wrap my arms around her and wait until she's ready to pull away. Tok watches us, joy shining in his eyes. As soon as Marn releases me, he steps in for a hug too. I feel his chest shake against mine as he hugs me hard. I'm pretty sure he's crying, and he holds onto me until his breathing is more normal. He steps back and wipes at his face.

He claps suddenly, and the loud sound fragments the heavy emotions wafting around us. I jump from the noise and then try to not look like such a scaredy-cat.

"Ory, call the families," Tok orders. "Announce that one of ours has returned home."

I expect Ory to mouth off about the command, but he takes off into the air before I can even look his way.

"Come, Vinna, let us show you around. All this is yours now, and you should get familiar with it," Tok states, and I try to cover up a choking sound with a cough.

"I hope you will join us," Tok offers Sauriel in invitation.

"I'd be honored," he answers back.

Tok puts an arm around me, and I try not to stiffen. He doesn't say anything if he notices and proceeds to lead me into his house. I renew my plea to the universe that somehow this won't take a turn for the worse as I take in the ornate entrance with my grandfather's arm around my shoulder. So far so good. Here's to hoping it stays that way.

22

"Are you thirsty or hungry?" Marn asks me as we make our way up a massive staircase. "Grier always liked caro water and zah. Would you like caro water?" she presses.

"I'm okay," I tell her politely. I have no idea what either of those things are, but I couldn't eat or drink with my stomach all in knots the way it is right now.

"You guys want anything?" I ask Bastien and Knox. They just shake their heads as they look around.

We've toured the elaborate stadium sized main floor and are now venturing into the upper levels of the First Palace. They don't call it that, of course, but a spade is a fucking spade. I'm pretty sure the railings are solid gold, and everything about this place is well past over-the-top. They open the door to a room on the right, and my eyes light up with recognition and excitement.

"Grier insisted we have it close by her room. She said it helped her think when she moved and pushed herself," Tok tells me, and I take in the combat equipment in the room.

It's not state of the art punching bags and combat

dummies like my space back home is, but it's the Sentinel version of all that. Padded poles in all sizes and heights, pulleys that would make targets move, another large mechanism that looks like it would refine agility, all fill the room, and an odd sense of giddiness and belonging trickles through me. I can picture a girl in here working out her frustrations, and I feel a sense of camaraderie with my mother that I've never felt before outside of us both being Sentinels.

Tok closes the door and leads me further down the large hall. He opens another large gold door, and he and Marn show me into a room that's light and airy with pastel colors. There's feminine touches in the bedding and wall fabrics, but other things, like well-used targets spread out on the walls, give me a peek at the depth of the woman who grew up in this room.

"This is Grier's room," Marn tells me reverently, confirming my hunch.

She runs her hand over a dressing table lovingly and blinks away the emotion I see pooling in her eyes.

"We've kept it ready, just in case," Tok informs me as he studies the space. "We've arranged for your belongings, which should arrive shortly, and if there's anything else you need in here, just let us know and we'll get it sorted," he tells me matter-of-factly, and I choke on a cough again.

"Say what?" I ask as I slap a fist to my chest in an effort to clear my airway of shock.

"You'll be staying with us now," he declares, and I study his face for a beat, not sure what to say about that.

"You are of the First House and should be here with your family, where we can protect you and guide you. The Sovereign's castle is not your place yet, and until it is, this is where you should be," he adds.

"I don't have any belongings," I croak out awkwardly, shooting Bastien and Knox an uneasy glance.

I don't know if I want to stay here. I especially don't know if I want to stay in my dead mother's old room. I want to spend time in it and get a feel for her, but sleep here? I look over at the bed and realize it will fit me and about one and a half of my Chosen. Yeah, that's not going to work.

"Well, then moving you here won't be too difficult," Tok tells me with a smile, answering my previous statement.

"Um...how are my Chosen supposed to stay here? The bed wouldn't fit..." I trail off, not sure how to say, *yeah this room is not right for me.*

"Your Chosen..." Marn repeats, trailing off as she glances at Knox and Bastien and then quickly looks away. "Right, yes. Your Chosen. We can arrange accommodation for them in the guest wing," she adds, quickly sharing a look with Tok that I can't discern.

"Oookay," I answer, feeling like I'm missing something. "We can stay in the guest wing, that's not a problem. I'll need space for my Shields too though," I add.

"You *all* will stay in the guest wing?" Marn questions, looking from me to Grier's room, like she's searching for the reason I wouldn't want to stay in here.

Shit.

"Yeah, well, I stay with my Chosen. So if they're in the guest wing, then I'm good to be there too," I explain, hoping it's enough and doesn't hurt her feelings.

"Right, that's totally understandable," Tok states and pulls Marn into his side. "We can get all of that arranged for you," he reassures me, and I give him a small smile.

"Well, it's getting late, and you must be starving. Let's go down for some dinner, shall we? We had the cooks prepare Illish which is Grier's favorite. I'm sure you're just going to love it," he tells me as he guides Marn out the door.

I turn to Knox and Bastien and make a face. *Illish*, I mouth to them, and Bastien pretends to get the shivers.

"You okay?" Knox asks me and opens his arms.

I step into them, and he surrounds me with his strong hold that helps me feel centered.

"Yeah...they seem nice," I observe. "It's just weird, I guess," I admit.

Knox kisses the top of my head as I nuzzle against his chest.

"Go easy on yourself, Bruiser. There's no rush to build bonds, it will take time," Bastien tells me, and I nod my head in agreement.

"If you don't want to stay here..." Knox starts.

"Here, the castle, it doesn't *really* matter to me. I just don't want to stay in my mother's old room. That feels kind of wrong in a way," I tell them. I'm probably not making a ton of sense, but Bastien and Knox nod their understanding, and I breathe out a sigh of relief.

"Grier...I mean...Vinna, are you coming down for dinner?" Tok asks me, and I look up from my hug with Knox.

Tok runs his gaze over our position, and I get the impression that he's uncomfortable with the display of affection.

"Yeah, coming," I say, stepping out of Knox's comforting embrace.

I move to follow Tok out the door. "So what exactly is Illish?"

"Can you see my ass crack?" I whisper to Knox as he tightens the ties on the new red-grape colored armor he's been given. I swear these Sentinel clothes are spelled to fit somehow, or these people are hella good at guessing sizes.

Knox looks back at my ass, and I stick it out a little so he can be extra sure. Marn and her people jacked my black armor, my sports bra and my underwear when I was changing into the dress they shoved into my hands and told me I *had* to wear.

"No crack is visible to me," he reports, and then he slaps my ass. "Your nipples however are going to be an issue," he adds, running the back of his hand against one of the hardened peaks.

I slap his hand away and look down. Yep, that's going to be a problem. Nipping out in front of my newly introduced grandparents has to be some kind of major faux pas. I cover my breasts with my hands and glare at Knox and Bastien as they both chortle.

I grumble as I move back toward the large mirror leaning in the corner and try to see if there's another way to wrap this dress so that I don't become an utter embarrassment to myself and my newfound family. The dress is a deep plum and has a very Grecian feel to the fabric and style. The material is very thin and very soft, but it shows a lot. It wouldn't have been my first pick for a night with the relatives, but Marn gave it to me, so I'm stuck.

I've officially lived in the house of the First for less than twenty-four hours. It's been nice getting to know Tok and Marn. I've heard all kinds of stories about things my mom got up to and her accomplishments. So far it's been really nice, all very surface level, but nice. Things are still stiff, but that's bound to be par for the course as we both figure each other out. I figure as we get more comfortable with each other, the more they'll tell me about what happened. I haven't wanted to push for too much information, but I'm dying to get into the deep shit of how Grier ended up where she did.

I haven't seen Tok and Marn much today. They announced at breakfast that they were throwing a party for me tonight, and since then, they've been fluttering around dealing with that. A little down time has been nice. I want to hear about Grier and her life, but I think it's hard on Tok and Marn too. They call me Grier a lot, and I can tell that they *really* miss her.

A tentative knock sounds on the door, and I look to make sure Bastien and Knox are both decent.

"Come in," I shout out as I attempt to flatten my annoying nipples. I don't think touching them is doing anything other than motivating me to figure out how I can get either Knox or Bastien alone in a bathroom somewhere, so I stop.

The door to the room we've been left in swings open, and in walks Marn and two other females. They all have full hands, and I watch as two of them set brushes and other things down at a table, and Marn makes her way over to me. Her eyes light up and fill with emotion.

"You look stunning, Vinna," she tells me, and her voice cracks as she says my name.

She quickly clears it and offers me a sweet smile. "This dress was your mothers," she informs me, and my eyes go wide with surprise.

Marn pulls on a long chain around her neck until a locket is revealed. She unclasps the jewelry from around her neck and hands it to me. "Open it," she encourages, so I do.

The round silver locket clicks open. Both sides separate from one another and reveal an image of a woman that really does look a lot like me. I study her face. Her skin was darker than mine, her hair lighter with a wavy texture mine gets when it dries naturally. Her eyes were the teal of her father's. Her lips, thinner than mine, are turned up into a breathtaking smile. When I saw Lachlan and was told he was my father's identical twin, I thought I clearly looked like my father. But as I stare at the picture of my mother, I realize I'm a good mix of both their coloring and features.

Breath whooshes out of me as I stare at her. I stumble back until the back of my legs hit something, and I sit down hard. Bastien barely gets the chair underneath me as I plop down, saving me from ass planting, but all I can do is stare at Grier in the palm of my hands.

My throat grows tight, and I can tell from the sniffling in the room that I'm not the only one affected by this moment. I'm quiet for a long time as I battle the grief that tries to leak out of me. I swipe at a stray tear that defies my order to *fuck off* and battle the others that are pricking to come out.

"I've never seen her before," I admit finally, and those words become an unknown key that unlocks so much pain.

I lose the war with my tears, and they stream down my face unhindered. Finally I have a face to replace Beth's in my mind when I think of the term *mother*. I haven't called Beth that ever, and yet when I think of the word, it was always her face that popped up unbidden. Beth's image mocked me and tainted that word for so long. I had no way to combat it. Now I do.

I caress my mom's face, and I can't help but wonder again what life would have been like if we could have just been together. Like Marn can read my thoughts, she sits down next to me and starts to speak.

"Grier was a good baby. Smart and kind and obstinate," she tells me with a sniffle and a warm smile. "When she got it in her mind to do something, it was as good as done.

Whether it be rearranging all the pots and pans in the kitchens as a child or going off in search of her Chosen when she was grown. Your Tok and I learned there was no talking her out of anything. If she had decided, all we could do was hope for the best."

I smile and hear Knox give a snort like he's commiserating with Marn. Marn laughs and wipes at her distant eyes, like she can see it all playing out in her mind like a movie. She always looks like this when she talks about her daughter, and I feel for her.

"Grier was our only, I know we've told you that, but she was more than enough. She was always training and pushing and searching for more. It didn't surprise us that she volunteered to go out in the world. We saw it as one last adventure where she could find her Chosen and then come back and lead our people into a new age. She was primed and ready to take on the role of Sovereign, but she never sparked for any of the Sentinels here, and she needed mates to help lead and carry on her line."

My gaze shoots to Marn in surprise. She just nods her head, sadly confirming my unvoiced question.

"She was the first girl our line had seen in almost seven-hundred years. Our people are always led by the females, and it was known that as soon as our House bore a girl, she would take back the throne from the House of the Second, who served as stewards while we waited for the rightful bond-laced heir to be born. When she didn't return, we were devastated, not only on a personal level, but the people she was meant to lead would remain lost without her."

Marn reaches over and strokes the image in the locket fondly. "But now she's left us you, and I don't need to consult a Bond Weaver to be certain that this is just as it's meant to be." I open my mouth to ask what that means, but Marn stands up and does that same loud clap thing that Tok did yesterday. I jump once again and almost drop the locket.

"That's enough of a stroll down memory lane for now. We'll have plenty of time to do that later. Tonight is about celebrating that you've come home to us and all is not lost." She gives me a huge smile and picks up something one of the ladies set on the table. "Now let's get you ready to meet your people properly."

She shuffles over to me and holds up what looks like an armored corset. "That is yours now, my dear," she tells me, gesturing to the locket.

"I can't take this from you," I argue and reach out in an effort to hand it back.

"Nonsense. I won't hear of it. I am your Marn, and you will mind me," she scolds me playfully, and I give her an awkward smile, not sure what the hell to say to that.

"Go on, you should have that," she insists again, and I give up and place the long chain around my neck.

The locket is hidden low in my cleavage, and the silver chain is somewhat hidden in the *V* of the neck of the dress. Marn manhandles me until I'm up out of the chair and once again facing the mirror. She's fucking strong for an old ass lady, I'll give her that. The thought has Getta's face popping up in my head, and I wonder if Sentinels get stronger and faster with age?

Marn and another lady reach around my waist and place the plum colored, braided leather corset around my torso. It cinches all the soft flowing fabric around my torso and chest. The deep purple leather adds a very kickass vibe to the otherwise flowy feminine dress, and I approve. As they tie the corset tighter, it sits just below my breasts, pushing them up. The fabric at my boobs gathers, helping to hide my nipple situation—*thank fuck*. One shoulder is covered by the gauzy plum colored fabric, and the other shoulder is completely bare showing off my runes.

I look like a Grecian goddess who couldn't decide if she was ready to party or battle. I like it. Well, maybe not the slit that runs up one side and into the bottom of the corset. One of the other women with Marn bats my hand away when she sees me trying to pull the slit sides of the fabric together.

"You need to show off those runes, not hide them," she scolds me.

I grumble my disagreement but stop fucking with the bottom of the dress. My hair is parted, a braid wrapped around my head like a headband, and the remaining strands swept up in a textured bun at the back of my neck. It all makes me look older and more sophisticated than I am. I'm sure the illusion will be ruined as soon as I drop my first *fuck* amidst Tierit's finest Sentinels. Or, as Tok and Marn keep referring to them, *my people.*

Another knock sounds at the door, and this time when it opens, my heart goes mental. Valen, Sabin, Torrez, Siah, and Ryker all are practically shoved into the room. I stand up from the chair I've been pinned in while they do my hair and bat at one of the ladies when they try to get me to sit back down.

Wolf whistles fill the air, and heat fills my Chosen's eyes. I smile and do a quick twirl, making sure the image of me in this dress gets seared into their brains. I point to the slit.

"Maybe this won't be as annoying as I thought," I announce as I picture any one of them sweeping the fabric aside for easy access.

"Dibs!" echo around the room, and Marn makes a choking cough sound at my implication.

I give her a quizzical look. Her and Tok keep doing that whenever I'm affectionate, and it's really something they need to get over. "I have seven Chosen; what did you think I did with them?" I ask her, and she turns red and titters awkwardly.

I study her, confused. She had a baby, for crying out loud, what's there to blush about?

"Well, your Chosen have their clothing there on the bed. Please get changed and make your way to the gathering room. Guests are arriving as we speak." With that, Marn nods at the other two ladies, and they rush out of the room.

"Nice to"—the door clicks shut—"see you again," Torrez states.

"Careful, they get jumpy when we try to talk to them," Knox teases, and Valen laughs.

"How was the tribunal?" I ask.

I've been worried all day since their summons came early this morning.

"Hostile," Siah reveals.

"They weren't happy that Bastien and Knox weren't there. We explained that we weren't going to leave you unprotected and they could call Bas and Knox another day, but that didn't go over so well," Ryker explains.

"They asked us what your Shields were even for. We just said *extra* protection, but I don't know if they're buying it," Valen adds.

I take a deep breath and go to run my fingers through my hair. I remember just in time that it's up and fancy and drop my arms to my sides instead.

"I'll talk to Tok and Marn tomorrow. I'll tell them about Sorik and explain Vaughn and his situation. We'll just have to hope they stay quiet about it. We can get him and Sorik moved over here, then the Shields won't have to guard them at the castle separately, and no one will be the wiser," I lay out and hope it all goes so easily.

The guys and I came up with this game plan last night. With Tok and Marn seeming to struggle with the existence of my Chosen, we thought it best to let the dust settle a little bit before dropping the bomb that Grier's Chosen were here too.

"Well, boys, strip down," I instruct excitedly. "Marn will probably be back soon to see what's taking so long. And a certain Sentinel I know let the cat out of the bag about shimmies and hair flips. Let's see what you got!" I tell them, rubbing my hands together.

They look at me like I've lost it, utter confusion written all over their faces. Well, all except Valen, who cracks up laughing.

"You two have some weird inside jokes," Siah observes, and then I crack up too.

I watch with greedy eyes and vagina, as my Chosen get dressed. Yep, they have to be magicked clothes, because each set of dark purple armor fits them like a glove. I'm tempted to say *fuck this party* and tackle each of them like a hungry velociraptor. The door swings open just as that thought enters my head, and Marn comes sweeping in, her lavender gown flowing around her legs.

Sabin gives a girly squeal. He's still shirtless and covers his nipples with his hands playfully. Marn goes beet red when she realizes not everyone is dressed and backtracks out of the room like someone hit her rewind button. The exchange is so weird that as soon as the door snicks shut, we all lose it. I keep picturing Sabin's wide-eyed surprise and squeak as he covers his chest, and the giggles run away with me.

"That'll teach her to knock," Bastien cackles, laugh tears dripping down his face, and it sets the whole room off again.

I think we laugh for about ten minutes straight before we pour out of the room, drunk on laughter. Marn stands demurely waiting for us at the top of the stairs, Tok at her side. I have to fight to keep the sight of her from sending me back down the slap happy rabbit hole. She reaches out for my hand, and I hesitate slightly before giving it to her.

"Are you ready to take your place amongst your people?" she asks me, an eager glint in her lilac gaze.

I take a deep breath and square my shoulders. I look back at my gorgeous Chosen, grateful for their presence and their ability to make me laugh and live in the moment. My gaze lands back on my grandmother's, and I give her a smile.

"Let's do it."

23

"It was nice to meet you," I call over my shoulder as Tok and Marn usher me away from the Sentinel they just introduced me to five minutes ago and point me in the direction of someone else they want me to meet.

"Vinna, this is Aern. Aern, this is Vinna of the First," Marn recites politely, and then she does what she's been doing all night, she watches us expectantly as we say our hellos and dive into the small talk.

I feel like I've spent the last two hours in a speed dating round of meet-and-greets. I'm introduced to someone, watched like I'm going to do something crazy, and then pulled away from them before I can even discover anything interesting about them. I'm trying to go with the flow for the sake of my newly discovered grandparents, but it's starting to wear on me.

"Aern owns some of the finest stables in Tierit," Tok tells me, and my face lights up. Finally, a topic I know a little about.

"Oh really? That's cool. Sabin has a couple of horses. He

just started to teach me how to ride. Horses are incredible," I remark politely.

"Who is Sabin?" Marn asks, and my eyes widen in surprise.

"One of my Chosen," I remind her.

"Ah yes. Well, Aern breeds the finest riding animals I would venture to say in this world," Marn shifts, patting Aern's arm affectionately.

The Sentinel says something I don't hear to Tok, and they're quickly wrapped up in a conversation I have no context for and could never hope to follow. I stand there and start to count down until it's time to be introduced to someone else. I scan the crowd for my Chosen, knowing they're close by. I spot them together, talking and scoping things out, their eyes wandering to me every minute or so.

I feel bad, they've got to be bored out of their mind. Tok and Marn seem to be playing interception with them tonight, and if the conversations I was being pulled into weren't mind numbingly boring, it might bug me. At least they're being saved from the mind-numbing political talk I don't understand, riveting conversations around crop yields, or being ignored all together.

Right on time, I'm pulled away from Aern and introduced to Para. The female and I exchange pleasantries and then slip into awkward silence when I run out of shit to talk about with her.

"So, uh, are these parties normally like this?" I ask her, struggling to find any better small talk topics.

"Yes and no," she responds and steps closer to me. "Sentinels of this rank only come out for the best of the best, and it's exciting when we all get together like this."

I try not to cringe at the word *exciting*. If this kind of shit is what licks her pickle, who am I to judge? A hand traces up the outside of my arm, and I step back to find Para tracing my runes.

"Your markings are quite extraordinary," she tells me, and I work to keep a scowl off my face.

Maybe it's not rude to touch other Sentinels' runes here?

"So what do you do here?" I ask, dodging her comment.

"I'm a hunter."

This piques my interest, and I smile. "What do you hunt?"

"Anything that's in season. It's all prey to me," she purrs.

Marn pops back up, and I've never been so relieved to see her. I'm obviously missing something here with this Para chick, and I'm ready to move on. Marn politely excuses me, but as we pull away, Para catches my hand. She tries to pull me toward her, a determined look in her eyes. I tense, ready for some kind of attack. She leans in toward me, and I lean back.

"Um...what the hell are you doing?" I question.

"I, I was just going to kiss you," she tells me, her voice raspy and her eyes filled with heat. I step back, confused.

"Why?" I ask awkwardly.

"To see if the sparks fly," she replies, like that should somehow be obvious to me.

"I have Chosen," I tell her, and I look across the ball-room, like I'm sending an SOS and need them to come rescue me from chicks who fuck up their signals.

Para follows my gaze and gives an incredulous snort. "You're Vinna of the *First* now," she tells me, stepping closer. "You have the world in your hands with a title like that, and all I know is I'd love to have my hands all over you."

Para tries to push up against me. I step back, removing my hand from her grip. My forearm grazes her breasts as I pull away, and she gives an exaggerated moan that has me seriously judging her acting skills.

"Like I said, I have Chosen. I'm not interested."

I move away, and Para reaches out for me again.

I turn back to her. "Touch me again, and you won't like what happens to you," I warn her.

She throws her hands up in surrender but blows me a kiss before she walks away.

Fucking hell.

I'm silently reeling over what just happened. When I look up to see who Marn and Tok are parading me in front of now, I'm taken aback to find Ory.

"Oh," I chirp with recognition.

"Oh, yourself," he parrots back.

"What are you doing here?" I ask as Tok and Marn dart away.

"I was invited," he snarks.

I roll my eyes and scan the room for my Chosen again.

"So how's your first First party going?" Ory asks me casually.

"Fucking sucks," I confess and then slam my lips closed. "Shit, don't tell Tok and Marn I said that. I don't want to hurt their feelings."

Ory scrutinizes me with his bright purple gaze for a moment. He dips his chin and then starts to scan the room like he's looking for someone cooler to talk to.

"So you light up for anyone yet?" Ory asks me, and my brow dips in confusion.

"Um no, am I supposed to be?"

He gets a mischievous grin on his face and shakes his head at me.

Fuck. How long have I been standing here? How much more time do I have to put up with this dude?

"They'll give you more time with me," Ory tells me cryptically.

"Who will?"

"Your Marn and Tok. They will give you more time with me because our match would be the most beneficial to them."

Whatever I was about to say falls silently out of my open mouth. I just stare at him, replaying his words in my head.

"I have Chosen," I answer simply, trying and failing to not feel bewildered.

Ory shrugs again. "I didn't say I was interested, I just explained why they would give you more time with me."

Irritation simmers in me, but for the first time since I met Ory, it's not for him. I release a deep sigh and shake my head. All the Grier talk focused around her place and that she was the next in line. Their dismissal of my Chosen. Fuck, they get my name wrong a quarter of the time. They want me to pick up where Grier left off. I sigh.

"So are they thinking they can convince me to ditch my Chosen and choose new ones? That's a thing here, isn't it? Or are they hoping that I'll just add a few advantageous matches for the fun of it?" I ask him flatly.

"From the looks of things, they're just waiting to see if you'll spark up for someone," he tells me, and suddenly their eager looks and hawk-like observation make sense.

"I'm so dumb," I confess. "It was all there, right in front of my face, and I just didn't see it."

I growl internally at myself.

"They're ambitious; there are worse things out there," Ory observes dismissively.

I shake my head and try to push down my frustration and anger. "They're my *Chosen*," I snap at him. "I love them. Tok and Marn can't just dismiss that or them like it's nothing. Not when they're *everything* to me."

"They're doing what they think is best," Ory tells me, and I bristle.

When are people who don't know me going to stop thinking they know what's best for me?

"Despite what they think, I'm not Grier," I tell him. "Maybe she wanted this life, but I don't."

"It's in your blood; you may not have much choice in the matter."

"There's always a choice," I counter. "Besides, you wanted to kill me a week ago, but now you're going to wax poetic about my destiny and place here? That makes zero fucking sense."

"I was *ordered* to kill you; there was nothing personal about it," he corrects, still scanning the crowd over my head.

"Riiight," I drawl. "Well, I wish I could say this was fun, but it wasn't. I'd say have a good night, but I really don't hope you will. Nothing personal," I quip with an amused smile and step away from him.

Ory chuckles as I turn around and walk away from him in search of my Chosen. I'm officially done with this night. I maneuver my way through the crowded ballroom, ignoring invitations to stop and talk with people I've already met throughout the night. I approach my guys and give them a huge smile.

"Let's get the fuck out of here," I tell them.

"Finally," Bastien states with a relieved sigh.

Knox's "it's about time" makes me chuckle.

And Torrez's "thank fuck" has me raising a hand as if to say preach.

"You okay?" Ryker asks me.

We move as a group away from the party, and I intertwine my fingers with his. "I don't know," I admit. "I'm irritated. I'm tired. And I'm not sure what to do about all of this," I tell him, gesturing to the ballroom full of Sentinels at our back.

"It's been a long day. Let's leave it for tomorrow to sort

out," he says. I nod and give him a quick peck as we head in the direction of the stairs.

"Vinna," Marn shouts behind me, her footsteps quickly approaching us from behind, and Tok and Marn cut us off. They're both flustered and sputtering.

"Where are you going?" Marn finally manages to string together.

"To our rooms," I state simply and move to go around them.

Tok steps in my way. "Ory is the Commander of Arms and a member of the First House. It's rude to just walk away from him," he scolds me.

I cringe. *Does that make us related somehow?* I shake off the thought and focus on Tok and Marn. I don't think they're bad people, but I'm also not cool with what's going down.

"I suppose it's rude, but honestly, I don't care and neither does Ory. Setting me up to potentially *light up* for other people I don't know is considered rude in some circles of the world too," I point out, making it clear I'm onto them.

Tok stutters for something to say. "Gri—Vinna, we—"

"Save it," I declare, cutting him off. "I'm sure you are used to doing things a certain way, and I have a lot to learn about you and this place, but I have Chosen, and I have a mind of my own. I'm not going to just pick up where you left off with Grier's life," I tell them, my voice kind but firm.

"How can you say that?" Marn demands, stepping toward me. "You were born for this. To be here. To lead them!"

"No, I wasn't," I tell her simply.

"You're just going to walk away from your birthright? Let your people continue to be led by corruption and fear?"

"This wasn't my birthright, it was Grier's. You need to see that. I know you miss her, and this feels like a second chance to recover all that you've lost, but it's not. I'm Vinna. This is your first chance with *me*."

Tok and Marn pause, their eyes filling with grief. My own eyes well up in response, my soul called to hurt simply because they are. I take a breath and rub at my chest. I look up the stairs in the direction of the wing we're supposed to be staying in, and I feel lost. It doesn't feel like home, like where I'm supposed to be.

"I can't stay here," I admit quietly.

I've been trying so hard to go with the flow and be what they needed, but this isn't going to work unless I can be who I am and they can accept me for that.

"But we're your family, this is where you should be," Marn argues, swiping tears from her cheeks.

"We don't even know each other," I point out.

"That will take time though, Vinna," Tok tells me.

"You're right, but it will also take effort too," I tell them. I gesture to my Chosen. "Can you tell me their names?"

Tok stares at me, confused for a second, and then looks around me to where my guys all stand. They all give a friendly wave, which makes me smile. The smile fades as I watch Tok struggle to answer me.

"So here's the thing. It's been a couple of crazy days, and I think we need to start over. I'll get to know you, and you'll get to know me. We can just take it one day at a time and see where it leads us," I tell them with a sympathetic smile, and then I let it fade from my face so I can hammer my next point home.

"With that said, I'm going to say this next part once, and if you want to have *any* kind of relationship with me, you will etch every word into your soul," I state, locking eyes with Marn and Tok in turn.

"These are *my* Chosen. I am theirs and they are mine. Nothing will push me further away than disrespecting or disregarding the people that I love, and I love these males more than *anything* in existence. If you ever try to set me up in any kind of way that disrespects my bond with these males, you and I will be through. That's a deal breaker for me. Do you understand?"

The room grows quiet for a minute, and I wait to see if they get it, because if they don't, there's no hope from here on out that we'll ever be anything to each other.

"We're sorry," Marn offers me after a couple beats, and she sounds so broken that it kills me. I pull away from Ryker and step to give her a hug.

"I know this is hard. How are any of us supposed to know how to navigate this shit?" I tell her, and she gives me a watery laugh. I look at Tok over Marn's head. "We'll fuck it up, and that's fine. As long as it's not a deal breaker, we'll figure out how to make it better. It's going to take all of us being honest and really trying."

"Wise words," Tok tells me warmly, and he swipes at a tear that sneaks down his face.

"I'll check in with you guys tomorrow, and then we can start operation *figure all this shit out together*."

Marn nods and gives me another squeeze before she pulls away. I open my arms to Tok, and he wraps me up in an epic bear hug that could rival one of Aydin's.

"We'll see you tomorrow, Vinna," Tok assures me, and I give him a big smile.

"Tomorrow," I agree, and then my Chosen and I leave.

We step out into a cool starlit night, and I feel both relieved and sad at the same time.

"I'm sorry, Squeaks," Ryker offers, and as soon as we're out of the gates, I take a moment to find the home I always feel in his arms.

"I kept telling myself that they were nice and to just appreciate that they didn't hate me on sight. I mean, things could have been worse. But what the fuck were they thinking?" I ask no one in particular.

"I think they just had high hopes for your mom," Valen offers.

"They've been grieving her and the loss of what they wanted her to become this whole time," Bastien adds.

"Then you show up, and they go into overdrive trying to push it all in your lap," Knox finishes.

"They didn't even talk to you guys," I lament.

"I think they will, though," Siah offers. "Their hearts seem like they're in the right place, and after what you just said in there, I think you guys will be able to figure it out."

I tilt my head up and pucker my lips. Siah grins and leans down to give me a soft sweet kiss.

"Then they'll learn that you all are the best fucking males in this whole place and that I'd be fucked in all the worst ways without you!"

I shout that to the empty fairy light lit streets, and it bounces back to me on a fading echo. My words reverberate around me, and I suddenly feel like they just slapped me across the face.

"Holy shit, that's it!" I realize. I turn to the guys. "You've been telling me over and over again that we're a family, a unit, stronger and better together, but I just wasn't getting it. That's it!" I shout again, and then I take off running down the street.

Shouts of confusion and my name sound off behind me, but I know they'll catch up. Excitement surges through me, and I feel like an idiot. I've been trying to do this all on my own, but I'm not on my own anymore. I'm an idiot for not seeing it sooner, but now that I have, I don't want to waste another second.

I barrel down the streets, careening through the empty market place that was bustling the last time we came through here. Torrez sprints up next to me, followed by Siah and then Bastien.

"Come on, slow pokes," I shout over my shoulder, and I hear Sabin grumble, "I'll show you slow poke."

I laugh, which probably makes me look as unhinged as fuck, but I don't care. I call on my runes and move faster.

"Care to tell us why we're running down the streets in the middle of the night?" Siah asks me casually.

"Because I figured it out," I offer vaguely, pressing to move even faster.

Getta's gate comes into view in the distance, swaying like it's a finish line banner. I hurtle over it, almost clipping my foot and dress on an iron rod and face planting. I pound on Getta's door, my knock urgent and demanding.

"She's probably sleeping," Sabin tells me when no one answers after a couple minutes, and I bang on the door again.

"Then she'll wake up," I tell him, and he shakes his head.

"Did I not just tell you Sentinels have a superiority complex?" Torrez teases, and I elbow him as I raise my hand to knock again.

The door swings open, and Issak peers down at all of us irritably.

"I need to speak with Getta," I tell him, and he studies me for a long drawn out moment before nodding once and then slamming the door in my face.

I squeal in excitement at what I know is going to go down next, and I move away from the door and head in the direction of the backyard. I call on my staff and wait patiently like the good grasshopper I am. After a handful of minutes, Issak exits out of a back door, cradling a feeble looking Getta.

"Ah, so the girl is back for more, I see," she announces, and I don't miss the excitement in her tone.

I've spent my whole life proving to people that they should never underestimate me, and then what did I go and do? I underestimated Getta the first chance I had to get some answers. Well, not this time.

Issak sets Getta down gently on the packed dirt, and she stretches out her back and lifts her head to the sky.

"It's a mighty fine night for an ass kicking, don't you agree, Issak?"

Issak smiles and moves to lean casually against the back of the house. I laugh and shake my head at Getta. Too bad I'm not related to her. She feels more like my people than anyone I've met on this side of the barrier.

"Well, girl, I don't know why you'd get all fancied up for another lesson in losing, but whatever blows your skirt up, I suppose." She eyes my clothing. "Judging by the look of that thing, it wouldn't take much to blow it clean off. Issak, close your eyes," she instructs.

I look over at Issak, and he just rolls his eyes.

I ignore her efforts to get me all riled, and wait patiently for what I know is coming. She smiles at me when I don't take her bait, and I can almost feel pride rippling off of her. She nods at me and then calls on her staff. She studies it for a beat and then presses one end into the dirt and leans on it.

"Tell me, girl, are you worthy?" she finally asks me, and anticipation strikes through me, sending my heart racing.

"Alone, maybe not, but together," I tell her, gesturing with my staff to my Chosen, "*we* are."

Getta stares at me intensely for what seems like forever. I feel like she dives into my soul, swims around for a bit, and then climbs back out to dry off. She twirls her staff in her hands expertly, and I tense, waiting for the attack that I know is coming.

She reaches out, slow as cold honey, and then flicks the end of my nose. I reel back.

"So you do have a brain in that pretty little head of yours," she cackles. "Glad to see you're using it now. Very well then, follow me," she instructs.

With that, her staff disappears and she starts to hobble away.

I stare at her, open mouthed and dumbfounded.

Wait. What the fuck just happened?

24

I look back at the guys, completely bewildered, as Issak swoops in and picks up Getta.

"Wait. Are we not fighting?" I ask, and there's a tinge of disappointment in my voice that has me questioning my own sanity.

Getta's backing down, Vinna, this is a good thing. Shut the fuck up!

She cackles from the safety of Issak's arms and motions for me to follow her. "The fighting was just for fun. If you've decided you're worthy, who am I to say otherwise?"

I stop mid step with those words, and Ryker slams into my back, creating a domino effect of crashing Chosen. "Hold up," I call out to Getta, and Issak turns around to face me. "If *I've* decided I'm worthy? Is the fight not a test?"

"Oh, no, that's just to get these old bones a moving."

"But...but you said I wasn't worthy," I ask confused.

"No, girl, *you* said you weren't worthy. Like I said, who am I to argue?"

Issak once again turns around and angles his large frame into the back door of the house. I turn to look at the guys, incredulous squeaks coming out of my open mouth.

"Is she seriously fucking telling me that if I had just said *yes, I'm worthy* in answer to her question last time that we'd already have answers?"

"Sounds like it," Torrez confirms.

I groan and rub at my face.

"Seems like that existential crisis you've been wrestling with was all for nothing," he adds.

"All that brooding for nothing?" I squeak out.

"Don't forget the pouting too," Bastien adds, and I slap his pec and try not to smile.

I don't know if I want to scream or crack up right now.

"You kids coming?" Getta hollers out from the open back door, and I glare at her house.

Well played, you wrinkled old ninja. Well fucking played.

Knox slaps me on the ass as he passes, and like an obedient steed, it gets me moving. I rub my cheek and follow him into Getta's house, the lights dim and the furnishings quaint. There's a very warm and homey feel to the inside of her cottage that makes me want to sink into a big chair and just chill. There are books everywhere and the kind of clutter it seems all elderly people tend to have. Issak sets Getta into a rocking chair that has intricate carvings of deer and other creatures all over it, and she's wiggling around to get comfortable.

He sits at her feet, and even sitting, he's still taller than she is. I stare at his gargantuan size before Getta motions for all of us to sit down, and it pulls me from my gawking. There's a fire going, and it gives off a comforting glow as shadows dance on the cottage walls. I sit next to Getta on a small stool, and the guys all find perches here and there too.

"So, girl, tell me what it is you want to know, or do you expect me to read your mind as well as your heart?"

I shake my head again at the realization that Getta got me, and I sort through the lists of questions I've been

235

making note of in my mind since I was young. I start at the top.

"What are Sentinels, and where do we come from?" I ask, my voice strong and clear, and the room goes quiet with anticipation.

"Well, fuck, you don't have anything smaller we can start with?" she asks. "No foreplay questions?"

Knox busts out laughing and promptly tries to cover it up when Getta gives him a glare.

"Issak, be a good lad and make some tea for everyone. I have a feeling it's going to be a long night if that's where we're starting," she giggles.

Issak says nothing as he rises and ducks through a doorway that leads out of the room. I hear the clanging of dishes and water filling something.

Getta clears her throat and begins to rock her chair rhythmically back and forth. "We come from a different place whose name most no longer remember. We were one branch of many magical branches, but we got it in our heads that we should always be at the top the tree. With promises and power, we enslaved others, and we lived that way for a very long time."

Getta stares at the fire as she talks, and I find myself hypnotized by the light flickering over her worn face as she starts to weave it all together.

"With time, the people we squashed under our boot— for no one's sake aside from our own—rose up and demanded *no more*. It started with battles and quickly turned into wars. We were arrogant and powerful, but our numbers have always grown slowly. That, however, was not the case for the ones who we fought against. In less than a century, we went from hunter to hunted, and our people were desperate."

I lean forward, my heart hammering in my chest. I have

to keep from pinching myself just to make sure this is actually happening. I've waited so long for answers, and here they are, spilling so freely from Getta's thin aged lips.

"We awoke the gates of old, the ones that first brought beings to our land, and fled everything we ever knew to start over. But did we learn our lesson? Did we change our ways?"

Getta scoffs and shakes her head.

"I'm going to go with *no* on that one," Valen states, and laughter flutters around the room.

"You would be right, boy. Because when we arrived here, we once again wanted to be the top of the tree. It wasn't enough that we could be the root or the trunk. The Ouphe of old didn't see that as a position of strength. They just saw the surrounding branches and wanted to top them all. And so history repeated itself until we were once again forced to flee. By then, the gates were closed to us. There weren't enough with the Bonds to open them, so we hid, and thus Tierit was created."

"What is the Ow-f?" I ask, trying to repeat a word she used to describe the older generation.

"The Ouphe is what we once were and must fight to never become again. We have abandoned those ways of thinking and the magic that made it all possible. Only a handful of Bond Weavers still exist. They keep to themselves and only use their light rarely as it now sparks fear in most."

Issak stalks into the room and hands Getta a cup and saucer. She takes it with a grateful smile, and then he turns and presses another cup and saucer into my hands.

"Oh, thank you," I tell him, to which he grunts and disappears back into what I assume is the kitchen.

He returns several more times until everyone has tea, and then he once again takes his place at Getta's feet. I sip my tea and have to fight every instinct in my body not to spit it back out. I swallow and try not to gag. I give the cup and then Issak a dirty look for trying to poison me.

"What exactly is this tea?" I ask, trying to sound polite and failing.

Getta laughs. "Best to shoot it straight back if you're not used to it. It's good for the circulation."

I stare at my cup and cringe. *Eh, what the hell.* Bottoms up.

I toss back the tea that tastes like moldy farts and hold my breath. As I swallow it, I secretly try to wipe my tongue with the skirt of my dress before giving up on the discreet part of that plan and just going for it. I see out of the corner of my eye some of the guys gagging and cringing, and I chuckle knowing my taste buds are not alone in their suffering.

"Interesting," I croak out as Getta looks at me with raised eyebrows like she's asking me what I think.

She sips her tea with not even a trace of a grimace, and I have to stop myself from rolling my eyes. Like she really needs to prove she's more of a badass than me. We all already know it.

"You have traces of the old magic in your veins, girl," she tells me, jerking her chin toward my lap where my hands are folded.

I look down to see what she's gesturing at and see the new rune on my palm that none of us have tested out yet. "Do you mean this?" I ask, holding the rune up.

"I do."

"What does it mean...and do?"

"It's very rare. It means you not only claim your Chosen with your marks, but with your magic as well."

My brow furrows with confusion. "I thought all Sentinels used magic to mark their Chosen?"

"That they do," Getta agrees. "But they can only share

238

their marks. You can share your marks and your magic. *That* is what is rare. Your mama could do it too."

"Hold up, are you saying that all of us now have the same branches of magic that Vinna does?" Sabin asks, the surprise in his tone reflecting the look on the rest of our faces.

"Yes," Getta replies simply as she takes another sip of her fuck nasty tea. "It also means that you can pull and give power at will to each other. Each member of your Chosen will be able to share their abilities when this rune is activated."

"So they could become wolves?" Torrez asks excitedly.

"Yes," Getta once again answers simply.

"Holy shit!" I exclaim, and we all look at each other even more wide-eyed.

"Now, before you go start playing around with this and get yourselves killed, this kind of magic is rare for a reason. Like with all things, it can be used for good and for bad. In the past, the bad has prevailed, which is why Bond users are hunted by many kinds. You need to keep these abilities quiet and watch yourselves. Not many know what the runes of that branch look like anymore, but they do know what the light does, and they will snuff it out if they find it."

Getta's ominous words settle in the room, and we all grow quiet and contemplative.

"What about my Shields?"

Getta looks down at my unmarked middle finger. "What about them?"

"I have marked four Shields—"

"But not sealed them, I see," she observes, and I nod.

"The thing is, they were marked by another Sentinel when we got here."

"As Shields?" Getta asks, surprised.

"No, as Chosen," I explain.

"Ahhh, I see," she tells me. "The people of this world can only be marked by one Sentinel. Whether that be as a Shield or as a Chosen. If you complete what you started and make them true Shields, then the Chosen claim will sever."

Relief washes through me, and I let out a long exhale. We can all get out of here. I just need to do whatever it is that needs to be done to complete my marking of Enoch, Nash, Kallan, and Becket.

"Now, girl, I can see that you are a purveyor of excellent male specimens."

Torrez, Bastien, and Knox all snort out laughs. I roll my eyes at them.

"If Issak here wasn't already spoken for, he would be a good fit for you and your Chosen."

This time *I* give a surprised snort, and Issak gives me a look.

"No offense, she just took me by surprise. I'm sure you'd be an excellent mate," I tell him. He blinks once and then turns away.

"My point is, girl, that you have an excellent and deliciously varied selection of Chosen. Why exactly do you need Shields?"

Getta's question takes me aback. "But I marked them; clearly, my magic felt that I needed them," I defend.

"Oh I agree that they are needed, but is it truly by you, or is it by the other Sentinel that marked them?" She poses the question, and I pause to really think about it.

I notice out of the corner of my eye that Bastien is fidgeting in his chair. I ignore it and think through my connection with Enoch, Nash, Kallan, and Becket. I look at them like brothers and good friends. They've never felt like Chosen to me, and yet I've always felt compelled to bring them along with me from the moment their marks showed up.

Valen and Sabin seem to get wiggly in their seats too, and I wonder if they have to pee.

"If they could have more than what they would have being my Shields, then I would want that for them," I admit, and Getta nods. "But will they have that with this Sentinel? She seems like she hates them," I add, hoping Getta can offer some kind of reassurance or guidance.

Ryker proceeds to start crossing and uncrossing his legs, and I look over at him.

Did these dudes get ants in their pants or something?

"That is an excellent question," Getta declares, and I focus back on her. "An excellent question that's really none of your fucking business," she finishes, and I chuckle and shake my head at her.

Torrez and Siah move like they're uncomfortable, and I look over at them, puzzled. *Fuck, the wiggles got them too?*

Getta starts to say something else, but I don't pay attention to it as I'm too busy watching all of my Chosen fidget and move like they're going to pee their pants at any moment. They look uncomfortable as fuck, and I can't figure out what's going on.

"It's the tea," Sabin's voice shouts in my mind.

"What?" I ask, even more confused.

"There must have been something in the tea, because we're all sporting major wood right now!" he declares.

I look down at his crotch and then Bastien's. I bust out laughing.

Getta gives me a knowing look, and I crack up even harder. "You brew your tea with Viagra?" I ask her, and she giggles.

"I don't know what that is, but I did tell you it was good for the circulation, didn't I?" Getta cackles, and all the guys look even more uncomfortable.

"Go, girl, have your way with them, and then come back and tell me all about it."

My head jerks to Getta, shocked. Did this crazy old lady just say that? She nods like she's confirming my unspoken thought, and I don't know if she is *goals* or if she should be avoided at all cost.

"I guess that's our cue to go," I announce to my Chosen. They all slowly get up, shielding themselves with throw pillows and hands and quickly turn their backs on the very dirty old lady.

She watches them, pure amusement seeping out of every pore. "That view isn't so bad either," she declares, her eyes fixed on Ryker's ass. I don't know if I should cover her eyes, high-five her, or hurry my guys out the door. I decide on stepping in front of her to block her view and mouthing *run* to the guys. I wait until they're all out of sight, and turn around to find Getta laughing her ass off.

"Is that tea going to fuck me up too?" I ask, resisting the urge to drop my hands in solidarity with the guys and cover up my nonexistent boner.

"Well, you won't grow a penis, if that's what you're asking," she teases.

I snort out a laugh and shake my head.

"Your clit will thank me later," Getta adds, and I'm simultaneously mortified and intrigued by her vague statement.

"This Q and A isn't over just because you drugged my Chosen," I tell her with a finger wag.

"Next time, you'll have to fight me for it," she challenges, and I laugh.

"Fine by me. I'm a mimic, so everything you did last time is now in my repertoire," I tell her.

"Doesn't mean I'm not going to hand you your ass again," she retorts.

"Maybe, but eventually you'll run out of tricks, and it'll be your ass in the trough."

"Careful, girl, don't make me neuter those big lady balls you have."

I crack up, not able to help myself.

Goals. Getta is goals. It's official.

I turn to leave, but I'm stopped by a strong grip on my arm. I turn expecting to see Issak's hand, but instead find Getta's. "My Issak's mate will find herself at a crossroads. Both options will suffocate her slowly. I need you to show her the path here," she tells me.

I study Getta for a beat. All traces of humor have left her lined face and her light gray eyes. I can feel in my bones that whatever she's telling me right now is *very* important.

"Okay, but how will I knew who she is?"

"Oh, you already know her." And with that, Getta's head lolls, and a tiny snore comes out of her open mouth. Issak rises from the floor and picks Getta up out of her chair. I brush hair off her forehead and once again marvel at how deceivingly fragile she looks.

"I'll send her your way, Bond Weaver," I whisper to her, and Issak lifts an eyebrow in question at me.

"Yeah, I figured out who she is. It was the way she touched my rune the first time I met her..." I explain, skimming a finger over the rune on my palm that showed up when I marked Siah. "And what she told us today made it all click. She's one of the last, isn't she?" I ask him, and he stares at me for a moment before giving me a small nod.

"Don't worry, her secret is safe with me," I tell him softly, and then I turn and follow my Chosen out the back door.

25

Heavy breathing and light snores serenade me as I unwrap Siah's arm from around my waist and push off Torrez's hand from my chest. I pause when Torrez grumbles something about *cock chi* and rolls over. I shake with restrained laughter when he buries his hand in Valen's hair and purrs that it's *soft* before smacking his lips a couple of times and falling back into a deep sleep. Looking around at the night soaked room of our castle suite, I try not to feel weird about the fact that we're here again instead of at Tok and Marn's house. Slipping out of my place on the mattresses that have been pushed together on the floor of the large room, I tiptoe to the bathroom to shower.

I pull the levers on the wall that get the water flowing. Steam wafts from the downpour after a couple minutes and I check the temperature of the water with my hand. I adjust the levers to make it even hotter and step under the steady stream. Heat envelops me. As I stand under the sweltering torrent, I hope it will sap the restless energy slithering through my veins, but it has the opposite effect. I'm now even more awake.

I dry off, get dressed, and shake my limbs out. Even

though I'm tired, my body and mind won't shut down long enough for me to get any amount of rest. I've been up all night, listening to the deep breathing of my Chosen as they sleep. Images and voices swirled around in my head as I relived everything that happened today. I rub at my chest and the unease I feel there. I'm anxious, and I can't figure out exactly why.

It could be this situation in general, or maybe something happened back home. I fucking wish my phone had service so I could call and check in with everyone. I'm itching to hear the sisters' voices and to hear from Aydin and Evrin what's going on there without us. I need to hear Mave's laugh and check in on Cyndol and see if she's ready for a new circuit.

The door to our room creaks as I open it, and I pause and quietly wait to see if it woke anyone up. No one stirs, so I squeeze out and shut it behind me with a soft snick. I move silently to Sorik and my dad's room. I open the thankfully silent door and peek in. Vaughn is asleep in the bed, or I assume he sleeps. We tell him to close his eyes and sleep, but I don't know if he actually does. Sorik is passed out in a chair, a book in his lap. I smile at the sight and back out of the room.

I move to the room my Shields claimed and slowly twist the knob and push it open. It gives a tiny squeal of protest, but the knife now being pointed at my throat is what makes me stop in my tracks. Nash realizes that it's me and breathes out a sigh. The short sword disappears, and he takes a step back.

"Why are you sneaking around at three in the morning?" he demands on a whisper.

He pushes the door open wider to let me in, and I see Enoch, Kallan, and Becket in chairs that are positioned in front of the large fireplace in their room.

"I was checking on you guys," I whisper yell back as I step into the room.

"How do you know what time it is, anyway? I can't find a clock to save my life."

"The fairy light flickers the number of the hour when you look at it," he tells me casually and shuts the door behind me.

"Really?" I ask.

I turn to the wall sconce just by the door. Sure enough, it flickers three times. Well, shit, that would have been nice to know before now. I move toward them and perch on the arm of the chair Kallan is sitting in.

"How the hell do you know that about the lights? And what are you guys doing up?"

"Sauriel told us about it when he stopped by yesterday evening," Kallan answers.

My brow furrows. "What did he want?"

"To talk to us about Suryn, and he sort of just wanted to get to know us, I guess," Enoch tells me with a shrug.

"Oh," I respond, a little surprised.

I look around at all of them, scanning the situation again. Becket is tense and so is Kallan. Enoch is leaning forward in his chair like he was listening to something with rapt attention or maybe communicating something passionately. Nash looks relaxed, but he always looks that way.

"What's going on here?" I ask again, my tone this time more suspicious.

"We were just talking," Enoch tells me as he leans back in his chair, defeat radiating in the sudden slump of his shoulders.

"Oookay," I respond, unsure.

"Why don't you fill her in, Enoch? I mean, ultimately this does affect her too. Shouldn't Vinna get a say in all of this?" Kallan asks Enoch, and the anger in his tone takes me by surprise.

I study Kallan for a minute and then look expectantly at Enoch.

What the hell is going on?

Enoch runs a tired hand over his face. "Sauriel thinks the tribunal will vote against the Sovereign's order to have us all killed." He pauses and then doesn't say anymore.

"And that's a bad thing?" I ask, perplexed as to why there'd be an issue with that.

"No, of course not. But once that happens, we have a decision to make," Enoch goes on, and a light bulb goes off in my head.

"Ah, okay, I get it."

We all go quiet, and uncertainty and tension settle at the nape of my neck. I open my mouth to say something and then close it, Getta's words from earlier resonating in my mind. I stare at the flickering fire for a minute and swallow down my feelings about the situation. Kallan's right in the sense that this does affect me, but he's wrong when he says I have any say in the matter.

"Have you guys pro-conned it?" I ask quietly.

Becket snorts and leans his elbows on his knees. He cradles his head in his hands and chortles. "That's pretty much what we're doing now," he informs me, and I give him an understanding nod.

"Should I go?" I ask them awkwardly, getting the impression that I might not be welcome in this conversation. I feel like I'm intruding, and this is now uncomfortable as fuck. Part of me wants to know just what pros Suryn could possibly have in their eyes, but the logical side of me is screaming that it's none of my business. I push off from my armchair perch and stand up.

Enoch jumps up out of his chair at the same time. "No.

Kallan is right. We should be talking to you about this too. Don't leave," he implores, and I'm stuck between listening to him and bolting for the door anyway.

We stare at each other for a moment, and then I slowly sink back down onto the arm of Kallan's chair. Oddly, Enoch doesn't look relieved. He does, however, look seriously fucking nervous as he also sinks back down onto the cushions of his chair. Nobody speaks for a bit, and I'm left looking around at all of them, not sure where it's safe for my gaze to land.

"Why does this feel so fucking weird?" I ask in an effort to lighten the mood and gauge what's going on.

Nash and Becket both give me a gratuitous amused snort, but Enoch and Kallan both just sit there staring off at nothing.

"Because it's all like some fucked up arranged marriage, and none of us can agree on what to do," Becket supplies, and this time I give him a humorless chuckle.

"Well, we're all adults here. We've been through some shit together, and we all care about each other. So just get it all out there. This room is officially a safe space, and what's said in here will stay in here," I offer.

"Fuck, this is weird," Kallan admits as he breathes out a sigh. "Okay fine, we're all adults, and we can be mature about this shit. We're split fifty-fifty on whether to stick with you or jump ship and go with Suryn."

"It's not jumping ship, stop calling it that," Nash irritably growls.

"Maybe not to you, but that doesn't mean *I'm* not allowed to feel that way," Kallan snaps back.

"Okay..." I interrupt, seeing why things felt so strained when I walked in here. "I'm assuming Becket and Nash are for Suryn and you and Enoch are for me?" I query in an effort to get the lay of things.

They all go quiet again, and it's clear I just got the split wrong.

"Becket and I are for you. Nash and Enoch are for Suryn."

"Oh," I chirp, surprised by that information. I look at Becket, who kind of just glowers at me, and then to Enoch, who won't make eye contact. I'm not sure how I feel about this. Enoch was so insistent before that he and I were *something*, and I'm shocked that he would choose Suryn over me.

"Are you pissed?" Enoch asks me as he stares at the fire.

"No...I'm just confused," I answer honestly. "You've been pushing so hard to convince me that you are my Chosen..." I trail off.

"Yeah, but you've been telling me that it doesn't feel that way for you. I can stay with you and be on the outside of what I want forever. Or go with her and...who knows?" Enoch replies.

"And who knows?" I parrot back quietly. "She thinks you're filth. What the fuck kind of relationship do you think you'll have with her?" I ask him, suddenly irritated and trying to understand why.

Why is this pissing me off?

"Are you pissed because you care or because you don't like someone else playing with your toys?" Enoch snaps at me, and I reel back.

"Watch it," Becket warns Enoch.

"When the fuck have I treated any of you like toys?" I demand. "I don't play with you and set you down. I don't string you along."

"You sure were quick to mark us as your territory though," Nash tells me.

"I was protecting you. She tried to kill us! How the hell did I become the bad guy in this scenario?"

"You're not, but I don't understand why you'd want to

keep us tied to you, knowing that we aren't your Chosen. We could never have what you have with your guys if we commit ourselves to you," Enoch explains.

"I am not trying to force you into anything with me, Enoch. But if you think Suryn is going to make you Chosen, I think you're delusional. She hates us."

"Sauriel thinks she will come around," Enoch defends.

I scoff, "Oh, does he now?"

"What does that mean?" Enoch demands.

"Look at the fucking source there. You're going to blindly trust Adriel's brother?"

"They're nothing alike, Vinna. You don't know Sauriel, and you know nothing about Suryn," he defends.

"And just what the fuck do you know about her, other than she can get you where you want to go faster than I can?" I growl at him.

"What the fuck does that mean?"

"What the fuck do you think it means, Enoch?"

"Both of you stop! This isn't getting us anywhere," Nash orders.

"Well, where the fuck did you want this to get you? Do you want my permission? Fine, you've got it. Do what you want to do, but let's not pretend it's something that it's not," I snap as I get up and move toward the door.

"And just what the fuck is that?" Enoch snaps back.

"A power grab," I state simply. "You weren't getting it from me, and this opportunity is just too good to pass up, isn't it, Enoch?"

I don't wait for him to answer. I slip out of their room and have to stop myself from slamming the door. Our suite is quiet and peaceful, which is the exact opposite of how I feel inside. I'm fucking pissed, and I storm out the front door without a second thought. The halls of the castle are quiet, and there's a sleepy quality to the air as I silently navigate away from the rooms. I feel like I can't get away fast enough.

I want to scream and pound on something. Knox was right all along about Enoch. But even as I think those words, they feel wrong. There's more here, and I'm just not seeing it. I retrace the path that Suryn took us the first time. If I can get back down to the throne room, then I know how to get out of the castle. From there, I can get back to that training facility. Maybe they'll have replaced the poles I broke last time, and I'll have something new to break again. Worst case scenario, I'll find a tree and just punch the shit out of that.

I turn left and right, the way that I remember, but instead of finding the flight of stairs that I expect to be there, I find myself in a dark corridor. Was this here last time? I keep going. Maybe it all just looks different at night. I walk silently and swiftly until the area starts to look somewhat more familiar, or perhaps this place has oil paintings similar to the other parts of the castle that I know.

I trek on for another twenty minutes before finally accepting that I'm lost. I huff out an irritated breath and turn around to retrace my steps. I pause when I notice a ball of fairy light slowly moving in my direction. My first thought is that it's Enoch or one of the other guys chasing after me, but I quickly realize that they don't know how to make fairy light and wouldn't be using it to guide their way.

Unease flares inside of me, and I slink back into a corner and activate the runes that increase my hearing, vision, and smell.

"Only another day or so, and then their deliberations will be complete," a male voice explains.

"And will they do the right thing?" a female voice inquires.

"The outcome is not as sure as we would like. She is

close with members of the old Houses, and with a *tainted* in the tribunal..." the male trails off.

"So it will be up to us then," the female declares, and the man gives an affirming grunt.

"Arrange it," she orders, and goosebumps prickle up my arms and neck.

"And your niece?" the male asks.

"I've made our position clear, and she's agreed, but maybe it's time for her to go too. We could always blame it on the vermin."

They get closer, and as I make out the Sovereign's face, rage begins to percolate in my soul. She's going to try to kill us regardless of what the tribunal decides. She unties her dress at her shoulders, and it falls to pool at her feet. She's completely naked in the middle of a corridor where anyone could come across them. The male, who I don't recognize, hums his appreciation and licks his lips.

"On your knees," he commands her, and she titters out an annoying little giggle.

The Sovereign does as she's told, and the male unties his pants. He starts stroking his cock as the Sovereign reaches between her thighs and starts playing with herself.

"Did I tell you to play with that filthy cunt of yours?" he asks her, annoyance ringing in his tone. "Move against the wall. I'm going to fuck your face. I want fingers in my ass at all times, do you understand?"

The Sovereign nods excitedly and opens her mouth. The male grumbles, "Good girl," and then grabs her hair roughly and shoves his dick down her throat. I look away as she reaches around and shoves her hand between his cheeks. I look down the hall in the direction I just came from and wonder if I keep going, will I find my way out or just end up in a worse situation than listening to the Sovereign gag and moan around this guy's dick?

I look back and cringe. He has a hold of her hair, and he's slamming into her mouth so hard that I can hear his balls slap against her chin. It looks fucking painful, and I have no idea how she's not puking with the amount of gagging she's doing.

"Fuck my ass harder," the male demands, and he pins the Sovereign against the wall and hammers into her mouth.

She must do what he says, because he starts moaning and talking about her tits and her dirty cunt and all the things he's going to do to them later. He lasts for another minute, and then the telltale grunts that indicate he's coming fill the hallway.

"Lick your fingers clean," he tells her, and I have to fight to keep from gagging myself now. I look away, not wanting that image to be seared into my mind. Pretty sure this is going to haunt me regardless though.

"Phip and Lanis wake up in an hour," I hear her tell him, and he scoffs.

"You want me or Thessa to make you scream before your Chosen wake up?"

"Both," she cackles again, and he grabs her by the hair and starts dragging her down the hall.

"I'll fuck your ass while she licks your cunt, and then..."

I don't hear what he plans to do after that as I disconnect my runes. I've been traumatized enough for one night. I shudder as sounds and images I want to scrub from my brain replay. That female is fucked up. She's going to take us all out for no reason other than she wants to. She cheats on her Chosen and would be the perfect candidate for the next *Two Girls One Cup* video.

Fucking hell.

Tok and Marn talked about corruption being an issue here, but seeing it right in my face like that is brutal. The fairy light disappears in the distance, and I count to twenty before slinking out of my shadow-dipped hiding spot and retracing my steps. I keep looking over my shoulder, worried that somehow someone will see me.

Hands reach out of a dark alcove and snatch me into it. I call on a knife and bite back a scream as a hand clamps over my mouth.

"It's me, Vinna," Enoch whispers in my ear.

I slam an elbow into his side, and he grunts and lets me go.

"What the fuck, Enoch, you scared the shit out of me!" I whisper screech at him.

He puts a finger to his lips, and I immediately rage at him more quietly.

"We're not supposed to be in this part of the castle. If anyone catches us, we'll be fucked," he tells me.

"No shit. I was well on my way to getting the fuck away from here until you jumped me."

Enoch snorts quietly and rolls his eyes. "I didn't jump you, you big baby."

I glare at him, suddenly remembering why I'm out roaming the halls at this time of night.

"Don't look at me like that, Vinna. We both said some shit, and we're both going to get over it, because that's what real friends do."

"Oh, so we're friends? No more trying to kiss me or earn your place?" I angrily whisper back.

"Is that really what this is? You want me to want you?" he hisses back.

"No."

"Then what?"

"I just don't want you to leave," I tell him, the confession a little surprising.

"We wouldn't be leaving you like that, Vinna. We'd still

be in each other's lives; we just wouldn't be tied by magic. The issue is Shield versus Chosen, not Vinna versus Suryn. You said we were family, right?" he asks me, and I nod. "That's not going to change," he reassures me.

I lean back and study Enoch's gray-blue gaze. "You like her, don't you?" I ask him, the truth in his gaze shocking me more than anything. "How?"

Enoch scoffs and rolls his eyes. "I don't know, how do any of your Chosen like you?" he counters, and I snort.

"I'm a fucking delight, I'll have you know."

Enoch smiles and shakes his head. "I'm not doodling her name all over my notebooks or anything, but when she marked me, it just did something." Enoch rubs at his chest, and I give a weary exhale. I think back on the time I marked the guys. I was panicked and freaked out, but it also felt right in this weird inexplicable way.

"Does the rest of your coven know?"

"Yeah. They feel a pull, but Nash is the only one aside from me who seems interested in exploring what that means."

"What does Kallan say?"

"That you marked us first and that there had to be a reason for it. He thinks if we go the Chosen route, we're betraying you."

I nod absently as I listen. "And Becket?" I inquire, not attempting to mask my shock that he would take my side after what happened with his father.

Enoch grins like he can read my mind and was surprised too. "I think he just likes you better than Suryn," he tells me with a smile.

"Well, that's not exactly difficult when she's a nightmare and I'm—"

"A fucking delight?" Enoch adds in, and we both laugh.

"There's not much I can do about Becket recognizing

that I'm more fun than Suryn could ever be," I tell Enoch and give an exaggerated flip of my hair. "But I'll talk to Kallan. If all of you are drawn to her and this is what you guys want, then that's what you should have."

Enoch pulls me in for a hug.

"Thank you, Vinna," he whispers and kisses the top of my head.

I hug him tightly. "I'm sorry about the whole power grab thing. I don't really think that," I tell him, and I feel him breathe out a sigh.

"It's okay, you can't help that you're a girl and get all emotional and irrational at times," he teases, and I quietly laugh and pinch his side.

He squirms and then hugs me harder. I return the squeeze and then freeze when someone that isn't me or Enoch clears their throat. We pull apart with a jolt of shock, and my head snaps in the direction of the hallway this little alcove is attached to.

Fuck! Don't be the Sovereign. Don't be the Sovereign.

Relief washes through me when I realize that it's not the Sovereign. But it's quickly replaced by a decent amount of *oh shit* when my eyes connect with the angry hazel gaze of Suryn. A *this is not what it looks like* creeps up my throat, but before I can say anything, she takes a menacing step toward us.

"This area is off limits to the likes of *you*. Find some-where else to fuck," she seethes and then stomps off.

Enoch hesitates for a second. "Go after her," I tell him and shove him in the direction she just stormed off in. "It's okay, I'll find my way back," I reassure him, and he rushes off after what looked like a very pissed off Sentinel. Then again, she always seems to look like that, so who knows if she really cares about this or not? I slip out of the dark alcove and eventually find my way back to a side of the castle that I recognize. I don't run into anyone else, and I slip inside the suite we've been given just as the sun starts to peek over the horizon. I flop down onto a couch with a sigh.

I can already tell this is going to be one fucking long ass day.

26

I give a deep toe curling yawn as we make our way into
the throne room. I shake my cheeks in an effort to
wake the fuck up, but another yawn starts at the back
of my mouth, and resistance is futile.

"Someone please help me to wake the fuck up," I beg as
we take our place in front of the thrones.

We were summoned this afternoon by the tribunal.
Apparently, they're ready to make their decision. Unease
courses through me, but it doesn't seem enough to combat
my exhaustion. I'm way less nervous for this than I would
have thought. Pretty sure that has to do with what I overheard from the Sovereign herself. She wants us dead no
matter what. The order will probably come today, at least
that's what I expect.

I think back on our conversation this morning with Tok
and Marn.

*"If the decision is for the Sovereign and against you, don't
fight. They'll be ready for that and have measures in place that
you won't see coming," Tok tells me, his countenance urgent and
his tone critical.*

"They will take you and imprison you until they can make all

the arrangements they need to turn your deaths into a spectacle," Marn adds.

"What if they don't do that?" I ask. Knowing my luck, this will be the one time she deviates from protocol and cuts us all down.

"The Sovereign rules with fear. She needs to keep the people scared of outsiders and of each other so they don't look too closely at her. She won't miss an opportunity to show Tierit the big bad outsiders who dared to attack her and were defeated," Marn explains.

"So we go quietly, and then what?" Valen asks.

"You wait for us to get you out," Tok answers, looking at each of us in turn. "We have connections and power we don't often flex, but we will. We will get you out, and then we will all run. The Sovereign may send Sentinels after us, but it won't be anyone that isn't already expendable to her. So we'll have an opportunity to flip them, or I'm sure between all of us, they can be dealt with."

"The only issue is the barrier, but we have some people looking into that as we speak," Marn informs us.

"I don't think the barrier will be an issue," I declare.

Tok and Marn both look at me curiously with a hint of skepticism in their gazes.

"When we came through, we did something to it. That was the bright light that gave away that we were even here. If that hadn't happened, I don't think you guys would have known the barrier had been breached until we were walking into the city and announcing where we were from and what we were doing there. I'm not certain of what we did exactly, but I feel in my bones that we'll be able to get out when we need to," I tell them.

Tok leans back in his chair and stares out the window in contemplation. "Well, let's hope you're right."

Another jaw cracking yawn pulls me from my thoughts, and I roll my neck and try to convince my body it needs to be on alert.

"If you stop yawning, I'll do that thing with the chocolate that you love so much," Ryker leans down and whispers in my ear.

His blond shoulder-length hair tickles the side of my neck, and I get chills as his words skim my ear.

"Whipped cream too?" I ask, excitement now strumming through my veins.

"Of course. I'll make sure it's hot as fuck and overwhelming to every sense you possess. And just when you can't take anymore—"

I moan, cutting him off. "Don't you fucking tease me, Ryker."

He laughs. "I would never, Squeaks. It'll be everything you've been dreaming about and so much more."

I release a dreamy sigh that makes Ryker crack up again.

"But where are you getting the brownies from?" I ask, my mouth watering.

"I have a hookup with the kitchen," he beams proudly.

"Oh you do, do you? And how did you come by said hookup?"

"Well, really we have Sorik to thank and technically, Sauriel too."

I look up at Ryker, now suddenly very curious.

"Sauriel arranged for blood for Sorik. The female who volunteered also works in the kitchen. She and Sorik have struck up a friendship, and she mentioned if there's anything we need, to let her know. So if I were to, say...ask for a brownie sundae, then you, Squeaks, would have your brownie sundae."

I stare into his sky-blue eyes for a moment and then reach up on my tiptoes and kiss him. "You're too fucking good to me," I tell him against his lips, and he nips at my mouth before I pull away and drop back flat on my feet.

The side door opens, and in walks a couple of guards

followed by Mote, Naree, Port, Wella and Sabin. They're led to the side of the room, and they no sooner take their place there than a guard steps forward and announces the Sovereign.

"All hail Sovereign Finella, Leader of the Marked, Ruler of Tierit, Blood Savior, Walker of Realms and Gate Keeper," he announces, and the side door opens again to present a large show of force.

The guards march in step as they lead Tawv and Sauriel in before the Sovereign this time. I realize, as I watch them walk up to their thrones, that no one ever introduces them with a title. They're clearly important as they're part of this Quorum of leadership, but I have no idea what they really do. Are they the checks and balances to the Sovereign? I think about that for a minute and decide that it seems about right from what I've witnessed so far.

There seems to be an extra show of force around the Sovereign today, and I tense, wondering if it's because she's expecting trouble or about to cause it.

Her dress is light pink, but her deathly pale pallor and bright white hair make her look washed out regardless of what color she's wearing. It once again has slits, which Sentinels here seem to be a big fan of, and the material is very thin. It's not see through but pretty damn close. Put this chick in front of a sunny window, and you could probably count her pubes.

She glides up the stairs to her throne and reaches up to touch her crown, like she's making sure it's still there, as she sits. Suryn comes through the side door next, and I choke when I see that she's in a wispy barely there dress too. I've only seen her in the black armored clothing that all my guys and I are now rocking, and it shocks the fuck out of me to see her looking so completely different.

Ory saunters in behind her, and they both take their

place on the opposite side of the room from where the tribunal is standing. A boom resonates around the room as the side door is closed. The loud noise slowly settles, and we all wait for the Sovereign to speak. She takes her time like she's in no rush, or more likely she just likes to make it clear who's in control here.

An image of the man from the hallway thrusting into her mouth so hard and so deep that tears streamed down her face as she gagged, fills my mind. I blink and mentally shove it the fuck away. *Ugh.*

"I have been informed the tribunal has come to a decision, is that correct?" the Sovereign asks.

She looks over at them, her focus honed in on Mote and Port specifically.

"Yes," Naree announces with a nod.

The Sovereign and she stare at each other for a moment before the ruler of the Sentinels irritably asks, "Well, what is it then?"

"We unanimously rule against the order of death," Naree declares, and the Sovereign narrows her eyes.

The decision rings in my ears, and I'm beyond stunned. I know Enoch said that Sauriel thought this would go in our favor, but I thought for sure we were going to be fucked. My breaths become short, and I have to focus on pulling enough air in.

"Unanimously?" the Sovereign questions.

"Yes, unanimously," Naree answers.

"Very well then, I dismiss you from your service on the tribunal and will lay the responsibility at your feet if this decision proves as catastrophic as I suspect it will be."

"Sovereign Finella, that is uncalled for," Tawv admonishes, and she turns her glare on him.

"No, what is uncalled for is your putting the people of Tierit at risk for your own political gain," she volleys.

Tawv laughs. "Are you addled? Exactly what would I do with any level of political gain? I am not the next in line. Or rather, the one whose grip is slipping from the crown. I upheld the laws as they are written. The tribunal has made their decision based off of facts and reason, which I dare say will serve the people much better than decisions based off of insecurity and fear. She is a powerful Lost Sentinel that's come home, and *we* need her."

"Damn," I hear Knox whisper behind me, and I couldn't agree more.

Note to self, fist bump that creepy eyed hero of a male later for the verbal bitch slap he just delivered to the Sovereign.

"How dare you," she hisses at him, shoving out of her throne to tower over him, her pale skin getting redder by the moment.

"No. How dare *you*," he growls back, rising from his throne and forcing her to look up at him.

Our eyes bounce from the Sovereign to Tawv, waiting to see who will say something next. The whole room seems to hold their breath. *Is this it?* I think as I survey the room. Is this where she goes full tyrant and tries to slaughter us all? It sure fucking feels like it's headed in that direction. Tension fills my every cell. My magic is ready to call on whatever I may need in a fight, but I calm my bloodlust. We all just watch and wait.

I'm surprised when the Sovereign turns and storms out of the room. The large door slams behind her, and the guards scramble to follow after her hasty retreat.

"Awkward," Bastien singsongs quietly behind me, and I have to bite my tongue to keep from laughing.

I shake the tension and need for action out of my limbs and listen to the Sovereign's angry footsteps on the other side of the door. I swear I can hear the *you haven't seen the last of me* vow in the rhythm of her departure.

"Tribunal," Tawv's warm voice breaks the uncomfortable silence. "We thank you for your service and dismiss you back to your lives."

Naree, Mote, Port, and Wella give him a nod and then surprisingly look over at me and place their fists over their biceps. Shock strikes through me, and judging by the gasps that ring out through the room, I'm not the only one. None of them wait for me to respond in any way before they turn and head out the front doors. I watch them go, conflicted by what the hell just happened.

I turn forward, my questioning gaze in search of Tawv, but I find Suryn instead. She stares daggers at me, every inch of her radiating fury, and it sends prickles of warning all over my body. Ory steps into my line of sight and whispers something to her. I can't tell what he says, but whatever it is, it's enough to snap her out of our little staring contest. Suryn nods her head once at Ory, and then they both rush off exactly like the Sovereign just did.

"Well, that was fun," Valen quips. "Raise your hand if you're in favor of getting the fuck out of this place before they change their minds."

My hand snaps up without hesitation as do all of my Chosen's hands.

"Actually," Tawv interjects. "In order to leave, you have to have permission from the ruling body." He gestures toward the side door. "I wouldn't be in a hurry to ask her any favors," he adds.

"Okay then," I tell him simply, and he narrows his eyes at me, suspicious of my lack of argument.

"No, I'm saying you physically can't leave; the barrier won't allow it unless she grants you access to it," Tawv reiterates, his face filled with concern.

I stare at him for a moment, reading the worry on his face, and decide to let him in on our possible advantage.

"Actually, I'm pretty sure I claimed your barrier when I came through, so I think we'll be fine," I explain, my eyes filled with reassurance and confidence.

"That's not possible," Tawv argues.

"Saw it with my own eyes, bud," I counter. "We all lit up like supernovas and..."

I trail off, not wanting to mention about the thing that happened with the rune on our palms and how I drained my Chosen dry, doing whatever I did to the barrier. I know Tawv took us to go see Getta in the first place, and he might be Bond magic friendly. But I'm taking Getta's warning seriously to keep our mouths shut about this to everyone. I freeze when something dawns on me. I hurriedly play back that moment in my mind again and add the soundtrack of Getta explaining how it all worked.

"You can pull and give magic at will to each other. Each member of your Chosen will be able to share their abilities when this rune is activated."

Tawv says something to me, but I can't focus on what past the ring of realization that's happening in my head right now.

Holy shit, could that really be it?

I turn to Ryker, my eyes filled with exhilaration and shock. "I think I know how we can fix my dad."

His eyes snap to mine. "What?" he asks, his tone just as stunned as mine is.

Tawv is still going on about something, and I cut him off. "Okay, yeah, we'll do that. Um, we gotta go...nap. Yeah, slept like shit last night, so naps for all. Let's put a pin in this and pick the discussion back up later. Cool? Okay, cool." And with that, I turn around and bolt for the door.

27

I sprint for our rooms, and it doesn't take long for the guys to be right on my heels.

"Vinna, what's going on?" Ryker asks as he pushes to catch up with me from behind.

"I'm all for a good chase, but this vague-dashing is getting old," Torrez grumbles.

"I'll explain when we get to the room. We don't need any extra ears hearing," I tell him over my shoulder, and thankfully, everyone keeps their questions to themselves until we get to the room.

Chosen and Shields pour through the door to our suite, and as soon as they shut the door behind them, I call up a barrier to keep anyone from listening or looking in. The yellow-orange barrier coats the floor, crawls up the walls, and colors across the ceiling. As soon as we're encased, questions come firing my way.

"Okay, hold up," I order. "I'll explain." I wait for everyone to quiet, and then I take a deep breath and start pacing as I explain.

"Siah, when we were driving to Adriel's cave compound, you told me about how lamia are made."

"Right," he agrees, his tone perplexed.

"You said that not everyone can do it, because you have to drain the other person of their magic without overloading yours and killing yourself, and then you need to feed your magic back into the person without draining yourself too much, which would also result in your death.

"Yes, that's right," he confirms.

"Well, when Adriel tried to turn Vaughn, he didn't have enough magic to complete it. That's probably because Vaughn is a Sentinel, and if his source is anything like ours, it's massive. It would take a fuck-ton of magic to complete the process, and Adriel didn't have that even on his best day. But guess who does?" I ask them.

I'm too excited to wait for anyone to guess, so I hurry and solve the mystery. "We do," I tell them like a magician that's setting up a mind-blowing trick.

"Wait. What?" Becket asks.

"Getta said that when we activate this rune"—I hold up my hand and point to the six diamonds in a circle on my palm—"we could share magic; we can pull from each other or push it into each other. That means that we could send the fuck-ton of magic that my dad needs to complete his turn using this." I wave my hand at all of them and watch what I'm saying soak in.

"It could work," Sorik says, stepping out of his room and into the conversation. "But we're assuming that's what's wrong with Vaughn, that he's stuck in the transition somehow."

"But what else could it be?" I ask, my hope deflating slightly. "He became like this after Adriel tried to turn him. Isn't being stuck in the transition the most logical conclusion?"

"Maybe, Squeaks, but it could be because he's a Sentinel too. Lamia can be turned to Sentinels, but maybe Sentinels can't be turned into lamia. This could be what happens instead," Ryker tells me.

"It's worth a shot, don't you think though?" Valen asks Ryker.

"I mean, if it doesn't work, it doesn't work, but at least we tried," Bastien adds, agreeing with his brother.

"But what if this could hurt us? None of us knows how much power it would take to complete Vaughn's transition into a lamia. Even if we can pull it off, it could drain all of us badly. We'd be vulnerable in a time that we really can't afford to be vulnerable. What if the Sovereign comes for us?" Sabin asks.

Everyone goes quiet as they think through the shit ton of info I've just dumped all over them. My heart speeds up, but the hopeful little shit has gotten me in trouble too many times for me to just follow it blindly.

"So we're smart about it. We set up barriers around us, and we don't push past what happened to all of us when we crossed over into Tierit and altered their barrier. You guys were out for about three hours. Enoch, Kallan, Becket, Nash and Sorik can watch our back for that long," I propose.

"So what would we do?" Siah asks hesitantly, and I try to take a deep breath and calm myself down. This is going to happen. I can feel it, but I don't need to get carried away with excitement until it works.

"We would push our magic into you, and you would push it into Vaughn."

"That's it?" Knox queries.

"That's it," I confirm. "Siah would finish the turning with our help."

"Is that safe for Siah?" Kallan asks.

"I would never do anything to hurt any of you," I defend.

"I know you wouldn't purposely do something, but

didn't you say if he has too much magic or too little, he could die?"

"That was before though. He's Chosen now. He's a lamia Sentinel hybrid who can share magic with me and his compeers. There should be zero risk. At least not to him."

"So what if Vaughn needs more magic to heal him than the barrier did, what then?" Nash asks.

"I don't know. We won't know what might or might not work without trying," I counter.

"So should we try to drain him again and start the process all over or just push magic into him and see if anything happens?" Valen asks.

"I think we should push magic into him and see if that heals his mind enough to pull him out of this functioning catatonic state," Sorik proposes, and I nod my head agreeing with him.

"So do we want to do this now or wait until after we get out of here?" Sabin questions.

Mentally, I try to weigh the pros and cons of attempting this now versus waiting. Maybe it's dumb to push for it now with everything going on around us, but I just feel in my gut that we need to try and now is the time to do it.

"I feel like now is the best option," I tell them. "Enoch, Becket, Nash and Kallan, would you be okay to stand guard in case any of us go down for a while?" I ask.

They nod, and Becket immediately starts setting up additional barriers around our suite.

"Well, okay then, let's see if this works," Torrez announces, and he pushes out of his seat on the couch and saunters over to Vaughn and Sorik's room.

The rest of my Chosen follow Torrez, and nerves trickle through me as I bring up the rear. Vaughn is sitting in a chair, staring at the empty fireplace, and anxiety begins to gnaw at my gut. What if this doesn't work? What if it does? What happens then? Will he know what's going on, be aware of everything he's lost or that's changed around him?

I honestly don't know which would be worse, him being *stuck* in there this whole time or him waking up to all of this like he's been asleep through everything that's happened. What if he doesn't know that Grier is gone? My heart aches, and my mind whirls with all the endless possibilities. For a brief moment, I wonder if it would be better to leave things as they are. Waking him up could be devastating, but I banish that thought and hope that if this does work, he can overcome everything that's happened.

I wipe my suddenly sweaty palms on my armored pants as Sorik instructs Vaughn to move to the bed and lie down. I'm oddly aware of my breathing as Vaughn does as he's told, and I feel like my heart's going to beat out of my chest. I keep telling it to calm the fuck down. This may not even work. There's also the possibility that if it does, I could be diving head first into another Lachlan situation.

I beg my heart to stop with the hope, but each beat is filled with it anyway.

"Okay, everyone ready?" Siah asks.

He rolls his neck and shakes nervous energy out of his arms. I'm tempted to mimic him as my body starts to hum with adrenaline. Bastien's palm lights up as he activates the six circular diamond runes. Slowly one by one, each of their palms light up. A blue glow fills the room, and it feels like everyone is holding their breath and waiting to see what will happen next.

Siah watches me as I activate my rune, and then his palm lights up with that same eerie blue light.

"I've never changed anyone before," he admits, looking to Sorik for help.

"You know when you're feeding and you can feel something inside of you latch on to the power in the blood?" Sorik asks.

Siah nods and looks at me quickly before looking back at Sorik.

"You'll do that, but instead of pulling the power into you, you'll push it further into him. You'll keep doing that until Vaughn is full. If it works, he should wake up a lamia, and hungry."

"Okay," Siah agrees, and then quick as lightning, he slashes across Vaughn's forearm.

My initial reaction is to defend Vaughn from any more injury, and I have to talk myself down from reacting the way my instincts are screaming for me to react. *He's okay, Vinna. Siah needs his blood. Would you rather he bit him, knowing what that bite can do?* I roll my neck and open and close my fists in an effort to regain control of myself.

Siah focuses on the line of blood that's seeped into the scratch, and it's as if time stands still. I don't feel anything at first, but after maybe ten minutes or so, I start to feel tiny tugs right in the middle of my chest. The pull is soft, and even though I can't physically see any evidence of the magic that Siah is pushing into Vaughn, I can picture it in my mind. I imagine that there's a steady flow of blue light running from Siah's hands into Vaughn's chest. I can picture Vaughn filled to the brink inside and then sitting up, gasping for air.

Sorik watches Vaughn and Siah closely, and I wonder what's going through his mind. Is he as tangled up inside with conflicting emotions as I am?

Torrez goes down first. My heart hammers with alarm, but Sorik gets to him before he can crumble all the way to the ground. Sorik lays him down gently and whispers something to him that I can't make out. Knox is next, and then Sabin. Worry begins to consume me as one by one, Siah drains each of them, and there's still no hint that any of this is working.

"They're okay, just sleeping like before," Sorik reassures me.

I nod and try to convince my heart that this will all be okay.

Bastien and Valen both look pained, like they're fighting what we all know is inevitable. Bastien grunts, and the next thing I know, Sorik is positioning both of the twins on the floor. I fall forward and grab onto the side of the bed to keep me from going all the way over. I don't feel like I'm going to pass out, but the tug at the middle of my chest just got infinitely stronger. I feel like someone just harpooned me and is trying to drag me through the water to them.

Ryker sways on his feet, and I prepare myself for the increase in the intensity of the magic pull when he goes down.

"Vinna," Ryker calls to me through gritted teeth. My eyes snap to his. "Call on the runes Siah gave you. I think they might heal. Lace that in your magic and see if it helps," he tells me, and then he's down for the count.

I gasp as the harpoon in my chest gives another hard yank, and then I do what Ryker suggested. I activate the runes on my right shoulder that Siah's bite left behind.

I feel like someone just bitch slapped me with a lightning bolt. The runes I just activated said *hold my beer* as they shoved the harpoon out of my chest, cracked my rib cage in half and swung each side open like opulent French doors. Power pours out of me like I'm doing the fucking Care Bear Stare, and I grit my teeth and try to hold my ground. I look down at myself and see that my skin is still just kissed by the eerie blue light from the rune on my hand and shoulder, but I feel like I'm lit up like the fucking sun right now.

"He's close," Sorik announces, and Siah inclines his

chin, his teeth also ground together from the force I'm now feeding into him.

I begin to pant. My insides start to *feel* like the sun as a deep burning starts in my chest and works its way out into my limbs. The burn becomes searing, and pain radiates through everything that I am. I grit my teeth and will against it and keep shoving everything I have into Siah. He growls and a drop of blood spills out of his nose. His face is filled with strain and agony, and I know my features reflect the exact same thing. A keening starts in my chest as I keep pushing power out of me and into Siah. It fucking hurts, but we're so close.

Will this work? *Fuck, please let it work,* I beg as I burn from the inside out, my keening on the verge of a scream. I release my plea to float out into the universe, and just as I do, Siah disconnects his rune, and his legs give out. Like a rubber band from hell, the magic I was pouring into Siah snaps back at me, and I get hammered by the force of it. I gasp and then cry out from the impact, and then the next thing I know, everything goes black.

28

I open my eyes and squint against the bright sun
streaming through the windows. My Chosen are still
asleep around me, and I'm not sure how long we've
been out. I crawl out of bed and press Healing magic into
each of them, but they all seem to be okay aside from the
whole unconscious thing. I head out into the main room,
and Kallan and Becket leap up from the couches.

"She's up," Kallan announces, and then they both
become hovering mother hens.

"How are you feeling?" Becket asks at the same time I
ask, "How long was I out?"

"About seventeen hours now," Nash announces from the
doorway of Vaughn and Sorik's room.

My heart rate picks up like a galloping horse as I try to
see past Nash into the room. My hopeful gaze falls on Nash,
the question clear in my stare.

Nash shakes his head, and everything in me drops.

"Nothing?" I ask, my voice cracking with emotion.

I thought for sure this was going to work. It just felt so
right when we worked it out.

"He hasn't woken up; he seems to be in a deep sleep and doesn't respond to instructions the way he was before."

Nash's words feel like a sledgehammer to my heart. Each syllable pulverizing what I hoped would happen. We didn't make him better, we made him fucking worse. I step back away from them. I choke on the acceptance I know I need to swallow, but I just hate the fucking taste of it so much.

I really thought it would work.

I look up at them and then around the room. I can't be here right now. I need to go!

"I'm going to go for a run," I announce, and then I move out of the room and try to get as far away from my disappointment as fast as I can.

"Vinna, wait," Enoch calls, but I need to get out of here.

"Just guard my Chosen, okay? Please," I beg, and I'm out the door before anyone else can say another word.

Sun beams in through the windows that line the hallway, and I easily find the stairs that lead down and out of this fucking useless castle. If I ran the show here, this place would be the first thing I'd tear down. I'd build a house that was normal and functional and didn't have ostentatiousness vomited over every square inch. Fuck the First House and all these ancient assholes who think somehow their opinions and blood matter more than every other Sentinel within this barrier.

I make my way to the training facility I used the other day and once again wish I was home in my gym with a treadmill that won't quit and every kind of punching bag imaginable. I stop in my tracks when I find Ory standing solitary at the doors leading into the facility. He looks a little surprised to see me, but it's gone in a blink, just like every other emotion this guy shows.

We both just stand and stare at each other for a moment before he seems to come to some sort of a decision and steps aside. I reach for the handles on the doors to the entrance and pass by him warily. I'm not sure what his deal is, but honestly with the way I'm feeling, I'd be game to fuck him up once and for all if he tries anything. I step into the facility and don't hear any of the telltale signs that anyone else is in here like I heard last time I came.

Good. Time to fuck some shit up.

I start to stretch out and loosen my limbs. After sending a zap of Elemental magic into my phone, I turn it on and pull up Bring Me the Horizon's "Can You Feel My Heart," letting the lyrics scream me into action. I step into the arena-like facility and start to work out a circuit that will purge the frustration. Just as I'm about to get started, someone drops from the top of the tall wall that I'm pretty sure they practice flying over. They land and start sprinting for the next obstacle when they spot me and stop in their tracks.

I groan, irritated, when hazel eyes meet mine. *Fuck my life.* Of course this bitch Suryn is here.

I should fucking know by now that Ory is practically her personal guard. Where there's one, you'll find the other.

"How did you get in here?" she demands.

"Your boyfriend let me in."

She narrows her eyes at the word *boyfriend.* "Leave," she commands, and she turns and moves back in the direction of whatever course she's running, like she just expects to be obeyed.

"Unless you have another place erected somewhere in the city where I can work out, I'm good here, but thanks."

She goes stiff and then whirls around. Her nostrils flare with anger, and for some reason, I really like that. It feels good to get under this arrogant brat's skin.

"I said leave," she orders again.

"And I said no," I volley back.

"I am the second in line to the Sovereign, and I have given you an order," she growls.

"I am the first in line to *I don't give a fuck*. I'm not yours to command. This place is plenty big enough for both of us. You stay out of my way, and I'll stay out of yours."

Suryn takes a menacing step toward me, and it's obvious that she's fuming. "Who do you think you are, breaching our boundaries, waltzing up in here like you're owed something, tarnishing everything with your presence?" she seethes.

"First of all, I don't waltz, it's impossible to make that look badass. Second of all, from the sound of things, it's my bloodline that's due for a little Sovereign time. You may see tarnish but, bitch, I see a glow-up, and this place is in desperate need of a reality check."

"Oh yes, your reality, where spreading your thighs for filth is for the common good, right?"

I shake my head at her, *fucking brainwashed twit*. "Careful, Suryn, because your magic seems real fond of that filth you keep referring to. It was real quick to claim the first worthy males it could. Desperate much?"

She takes another step toward me. "Are you going to leave, or am I going to have to make you?" she threatens, and I snicker.

I run my eyes over her frame, sizing her up. She's a couple inches shorter than me and not quite as muscular, but I know she's good with weapons, and the bitch can fly.

Sounds like fun.

"Let's fight for it," I challenge.

"Done," she agrees, and with that, she closes the fifteen feet of distance between us in one magic fueled leap.

Fuck, I really need to figure this flying thing out.

She swipes at me with a katana as she lands, and I guess that solves the weapons or no weapons question. I lean

277

back, the blade slicing at the armor of my top, and call on my short swords. I cross them in an *X* and then arc them up, stopping her from trying to cut me in half. Her katana ricochets off of my blades, and I kick out at her. I land a foot square in her stomach, and my blade slices up her back in a clean line as she crumbles forward from the impact of the kick.

She hisses and spins away from me. I twirl my swords in my grip and let her go. I circle her slowly as she rubs a hand over her back and glares at her blood tipped fingers.

"First blood, you want to stop?" I snark with a raised eyebrow.

Suryn raises her own eyebrow haughtily and gestures with her sword to my chest. "Try again, you stray."

I look down and notice a bleeding cut through my shirt at the bottom of my ribs. *Well, shit, that'll teach me to get all braggy.*

I shake my head, amused. Round two.

I call on throwing knives and start to pelt her with them. She bats them away with her sword, and I up the ante by calling on Offensive magic. I rotate between throwing blades and orbs at her, and she rotates between calling up shields and batting away weapons. Suryn clearly has Elemental magic, hence the flying, and Defensive magic, hence the shields. I question whether or not she has anything else in her magical arsenal, when the ground under me goes from solid to ocean-like waves.

Conjuring a disk of magic directly under my feet, I do my best to ride the waves as I hurl balls of fire at her. Water shoots from Suryn's hands, dousing my assault, so I freeze her water into dagger-sharp points and fling them at her instead. One of the ice daggers nicks her cheek, but I have zero time to celebrate the hit as a broken pole comes hurtling my way. I dive to dodge it, but the ground where I'm about to land turns into rock spikes.

Air comes at my call, and I use it to blow me out of the way of the sharp points. I use a little too much force, and it sends me spinning, so I shove a barrier out around me to keep anything else from impaling me while I try to find my feet. Then I chuck another barrier her way. Suryn flies up, avoiding my magic, and throws an axe at me. It bounces off my shield as I shake away the dizziness I have from tornado-ing myself away from the land spikes.

My barrier fractures from the hit of the axe, and the next thing I know, Suryn is slamming into me. She punches at the cut she gave me on my ribs. I grunt in pain and hammer her with elbow after elbow to her neck and shoulders. She stabs me with something, and I can tell right away that she's hit a lung. She tries to fly up and off of me as I call on another dagger.

Oh no you don't!

A whip appears in my hand, and I crack it at her. The braided magic wraps around her neck, and I yank her back down to the ground. Dirt plumes around her as she crashes to the ground with an oomph and a painful sounding crunch. Suryn writhes on the ground, and I can see that she's struggling to catch her breath.

Well, that makes two of us.

I look down to see a long thin dagger shoved between my ribs. I pull it out with a grunt. The dagger poofs out of my hold, and I look over to see Suryn trying to get to her feet, watching me with a satisfied smile. I rip off my shirt to see how bad it is, but I can tell by how hard it is to breathe that it's a nasty one. Luckily for me, Ryker helped me to figure out what Siah's runes do. I activate his bite marks on my right shoulder and stare at Suryn with a big *fuck you* in my smile.

Her eyes go wide as both of my wounds knit together in front of her. I take a deep breath as my magic heals the damage to my lung and surrounding muscle and tissue. I wipe at the leftover blood on my side. My skin is once again smooth as I pull my soiled shirt back over my head.

"How?" Suryn asks as she gets all the way to her feet.

"I'd take any of my Chosen over your purest blooded Sentinels any day," I retort, and I call on another gust of wind and blast myself at her. It's not as kickass as flying, but it's effective. I go full missile and slam my fist against her cheek as I tackle her. She kicks me over her head. I flip and twist to right myself and then spin a roundhouse into her side.

Suryn grabs my ankle and drops an elbow into my knee. I call on my staff and swing it at her head, but she gets a shield up just in time. My staff connects to the magical barrier, and it sends nerve numbing vibrations up my arms and into my body. I let the staff go and shake out my arms. Suryn calls on her own staff, which has spikes ringing each end, and a flash of staff envy strikes through me.

I want spikes.

She steps back and starts spinning it expertly, like she expects the show alone to send me running. I smile.

"Whoa there, Gandalf. Please don't smite me with your sweet moves," I snark.

"You talk too much," she growls at me as she charges.

My own staff appears in time to stop her spikes from connecting with my head, and the crack of noise the two weapons make as they strike one another sounds like an explosion of thunder.

Booms ricochet all around us as we strike at each other, and it sounds like the heavens are beating the war drums in our honor.

"You know the Sovereign is going to kill you," I throw

out there randomly, feeling the urge to talk *more* now that I know it bugs her.

"Oh no!" she mocks. "I guess I'll just throw down my weapon and let you have the honor instead."

I snort and spin, bringing my staff down high. She blocks the hit, but I use the momentum to allow the opposite end of my staff to nail her in the stomach. She grunts but doesn't miss a beat as she swings her staff into my shoulder. The spikes don't connect, thank fuck. I'm too close for her to hit me with either end, but it still hurts. I activate Siah's runes again, and whatever injury was there heals.

These marks are the fucking shit!

"You think I'd really believe anything you say anyway?" she growls at me as our staffs meet in another boom.

"I don't really give a fuck what you believe. It's the truth. If you don't believe me now, you will. Right before she slits your throat or has that creep Ory take you out, you'll know then that the *stray* was right."

"Ory is loyal," she counters.

"Right, just like your aunt, the Sovereign, is?" I challenge.

Suryn backs away from me for a minute, and we both watch each other.

"How do you even know this?" she asks me after a couple beats.

"Overheard it one night."

She scoffs.

"Trust me, I wish I hadn't gotten myself lost in the castle. I would love to not know what the Sovereign sounds like while she lets some dude fuck her face," I confess, and we both cringe.

"Was this the same night you were fucking my...*your* Shield?" Suryn corrects herself.

I watch her for a moment, taking in the fire that lights up in her hazel eyes. *Is she jealous?*

"You've got it wrong," I tell her.

She gives me a sardonic smile. "What? That you weren't rubbing up all over your Shield?"

"That, for starters, but you're especially wrong about that whole filth mentality that's poisoning your brain. You think you're better than they are, but they've got you beat in every possible way. You're the one lacking, not them."

"Yes, and you know me so well," she bites back.

"I know enough to spot a close-minded hypocrite when I see one."

"And I know enough to spot a power hungry back dweller when I see one," Suryn snaps back.

"Now, now, now, don't go getting me confused with your aunt. Taking things that don't belong to them clearly runs in your family, I wonder what else does?" I jab.

"Fuck you, mongrel," she flings at me as we move to go head to head again.

"Better an honorable mongrel than a pureblood piece of shit," I proclaim.

I spin, dropping my staff and slicing across her stomach with the throwing knife I just called into my grip. "Oh wait, that's right, isn't your dad lamia?" I ask, my voice dripping with faux sweetness, as I move inside the strike she's trying to brain me with and cut up the inside of her arm. "Looks like we're both just a couple of mongrels," I observe, slamming my blade into her thigh and rolling away from her.

Suryn hisses and yanks the small dagger from the meat of her thigh. She throws it at me, and it goes wide. I pluck the handle out of the air and let the weapon disappear as I disengage the runes. She sways on her feet, and I can tell from the blood dripping down her arm that the cut up the inside of her bicep is the one that's about to bring her to her knees.

I brush myself off and walk slowly toward her. She drops to one knee and shakes her head like she's struggling to stay conscious. Suryn calls on her katana as I get close, but I push it aside like it's nothing. I reach for her throat, recognizing the resignation I see in her eyes. She knows this is it.

I shake my head at her presumption and shove magic into her. I feel for her wounds, healing them one by one, and shove away any respect I might feel over the fact that she fought as well as she did when she's this beat up.

"What are you doing?" she asks me, her tone laced with confusion.

"What does it look like? I'm healing you."

"I know, but why?"

I crouch down to look her straight in the eyes. "Because I'm not actually trying to kill you. I just needed to blow off some steam. You need to broaden your horizons and open your mind, not die."

I finish mending all of her injuries and shove her away from me a little harder than is necessary as I stand up. Suryn rubs at her throat and shakes her head at me. She watches me for a moment like I'm a puzzle she just now realizes she hasn't figured out. She rolls over and pushes up from the ground slowly. But as she gets back on her feet, she hisses and clutches at her chest. She looks over at me, her gaze filled with agony.

Fuck, did I miss something?

I move toward her and open my mouth to ask her what's going on.

"My Chosen," she whimpers, and then just like that, she shoots into the sky and takes off like a fighter jet.

I stare at her wake, confused. *Her Chosen?* Does she have

more than just... My thoughts trail off as I realize what just happened.

The guys are in trouble.

I shove magic into my legs and sprint for the door. I seriously need to fucking learn how to fly. I slam through the wood out into the open air and scare the shit out of Ory, who was standing there looking at the sky. I skid to a stop.

"Fly me to where she's going!" I shout at him.

"What?" he asks. "What happened? Where is she going?" he demands, looking back up at the sky like he expects Suryn to be there.

"I don't fucking know, but someone must be hurt. Follow her and take me with you!" I scream at him again, panic burning up my throat. I'm wasting time here, but if this birdbrain can pull his head out of his ass, he'll get me wherever she's going faster than running will.

I stomp over to him and wrap my arms around his neck without waiting for his permission. "Go!" I bellow at him, and the order finally spurs him to action. Ory wraps strong arms around my waist, crouches down slightly, and then blasts us up into the air like a fucking rocket. I tighten my hold around his neck and try to search the sky for Suryn.

The flap of his massive wings blocks my view, but I don't risk trying to turn around midair so I can track the Sentinel that's tied to my Shields. Ory pulls me tighter against him, and we snap right. I think we're headed in the direction of the castle, which sends fear crawling up my insides.

Stupid, stupid, stupid fucking Sentinel. You left your Chosen and Shields behind so you could have a temper tantrum in private. I fucking knew the Sovereign was going to try something. I'm a fucking idiot.

"You don't know that's what's happening," Ory tells me as we drop slightly, and I tighten my grip even more.

"Are you reading my mind?" I demand as I try to get my bearings.

"No, you're screaming into my ear. Something else could be happening, so just calm your glowy shit down so we can assess the situation before you magic fry people," he tells me.

Sure enough, when I look down, I see that my runes are glowing purple. I have to stop myself from reaching out to the guys mentally. *What have I always said about distractions in the middle of a fight?* I remind myself over and over as Ory circles the side of the castle and aims for a broken wall of windows that looks terrifyingly familiar.

I don't feel anything that would indicate that my Chosen are hurt, but that doesn't reassure me as much as I'd like as we dive through the wall of shattered glass, passing the table that's pushed up against it. I immediately recognize what was my suite of rooms in the castle, but it's pure fucking pandemonium inside. I call on my long sword and clap the hilt to make it two weapons. I send out a pulse of Sentinel magic that sends fighters in my immediate vicinity flying through the air, and then I stop in my tracks as sky-blue eyes and blonde hair come walking toward me out of the crowd.

I shake my head, trying to understand what I'm seeing. No. No, no, no, no, no… It's not fucking possible. I take a step back and try to understand what's happening. Laiken? How the fuck is my dead little sister here?

29

She walks slowly toward me, and I can feel a sob working its way up my throat.

"How?" I ask her, lowering my weapons as I search her face for some kind of explanation.

Her soft giggle fills my mind as she begs me to play the slap game. She places her small hands in mine, and I wait to pounce on her and tap her hands before she can pull them away. She laughs and laughs as I get her over and over again. We're so carefree and happy in this moment that I never want it to end. I blink and that memory fades. *I'm back in the field with the soft green grass and little white flowers.*

"I spread your ashes," I tell her, stunned, as I try to make sense of what's going on, her happy giggle still ringing in my ears.

Ory is in the background, spinning so fast that his wings are cutting people down. But I can't focus on him or the other fights going on all around me—all I can see is her.

Laiken doesn't say anything as she closes the distance. The look in her eyes is hard, which confuses me even more. Why is she mad? But before I can ask her any of this, she shoves a sword through my chest. I gasp, shocked by the pain of the wound. The pain in my soul as my Laiken twists the blade and leans into me.

"Die," she growls at me, spittle flying from her rose pink lips to land on my tear-streaked cheeks.

I choke on pain and sorrow as her hate-filled gaze bores into me. Gone are my memories of her sweet laugh and her kind voice. In this moment, as Laiken looks me in the eye and demands my death, all the good I know of her turns to ash in my mind. I'm so fucking confused, and everything inside of me feels like it's fracturing.

"No," I plead, and I can't tell if I'm answering her order or begging for this not to be happening.

This isn't right. None of this is right. Wake up, Vinna. Wake the fuck up!

Laiken pulls the sword from my chest, a sickening smile on her face. She pulls her arm back, and I can tell from the angle that my little sister, my guardian angel, is about to cut off my head. My instincts scream for me to do something, and just as the blade arcs down toward me, I lift one hand to block it and shove my long sword through her throat with the other. I scream as I watch her eyes go from merciless to shocked. She collapses, and I let go of my weapons to catch her and pull her into my lap.

Tears stream down my face and drip onto her as she gasps for air and chokes on her own blood.

"I'm sorry. Oh fuck, I'm so sorry," I tell her over and over again, my soul slowly being pulverized with each empty gasp she takes.

I go to heal her wound, not caring if she tries to kill me again. I can't just sit and watch her die. I can't kill her. She's my Little Laik. I reach up to her throat, but in a blink, I'm suddenly staring at a man.

What the fuck?

Terror floods me, and I push him out of my lap and

scramble back away from the still gasping body. My body lights up with pain, and I call on Siah's runes and fix myself. I search the room for Laiken, trying to understand what the fuck just happened. Then it dawns on me. It was never her.

A gasping sob tears out of me with the realization. And I cover my mouth to trap another one trying to escape. It's chaos and mayhem all around me, but all I can do is try to hold the pieces of me together and watch the man I stabbed in the throat take his last breath. I look up and see Talon across the room, fighting Sorik. I don't spot Suryn or any of my Shields, but my blood runs cold when Bastien screams, "Vinna, no, it's me!"

The anguish and betrayal that rings out in his voice hit me like a truck. I'm on my feet in seconds, running for him as he drops his sword and shakes his head. He's fighting a woman who looks nothing like me, and if I hadn't just had my heart shredded by what just happened with Laiken, I wouldn't understand anything that's going on right now.

I scream in rage as I bring my sword down and cut the bitch fighting Bastien in two. Bastien roars out a lament and reaches for imposter me as he looks up with vengeance in his gaze. His pain and anger tear at me, but when his agonized and enraged hazel stare meets mine, shock and disbelief are suddenly all I see. He reaches for me and pulls me to him.

"What just happened?" he begs me as he runs his hands and eyes all over my body to make sure I'm actually there and okay.

"They're illusions. Very, very fucking good illusions," I pant at him as he wraps his arm around me. "Bastien, if you see me again, ask me what the code word is, and if I don't say pineapple, kill me. Okay?" I tell him, but he looks so fucking haunted, I don't think anything is sinking in.

"Bastien!" I yell in his head, and he blinks out of his

horrified stupor. *"Use the runes. We need to talk in each other's heads. There's no way to know what's really going on otherwise."*

I light up all my runes and shout into my Chosen's heads. It goes against every instinct not to distract them, but how else are we going to be able to tell what's happening?

"If any of you are fighting me right now, kill her. Someone here is creating very powerful illusions, and what's in front of you is not what you think!" I tell them.

"You mean Bastien is not trying to kill me?" Valen asks, his mental tone filled with heartache and confusion.

"Never, Val! I would never!" Bastien confirms, and then he runs off in the direction of where Valen is and cuts off the head of the Sentinel he's fighting.

"Vinna, go wolf mode!" Torrez yells in my head. *"You can smell whether it's us or not if we try to approach you."*

"Got it," I confirm as I activate Torrez's marks on my shoulder, tapping into the extra smell and deactivating the change in sight it usually causes. Wolf vision is not going to help me in this cluster fuck of a battle.

I wrinkle my nose as the sour stench of fear and the metallic tang of anger flood my senses. I stab through the back of Talon, telling myself over and over again it's not him. I invite fury and wrath to take over everything inside of me. Sorik holds up his short swords threateningly as I approach him.

"Sorik, it's me, Vinna. I'm not going to hurt you," I tell him as I drop my weapon.

"Yeah, not buying that since that's what the last you told me," he growls, and my heart hurts for him.

"You are my mom's Chosen. I first saw you in a club. I thought you looked like an ancient Viking. You helped save me when Faron kidnapped me. You crossed into Silas pack territory where you showed me your runes and told me who you were. That was the first time I saw Siah."

"Thank fuck," Sorik declares as he steps in to give me a tight desperate hug. "They can't answer personal things. They look like other people and sound like other people, but they don't know details," he tells me, and I immediately relay that back to my Chosen.

Someone charges me from behind, and I spin and slam my sword through the chest of the Colossal Douche I fought and beat the night I met Lachlan and his coven. *Whoever is doing this can't differentiate between people we care about and just people in our past.* There's a flaw in however their ability works. Ryker moves toward me, his face haunted. I breathe in deeply and get a nose full of fear and disbelief. Under that though is a clean scent of sun-dried cotton, santolina, and amber.

"Ryker!" I shout into his mind and release the magic to any weapons in my hands. *"It's me,"* I reassure him, and he crashes into me, burying his head in my neck and squeezing me so hard my bones are protesting. Shouts and the clang of weapons all around us keep me centered in the battle raging all around us and keep me from getting lost in his hold the way I want to.

"I've killed you three times," he confesses, his bright blue eyes haunted. "I knew it wasn't you, you would never attack us, but I don't think I'm ever going to get the image of you dying out of my head."

"I'm so fucking sorry," I tell him, squeezing him tighter. "I'm here, I'm in your arms. I'm safe. We need to make sure everyone else is too though," I explain, pushing out of his hold.

Ryker nods and sticks with me as we cut our way through the fighting. Sabin comes running for us. I breathe him in, but the scent is all wrong. I throw a dagger, and Sabin's feet go out from under him as it hits him so hard in the throat he flies back. Ryker's words and tormented gaze resonate through me as I watch Sabin die. I know it's not him, but it doesn't make the visual any less fucking traumatizing.

"Vinna, Enoch and his coven are cornered in the back bedroom on your left," Siah tells me. *"I'm trying to get through to them, but I have to kill off my whole family..."* he trails off, and white hot rage surges through me.

When I find whoever the fuck is responsible for this repeating nightmare, I'm going to strangle them with their own guts. I run in the direction where Siah must be. I don't know what's going to be more fucked up to him, having to kill people that look like his long lost, dead family or watching your mate cut them down. I don't see what Siah sees, thank fuck, but I know his siblings were kids when some of them died, and I don't want to think of the scar it will leave on him to watch them cut down, even when he knows it's not actually them.

"Siah, close your eyes," I mentally shout at him as I break through the ring of Sentinels that are surrounding him.

He does it without question, and I'm so fucking grateful and honored by his trust. Ryker and I start cutting them down, and they go from random strangers I don't recognize to people I know in a blink. I cut off Mave's arm and then stab her through the heart. The sisters lose their heads one by one, and then Beth steps into my path.

I shake my head at this illusion. "You got the wrong face," I tell the Sentinel behind the illusion. Beth stabs me in the stomach with a short spear-looking thing. I push forward against it and shove my hands against her chest. Flames erupt all over her, and she screams as they lick up her body and catch her hair on fire.

I've always wondered how I would feel if I could give Beth a taste of what she dished out to me my whole life. Would it make me feel better to starve her and beat her?

Would I find comfort in verbally tearing her down and breaking her like she so often tried to do with me? I watch Beth fall to the ground, completely engulfed in flames, and realize the answer is *no*. It doesn't change anything.

Ryker quickly dispatches the last of Siah's attackers, and I reach up and caress Siah's face.

"It's over," I tell him softly, and he opens his eyes and leans into my hand.

"Thank you," he whispers, his voice pained.

"I've got you," I tell him, our vow coming full circle.

I give him a soft smile and then move away in the direction of the room he said Enoch and the others are trapped in. Valen and Bastien join us, and relief spreads through me when they smell right. There's a bottleneck of people at the doorway into the room. The presence of so many of us makes it easier to identify the enemy. The illusions seem to work better when it's more one on one. It's as if the magic can really only focus on the people in one person's life at a time.

With me, Ryker, Siah, Valen and Bastien there, the people stuffed in and around the entryway take on various identities. Laiken comes for me again, as does Keegan. Bastien cuts them both down before they can take two steps in my direction. Ryker cuts through Silva and a woman I recognize from a picture Bastien has in his room.

"It's not real," I yell at Bastien and Valen as they both watch Ryker slit their mother's throat.

Tears well in Valen's eyes, and he blinks rapidly to clear the emotion away. My throat gets tight. I want to scream and punish and kill these fuckers for putting the ones I love through this torture.

I call on my short swords and get to work. My Chosen and I move like the unit we are as we weave in and out of each other, spinning, dipping, bending and leading in a death dance. One dead Sentinel at a time, we make it inside the room. I step over bodies and through the doorway. I find Enoch, Kallan, Nash and Becket each battling several Sentinels, while Suryn stands there...guarding the fucking Sovereign.

I take one look at the leader of the Sentinels and know exactly who we have to thank for today's trauma fest. I'm surprised she's even down here getting her hands dirty, but maybe she has to be within a certain proximity to keep the illusions up. Neither she nor Suryn have noticed that we've just walked in on their little party. The Sovereign's entire focus is on Suryn, while her stare is locked on my Shields.

I don't know what illusion the Sovereign is making Suryn see or if she's even making her see an illusion. Didn't she say something in the hall that night about getting Suryn on board. Maybe Suryn, the first in line to rule the Sentinels, doesn't give two fucks about the males her magic has marked getting slaughtered in front of her.

As soon as that thought enters my mind, it feels wrong. The way she reacted at the training facility isn't the way someone reacts when they don't care. She may talk the Sovereign's talk when it comes to Enoch, Kallan, Becket, and Nash, but I don't actually think she believes it. At least not the way the Sovereign and her cronies do.

There's a glimmer in the air around the Sovereign and Suryn. I study them and try to drown out the battle cries and sounds of weapons and magic clashing all around me as my Chosen unleash hell on the Sentinels attacking my Shields. Suryn doesn't take her eyes off of what's happening, and the Sovereign stares at her with such intensity it makes the hair on my arms rise. I move fluidly against the wall, chanting a steady mantra of *you don't see me, you don't see me.*

The massive bed in the room splinters as Sabin picks up a Sentinel by the throat and slams him down on top of it.

Furniture is reduced to a pile of rubble as it's used as a weapon or a projectile, and still Suryn and the Sovereign seem unfazed. I push magic out toward the barrier, but I can't get a feel for what comprises it. It doesn't feel threatening, more like a magic brick wall of some sort. I approach from behind and place a hand against the barrier.

It gives as I push against it, and I hesitate. I can get through here. Unease strikes through me as the words *too easy* twist around in my head. No one has noticed that I'm here, and I push further into the magic wall around the Sovereign. It feels similar to when I walked through the barrier into Tierit. I shove through it and call on my throwing knives as I surface on the other side.

I shake off the staticky feeling that coats my limbs and pull my hand back, ready to end the Sovereign and her reign of terror. And that's when she looks over her shoulder at me and smiles.

30

Her lips pull back in a grin filled with pure malevolence, and my blood turns to ice in my veins.

"Nice of you to join us," she coos venomously, and then she flings out her palm and slams me square in the chest with a white bolt of pain. I'm shoved back against the now rock hard interior of the barrier, so hard I can hear my bones crack.

I can't even scream, it all happens so fast. I make a haunting, gurgling sound as my vision tunnels, and my skin starts to feel like it's melting off my fracturing bones. I can't think through what the fuck is happening, my mind is so overwhelmed by pain.

A tinkling laugh fills my ears. "Thought you could just waltz in here and play the hero," the Sovereign tuts and then sends another bolt of pure torture into me with her other hand.

I can taste the blood gurgling up my throat, and whatever it is she's doing...is killing me. I try to call on my weapons, but nothing happens. I beg my runes to give me their shields and protect me, but my magic doesn't respond.

I grit my teeth until they feel like they're going to crumble to nothing in my mouth, and reach out to grasp the white bolt hammering into my chest.

It feels like lava in my hand, and I look down, fully expecting my limb to crumble to ash, but it doesn't. It fucking hurts, but it's still there. I tighten my grasp, and like I'm kinking a hose, the stream of agony flowing into me tapers. I reach out with my other hand and grab the second bolt the Sovereign shot into me. I grip it as tightly as I can, and the mind-numbing pain diminishes just enough to give me hope that there's some way to survive this.

I hold onto the bolts like the misery-filled lifelines they are. I push away from the barrier I'm pancaked against, each step feeling like it's taking every ounce of energy I have. I stare at the Sovereign, her waning sneer my only goal. Surprise flickers through her eyes as I hold onto the bolts and take one more staggering step toward her.

She tries to close her palm but can't. She stares down at her hand like it's betrayed her, and I can see her try to force it into a fist. I think she's trying to cut off whatever she's doing to me, but she can't. She scowls up at me, her eyes glittering with malice. She looks down at where I have a stranglehold on her magic, and snarls.

The Sovereign yanks her hand back, and the bolt of torment slips slightly out of my grip. I don't know what will happen if she can retract the crackling pain filled strikes, but I'm not about to find out. She tries to dislodge them from my grasp again, and I almost lose my balance, trying to hold on to them, and I cry out as I struggle to keep my feet underneath me.

"Suryn!" the Sovereign screams out.

I look over and watch as Suryn's head snaps from where she's still watching the fighting, over to us. She blinks and shakes her head like she's trying to clear it, and then it registers in her eyes and features what's going on. Suryn looks away from the struggle between the Sovereign and me out into the room. She cries out and slams a hand against the barrier. She slams a fist and then another against the magic trapping her and growls out her frustration.

I look away from Suryn's struggle to get out, and wrap the beam of agony around one wrist and then the other. Anguish sears through me at the contact, but I use the white bolts as leverage to get me closer to the Sovereign. If I can just get within striking distance. I don't fucking care if it kills me in the end to try, but at least I can take the bitch with me.

I glare at the Sovereign, vengeance and death flaring in my eyes.

Let's see how good this bitch is at tug of war.

I wrap the beams around my arms again and scream from the pain that hammers through me.

"Suryn!" the Sovereign shrieks in time with my voiced agony. "Kill her and I'll spare your Marked," she offers, and Suryn turns away from the barrier back to us. "Kill her and no one will ever touch your Chosen again. I vow it, Suryn!" the Sovereign bellows, and my screams rip my voice in half. Blood dribbles out from my clenched teeth. I'm dying, but I can't let go.

Something massive slams against the barrier. I look to find Sabin tearing at the magic and shouting my name. I can't hear him, but I can see his lips call out to me, his eyes frenzied and anguished. Bastien shoulders the barrier next to him, and not too far away from them, I spot Becket hammering the magic with his mace.

My screams are nothing but blood-filled gurgles as I tense and make another loop around my arms, bringing myself one step closer to the Sovereign. My legs feel jellied, and I know I won't be able to stay on my feet much longer. Deafening thumps sound off all around me as the barrier is hammered by all of my Chosen and my Shields. Rage and terror streak through them as they soundlessly scream and scramble to get in.

"Swear a blood oath that all of us will be safe, Aunt. That no one will lay a hand on them or on me," Suryn shouts out, her words partially drowned out by the booming efforts of all the guys trying to force their way in here.

The Sovereign narrows her eyes, and her pursed lips form a snarl.

"That's what I thought," Suryn growls, and then she leaps for the Sovereign, her katana glinting in the flashing magic that's doing its best to kill me.

I hold my breath and will her to close the distance and end this once and for all. My knees give out. I fall to the floor and lose my hold on one of the bolts. It snaps back to the Sovereign. I try—and fail—to get to my feet to stop her from shoving her palm out at Suryn. The strike of white undiluted pain surges out of the Sovereign's palm. I watch like it's in slow motion as it crackles toward Suryn. It slams into her mid-leap, and it's like watching someone get hit by a semi-truck. Suryn folds in on herself and is thrown back, the katana blinking to nothing in her grip. She screams a blood curdling scream that I feel scar my soul.

The Sovereign watches her niece writhing in pain, with an unhinged look of glee that makes me feel sick and tainted just from witnessing it. I grab the bolt of pain still wrapped around my right arm with my other hand and pull at it, using it to help me get to my feet. I wrap it around my arm again and close the distance even more.

Five feet.

Four.

Suryn's screams make my ears bleed.

Three.

I look over at the thundering fists against the barrier.

Two.

Tears stream down my face. Blood seeps out of my mouth. I try to call a weapon, any weapon, into my hands. Nothing comes.

One.

The Sovereign looks away from Suryn and right at me. Her brown eyes gleam with victory. She knows I've got nothing left. The ones I love pound impotently on the barrier all around us, and Suryn's screams are cracking and splintering as her voice starts to give out.

I look away from her hate filled triumph and look to my Chosen.

"I love you," I mouth, blood spattering my chin and chest as my eyes connect with each of them in turn.

Ryker places his hands helplessly against the barrier, agony twisting his features and soundlessly screams out *no*. Torrez howls out his frustration and hurt and slams against the barrier harder and harder. Siah's features morph into a snarl as he claws at the magic in an effort to get to me. Valen screams for me to hold on as his eyes pool with pain. Knox roars, his face filled with rage as he prowls like a caged tiger, trying to find a way in. Bastien's cheeks are streaked with tears, and he begs me to stay, over and over. Sabin shakes his head as he cries, and he mouths "I love you" back.

"I'm sorry," I tell them, my heart breaking as I do. I can feel my soul fracturing as I turn away from them and focus back on the Sovereign.

Suryn's screams have morphed into a gravelly keening, and the Sovereign's gaze flits from her to me again. I tighten my hold on the beam wrapped around my arm with my right hand and let go with my left. The Sovereign's eyes widen with surprise as I reach out and grab onto the other bolt she's feeding into Suryn. I yank it as hard as I can, and it snaps from Suryn, to me. I throw my head back in a silent scream as the beam of white pain slams into me.

My legs give out once again, and I crumble to the ground, but this time I keep my hold on the Sovereign's lethal magic. There's nothing I can do to stop her, but maybe I can buy Suryn more time. Maybe they'll figure out a way to break through the barrier and get to her. I just need to hold on to the Sovereign's magic as long as possible.

Black dots swarm my vision, and I start to go numb. I tighten my hold on the Sovereign's magic and sway as I try to stay on my knees at her feet. She stares down at me, as life leaks out of me, and says something my ears can no longer hear. I open my blood stained lips to mouth one last "fuck you" to her, when out of nowhere, her head leans to the side at an odd, unnatural angle. I watch it, confusion sparking through my pain muddled mind, and then the Sovereign's head slips off her shoulders all together and falls to the ground next to me.

The Sovereign's headless body falls a moment later, revealing Suryn behind it. My body gives out, and I completely collapse. I stare at the dead eyes in the Sovereign's severed head, and relief wafts through me. I close my eyes, no longer able to keep them open.

I can go now. They'll be safe.

And that's the last thought I can think as death reaches out and wraps its cloak all around me. I snuggle into it as it warms me, and then the blackness takes over everything that I am.

* * *

Bright light flashes on the other side of my closed lids. I try to turn away from it, but no matter what I do, I can't seem to escape it. I breathe out a deep irritated sigh and open my eyes. The light is blinding, and I quickly slam my lids shut.

"Fuck, someone turn down the light," I grumble, and a deep laugh resonates around me. I squint to see where it's coming from and can make out blurry black hair, olive-toned skin, and green eyes.

Surprise flashes through me, along with resignation and peace.

"Hey, where's Keegan?" I ask Lachlan as his lips stretch into a happy and welcoming smile.

I try to sit up and grunt from how stiff I feel. He leaps out of his chair and helps me.

"He's not here, Vinna," Lachlan tells me, his tone solemn, and my throat gets tight.

"Shit. I'm so sorry. Maybe we can find him together," I offer, and my uncle's eyes fill with warmth and emotion.

"You don't have to worry about that," he tells me. "Just rest, and I'll be right here if you need anything," he reassures me, and I can't help but give him the side eye.

Lachlan sure is a fuck-ton nicer now that he's dead. Although I suppose whatever happens after we die could maybe do that to a person. I take stock of myself, and I'm not surprised to feel a million times better than I did before I ended up here. Wherever here is.

I look around and snort at the cliché tones of cream and white that cover everything. Why do I have to pee? Guess that kind of crap stays with you in the afterlife, go figure.

"So how are you?" I ask Lachlan as I double-check that I'm dressed and then push the covers off of me.

I'm decked out in some kind of shift—it's white of

course. The color palette is definitely going to get old around here quick.

Lachlan snorts and rubs his hand over his face. "I'm good. Adjusting. It's all a lot to take in," he confesses, and I nod my head.

"How are you?" he asks me, his earnest gaze searching my face. "I still can't even believe you're here and that I'm talking to you."

I mirror his actions and rub a hand over my face. "I honestly don't know. I feel better, which is good. Nothing hurts. I guess I just don't know what happens now...you know?" I ask him, running my gaze around the room like the answers will come floating out of the walls.

The door opens, and more light floods into the room. I hold my breath to see who will walk in. Some kind of spirit guide? My mom? Laiken? Ryker walks in, and his eyes go wide. He leaps for me, and I'm wrapped up in his arms so fast, *home* slamming into me with his tight embrace.

"Fuck, Squeaks, that was the worst fucking thing I've ever been through," he whispers against my hair, and then his lips are on mine.

His kiss is reverent, and I reach up and wipe the tears off his cheeks as he pours his sadness and joy into me. I get lost in his lips, and then it hits me like a ton of bricks.

Ryker is *here.*

I push back, separating myself from him, panic in my eyes as I trace his face with a heartbroken gaze.

"No, no, no, no, no! You were supposed to be okay. How are you here?" I shout and spring up on the bed.

Ryker looks confused for a moment, but before he can say anything, Bastien, Valen, Knox, Siah, Sabin, and Torrez come barging into the room. They look exhausted. Relief, sadness, excitement and several other things haunt their eyes and expressions. I want to scream.

Tears pour out of me, and I scramble back when Bastien reaches for me.

"No," I yell at him, and he jerks back, hurt flickering in his eyes. "You shouldn't be here!"

I pull at my hair, my chest heavy. I watched the Sovereign die...

"Who was it?" I demand. "Was it Suryn? I swear to fuck if it was her, I'm haunting her ass forever! What a fucking cunt! I save her ass, and she pulls this?"

"Vinna, what the fuck are you talking about?" Valen questions, and I pause.

"Who killed you?" I demand again, and he reels back, dumbfounded. "We're going to fuck them up; I don't care if we're all ghosts or angels or whatever, we will find a way to make it happen," I tell them.

I spin to see if I have wings or anything on my back. "Do we get wings and shit?" I ask, turning to look at Lachlan. He's been doing this whole afterlife thing longer and would know.

"Bruiser, we're not dead," Bastien declares.

My gaze snaps to his, and I stare at him for a moment, confused.

Shit, do they not know they're dead? Maybe they didn't see it coming like I did. Fucking Suryn.

"I'm sorry, Bas, but you are," I tell him softly, moving toward the end of the bed so I can hug him.

"No, I'm not," he repeats with an incredulous snort.

My eyes fill with pity. Poor guy's in denial. I look for Sabin. He's always rational, he'll help everyone to see. I find his forest green gaze. It's filled with love and warmth, and it makes my stomach go all gooey.

"You know you're dead, right?" I ask him, and his eyes search both of mine for a beat.

"Why do you think you're dead, Vinna?" he asks me

303

simply, and I snort out a humorless laugh.

"Because I felt myself die. I got all warm and fuzzy. Everything went black. I woke up in the white monochromatic room and had a whole conversation with Lachlan," I tell him, and understanding flares in his eyes.

Finally. Now we can get past this whole *shit, I'm dead* thing and get right into *who the fuck do we need to haunt for making it happen.*

"Vinna, I'm not Lachlan," Lachlan says, stepping toward me.

"Oookay," I drawl with a titter. "Who the fuck are you then?"

"I'm...I'm your dad. I'm Vaughn," he answers, and my amused smile falls right off my face.

"What?" I whisper, stunned.

I take a step back away from everyone and look around confused.

"I'm not dead?" I croak, my voice bleeding emotion and shock.

Valen reaches for me, but I back away, feeling overwhelmed and reeling.

What the fuck is going on?

My eyes well up, and I look from Vaughn to my Chosen, completely lost.

"How?" I ask, and everyone's eyes soften.

"When the Sovereign died, the barrier fell. That warm feeling you felt was all of us pushing Healing magic in to you. The blackness was you passing out, not dying," Sabin tells me, his eyes suddenly filled with unshed tears. He reaches out, and this time I take his hand. I need him to help me feel tethered, to help me process what the fuck he's saying.

Emotion slams into me, and a sob works its way out of my mouth. I slam my hand over it and then fall on the bed and cry. I'm so fucking happy and shattered and over-whelmed that I just collapse into a pile of sobs. Comforting hands rub my back and arms and legs. Someone strokes my hair slowly, and they all just let me break, their touch and reassuring words promising they'll help me put it all back together again.

Gradually my soul-racking sobs taper, and my tears slow. I purge the desolation and anguish one salty drop at a time until it no longer weighs me down. I wipe at my face and lift my head. My eyes lock on Vaughn's, and he wipes at his wet cheeks.

"Hi," I tell him, no clue what else to say in this situation.

He smiles, and we both give a watery chuckle. "Hi," he answers back, and then he hugs me.

His arms lock in a vice-like grip around me, and his chest shakes from the sobs working their way out of him. I hold my dad as he takes his turn breaking. I hold him tight and let him know it's okay, because we'll help him put it all back together when he's done. I have no idea how he's here, holding me, but it's a story that can wait. I can't even imagine what he's been through. But in this moment, his embrace is so much more than I could have ever hoped for.

I don't know how long we stay like that. Father and daughter slowly piecing themselves back together. When we separate, I'm immediately pulled into another set of waiting arms. I hug Bastien hard, and we breathe each other in. Valen steals me next, burying his hands in my hair and kissing me gently. Knox shoves his way in and lifts me into his arms. My feet dangle as he holds me, our locked arms offering the reassurance that we're both desperate for.

Torrez peels Knox's arms from around me and sits down on the bed and pulls me into his lap. He tears the neck of my shirt and rests his head against his runes on my shoulder. I run my fingers through his black hair, fortifying our bond with each breath and each stroke of my fingers.

Siah sinks down next to Torrez and pulls me in to his own lap. We stare at each other for a while, and I take this moment to replace the last memory I had of his pained face on the other side of the barrier with this image of his love-filled features.

Ryker extends his hand out to me, and I take it and step out of Siah's hold. Ryker cradles my face and kisses me again softly. None of us say anything. We don't need to. I can feel and see what this did to all of them. The relief is palpable. It was a close call, and none of us will ever be the same because of it. We take time and breathe each other in. We offer what physical reassurances we can in this moment. It's going to take time to feel secure again and not haunted by the way death was breathing down my back. But we'll get there, and when we do, we'll be even stronger for it.

31

I stare at myself in the steamy mirror, studying my face. I look rested and as far from the deathbed as I can get. The guys told me I had been out for three days. Three agonizing days when they weren't sure I would wake up at all. It felt like a blink to me. I tilt my chin back and study the new rune on the underside of my chin. The line of the simple circle is thick and black, and when I tilt my head back down you can't even tell it's there. The guys said it showed up as they were trying to heal me. None of us are sure exactly what it does, but I have an idea. One I'm not ready to think too hard about yet.

I run my fingers through my wet hair, and a soft knock sounds on the door. It cracks open, and Ryker's gorgeous blue eyes meet mine in the mirror.

"I brought you clothes," he announces as he steps into the bathroom.

I look down at the pile, expecting black and leather, but instead Ryker is holding soft looking magenta fabric. I make an icked out face, and Ryker chortles.

"Marn told me you had to wear a dress for this," he tells

me sheepishly. "You know there's no arguing with her when it comes to this shit," he adds, and I chuckle.

He sets it on the bathroom counter and turns to leave.

"Where do you think you're going?" I tease. "Who's going to help me get this thing on? The dresses here are always complicated."

Sure enough, I hold it up and immediately think there's not enough fabric here. The dresses themselves are relatively simple and Grecian-esque; what's complicated is making sure all my bits are fucking covered.

Ryker grins and steps back toward me. I slip the thin material over my head. It's softer than silk as it caresses down my body and pools at the ground. The straps on each of my shoulders have magenta leather wrapped around them at the top of my shoulder. The gathered fabric dips down my chest into a *V* and leads into a flowy skirt that has the ever popular slit up to my hip bone on one side. The *V* of the top plunges so low that all of my Chosen marks are visible between my breasts.

Ryker holds up a smooth leather piece with braided ties on each end. It's too small to be a corset but way too big to be a belt. I shrug, not sure how it's supposed to be worn. Ryker steps up behind me, his chest skimming my bare back as the dress dips deeply on that side too. He wraps his arms around me until the leather piece rests against my stomach. The top of it sits a couple inches below my boobs, and the bottom ends exactly at my waist.

Ryker wraps the braided ties behind me until it's tight but not too binding. The ties crisscross at the back, and he brings them forward and ties them together at the front. He makes a bow and the long ends of the two braided ties hang down the front of the dress. Ryker flattens his hands against my torso, and our eyes find each other's in the mirror again. We stare at each other, heat slowly building in our gazes and every part of my body that's touching his. He leans down slowly, his eyes never leaving mine, and kisses where my neck meets my shoulder.

Goosebumps rise up on my arms, and my nipples grow harder with each breath against my skin. I reach up and cup his head as he nips at my shoulder. With my other hand, I reach up and guide one of his hands from my torso slowly down my body. The air around us becomes heavy as his hand finds the slit in my dress. His fingertips move languidly across my lower abdomen.

My muscles twitch from the ticklish attention, and I rest my head back against his shoulder as we continue to stare at one another in the mirror. Ryker slips a finger between the lips of my pussy and strokes me reverently. I hum my approval and sink my fingers in the strands of his soft blond hair. As he trails kisses up my neck, he pulls the wet evidence of my desire up over my clit and begins to circle it slowly.

Someone knocks at the door and opens it before either Ryker or I can say anything. Sabin pokes his head in to say something, but he pauses when he takes in Ryker's hand and my hooded gaze. Ryker's small circles around my clit never even pause, and I try to bite back a moan as I wait for the Captain to tell us it's time to go or something else that puts a stop to the orgasm that Ryker's touch is working to coax out of me. Instead, Sabin steps into the bathroom and closes the door behind him.

In three steps, he's cradling my face and kissing me so thoroughly that it's making my head swim. His tongue plays with mine as Ryker's fingers tease my clit and dip back down between my wet lips. Sabin swallows my moan as Ryker pushes his finger into me. He skims my hips with his other hand and pulls the fabric of the dress all the way to the side. Sabin pulls away from my mouth as Ryker pushes two fingers inside of me and begins to circle my clit with his other hand. I turn to Ryker over my shoulder, and his lips are on mine before I even have to ask.

Sabin runs the tip of his nose around my hard, fabric-covered nipple and holds onto my hips as Ryker's mouth leaves me panting. He pulls away, and I turn to watch him play with my pussy in the mirror. Sabin pushes the deep *V* of my dress to the side and sucks my nipple into his mouth. Every part of me feels needy and heavy, and I squirm and revel in the feel of them. Their attentions are slow, reverent, and I feel precious and fragile in their hands.

An orgasm cascades through me, and Ryker whispers, "I love you," in my ear. I turn to kiss him again, and Sabin pulls my other breast free of my dress and moves his full lips to it. Ryker pulls the skirt of my dress up inch by unhurried inch. His touch falls away from me as he unties his pants. Sabin pulls away from my breast and looks up at me, his forest green gaze blazing with tender affection.

He grabs my face and pulls it down as he drops to his knees. I bend over in pursuit of his lips, and Ryker bunches my dress up above my hips. I spread my legs in invitation and steady myself on Sabin's shoulders. Ryker strokes my hips and lines himself up. He pushes inside of me, and I break away from my kiss with Sabin to moan.

"Fuck, you feel good," Ryker tells me as he pulls out and grinds back in.

I moan, and Sabin sucks on my bottom lip and then peppers kisses across my jaw. He pinches my nipples as Ryker increases his speed, and I cry out, loving every touch and stroke and thrust.

"That's it, Vinna," Sabin encourages as I mewl and groan and gasp. Ryker grips my hips tightly as he fucks me faster and harder with each thrust. I hold onto Sabin's shoulders as he moves his mouth to my ear.

"Do you know how beautiful you are right now?" he whispers into my ear and then nips at my lobe. I moan, and Ryker groans behind me. The sound of Ryker's hips slapping against my ass gets louder and louder as he fucks me harder and harder.

"Come, Vinna," Sabin tells me quietly, his mouth inches from my ear. "Come all over your mate's dick. Call his name as he worships your pussy."

Sabin's words push me over the edge, and I call out for Ryker and come all over his dick just as instructed. Ryker moans out my name in return as he thrusts in deeply and comes. I push off of Sabin's shoulders, arching my back to keep Ryker deep inside of me and reach for his face. I kiss him and whisper my "I love you" against his mouth as we pull apart to catch our breath.

Ryker pulls out of me, and the next thing I know, Sabin's lifting me up on the counter of the bathroom. My bare ass hits the cold stone of the counter, and I squeak out a protest. Sabin thrusts into me, turning that protest into a breathy moan. Ryker gives an amused snort as he watches us, and I flip him off playfully. Sabin bends down and sucks a nipple into his mouth at the same time he buries himself deep inside of me and grinds against my clit. I pant and throw my head back, relishing the feel of him.

"Eyes on mine, Vinna," he tells me. "You know how much I love to watch you come."

"Then make me come, Sabin," I order.

I pull his lips to mine and moan my encouragement as he speeds up. "I can't believe we almost lost you," he laments against my lips.

"I'm here. I'm not going anywhere," I promise, looking from his forest green gaze to Ryker's sky-blue one. "I'm here," I repeat, and Ryker steps to my side and kisses me deeply. I can taste the fear and worry in his kiss. I steal it from his lips and replace it with reassurance and devotion.

Sabin changes the angle of his thrusts, and I pull away from Ryker and ride the edge of another impending orgasm.

"Right there," I urge and run my nails up his back the way I know he loves.

"Never letting you out of my sight again," Sabin growls out, and I fall into bliss and sensation as I come again.

He stills deep inside of me, and I watch him lose himself to his orgasm. His cheeks are flushed and his hair disheveled. I look at Ryker, surveying his *kiss swollen lips* and *just fucked hair*. I chuckle, loving it when my Chosen look like this.

"Fuck, we're going to be late," Sabin comments as he grinds against me again.

I laugh and roll my eyes. "I'm game for round two if you guys are."

Sabin nips at my bottom lip and boops my nose. He pulls out of me and steps back, grinning at the overexaggerated pout I give him.

"Nope, you have to go, and you know it," Sabin states, his tone brooking no argument. My greedy vagina clenches, loving it when he gets all growly and demanding.

"Tok and Marn would have our heads, and I for one like where my head currently is, thank you very much," Ryker declares.

I look down at his pants-clad crotch and arch an eyebrow. "I personally like it better when your head is buried deep inside of me, but maybe that's just me."

I wink and hop off the counter as he swats me with a towel. I snag it from his hands and clean up. I tuck my breasts back into my dress and straighten everything the way it should be. *Maybe these slits and deep Vs aren't so bad after all.*

I quickly dry my hair into loose flowing curls and step back to study my reflection. Ryker and Sabin watch me, and I tilt my head appreciatively, a salacious smile slowly spreading across my face.

"No," Sabin commands, and I roll my eyes.

I salute him. "Aye, aye, Captain!"

Sabin shakes his head and fights a smile. "Be good and we'll all make sure you're screaming our names *all* night long," he tells me, and a shiver of desire snakes up my spine.

"Fine, but if this goes bad, you guys are going to owe me non-stop orgasms every day for fucking ever," I warn them both.

"Pshhh, pretty sure you're in for that even if this goes well," Ryker tells me. "Sabin's right, none of us have any intention of letting you out of our sight again, and the easiest way to do that is to never let you out of bed. Now let's go," Ryker orders, and I squeak again as he slaps me on the ass.

"They're gonna kick our asses, aren't they?" Ryker asks Sabin as we make our way out of the bathroom.

"They knew you were a goner when you didn't come back out five seconds after you went in. It's me they're gonna harass. I was supposed to be the levelheaded one."

I chuckle and internally high-five my vagina. *Go us, corrupting the incorruptible.*

Sabin steps in front of me and opens the bedroom door for me. "You look ravishing, Vinna," he tells me as I walk past, and I get all girly and smiley.

"Mm-hmmm," Ryker agrees from behind me. "I'm looking forward to eating you all up later."

Heat burns low in my stomach, but I don't have enough time to say anything that will get him as equally hot and bothered as he just got me. The rest of my Chosen are all lounging in the massive main room that our new bedroom feeds into. After the battle in our old suite, we've been moved and massively upgraded. Bastien, Valen and Torrez rise to their feet from the plush cream sofas. Siah and Knox push off from the walls they're leaning against.

Knox reaches for my hand and gives me a good twirl.

"You look stunning," he tells me. "No wonder they caved. Fuck, I'd still have you in there." I laugh and give him a quick peck.

"Fuck it, let's go!" he declares and moves to throw me over his shoulder.

"Whoa!" the guys all shout out and intercept him.

"Everyone is already down there, we're late, let's go," Siah announces and pulls a grumbling Knox away from me.

I huff but fall in step with them as they lead the way out of our suite. Our new digs put us closer to all the action, and in less than five minutes, we're standing outside of tall, black, ornately carved doors. My guys surround me, and I'm nestled in the middle of all their strength and support. I take a deep breath and blow it out slowly. The doors open, and Bastien and Valen step to the side so I can walk forward.

A guard slams his fist over his bicep and then turns to announce my arrival.

"All hail Sovereign Aylin, Ruler of Tierit, Bond Restorer, Liberator of Illusions, the Found Sentinel, Collar Breaker, the Prime Marked, and Gate Keeper."

He steps aside with a nod, his booming announcement still echoing around the walls of the packed room. I swallow back my unease.

Fuck, I'm pretty much never going to get used to that.

32

I step into the room. At once, everyone places their fist over their bicep in greeting. They move so precisely and in sync that it gives me the chills, and I'm honored by the show of respect. It's a far cry from how I thought I'd be received, that's for fucking sure. It's standing room only, it seems, in here, but the crowd parts as much as they can to allow me through to the large round table at the center. This space feels very different from the last time I was here being questioned by the tribunal. There's a vitality and hum of excitement around me that feels contagious.

Tok pulls out a chair next to him, and I give him a happy smile as I make my way over to it and sit down.

"You look absolutely regal, Vinna," he tells me.

I snort and try not to roll my eyes. No matter what I tell him, he's still convinced that the *Sovereign* title is going to stick.

The room starts to settle as we all take our seats. I look over to see Suryn on the other side of the table, Tawv and her dad, Sauriel, on each side of her. Enoch, Nash, Kallan, and Becket are seated off to her right, and I study them and then her. I haven't seen any of them since the big turn up in my room after I woke up, and I wonder how everyone has been doing since then.

"You look well," Suryn tells me with a polite nod.

I give her an equally polite nod in return. "You do too," I reply.

Tawv rises from his seat, and the quiet muttering in the room stops. "We are gathered here today to come to discuss which of the interim Sovereigns should lead the people. We will hear arguments for and against, with a final vote being cast three days from now. Let us begin."

Tawv sits down, and Tok springs out of his seat like a bullet. He starts in on our lineage and the way of our people, talking about the Ouphe, The Light Marked, and the Sentinels as if they represented different times in our past. I tune him out and watch as Enoch, Kallan, and Nash sneak side glances at Suryn. What's funny to me is that she sneaks glances at them too when they're not looking. They play an entertaining game of cat and mouse with their peeks at one another. I watch them, oddly riveted, and find I'm quickly invested in whether or not they'll get caught looking at each other.

"You perving out on Enoch and his crew?" Bastien asks me in my mind, his teasing tone making me chuckle.

"You know it," I joke back. *"Dude, just watch them. Enoch and his coven are sneakily making eyes at Suryn, but they're completely oblivious that she's making eyes at them too."*

Bastien looks at me with clear judgment in his gaze. I may have just sounded like a kid who was about to be handed a puppy. I clear my throat and try to rein in the ridiculous levels of excitement I just spewed out. Bastien laughs and then proceeds to watch them for a couple of minutes.

"How have they not made eye contact yet? It's like they have a sixth sense that tells them when it's safe to look."

"*Right! It's completely weird,*" I agree, loving that he gets it.

Tok sits down after a while, and Sauriel jumps to his feet and starts in.

"*I want to try,*" I announce, and then I start sneaking glances at Ryker, Valen, Siah, Torrez, Knox, and Sabin.

I only make it one round of glances until Knox's gray eyes catch mine.

Dammit. Busted.

Bastien laughs, and Knox gives me a confused half smile.

"*What are you weirdos doing?*" Knox asks.

"*You guys should really be paying attention to what's going on, Vinna. They're only discussing your potential reign over the Sentinels,*" Sabin dutifully points out.

In response, I send him a mental image of what he looked like with my nipple in his mouth earlier. Sabin coughs, choking on air, and hits his chest to clear it. All of my Chosen's heads snap over to me. I sigh.

"*I sent that to all of you guys, didn't I?*" I ask.

It was only supposed to go to Sabin, but I swear my magic likes to fuck with me. Their laughter and salacious smiles are all the answer I need.

I shrug. "*Sorry, not sorry,*" I declare with a mischievous smile.

"*What'd he do to deserve that? I want to do it too,*" Torrez asks, and I crack up.

I put my hand over my mouth to try and hide it, but Suryn looks over at me. I cough and then give her an innocent smile. Her brow furrows, slightly perplexed, but she returns my small smile and looks away. Sauriel sits down, and someone else already standing starts to talk.

"*He was lecturing me on the importance of this meeting,*" I explain to all of them, and they all make noises expressing that they're not surprised by that. Sabin shakes his head.

"In a couple of days, they'll vote Suryn in. I'm not worried," I tell Sabin.

"I don't know, Squeaks. A lot of people are nodding their head and agreeing to arguments for new blood. A good chunk of the room agreed when Tok pointed out that because you're of the First, you're technically the rightful heir," Ryker tells me, and nerves flurry up in my chest.

"I don't want to be the Sovereign though," I state. "I'm sure that has to factor in at some point, doesn't it?" I ask, searching their faces.

"I know you keep saying that it's not your thing, but you could be really good for these people," Sabin tells me.

I shake my head.

"I'm not cut out for that, Sabin. I don't want to rule anyone. I don't want to be responsible for their futures. It just doesn't feel right to me."

Someone shouts out something that has the room grumbling, and it pulls my attention away. Tawv stands up to quiet whatever it was that set people off, and the crowd calms down again.

"If this doesn't feel right to you, then what are you thinking does feel like the next right move?" Valen asks me.

I think about the question for a minute.

"I'm not really sure," I admit. "And really, it's not like it's up to me either. We're a team. Shouldn't we be deciding that together?"

Tawv calls on a female leaning casually against the wall, and she dives right into voicing her concerns.

"True," Ryker and the others agree in my mind. "So what do we want to be when we grow up?" he throws out there, and we all snicker.

"I don't want to settle down here, but I can't picture us only living in Solace either. I still feel like a paladin even though I *know we'll never have that title. It's hard for me to picture a life that doesn't include that kind of work,*" Knox confesses.

"*I feel the same way,*" Valen states.

Bastien, Sabin, and Ryker all voice their agreement too.

"*I was a beta in the Silas pack, and what that involved was similar to what paladin do. We police the pack, protect and defend as needed. We help broker deals with other territories and back up the alpha at all times. Obviously, my role as a mate is different, but I was built for what I did as a beta. I was good at it, and I liked it,*" Torrez tells us.

The guys grunt their understanding.

"*So we need to find a job that fits a beta, paladin, enforcer... and whatever Vinna is,*" Siah adds, smiling at me.

"*Badass. I think the word you're looking for is badass,*" I tease him with a wink.

"*So a job fit for a beta, paladin, enforcer, and one all around badass,*" Siah recounts with an amused tone. "*Well, that shouldn't be too hard,*" he jokes, and we all give an incredulous grunt.

"*What if it wasn't though?*" I ask after a couple of minutes.

My mind whirls with the possibility of something, and I'm not quite sure what to make of it.

"*What do you mean?*" Bastien asks me.

"*I mean...*" I trail off for a moment as I try to piece it all together in a way that makes sense. "*The casters have the paladin, but really paladin only get involved with caster issues. Same goes for the shifter hierarchy and the lamia hierarchy. But what's the problem we all have in common, including the Sentinels?*" I ask.

They all look away, thoughtful.

"*Corruption?*" Knox points out on a snort.

"*Exactly!*" I exclaim.

"*Wait. That was really the answer? I was kidding,*" Knox declares.

"Kidding or not, it's true. How many fucked up situations have we run into because people in power were abusing it?" I ask.

"I'd say like eighty-seven percent of our problems come from that," Valen points out with a hollow laugh.

"So what are you saying? We go around and try to weed out all the corruption?" Siah asks, his eyes filled with doubt.

"Hell no, that's pretty much impossible. But what if we were an alternative force that could somehow help if the case was bad enough? Like beta, paladin, enforcer, badasses, but for anyone who needs it, not just one kind of supe," I explain.

Everyone goes quiet, and it's not just the guys. *Everyone* in the room is suddenly quiet. I look up, and the whole room is staring at me.

Shit. I wasn't paying attention.

"Um, sorry, what was that?" I ask in an effort to cover my ass.

Fuck, I hope it was a question that has them all staring at me, and I didn't just do that thing where I think I'm talking in my head, but I'm really talking out loud.

"The Seventh House was asking, if they vote for you to be the Sovereign, will you open up the barrier?" Tok tells me, and I flash him a grateful smile.

"That's an excellent question," I announce, stalling as I figure out what the fuck to say. "I think that's an issue that needs to be discussed in greater detail before I could truly decide," I start to say.

Several people narrow their gazes at me, and I quickly rethink my plan to spout off some polite political bullshit.

See, this is why I would suck at this job.

"I think the people of this city should have a say in what they think is best for them. I personally think it would be a good thing for Sentinels to get reacquainted with the world. We could open up the barrier so that the Sentinels who want to do that, can. And for those that don't, Tierit could still be a safe haven for them. I think there's probably a way to make both sides of the argument feel safe and happy."

I lean back in my chair and close my mouth. Murmuring starts up in the room, and I look over to find Tok and Marn beaming at me.

Well, shit.

If they're happy with that, then I didn't help my *I don't want this job* argument.

"*Okay, let's come back to what you said, Bruiser,*" Bastien requests, pulling my attention back to him.

"*About the barrier?*" I ask.

"*No, about the beta, paladin, enforcer, badass thing. So do supes hire us?*" he queries.

"*Um...we're like hella rich already,*" I point out, and some of the guys smile, while Siah says, "*We are?*"

"*Yeah, we haven't had much need to dive into the finances side of things yet, but the readers left me a fuck ton of money. Like our children's children to infinity and beyond are going to be good, and I mean reaaallllyyyy good,*" I tell him.

"*So you want kids?*" Sabin asks me, and I choke on nothing.

The room looks over at me as I try to get a hold of myself, and Enoch stands up and brings me a glass of water. I stop coughing and hold the glass up like I'm toasting the room and announcing that I'm going to be just fine. I take a sip, and Sauriel gets the conversation started again.

"*Where the fuck did that come from?*" I ask Sabin.

He shrugs. "*You're the one that brought up kids.*"

I glare at him. "*Only in the sense that generations long after ours will be set up financially.*"

"*You still brought them up,*" he counters, and I roll my eyes.

"*I thought we were supposed to be paying attention to the Sovereign discussion,*" I snark.

"And I thought they were going to crown Suryn, so we didn't need to," he counters.

I huff out my irritation. "I don't know how I feel about the whole kids thing. For sure not now. Maybe not ever. I don't know."

"Okay," he answers simply.

I stare at him for a minute, trying to figure out what the catch is. What am I missing?

"Okay? Just like that?" I question suspiciously.

"I don't want kids now. My biological clock is still on its spring daisy setting. We just never talked about it, and you brought it up."

I flip him the bird, and he chuckles.

"Anyway..." I drawl, aiming one last glare at Sabin, "I told Suryn and Sauriel about the money the readers saved and invested on behalf of the Sentinels. They said they had no idea who would have set that up and that Tierit didn't want it or need it. So, finders keepers officially applies," I finish, and Siah raises his eyebrows with surprise and gives an approving nod.

"Okay, so nobody pays us cash, but maybe the people we help owe us a favor instead. Not in the mob boss kind of way, but in a way that helps us build a network that could do good or help others down the road," Valen states.

"That could work," I agree.

"But who decides who we help and how we help them?" Ryker asks.

"We would," Sabin answers after a moment. "We could set up some kind of referral situation. Aydin, Evrin, Sorik and Vaughn could help us vet things if a lot of requests came in, and we would decide what to work on and how," he adds thoughtfully.

Sabin's statement warms me. I really like the idea of

getting Aydin, Evrin, Vaughn, and Sorik involved in whatever this is that we're trying to do.

"*That's...a really good plan,*" I beam at Sabin, forgiving him for the baby bomb he just threw out there.

All this talk stokes a fire in me. It all feels so right that I want to run out of this room right fucking now, make a plan, and go for it. I look around the table at my Chosen, and I can tell by the excited light I see in all of their gazes that they're feeling the same way.

"*Okay, so that's it. We walk away from this table and figure out how to make BBEP happen.*"

"*What the hell is ba-bep?*" Knox asks with a wide smile and a confused glint in his eyes.

"*You know...Beta, Badass, Enforcer, and Paladin. I had to switch it around a little so it could make some kind of logical sound...*" I trail off when the guys start snickering. "*I was making an initialism or an acronym or whatever the fuck it's called,*" I defend.

They start to shake with suppressed laughter, and I glare at them.

"*Witch, I already told you, you are not allowed to name anything, ever!*" Torrez tells me, and the angry veneer I'm trying to keep in place cracks.

"*Fuck off, Geriatric Wolf,*" I tease.

"*That's The Geriatric Wolf to you, Witch,*" he corrects, and I crack up.

A couple people turn to me, including Marn and Tok, and give me a bewildered look. I offer a sheepish smile and try to remember that I look like a fucking loon sitting here laughing to myself. *Actually, that's not such a bad thing. People don't vote for crazy, do they?*

"*Okay, so my name is off the table—what would you guys call us?*" I challenge.

Bastien throws out, "*The Super Saver Squad,*" and then

gives himself a look like his mind just had some kind of meltdown. I can tell he's hardcore judging what just came out of it, and it's fucking hilarious.

"You've made us sound like extreme couponers," Valen points out, and then he fucking loses it.

Half the room turns to see what's going on. He waves them off and apologizes as the rest of us try to keep from cracking the fuck up too.

"What about the Wet Bandits?" Knox pitches with a proud smile on his face.

We all stare at him for a moment with a giant *what the fuck* written across all of our faces.

"Is this some kind of reference to Vinna's vagina? Because I gotta say her TGV trumps the 'Wet Bandits' any day," Torrez tells Knox, and I snort.

He just shakes his head.

"Bro, it's from Home Alone. *You know, the robbers that break into the kid's house?"* Knox explains.

"We're not robbers though," Ryker points out, even more confused, but Torrez just looks blank, clearly out of the loop on this one.

Knox's eyes go wide with shock.

"Do not tell me you have never seen Home Alone. *It's a fucking Christmas pastime!"*

"Torrez is older than Christmas," I point out on a giggle. *"You know how old people are about keeping up with the times,"* I add.

Marn gives me a stern look that tells me to cut it the fuck out.

"Witch, you are just asking for it, aren't you," Torrez tells me.

My vagina contracts with excitement. I *love* when he tries to fuck me into submission.

Torrez's nostrils flare, and he gives me a knowing smile

and chuckles. All of a sudden, my six other Chosen shout in my mind, *"Dibs!"*

Tok and Sauriel leap out of their chairs and start arguing with another Sentinel in the room. I focus back in on what's going on, and when I hear the other male's voice, it makes my skin crawl. It's the male from the hallway that I overheard with the Sovereign. I wish I could scrub his voice and the shit he said from my mind, but unfortunately I don't have a rune for that.

"You all squabble back and forth like either of these females are worthy and didn't just commit regicide!" he bellows, spittle flying from his mouth. "They should be executed for their crimes, not rewarded," he snarls.

"The Sovereign broke the law when she attacked them with no cause. She went against the decree of the tribunal and violated her vows to her people and the laws she swore to uphold," Tok shouts back.

"They murdered her!" the male from the hallway accuses, his gaze filled with fury and his tone screaming for retribution.

"We defended ourselves and our Marked from an unprovoked attack, which we have every right under our laws to do," Suryn declares, rising up from her own chair.

"So you say. And we're just supposed to believe the word of the two females who are now both vying for her crown?" he accuses.

I push out of my chair.

"No, you should believe the evidence," I growl at him. "My Chosen were attacked in our rooms. The Sovereign brought a fight to us. Everyone who's reviewed the scene agrees. And if you don't want to trust them, then think back on the other night just before you shoved your dick down the Sovereign's throat in the hallway. Pretty sure she told you she was going to get rid of us and her niece if she couldn't get her on board with it."

"How dare you!" he screams at me and lunges.

He doesn't even make it a foot closer before the room converges on him. I expect them to carry him out kicking and screaming, put him in jail or something, but someone shoves a sword through his chest instead, and the male from the hallway is dead in seconds.

Well, okay then.

Guards carry out the body, and the back and forth about who should be Sovereign kicks up like nothing happened. I look around the room and then back to my Chosen.

"Let me make this easier for everyone," I declare.

Tok raises his arms to get everyone's attention, and the arguing slowly quiets. He looks over at me expectantly.

"I'm going to make this decision a whole lot easier for everyone," I repeat, and the quiet murmuring still going on gets slightly louder. "I remove my name from consideration for Sovereign," I announce.

"What?" Marn demands as she surges to her feet.

"I don't want the fucking crown!" I exclaim, and the room goes silent.

Tok and Marn gape at me like they don't know how to process what I'm saying.

"Suryn, I'd like to speak to you outside," I tell her, and then I turn and move toward the door.

"Vinna, wait!" Marn calls out to me, but I ignore it.

"What's going on?" someone else calls out, and I can hear whispers skittering across the room.

Chairs scrape and screech as they're pushed back, and I know that my Chosen are following me out. I step out of the door, and the room explodes with shocked and confused voices. I know I'm going to have to answer to Tok and Marn later, but right now I'm taking control of my future, and it feels fucking good. I'm tired of my next steps simply being a reaction or counter move to one fucked up thing or another. It's time to be proactive. To take control of who I am and who I want to be.

It's time to Sentinel the fuck up.

33

I walk out of the castle gates and pause. I turn to find my Chosen, and Suryn, Nash, Kallan, Becket, and Enoch all making their way over to me.

"I have no fucking clue where I'm going," I admit, gesturing around me and to where we're standing just outside of the castle gates.

My Chosen let loose an amused snort.

"We can just walk down the street, it circles back," Enoch points out, and I shrug and turn to Suryn.

She wobbles her head in a way that tells me she doesn't really care where we go, so I pick a direction and start going that way.

"Seems quiet out here today," I observe as we all start moving as a group.

"That's because a good majority of the Light Marked that live and travel in this part of the city are in that room we just left, speculating about what we're doing out here," Suryn points out.

A breeze picks up the skirts of both of our dresses and makes them dance lightly with its playful touch.

"I don't want to be the Sovereign," I start.

Suryn snorts. "Yeah, I got that much inside," she snarks, and I laugh.

"So I take it I'm out here to discuss what you *do* want?" she asks, and her eyes flick over to Kallan quickly before focusing back on the road in front of her. "Is this the part where you pitch a mutually beneficial relationship between the two of us?" Suryn asks, her tone cheeky with just a hint of uncertainty.

I shake my head, amused. If she wasn't such an uptight bitch, I might just like her.

"Well, I don't know about the two of us..." I half joke, trailing off. "But I think if we work together, we could make things much safer for Sentinels outside of the borders of Tierit."

"And how would *we* do that?" she questions, a hint of a grin peeking out of the corner of her mouth.

"My guys and I are going to leave," I start, and Suryn stares at me for a beat. I don't miss the flicker of unease that flashes through her eyes before she blinks it away. "We're working out the details, but we're going to start our own group that looks out for the welfare of *all* the supes out there, Sentinels included if they want."

"When did this get decided?" Becket asks, interrupting whatever Suryn is about to say.

I turn back to him. "Pretty much in there, just now," I explain.

"That's what all the giggling was about?" Kallan accuses.

"Well, that and some other things," I tell him and try hard not to smile.

"So we're going full vigilante?" Becket questions, his eyes thoughtful.

My gaze darts from Becket to Suryn, and I'm not sure what to say.

"Vinna's Vigilantes," Ryker throws out randomly.

We all turn to him.

"Has a ring to it," he announces with a shrug.

"Hard pass," I counter with a laugh.

Suryn looks at me, confused.

"Sorry, we suck at figuring out what we're going to call ourselves when we go rogue," I explain.

"You don't have to be rogue," she surprises me by saying.

I stare at her, perplexed, and she gives me a small smile and shakes her head.

"You saved my life, Vinna Aylin. You think something like that doesn't matter to me or the people of Tierit?" she asks me, and I don't know how to respond.

We walk side by side in silence for a minute. Suryn seems to be working something out in her mind, and I leave her to it.

"You won't be vigilantes," she declares after several quiet steps. "I'll make you official. You'll have the full weight of the Sentinels behind you, if you want it, that is," Suryn offers, and I stop dead in my tracks and stare at her.

"What do you mean?" I ask, unable to wrap my mind around what she's saying.

"Just what I said. I can make what you and your Chosen want to do official. You can be diplomats or something... I don't know, I'm just saying it can be worked out," she explains and continues to walk forward.

Her offer sends me reeling, and I get lost in thought for a moment as I fall in step next to her. We walk side by side, a hint of awkwardness between us. We were on two different sides up until the fight with the Sovereign happened. I don't think that either one of us quite knows what to do with each other now. There's a thread of cama-raderie that ties us together because of what happened with her aunt, but aside from that, we're strangers. Strangers that didn't like each other all that much not too long ago. And now we could be...what? Partners? Diplomats? The Muscle?

I try to think through what she's offering me, to see a downside or a catch, but right now I'm just not seeing it. Her backing could be just what the guys and I need to go up against the caster elders or any other leadership that could try to stand in our way.

"So does this mean you think it's time for the Sentinels to see what's outside of Tierit?" I ask.

She takes a deep breath. "I think our survival just might depend on it. Not everyone will be happy, but I think we can do this in a way that works for everyone," she explains.

"*We?*" I tease.

Suryn looks at me for a moment and then nods. "Yes, we," she declares, and then she fists her right hand and places it over her left bicep.

I don't know why the gesture touches me as much as it does, but my eyes sting, and I have to blink back my emotions. I fist my right hand and place it over my left bicep.

"I'd be honored, Sovereign..."

I trail off, trying to wrack my brain for what her last name is. Suryn of the Second is all I can come up with, but that's her family designation, not her last name.

"Shit, what's your last name again?" I ask, a sheepish look on my face.

She laughs, and I feel a little less like a dick for not knowing.

"My mother's last name was the same as my aunt's. Chosen and children take the surname of the female," she explains, and I try not to make a face.

"So you're Sovereign Finella too?" I confirm, and she nods. "Well, at least you won't have to change the stationary," I comment, and she snorts.

"I look forward to redeeming the name," she declares, and I put my fist out for her to bump her own fist against.

She just stares at it.

"Uh...you're supposed to bump your own fist against it," I explain. "It's a solidarity thing," I add when she still doesn't move.

She balls her hand and taps the top of my knuckles with it, like a fist boop. I smile and nod.

That'll work.

"I should get back and announce what we've discussed," Suryn states.

I nod and look over at my guys. "Would you guys go with her?" I ask. "Back up what she's saying and catch Marn and Tok when they pass out or implode," I add.

My Chosen laugh, and Suryn grins and shakes her head.

"I'm going to just have a chat with my Shields," I announce, and the irritation that flashes through Suryn's gaze when I call them *mine* is clear. "Promise I won't be long," I offer, and the guys give me nods and move to escort Suryn back to the castle.

"Are you sure about this?" Suryn stops and turns to ask me.

I see a hint of nerves or maybe uncertainty in her features.

"Yes," I confirm.

I watch her take a deep fortifying breath and then nod.

"Suryn," I call out as she starts to turn around, "we're here if you need anything," I offer.

She squares her shoulders and gives me a small smile. The *thank you* is evident in her eyes, but she doesn't say another word as she turns around and makes her way back to the castle. I watch her and my Chosen go, and feel a keen sense of peace wash over me. This is right, and I can feel the confirmation of that in my bones.

"So," I start as I turn to Enoch, Kallan, Becket and Nash, "let's talk about us."

I snort out a laugh at the needy girlfriend sounding shit that just came out of my mouth. They groan playfully and laugh too.

"The dreaded *where is this going* talk," Kallan teases, and I grin.

"The very one," I confirm and start walking down the street again.

They fall into step beside me, and we all go quiet for a bit.

"So what do you want to do?" I finally ask, and I don't know why, but the question makes me sad.

I feel like I already know what's going to happen, but I need to hear them say it. I'm excited for them, rooting for them, and I'm also bummed that we won't be around each other in the same way we have been since the elders moved me into their house.

"We're still not unanimous on that front yet," Kallan throws out there, and I meet each one of their gazes in turn.

"Still split down the middle?" I question.

"Uh...no. Becket is the only one who doesn't want to stay," Enoch informs me.

My eyebrows twitch up in surprise, and I turn to Becket. He rolls his eyes and huffs out a breath.

"I know I should hate you. The night you told me about my dad, I decided right then and there that I would always hate you." Becket trails off, his voice cracking with emotion, and I nod and look away, giving him space to collect his thoughts.

"When Adriel took me, when I found out that you were telling the truth about my dad, it didn't change things for me the way I thought it would. Truth or not, I was going to hate you all the same. But that plan got a lot harder when we were in the cell together, because I hated you, but I also started to respect you too," he tells me softly, and I can hear the conflict in his voice.

"I don't know Suryn, and I don't feel all twitterpated or curious about her like they do," he tells me, gesturing to the rest of his coven. "I respect you, Vinna. Fuck, I even admire you despite my efforts not to," he admits with an amused grunt.

I grin and shake my head.

"Your magic marked me as your Shield, and I just can't bring myself to abandon that or you in hopes that some other Sentinel chick will eventually throw us her occasional table scraps," Becket finishes.

Enoch scoffs and opens his mouth to say something, but I cut him off.

"I don't know if I would have come out of that cell the same, or maybe even at all, if it hadn't been for you being there, Becket. So I just want you to know that the feeling is mutual," I tell him, and he gives me a nod and a small smile.

"When Getta was telling me about where Sentinels come from and about my abilities, she said something about you guys that I've been thinking about ever since."

Someone steps out of their house on our right and fists their hand over their bicep to us. I smile at them and wonder if that gesture will ever stop meaning so much to me. We continue to stroll down the circular street, and I take another second to collect my thoughts.

"So I brought up the whole *trust the magic* thing to her. My magic marked you for a reason, and that was pretty much that to me. But she made a good point. Yes, I marked you guys for a reason, but was that reason really mine, or could it be something or someone else's? Maybe I marked you to lead you here. So you would meet Suryn."

They all kind of nod thoughtfully but stay quiet.

"I've been trying to think that through since then, and this is what I've come up with. When you all showed up at my house with marks, I felt this underlying need to keep you with me."

"You mean, after you felt the overwhelming need to gut us, right?" Kallan teases, and we all laugh.

"Yeah, after that part, of course," I joke back.

"I felt the pull in Solace and in Belarus when we decided to leave and look for Sentinel City." I pause.

"You don't feel it anymore, do you?" Enoch points out, and I shake my head.

"No. I don't," I confirm. "I'm not saying that you're not welcome with me and my Chosen. You don't even have to be tied to me or to Suryn if you don't want. Tawv says there are ways to unmark you, if that's what you'd like. All I'm saying is that, yes, my magic marked you, but I can't say for sure why that is now, any more than I could when it first happened."

We all fall silent again, walking and lost in thought.

"Suryn and I got in a fight over it," I announce out of nowhere.

"What?" Enoch asks.

"When?" Kallan demands.

"Who won?" Nash questions, and I shake my head and chuckle.

"She took off before it was really decided officially one way or the other."

"Why?" Becket asks, clearly judging her for leaving a fight.

"Because of you guys," I tell him, and confusion takes over Becket's face.

"She just gasped and called out *my Chosen* and then took off without a second's hesitation. It must have been right when the Sovereign attacked you guys," I finish, and I give them some time to let that soak in.

"I don't know what the future holds for you guys, but it might be worth trying to find out if that future could be here. I mean, worst case scenario, you can always meet up with me and the guys at any point. Or strip your runes and go home if you decide Sentinels are more trouble than they're worth," I tease, and they chortle. "I just think it might be good to see why her magic marked you too," I finish, looking over at Becket as we complete the circular path we've been traveling, and the castle's front gates can be spotted in the distance once again.

He and I stare at each other for several steps, and then he gives me a small nod and looks away.

"Besides, Getta could obviously use some worthy opponents. Fuck knows these Tierit Sentinels aren't giving her a run for her money," I joke, and we all crack up.

I leave it at that, not pressing them to make a decision or putting my nose any further into their business than I already have. Time will tell what they all choose to do. Whatever they decide, I'll be here to support it.

34

I fidget, wondering what the heck is taking so long. Marn reaches out for my hand and gives it a comforting squeeze. I squeeze her hand right back and then reach out and pull her into my side for a quick hug.

She and Tok took my *I'll pass on the Sovereign* announcement better than I expected they would. Suryn had already dropped the bomb when I walked back into the round table room. Maybe that gave them some time to wrap their minds around it, but when I confirmed what Suryn was saying was true and then mapped out what my Chosen and I wanted to do, Tok and Marn looked kind of proud and not at all upset like I thought they'd be.

Marn fixes the leather tie on the terracotta colored dress she forced me into. The dress is soft, flowy, and sleeveless, with a blackberry colored leather strap that comes forward from the back of my neck and crosses under my breasts and across my torso several times before tying at the back. I get a slit on *each* side of the skirt this time, which I wasn't a big fan of until Siah reminded me why easy access wasn't such a bad thing.

I can practically feel his fangs scraping against the inside of my thighs as he teased me right before—

"All hail Sovereign Finella, Ruler of Tierit, the Dawning of New Hope, Liberator of Illusions, Savior of the Sentinels, Light Blessed, and Gate Keeper," a guard bellows out, his announcement echoing around the walls of the packed throne room.

The hum of low murmuring that was just filling the room stops, and everyone goes quiet. Suryn walks steadily and gracefully into the long room, her emerald green dress strikingly similar to mine. I look over at Marn quickly to see if she's got a look of *who wore it better* on her face, but she seems excited rather than annoyed.

As Suryn walks, I notice rings of markings on her upper thighs, like she has several garter belts of runes wrapped around her legs. She has a couple more on her calves too. She's barefoot just like I am, but I don't spot any markings on her feet or toes. Suryn walks confidently up to her father, where he stands next to Tawv at the bottom of the stairs that lead up to the thrones. The old gilded chairs the previous Sovereign had up there are gone, and in their place are three large, light gray wooden high back chairs.

Suryn stops in front of Tawv and kneels, his almost white eerie gaze running over her. He gives a nod of satisfaction, and her shoulders seem to relax slightly. He reaches to his right and lifts a new gold crown over Suryn's head. Her red hair is reflected in the shine of what looks like vines and flowers that are twined around various runes.

I'm fascinated by all of this, but I'm also eager to get it over with. The guys and I agreed to stay until Suryn was crowned, but as soon as this is over with, we're out of here.

"I, a former member of the Quorum, crown you, Suryn Finella, the new Sovereign of the Sentinels. Do you swear to uphold the laws of our people?" he asks.

"I do," Suryn immediately responds.

"And do you swear to devote your life to leading your people into the light, to strengthen them, unite them, to know them and their needs?"

"I do."

"Do you swear not to allow your people to repeat the mistakes of the past? To be swift in action when called for against threats within or without the barrier, and to strive for peace and prosperity above all else?"

"I do."

"Then rise, Sovereign Finella, and lead us into a new age," Tawv commands.

Suryn does just that, and as she stands up, Tawv fits the crown on her head. She dips her feet in something next to Tawv and then makes her way up the steps to the middle throne. The room is so quiet I can hear her bare feet as they move across the stone of the floor. She turns around in front of the middle chair, and the room goes fucking mental.

Applause and cheers roar to life as Suryn fists her right hand and places it across her left bicep. The room grows even louder, and I add my own voice to Tok's and Marn's and my Chosen's. We all give Suryn the same gesture back, and I watch as she blinks away tears. She sits down on the throne, joy all over her face, and it's like a weight is lifted in the room.

I look around to see people openly weeping happy tears, and I can only imagine what this day feels like to them. There's a palpable *hope* floating around this place, and it's so different from the somber, almost beaten down feel that existed around Suryn's aunt. I can't help the massive smile on my face as I take it all in. I'm so fucking honored to see this, and I can't wait to see what's in store for these people in the future.

The room slowly quiets, and I spot Sauriel wiping at his

eyes as he stares up at his daughter, with pride and love shining in his eyes. I look over at Vaughn and smile when he notices me watching him. He gives me a smile back, and my chest grows tight when I see that same pride and love in his gaze.

"Sovereign Finella, have you selected your Quorum?" Tawv asks, his question booming through the long room filled to the brink with the Sentinels of Tierit.

"I have," she declares, and the room settles into silence once more. She looks through the crowd and smiles when she finds Ory. "To my left, I will call Ory Lark," she announces, and quiet excitement bubbles up in the room again.

Ory looks shocked as fuck by Suryn's announcement. I don't know why I find that amusing, because I don't think anyone here is surprised by it at all. He looks at Suryn, and I can tell he's asking her if she's sure with just a look. She smiles even wider at him and waves him forward.

"Why is he so shocked?" Sabin leans forward and quietly asks Tok.

"Because Ory will be the first of his kind to sit in a leadership position over the people who once enslaved his ancestors," Tok explains.

Surprise runs through me as Tok's words settle in my mind. Ory walks up slowly, shock still radiating out of his features. He kneels just like Suryn did, and Tawv starts the series of vows over.

"Wait, so what is he?" I ask, confused. I thought Ory was Light Born or Pure Blood or whatever the fuck they call a Born Sentinel instead of a marked one.

"Ory is part Ouphe of old and Gryphon," Tok whispers to me as Ory's *I do* rings out into the room.

Gryphon?

"I guess that explains the wings," I mumble, and Tok

nods. "Bummer, I was hoping it was a rune I could jack somehow," I admit, and Bastien and Knox both laugh quietly.

I lift a hand to rub at the rune under my chin but stop myself. I still haven't brought myself to touch it or activate it in any way to confirm what it is.

Ory rises, gets his crown, dips his feet and walks up to the chair on the left of Suryn. When he turns to face the room, the crowd goes wild again. Even Suryn claps hard and hoots her approval, and I can't help but join in again, even if the dude is a prick. Ory smiles and shakes his head as the Sentinels of Tierit make it clear that they're happy with the Sovereign's decision. I wish I knew what was going through his head; he looks so humbled and taken aback. It's a far cry from the cocky troublemaker mien he usually wears.

The room slowly quiets again, and Ory takes his seat. Tawv turns back to Suryn expectantly.

"To my right," she starts, looking down at Tawv with a wide smile.

I give a small nod, liking her next choice. Tawv is a good choice to help guide her.

"I will call Vinna Aylin," she announces, looking over at me, and my fucking heart plummets to my feet.

Wait. What?

My Chosen all voice their shock, and even Tok and Marn look over at me like they didn't see that coming. I stand there, doing my best impersonation of a confused statue and try to make sense of what the fuck is going on. Suryn chuckles, and the sound of it snaps me out of my stupor. Just like with Ory, she waves me down, and it's as if I've just been lassoed, because I automatically start moving toward her.

The crowd parts as I make my way through them until I find myself kneeling at the feet of a widely smiling Tawv. I look up to see the gold crown he's holding over my head is in fact vines and flowers intertwined with my symbol and with that of my Chosen. I feel breathless and unsure of what the fuck to do. Does this mean we aren't leaving as planned? Is this like a public proposal where you say yes so the other person can save face and then, behind closed doors, ask them what the fuck they were thinking?

"I, a former member of the Quorum, crown you, Vinna Aylin, a member of the Quorum and right hand to the Sovereign of the Sentinels. Do you swear to uphold the laws of our people?" he asks.

I pause. *Shit, do I? Can I swear to uphold them if I don't know what they are?*

"I swear to uphold the laws of our people as long as those laws are moral and don't hurt innocent people," I state, and then I wait for Tawv to throw my crown aside and tell Suryn she needs to pick someone else.

"And do you swear to devote your life to leading your people into the light, to strengthen them, unite them, to know them and their needs?" Tawv continues, instead of demanding someone else.

"I swear to devote my life to leading *all* people into the light; to strengthen them, unite them, to know them and their needs," I declare, once again waiting for someone to *boo* at me or call out the fact that I'm fucking with their vows.

"And do you swear not to allow your people to repeat the mistakes of the past? To be swift in action when called for against threats within or without the barrier, and to strive for peace and prosperity above all else?"

"I do," I answer, this time not feeling the need to alter any of the wording.

"Then rise, Vinna Aylin, and help to lead us into a new age," Tawv invites me.

I take a deep breath and get to my feet. He places the crown on my head, and I'm surprised by the weight of it. It looked so delicate but feels far from it. Tawv beams at me, but my smile is still radiating *what the fuck*.

"Now, Vinna, dip your feet in Dragon's Tears and make your way to your seat," he tells me, and my eyes go wide.

"Dragons are real?" I whisper, surprised, as I dip my bare feet in the same large bowl that Suryn and Ory did.

Tawv smiles. "It's actually sap from a Dragon plant," he explains. "We do it to clear away the remnants of the steps that have come before yours so that you can stand in your own reign and not someone else's," he tells me, and it makes goosebumps spring up on my arms.

I step away from him and make my way up the stairs. Suryn gives me a wide welcoming smile, and I have to stop myself from asking her what the hell she was thinking and flipping her off. My heart hammers against my ribs, tired after its climb from my feet back into my chest. I'm two steps from reaching my throne—*that's fucking weird to say*—and I don't know what's going to happen when I reach it and turn around to face the people of this city.

Will they glare at me? Shout out their rejection? Politely applaud? Just stare?

I take a deep breath, square my shoulders and turn around.

A wave of deafening sound blasts me. My dress flutters against my legs as cheers and applause reach out and blanket me in their approval. The Sentinels of Tierit don't hold back at all, letting me know loud and clear I am exactly where they want me to be. I fist my right hand over my bicep, and just when I think it can't get any louder or rowdier, the people take it to a whole new level. They salute me back, and I will never forget this moment for as long as I live. Just like Suryn and Ory before me, I have to fight back tears as I'm overwhelmed by the love and support of these people. I look over to find my Chosen bellowing their lungs out and saluting me back.

Tok and Marn are hugging, tears dripping down their cheeks and pride shining in their eyes. My smile is massive and genuine as they welcome me. I look at Becket and wonder if we just might get that parade he was hoping for. My cheeks ache by the time the crowd starts to wind down, and I sit on my throne to the right of Suryn.

She rises from her seat, and the room goes silent once more. "Sentinels..." she calls out, her clear voice ringing out into the crowd like a welcome and simultaneous call to action. "Today is the day we embrace the new, and prepare for a better future. We have long been safe within the borders of our barrier, but the time has come to see our seclusion for what it is: a death sentence," she declares, and a low rumble of agreement and nodding fills the room.

"Generation after generation thrives less and less within our magical walls, and we have to put a stop to the deterioration of our light and the slow depletion of our people. The leaders you see before you will be like none other as we pave the way for Sentinels not only here in Tierit but out there in the world."

The crowd explodes into cheers, and Suryn smiles and waits for them to settle. "It will take time. It will take your trust and support. But we will find a way to thrive again. We will find our way in the world again. We will lead ourselves into a new age where we can thrive and be better than we have ever been before. Are you with me, Tierit?" she shouts out into the room, and I bellow out my own approval.

She's good, I muse as she amps her people up and gives it to them straight. My worries about what will happen now fade as I realize that everything Suryn and I discussed before is still going to happen. I watch her saluting her people once again, and I can see it all clearly. She'll work within the barrier; I'll work outside of it. Ory will go where needed, and slowly but surely the Sentinels will come out of hiding.

The noise of the crowd dies down as Suryn raises her hands.

"Good," she proclaims. "Then let us celebrate tonight, because tomorrow we have work to do," she commands, and the room erupts again.

This time, the large doors in the back open, and people start flooding out of the throne room in the direction of wherever the party is going to get started. We watch them go, seated on thrones, and the realization hits me of what I'm responsible for. I'm humbled by it and slightly sobered by it too. My actions are not just mine and my Chosen's alone anymore. There's a whole race of people counting on us to make the world safe for them. I know it's not going to be easy, but I'm filled with so much hope that it'll be possible.

Suryn turns to Ory, and he gives her an incredulous look.

"You're a sneak," he accuses her playfully. "You said you were calling your dad and Tawv, you little chit."

Suryn laughs and moves toward him. He stands and wraps her up in a hug.

"You are the best male for the job, Ory. You get more than anyone what we're up against and just how important it is to get this all right," she tells him, and Ory nods and hugs her tighter.

A quiet, low, angry growl starts up, and I trace the sound back to Enoch who is glaring daggers at Ory. Ory looks over and sends his own threatening look at Enoch and his coven. An amused smile crawls over my face.

Glad I won't be here to referee all that shit.

Tawv walks up to us, a proud grin on his face. "We just need to wait for Wekun to give the three of you your joining marks, and then you can head to the festivities," he announces cheerily.

I raise my hand. "Um, what's a Wekun and what are joining marks?" I ask.

"Wekun is our official Bond Weaver. The Sovereign and her Quorum are marked with ways to contact one another and protect one another, and that's what he'll be here to do. It shouldn't take long," Tawv reassures me.

The side door to the throne room opens.

"Ah, there he is," Tawv declares, and for some reason, I expect a wizened old wizard to come shuffling out the door with the aid of a walking stick.

I could not have been any further off.

A tall drink of water with buzzed snow white hair, full lips, and a jaw that's clearly been chiseled by a very skilled sculptor steps out into the throne room. I freeze and can't seem to stop myself from open-mouth staring. It's like his mere presence has activated some creeper mode switch I didn't even know I had, while my brain hums a steady rhythm of *homina*. Like, my Chosen are standing just off to the side, and yet my mind gives no fucks.

"Tawv!" he greets with a deep voice that I just want to spread out like a blanket and roll myself in.

Burrito for two, please!

I watch Suryn shiver with pleasure and lick her lips as Tawv and the hot guy hug each other warmly and exchange pleasantries. Good to know I'm not the only one affected by this guy's presence. I giggle as Ory puffs out his chest in a testosterone infused cave-man-sensing-competition kind of way, and for some reason, that helps me slightly shake away the fog of lust clouding my thoughts.

Down, girl.

"Wekun, this is Suryn, our new Sovereign," Tawv introduces, and Wekun gives her a smile that makes Suryn's eyes widen. She slowly leans toward him as if she's a mere flower and he's the sun. Wekun places his fist over his bicep and slightly bows to Suryn.

"It's an honor to meet you," he tells her smoothly.

Suryn just blinks slowly like her brain has stalled somehow. Tawv clears his throat, and the sound has her looking over at him and then snapping out of whatever the fuck just hit her *pause and drool* button.

"And you," she stammers out after another awkward beat.

Tawv introduces Ory, and Suryn looks around like she's perplexed about what just happened. I chuckle, and she looks over at me. I wag my eyebrows at her, and she mock fans herself. We both giggle again and then shut the fuck up when Tawv says my name and Wekun turns to me, almost busting our fangirling.

"Ahhh, I was wondering when I'd get to meet you," Wekun tells me with a beaming smile that makes my synapses melt into a puddle of incoherent girly mush.

Fuck, he just hit my pause and drool *button too!*

He steps into my space and leans his forehead against mine. Several growls fill the room, but for some reason, I can't tear my eyes away from Wekun's champagne gaze and look to see what's going on. He inhales deeply, and the whole situation short circuits me. I basically become a broken toaster of a female that drools from multiple places as he stands there, his head against mine, just breathing me in like that's fucking normal.

"Welcome, sister," he tells me as he pulls his head away from mine.

The word *sister* has my lust screeching to a halt. My

vagina screams *oh hell nooooo* followed by a *whyyyy* aimed at the heavens as she reaches for a mop.

"What the fuck?" I ask, once again snapping myself out of whatever spell this dude's hotness puts on people.

Wekun laughs, and my vagina starts to judge herself when she responds regardless of the whole *brother* question still hanging in the air.

"Sister, as in fellow user of Bond magic, not as in an actual relation," he reassures me with a wink that my vagina's convinced is just for her.

"You have Bond magic?" Ory demands, his eyes going wide.

Well, shit.

I glare at Wekun for letting the cat out of the bag, but he just smiles that fucking smile at me, and my vagina convinces me we should forgive him.

"That actually makes a lot of sense," Suryn admits, studying me for a moment like she doesn't know why she didn't see the whole *Bond magic* thing sooner.

Wekun moves, and Suryn is once again lost like a moth to a flame.

"Are you like a fucking Siren or some kind of vagina whisperer?" I ask Wekun, his hotness melting any hope I have for manners.

He chuckles, and I involuntarily sigh dreamily at the sound of it.

What the fuck is going on with me?

I look over at my Chosen, and half of them look like they're about to brawl, while the other half look seriously amused. I watch as a rune on Wekun's beefy inner elbow lights up and then dims, and it's like he poured ice water on my libido.

"It's a failsafe my mother gave me," Wekun tells us, gesturing to the rune. "When activated, it makes anyone in my presence enamored. They're less likely to want to kill me if they want or admire me in some way," he explains, and I feel both severely irritated and impressed.

"Sorry to use it on you, but better to be safe than sorry when meeting new people," he throws out there, nonplussed.

I'm just grateful to have a non-simpering brain back, so I let it slide.

"Do you three have any questions before we start on your joining runes?" Wekun asks as the sound of dishes clinking around makes its way out of the kitchen.

I pull up my trusty mental list, but shock stirs through me when most of what I had has been crossed out and answered.

"What joining marks will you be giving us?" I ask, clearly the only one out of the loop here.

"The usual ones, mind speak, locators, emotional alarms. You'll be familiar with all of those already, Vinna, as you have similar pathways set up with your Chosen," he tells me.

"Suryn, you have mind speak with your Marked and of course the locators built into the finger runes. The emotional alarms will be new for you, and you and Vinna both will experience a gate rune for the first time," Wekun explains, his eyes kind and his tone patient. "Ory, this isn't going to be a whole lotta fun for you today, but just remember it will end and the pain will be worth it," he adds.

Ory visibly swallows and lets out a resigned exhale. I don't bother questioning how Wekun seems to know so much about us. From what I've been told about Bond Weavers and how they can see things, I figure it must just be part of his abilities.

"Any other questions?" Wekun asks, and we all look back and forth and then shake our heads. "Excellent, if you three are okay to start, we should get a move on. Vinna's mates are getting restless," he announces and winks over his shoulder at my guys.

"Now, hold hands so I can make this quick," Wekun commands with a clap of his hands.

He steps in front of me, and his champagne colored eyes feel like they look through me as he reaches up and touches under the spot behind my ear where my Chosen runes are.

"This rune will allow you three to speak in each other's heads when called on," Wekun explains.

A familiar burning starts at the tip of his finger. I grit my teeth against the pain as I feel two runes marking me there. It's there and gone in a couple of minutes. As soon as the pain fades for me, Suryn lets out a hiss of discomfort as she gets her marks. A few more minutes later, Ory grunts indicating that it's now his turn.

"Ready for the next?" Wekun asks when Ory unclenches his jaw.

I nod.

My heart rate picks up when I realize where Wekun has to touch to put the next rune. I look down at his inner elbow to make sure he's not working his failsafe mojo on me anymore, but nope, this is all the TGV's fault. Wekun presses his finger tip to my eight pointed star rune on my chest and then moves his finger down my sternum until he hits blank skin underneath the Chosen runes on my chest.

"This rune will work differently than the runes you have now, Vinna. If you are distressed, hurting in any way or scared, it will automatically call to the others. You won't have to call on it for it to work. It's a failsafe between the three of you," he explains, and the burning sensation starts again where his finger rests.

The rune moves through each of us one by one. Wekun

looks over me as it does, like he's searching my body for something.

"Are you okay with inner bicep?" he asks me after a minute, and I furrow my brow in confusion. "For the gate rune," he explains.

I look down at the inside of my arm. "Yeah, that's fine," I confirm.

Wekun doesn't ask Ory if he's ready this time. He just presses his palms to the inside of both of my biceps.

"This rune will be the hardest for all three of you to receive but possibly the most vital. It will allow you to jump to each other when called on."

"Like we can teleport to each other?" I ask, awe and astonishment in my tone.

"More or less. The marking will create a gate between the three of you. When you call on the marking, the gate pulls you through."

I don't get a chance to voice my amazement, because it feels like Wekun just shoved a white hot poker into the inside of both of my upper arms. My grip tightens on Suryn's hand, and I throw my head back and close my eyes in an effort to ride the searing pain out. The deep breaths I'm attempting turn into pants, and a quiet keening sneaks through my lips for a minute or so before the pain starts to fade.

I breathe heavy as the awful sensation starts to dissipate, and Suryn's hand becomes vice-like in mine. I squeeze her hand back and offer my own reassurances when her cries start to spill from her lips. More than five minutes go by, and her grip finally loosens. Ory yelps out a pained noise, and we watch and wait while trying to comfort him and tell him that it'll all be over soon. It feels like forever, but eventually Ory relaxes.

We let go of each other's hands, but none of us rushes to

move. The three of us stand there just taking it all in. We now have each other's symbols marked on our bodies, and I feel bonded to them and protective of them in a way I didn't before. Wekun claps his hands together loudly, and I jump with a squeak, not expecting the booming noise as we quietly inspect our new markings and what they mean for us.

Weeks ago we were all trying to kill each other. Now here we are, bonded forever as the new leaders of our people. It all feels so fucking surreal.

"I'm glad to have finally met you, Vinna," Wekun tells me, pulling me from my thoughts. "I think things will be busy for you for a while, but when they start to calm down, I'd like you to come here so I can teach you more about your Bond magic and how it works," Wekun offers.

I'm surprised for a moment and hesitate to say yes. My first reaction is to say that I may not be back in Tierit for a while. But I realize the new gate runes I now have on the inside of my arms will make it easier to pop in for a bit of training here and there. A wave of excitement rolls through me as I think about what I might learn. I'm sure Getta would be down for a good fight too when I'm in the neighborhood.

"I would appreciate that," I tell him, "so long as you promise not to use that rune on me again," I add.

Wekun grins, and then he tilts his head slightly, his prosecco toned eyes going distant like he's listening to something that only he can hear. After a beat of staring off at nothing, he gasps suddenly and grabs his throat. Worry strikes through me at the alarm I see flash in his distant stare.

"I have to go," he croaks out, and the next thing I know, he just disappears.

I blink and look around like somehow his sudden

absence is a trick of the light, but he's nowhere to be seen. My searching gaze lands on my guys, and I shrug.

"Who's ready to party?" I ask, hoping they can just let go of the fact that I went all drooly toaster about thirty minutes ago.

"I blame the failsafe," I declare as they prowl closer.

"Shots on me?" I try again when not all of them look as amused as I was hoping.

Shit, I might have to pull out the big guns.

"Fine, orgasms on me," I offer, and this time they all crack a smile even if some of them try to fight it.

35

"**V**inna, wake up, kiddo," someone tells me in an effort to get me to open my eyes.

I groan out an objection because I feel like I need to sleep for *at least* another week.

I was up during most of the flight, working out a plan in my head with Suryn and Ory for phase one of opening the barriers.

"Kiddo, you need to wake up, we have a bit of a situation," the voice I now recognize as my dad's tells me.

I sit up quickly and open my eyes. Vaughn snaps back, just narrowly avoiding an accidental head-butt. I try to blink through the exhaustion from hiking out of Tierit, the jet lag from the flight back to the US, and the interrupted nap I was trying to take during the long ass drive back to Solace. I look from my dad's concerned face to our surroundings in an effort to get my bearings. Tall trees and the two-lane road we're currently stopped on gives me a hint, but the collection of black Range Rovers blocking our path confirms it.

"What do you think they want?" Valen asks me from the driver's seat, his gaze fixed on the road block. I look over at

Sorik and Bastien who are also in the car and shake my head.

"Let's go find out," I grumble as I open the door and hop out of the SUV.

Sabin, Siah, Ryker, Knox and Torrez all pile out of the other SUV in front of us, and they look from me to the paladin now stepping out of the vehicles in our way. I don't recognize anyone, but I really only knew Lachlan's coven and Pebble's, so that doesn't really surprise me.

A light brown haired male locks eyes with me and steps forward. "Vinna Aylin, we are here to escort you to a meeting with the Elders Council," he informs me.

I make an irritated noise. Fucking hell, were they watching the airports for our return? Elder Cleary's face pops up in my mind, and I give an incredulous mental snort. I probably shouldn't be surprised.

"Fine," I relent.

Probably better to get this over with now anyway. Then maybe we can get home and have some uninterrupted sleep for a while before we get to work.

I turn to go back to the car, but the paladin's next sentence stops me.

"Lamia are not allowed within the barriers of Solace, so your companions will need to stay out here until the elders authorize their entry," he announces, eyeing Siah, Vaughn, and Sorik with clear distaste.

"My mate, father, and friend will go wherever the fuck I do," I state simply.

A few of the paladin bristle, but the leader just smiles. "If you want them to turn to ash when they cross into our territory uninvited, I'm fine with that."

I roll my eyes and give him a thumbs up. I'm too fucking tired to deal with this prick. I already know the barrier lets Sentinels through, but I'm not going to explain that to them.

They can wrack their judgmental little brains until they figure out that their barrier has some exploitable loopholes to its protections.

The paladin leader snickers and then shrugs as he turns to get back into his car.

"Do you think the elders are going to give us trouble?" Knox asks no one in particular.

"I think they're probably just nosy," I tell him as we walk slowly back to our vehicles.

"Enoch was keeping his dad in the loop before we left for Tierit. We're back now, and I'm sure the elders want first dibs on any information we have that they can exploit."

"Well, this should be interesting," Bastien observes, and a couple of us chuckle.

"I'm sure it will be, especially when Elder Cleary notices that his son isn't with us," Sabin adds, and I snort.

"Should we fill him in on what Enoch and his coven are doing? Or should we *really* annoy him by pretending it's top secret and shit?" Valen asks, and I laugh.

"Let's see how annoying he is and go from there," I tell them.

We separate into two cars again and move to follow the paladin into Solace.

"Did you get phase one worked out with Suryn and Ory?" my dad asks as we drive and I lean against the window and try not to fall back asleep.

"Close, we still need to work out some details. Ory suggested building another city just outside of Tierit," I explain, looking over at him and Sorik. "The new city would be a home base for Sentinels who want to integrate back into the supe world. It would be close enough to Tierit to take advantage of their resources and protections, while keeping Tierit separate and safe for the Sentinels who want that."

"Smart," Bastien observes.

I nod and try to stifle a yawn. Everyone else in the car starts yawning too like it's contagious, and I chuckle.

"So what do we do while all of that gets sorted out?" Valen asks.

"Well, first, we all sleep for like a month because we've fucking earned it," I announce.

Everyone laughs and voices their agreement.

"We get the word out slowly that the Sentinels are back, and then we start setting up the infrastructure *we* need to get Vigilantes R Us up and going."

Bastien and Valen both crack up at the name and shake their heads.

"We're not vigilantes, remember? We're all legit and shit now," Bastien teases.

"I know, but Legit Legion just didn't have the same ring to it," I joke, and we all dissolve into slaphappy, sleep-deprived giggles.

I'm pretty sure we're never going to find a name that encapsulates who we are and what we want to do. I wipe laugh tears from my face, and I'm not even sure what any of us are laughing about anymore. We turn down the road that leads to the main street that runs through the heart of Solace, and my dad grows quiet as he stares out the window.

"You okay?" I ask him quietly while the others pitch out more horrible names for our group and continue to crack themselves up.

He gives me a warm smile. "Yeah, kid, it's just weird being back here. It's as if nothing has changed, it all looks the same, and yet everything I know and everything I am is so...different."

I look around and understand exactly what he means. The guys and I drove away from Solace with nothing but questions and each other. Now we're back, and it makes everything we've gone through feel even more surreal.

The paladin drive into a parking garage, and we all park side by side. I smirk at the paladin as they unload from their SUVs with surprised looks on their faces. They look confused as fuck that Sorik, Siah, and Vaughn are alive and well.

"Sentinels," I call out to the paladin, and they turn to me.

"What?" the leader asks.

"We're Sentinels," I offer, but he just looks even more perplexed. "Don't worry, you'll be learning more about our kind soon," I explain.

Sabin puts an arm around me, and I lean into his side as the paladin escort us into the building. He smiles down at me, and I tilt my head up and purse my lips. He grins and leans down to give me the peck I'm demanding.

"What's that smile all about?" he asks, his eyes lighting with affection.

"Feels good not to have to hide what we are anymore," I answer simply, and he looks away in thought.

"It does," he agrees and then drops his lips to mine for another quick kiss.

We're led into an all too familiar room, and I try to shove away the memories that come surging back of the last time we were here. I can practically see Lachlan and his coven sitting off to the side of the room like they were last time. Images of my Chosen being forced away from me flash before my eyes, and I have to breathe deeply and let the panic and anger that surges through me settle.

There's a table where I sat last time and then the viewing area behind it, where the guys sat. I move to stand in front of the table, and my Chosen, dad, and Sorik arrange themselves on each side of me. Paladin settle into guard positions throughout the room, and thankfully we're not made to wait long before the door to the side of the elevated seats the elders like to sit in, opens.

The big Polynesian-looking Elder Kowka walks out first. I have to stop myself from rubbing the rune I now have because I magicjacked it from him. He's followed by Elder Nypan, who offers me a wide friendly smile. A younger gentleman walks out next, mushroom brown hair and dark chocolate eyes taking all of us in. He must be a replacement for Elder Balfour or Elder Albrecht now that they're dead.

Elder Cleary walks in fourth, his blue eyes immediately searching for his son. His brow furrows when he quickly notices that neither Enoch nor his coven are here. And lastly a familiar face joins the elders up on their dais of power. I give him a warm smile, and Paladin Ender quickly mirrors it.

"How much arm twisting was involved to get you to say yes to this gig?" I ask him, amusement ringing in my tone.

He chortles and looks over at his compeer, Elder Cleary. "I don't think anyone was more surprised by my getting voted in than me," he admits.

"So who's in charge of the paladin now?" I ask.

"Still me while we vet potential replacements," he answers with a tired smile.

Elder Cleary clears his throat and sends me and Paladin —or I guess he's now Elder Ender—a look that says it's time to get down to business.

I take a deep breath and wait.

"I see my son is not with you?" Elder Cleary starts.

"No, he and his coven stayed back to help with things there. I'm sure when he's able to call you, he will," I reassure him, and I can see concern leak out of his gaze.

"And exactly where is the *there* you're referring to?" Elder Kowka asks.

"*There* is Tierit, which we also call Sentinel City. And as far as its exact location...that's none of your business," I answer.

The term *Sentinel* doesn't seem to confuse any of the elders the way it did the paladin outside in the parking garage, and I figure it's safe to conclude that Elder Cleary has let them all in on what I am.

"We are your elders. You are required to answer our questions or face the consequences for refusal. You'd do well to remember that," Elder Kowka snaps at me.

"Actually..." Valen interjects. "We are a Diplomatic Envoy on behalf of the Sentinels of Tierit. You are speaking to Vinna Aylin of the Quorum, and the Right Hand to the Sovereign who rules over all Sentinels. And you'd do well to remember that," he finishes, glaring at Elder Kowka.

"Boom! Mic drop," Knox announces in my mind, and I have to try hard not to laugh. I look over and notice all my Chosen are working to keep smiles off their faces too. Elder Kowka narrows his eyes slightly but keeps his mouth shut. He looks over at Elder Clearly like he's no longer sure what to do. Elder Cleary leans back in his seat and studies us.

"So there are more?" Elder Nypan asks, his tone filled with awe.

"There are," I answer simply, loving the fact that it's true.

"And what is the purpose of your Diplomatic Envoy?" the elder I don't know asks.

"To establish relationships with other supernatural races and help pave the way for the safety of Sentinels in this world," Sabin recounts.

We sound legit as fuck, and I can't help the pride I feel looking over at my Chosen as we claim our seat at the table.

"Silva described you as catatonic, Paladin Aylin. I'm glad to see he was wrong," Elder Cleary states, changing the subject.

"That's Sentinel Aylin, Elder Cleary, and no one is as glad as I am that I'm perfectly well," my dad responds, and I don't miss the bite in his tone.

"Where is Silva?" Bastien asks.

"He is out on assignment with his new coven," Elder Ender answers simply.

Bastien looks over at me, and I shake my head. He was right. They're not going to punish his uncle for what he did. Irritation bubbles up inside of me.

"Well, you guys won't be the only deciding factor when it comes to shit like that anymore," I announce.

"And exactly what does that mean?" Elder Cleary demands.

"It means that there needs to be a shit ton more checks and balances to make sure situations like Elder Albrecht and Adriel don't happen again. Or where paladin are torturing lamia, or lamia hunting Sentinels, or any of the other fucked up things I've uncovered since I joined this community," I tell him.

"None of you are paladin," Elder Cleary announces. "You will not be allowed back in the Academy to become paladin either since you're no longer casters." He eyes my Chosen like he's looking to see if that hit landed. "You have no authority to weigh in on any decisions we make or how we make them."

"Fuck your Academy," I tell him dismissively. "We'll build our own if we want to." I take a step forward and feel every paladin in the room tense. "We may not have *your* authority, but don't think that means shit, because we don't need it. Feel free to test that anytime you want, we'd be happy to show you just what we're capable of."

"Is that a threat?" Elder Cleary asks.

"No, it's a warning. We'll be respectful and fair in our dealings with you, just like we will in our dealings with all supes. But if you fuck with us, you'll start a war I promise you won't be able to win. I want you to think long and hard about that before you attempt to flex any level of authority over us or try to tell us what we do and don't have a say in," I tell them, looking each of them in the eye, the *just try me* clear in my defiant gaze.

I don't want to start shit with the casters, but I can't have them thinking they're the top of the magical food chain anymore either. It's like Getta said, if you're not happy being the roots or the trunk, there's going to be problems. We all have to figure out a way to be happy being the roots so we can all grow together and make the strongest fucking tree out there. I release a weary breath.

"We're going to leave now. We've had a long trip, and we're tired. Elder Cleary, you're more than welcome to check your attitude and then stop by later in the week with your mate and compeers. I'll be happy to fill you in on what's going on with Enoch and his coven then. As for the rest of you, if you need something, send a *polite* request for a meeting. If you send paladin or attempt to escort us anywhere or limit our movements in any way, we'll consider it fucking with us and act accordingly."

I offer a stiff smile and turn around to leave. I pass the guys and walk toward the doors we entered through. A paladin male stands in front of them, and I watch the tic in his jaw as uncertainty flashes in his eyes. He looks past me, clearly searching for instruction. I don't slow or falter as I close the distance. This guard and whether or not he'll move or try to stop us is about to set the tone for our dealings with the Elders Council of the Solace casters.

I don't want to kill this guy, but I wasn't kidding when I told them not to fuck with us. I'm four feet away when I see the guard tense like he's readying for a fight. I get ready to call on weapons and warn the guys to do the same, when the guard reaches for the door handle and pulls it open. Relief washes through me, but I don't bat an eye as I walk right out the door and then out of the building to the parking garage. Thank fuck they chose the easy way. Here's to hoping they keep that shit up.

"Fuck that was hot," Torrez announces as we approach our SUVs.

I laugh and then roll my eyes. "Let's go home," I order, happiness and hope settling in my chest.

And in unison, my Chosen shout out, "*Dibs*!"

36

SIX MONTHS LATER

I park the Jeep and open my phone to double-check that this is where I'm supposed to be. I'm in the middle of fucking nowhere, staring at a small cabin that sure enough has the correct address carved into the side. I turn off my car and hop out, gravel crunching under my flip flops. I trudge down the thin path to the front door and knock hard.

"This better really be an emergency, Mave, because I was supposed to meet Cyndol for a super-secret training, and you know how hard it is to arrange those between her overprotective dads and the Captain," I shout out, banging on the door again when no one immediately answers.

"And this better not be another whine fest about the treaty with the Volkov pack. Tell Alpha Silas that he agreed to this months ago and they're going to be here next week no matter what. Even if they all do look like Brun, he still has to hold up his end of the bargain," I declare. "I should have never let the twins show him that picture of her. He's been a little bitch about all of this ever since," I grumble and finally hear footsteps hurrying to the door.

The door swings open, revealing my spitfire of a best

friend on the other side and the shit eating grin she's wearing on her face. I take one look at her and immediately get suspicious.

"Vinnnnnn," she coos at me, ushering me inside the small, mostly empty cabin.

"If this is you trying to convince me to talk to Pebble about the pros of a harem, I'm leaving now," I tell her, my tone adamant. "Once was bad enough. Never again."

She laughs and herds me further into the cabin. "No, this is not about that," she declares. "I already heart you fucking forever for doing that, and I have high hopes that fucker will pull his head out of his ass and embrace the ways of his people."

I chuckle and shake my head. "Yeah, I wouldn't hold your breath," I tell her.

She rolls her eyes. "He's not going to have any choice if my wolf claims another wolf. Even if we could convince my pack that a match between one of their precious females and a caster male was written in the stars, there's still a chance that someday my wolf might find another wolf and just decide they're hers," she tells me with an exasperated huff.

I pull her in for a hug, and then we both plop down on two wooden chairs.

"It'll work out the way it's supposed to," I reassure her.

I know Pebble is fucking madly in love with her, and I suspect Mave feels the same way about him, but their relationship is the definition of unconventional in these parts, and I don't think it's going to be the easiest road for either one of them. I wish I could smooth it all over, but that's just not how life fucking works. All I can do is support and be there for her and help her navigate the boulders that get thrown in their way.

"Anyway, this is not about me, this is about you," she tells me with a sneaky smile.

I narrow my eyes at her and lean back in my chair.

"Vinna. I am here to stage an intervention," she announces, and she looks proud as fuck as she does. Her milk chocolate brown eyes radiate excitement, and she grins and tucks her bright pink hair behind her ears.

I snort and look at her like she's lost her mind.

"Between your training with Hot Wekun and Beat Yo Ass Granny, Getta. The building of Sentinel City..."

I laugh just like I always do when someone mentions the name of the home base city the Sentinels have been working on. I still can't believe everyone agreed to just call it Sentinel City. I mean, yeah, I guess it is self-explanatory which is a good thing, and yes, that's what we called Tierit before we knew it was Tierit. I just really thought Suryn would choose something more flowery or regal sounding. But nope, now we have Tierit and an *official* Sentinel City.

Go figure.

Mave shakes her head at me, giving me a look that tells me she knows exactly where my mind just went.

"With the start of your Superhero Services and brokering deals with the other supes in the area, you aren't making time for your Bonding Ceremony," Mave scolds.

I huff and try not to roll my eyes.

"Mave, the guys and I decided it wasn't necessary. It's a caster tradition that connects mates in a way we're *already* connected. And don't worry, we do plenty of *bonding* every day. Like sooooo much bonding," I tease.

She snorts and slaps my leg. "God, I'm so jealous," she grumbles and stands up so she can pace and talk with her hands in a way that's all Mave. "Okay fine, you guys are all in loooove and the ceremony is redundant, but you all deserve a moment to just celebrate. *We* deserve a moment to just celebrate," she adds, circling a finger around her own head. "You've all been through so much; don't you just want to have a day to dance and laugh and enjoy what you all have together?" she asks me.

I smile as I watch her move around the room, and throw my head back in defeat.

"Okay fine," I relent. "I'll talk to the guys about it tonight. I can't promise anything, but if it will get you and the sisters off my back about this ceremony, then I'll try at least," I tell her with a playful glare.

The door opens, and in flit the sisters. Confusion streaks through me, and I look from them to Mave, trying to figure out what the hell is going on. Mave claps excitedly, and her voice goes all high-pitched.

"I was hoping you'd say that, Vin, because we already talked to your guys...welcome to your Bonding Ceremony!" she exclaims, and I look around the small empty cabin, even more confused.

"Here?" I ask, perplexed.

Mave rolls her eyes. "No, not here, silly. We're just getting you ready here. The party has been set up just inside the trees."

"Wait," I tell them, shooting out of my chair. "You planned a Bonding Ceremony, and you're just going to spring it on me like that?" I ask, looking at Mave, Lila, Adelaide and Birdie in turn.

"Pretty much," Mave confirms, and I snort out an incredulous laugh.

"Mave's right, my love, you all deserve a day to just celebrate what you have," Birdie tells me.

"And the guys are all cool with this?" I ask.

"They helped set everything up," Adelaide reassures me.

"So that's what they've been up to," I mumble, and the sisters giggle.

I laugh and shake my head. "Fine. Fuck it, let's do it," I tell them with a shrug.

Mave whoops and the sisters clap. Lila darts out of the cabin and comes back minutes later as Birdie and Adelaide are fussing over me in the chair. Mave already has a curling iron in my hair, and I'm still trying to figure out where it came from. Lila hangs a dress bag on the curtain rod above the front window, but Mave repositions my head to keep me from staring at it. The question of what's in the bag is gnawing on me despite everyone's efforts to chat and keep me distracted.

I never got to the *so what do we wear* part of the Bond Ceremony conversations. Is there a wedding dress, some kind of gown or robe that casters specifically wear? I have no fucking clue. I sit silently as they titter all around me, exuberant energy coating everything in the room. Mave parts my hair down the middle, and soft curls fall around my face and shoulders. She takes some of them and pins it back into a half-back, half-down style, while leaving pieces down to frame my face.

The sisters apply a little makeup, and the next thing I know, we're all staring at the dress bag, and I'm being asked if I'm ready. I shrug because I don't fucking know. Mave laughs at my response as Adelaide reaches up and slowly unzips the long bag hanging from the curtain rod.

My heart speeds up to a gallop as I stare at what is most definitely a wedding dress. It's a strapless dress covered in different patterns of intricate lace. The snow white lace lies over a nude underlay that just takes the dress to a whole other level of beautiful. It's exquisite, and I feel like I could sit here all night and just stare at the patterns. The room is oddly quiet as I take a step toward it and lift a hand to run my fingers over a familiar symbol.

"We had your Chosen runes hidden in the design of the lace," Birdie tells me, her voice reverent and loving.

"In caster tradition, the females in your family all sew blessings into the patterns of the lace," Lila explains, running a finger over small words that are hidden amidst a floral pattern.

I spot the word *love* and then *laughter* wrapped around the lace petals of a flower. *Home* and *family* peek out from some delicate leaves. There are sentences about always finding my way and trusting my bonds sewn into a line of lace that looks like beads. The more I look at the dress, the more I see messages of love and acceptance. I'm touching the hopes and dreams they have for me and my Chosen, and it's all woven into the very fabric of not only me but now this dress too. I blink back my emotions as I take it all in.

"I don't even know what to say," I tell them in a hushed tone filled with awe and appreciation.

I run my fingers over the word *treasured*. It's hidden in a pattern of lace that dips in a *V* down from my bust to my waist. It breaks up the floral patterns on the dress and is accentuated by the beaded patterns that *V* and crisscross in different places.

"It's so far beyond perfect," I tell them, and I know I'll feel more than treasured tonight and for the rest of my life.

I pull the sisters and Mave into a massive hug. "Thank you," I tell them, hoping those two words convey just how grateful I am for each of them. They all took me in and accepted me with no hesitation or reservations, and it changed everything for me.

"Let's get it on," Mave commands, her words more of a squeal as she pats her cheeks dry. I laugh and strip down, eager to see if this gorgeous dress will fit as perfectly as it looks like it will. I step into it, and Birdie zips me up. It hugs my body like a second skin until mid-thigh, where it slightly flares out. I feel dainty and feminine, and covered in the blessings and adoration of the women I love.

"You look stunning, Vinna," Lila tells me as she wipes at her eyes.

"Don't you start, Lila! You're going to set us all off, and then we'll really be in trouble," Mave scolds. We all chuckle and try to get a hold of ourselves.

Adelaide darts to the window and peeks out. She looks up at the sky and smiles. "Right on time," she announces.

She claps her hands together and orders her sisters and Mave to get dressed really quickly, and they all dart off. I run my hands down the tight bodice of the dress and feel...beautiful. Someone knocks on the door, and I debate for a second if I'm supposed to answer it. No one else comes out to do it, and I figure that pretty much solves that question. I pull the door open to find my dad. His face lights up when he sees me, and then he steps back so he can take me in.

"Kid..." he trails off, and then he takes a moment to breathe through the emotion I see take over.

"You're the most beautiful thing I've ever seen," he whispers, wiping at his eyes.

I blink back my own tears, and he pulls me in for a tight hug.

"Love you," he croaks as we pull apart.

"Love you," I counter and wipe at my cheeks.

Shit, I hope I didn't mess up anything the sisters did too badly.

"Ladies, I'm taking her down," my dad shouts into the small cabin.

"We'll meet you there," Mave hollers back, and he chortles and shuts the door behind us.

He puts his elbow out for me to take. I smile and wrap my arm around it. We start to walk toward the tree line, and I can tell sunset is quickly approaching.

"So were you in on all this too?" I ask as a welcome breeze winds around us to help chase some of the heat away.

"Guilty," he admits with a smile.

I shake my head and give his arm an affectionate squeeze. He squeezes me back and lets out a deep content sigh.

"Who would have thought this time last year that you and I would be here now...like this?" he states, gesturing to my hand in his.

"I know. I was training with Talon and fighting. I didn't really see anything beyond that," I confess.

"I'm glad he looked out for you," my dad states. "He was rough around the edges but a good guy nonetheless. I owe him a lot."

My grin grows wider. It's a perfect description of who Talon was.

"We both do," I agree.

We make our way slowly through the trees, and I take in the birds chirping and the smell of pine and soil.

"Thank you, Vinna," my dad tells me quietly, pulling me from my thoughts.

"For what?" I ask, searching his face for an answer.

"For finding me...fighting for me...giving me this," he tells me, patting my hand. "After how Lach was...well, you didn't have to believe in me the way that you did," he finishes quietly.

My dad has done nothing but apologize for Lachlan and what went down between us. No matter how much I try to make him understand that it's not his fault, I don't think he'll ever see it the way I do.

I can just make out some lights through the trees, but I stop and pull him to a stop too.

"Thank you for wanting to be a part of this," I tell him,

resting my palm on my chest. "With everything you went through, you could have seen me as a trigger, as something that reminded you of everything you lost..."

"No, kid, I could have never seen you that way. You were the light, Vinna. You always have been, and you always will be the light that came from the darkness."

I wipe at a tear that moves slowly down my cheek.

"Love you, dad."

"Love you, Vinna."

He pulls me in for another tight hug, and we stand there for a moment in the middle of dusk kissed trees, our love and gratitude radiating off both of us.

"Now..." he tells me as he pulls back, "let's go dance until we're sweaty and laugh until our cheeks hurt!"

37

We walk out of the trees to find people all gathered around in a massive circle. I'm not sure if one of my guys mastered fairy light or if there's a supe here that wrangles lightning bugs for fun, but tiny lights are everywhere, illuminating the ever growing night. Beautiful pinks, reds and oranges streak across the sky as the sun dips lower and lower. The entire scene is breathtaking.

My dad leads me toward the gathered people, and slowly they part to let us through. I spot members of the Silas Pack and the elders. Knox's family waves at me excitedly, and I return it as we move deeper and deeper through the gathered people. I spot Cyndol and Sabin's family, and I give her a teasing look that says *I know you were in on this*. She beams back at me, and I find myself once again wondering how long we're going to be able to keep our training together secret from her family.

Cyndol gets more and more shredded every month, and I know it's only a matter of time before someone asks why and how. I just hope by then they can all see her as more than some fragile caster female that needs to be coddled and caged. Cyndol is a warrior through and through.

My eyes land on Sorik. His blond hair is pulled back, and his face is lit up with happiness. I reach out the hand not holding my dad's and pull Sorik out of the gathered people. I wrap my arm around his just like I did with my dad's and let them both escort me to wherever it is we're going. Sorik may not be my biological father, but his love and protection is one of the reasons I'm even here. He's the most selfless being I've ever met and the best second father a girl could ever hope for.

He bumps his shoulder with mine, and his smile is beaming, and I mouth *love you* to him as we continue to make our way through the crowd.

"No fucking way!" I declare when my gaze lands on Tok and Marn.

I stop mid step and stare at them, worried if I blink, somehow they'll disappear. I step away from my dads and pull Tok and Marn into a tight hug.

"How are you here?" I ask, confused and elated.

"Suryn sends her best," she tells me simply, and I shake my head, stunned. My Tok and Marn are standing right in front of me—in Solace of all places. The reality that Sentinels are getting closer every day to re-entering the world hits me, and I'm simultaneously ecstatic and fucking nervous. I step back from them, and Tok immediately wraps Vaughn up in a hug, and Marn tackles Sorik.

Just when I think my smile can't get any wider, it does. I don't even have words for how it makes me feel to see Tok and Marn treat my dads like the sons they never had but always wanted. Over the past six months, the four of them have developed such a beautiful relationship that it just makes me grin like a fucking loon whenever I'm in its presence. The hug fest and subsequent tears wrap up, and I'm once again on my dads' arms, making my way to the center of the circle.

Mave and the sisters are somehow down here, and I look at them and then behind me, like somehow that's going to reveal how the hell they got down here so fast. I shrug and let it go. I'm sure it's the sisters' sneaky magic at work. Aydin's giant self is behind them, beaming at me like I'm all that's precious and good in the world. Evrin seems to be vacillating between elation for me and amusement for Aydin's over-the-top grin and leaking eyes. I chuckle and smile brightly at them both. Aydin wipes his eyes and then steps to the side.

Suddenly, there they are. My breath hitches as I take them in. They're in white also. Fitted, textured leather pants and a tunic-style linen shirt that comes down to their thighs. The hem of the shirt is asymmetrically longer on one side. A patterned leather vest tops it all off, buttons running from the top of their left shoulders to the bottom of the vest. There's an interesting kurta feel to the look and yet also a hint of Renaissance.

They look incredible, standing shoulder to shoulder in a circle, emotion swimming in their eyes as I make my way closer. I'm overwhelmed with gratitude for these males and everything we've been through together. I love them so much and can't even imagine a life or future without each of them in it.

The circle widens to let us through, and my dads place me in the very center of it all. I hug Sorik and then Vaughn and watch them leave to join the others all gathered around me. Bastien, Valen, Ryker, Knox, Sabin, Torrez, and Siah tighten their circle around me until their gorgeous and loving faces are all I see. I move in a slow spin as I look at each of my mates. Love and admiration war with so many other emotions that reinforce our connection and deep rooted bond, and I count my lucky fucking stars that they are mine.

"Vinna Aylin," Bastien starts, and I spin until my eyes are locked on his hazel gaze. The extra green around his pupils sparkles with happiness, and I grin like a love sick fool at him.

"You are my life. I love you, and I cannot wait to spend the rest of my life with you and with my compeers. I vow to honor and protect you. To guide you and to be guided by you. I vow to keep our bond strong and to be there for not only you, but for each other too," he tells me, gesturing to my other mates. "You are ours and we are yours. Nothing will change that until the day we both breathe our last breaths. I declare this bond unbreakable, and I will work to make it so."

My eyes well up at his declaration, and I move so that I can kiss him. Valen's voice ringing through the night stops me in my tracks though.

"Vinna Aylin, you are everything to me. I love you with everything that I am, and I know that love will still continue to grow as we tackle life together. I vow to honor and protect you. To guide you and to be guided by you. I vow to keep our bond strong and to be there for not only you, but for my compeers too. You, my love, are ours and we are yours. Nothing will change that until the day we both breathe our last breaths. I declare this bond unbreakable, and I will do everything in my power to make it so."

Valen's gaze is filled with fire, and it sears his vows into my soul. I stare back at him with the same intensity, making it clear that I feel exactly the same way.

"Vinna Aylin," Ryker calls out. I turn to him, my heart already filled to bursting with love. "You are my Squeaks," he announces, and a rumble of laughter moves through the crowd around us. I chuckle and shake my head.

Fuck, never going to get rid of that nickname now.

"You are strength and honor and all things right. I love you for all that you are and all that I am now because of you. I vow to honor and protect you. To guide you and to be guided by you. I vow to keep our bond strong and to be there for not only you, but for our family too. I vow to stand aside and let you claim who you were meant to be. And I vow to heal the hurts and make sure that we are always stronger because of them. You are ours and we are yours. Nothing will change that until the day we both breathe our last breaths. I declare this bond unbreakable, and I will always make it so."

Ryker's full lips taper up into a breathtaking smile that feels like home. I want to wrap myself in his arms and ensure that he always feels as cherished as he makes me feel.

"Vinna Aylin," Knox calls to me. I laugh when I turn to him, my favorite cheeky grin stretched across his beautiful face. His gray eyes are filled with love and mischief, and it's one of my favorite sights to see. "You were mine from the first minute I saw you," he declares, and I beam at him. "I claimed you right then and there in my mind, because I knew without a shadow of doubt that if I didn't live the rest of my life basking in your strong and beautiful soul, that I wouldn't be living at all."

I wipe at a tear that tries to sneak down my cheek and watch as Knox's stunning gray eyes well up with emotion.

"I vow to honor and protect you. To guide you and to be guided by you. I vow to keep our bond strong and to be there for not only you, but for my compeers too. I vow to trust you in all things, and I vow to always fight by your side. You are ours and we are yours. Nothing will change that until the day we both breathe our last breaths. I declare this bond unbreakable, and I will battle to make it so."

"Vinna Aylin," Sabin starts.

His smile grows even bigger as our eyes meet.

"I didn't know what to think when you first walked into our life. You were fierce, honest, stunning, and I was at a loss."

Sabin and I both chuckle.

"I'm not at a loss anymore. I know exactly what to do with the fierce, honest, stunning female before me. I simply love her. Vinna, I vow to honor and protect you. To guide you and to be guided by you. I vow to keep our bond strong and to be there for not only you, but for my compeers too. You are ours and we are yours. Nothing will change that until the day we both breathe our last breaths. I declare this bond unbreakable, and I will do everything possible to make it so."

"Witch," bellows out into the darkening night.

I laugh.

"You challenged me, called to my wolf, rejected me, and then saved me in every possible way. You came out of nowhere and hit me like a freight train."

Torrez clutches his jaw playfully, and people around us crack up.

"Where you go, I go. I will follow you to the ends of the earth and back again, grateful for every second because I get to claim you as mine. I vow to honor and protect you. To guide you and to be guided by you. I vow to keep our bond strong and to be there for not only you, but for our pack too. You are ours and we are yours. Nothing will change that until the day we both breathe our last breaths. I declare this bond unbreakable, and I will ensure that it always remains so."

A howl starts up around us, and goosebumps rise up on my arms. Torrez throws his head back and adds his voice to the call of his former pack, and I'm taken aback by how beautiful he is in this moment: wild, free, mine. I throw my head back and join in too, and one by one the rest of my Chosen add their voices. Out of nowhere, everyone around us joins in. I'm beyond touched by the beautiful way they support my Wolf, and us.

Fairy-light-fireflies float above our heads as the moon comes out to bless us and the stars start to blink away. Howls fill the night air and slowly begin to quiet and taper off. I look back to Torrez and wonder how there was ever a time I didn't see that he was mine and was always meant to be.

"Vinna Aylin," Siah declares with a sweet smile. "I was lost and then you found me. You are the compass that will always guide me home. I love you. I vow to honor and protect you. To guide you and to be guided by you. I vow to keep our bond strong and to be there for not only you, but for my compeers too. You, my mate, are ours and we are yours. Nothing will change that until the day we both breathe our last breaths. I declare this bond unbreakable, and I will do whatever is needed to make it so."

Siah's vow resonates around me, and I wipe at my eyes. Everyone grows quiet, and I look around to see what happens next.

"Bruiser," Bastien whispers, and my eyes snap to his. "It's your turn," he tells me, and my smile falters slightly.

"Shit! Okay," I state, and our friends and family laugh.

I want to punch Mave in the boob and ask her why she didn't warn me that I'd need to do a whole speech thing. I take a deep breath and look around at my Chosen.

"I love you, each of you, and I will live every day making sure all of you know and feel that. I vow to honor and protect you," I start, repeating the vow each of them made to me. "I vow to guide you and to be guided by you. I vow to keep our bond strong and to be there for all of you, no matter what. I vow to laugh with you, cry with you, fight *for* you and *beside* you. I vow to choose you today and everyday forever. You are mine and I am yours, and nothing will change that, ever. When we die, I'm tracking you fuckers down. There's no escape now," I tease, and my voice cracks with emotion. "We are unbreakable. What we have together is unbreakable, and we will fuck anyone up who tries to mess with that."

My Chosen laugh, and so does everyone around us.

"Do we get to make out now?" I whisper to Torrez, and he chortles and shakes his head.

"No, we get to party now," he shouts out into the crowd gathered around us, and everyone starts to cheer.

Torrez sweeps me up in a hug, and I'm promptly stolen from him and wrapped up in Siah's arms. I'm stolen and passed around until I've hugged and declared my *I love yous* to each of my guys.

"So was that it?" I ask Sabin as he sets me back down on my feet and plants a way too quick kiss on my lips.

"Well, normally there's the magic stuff that goes down after that, and then we'd all be expected to go to our designated bonding house and finalize the bonds the magic started to put into place, but we're already connected, so we're going to skip that part and celebrate with everyone else," he tells me, his smile contagious.

"So you're telling me that we could be off fucking right now, but instead, we're going to mingle and macarena instead?" I ask.

Sabin's features become horrified. "Of course not...we would *never* macarena, Vinna. That's not how Sentinels roll," he deadpans, and I pinch his nipple.

Sabin hops back away from me with a wide grin, and I glare at him. Ryker watches the exchange and laughs.

"What's wrong, Squeaks? We thought group sex freaked

you out?" he asks innocently, but the amused twinkle in his eyes gives him away.

"We were just looking out for you, Witch," Torrez teases, and somewhere behind us music starts up.

"Mi Gente" by J Balvin and Willy William starts up, and Torrez's eyes flash with excitement.

"That's my jam," he declares and reaches for my hand. "Come grind on me, Witch," he tells me and starts pulling me toward the area that's slowly gathering dancers.

"Don't worry, Vinna," Knox calls out to me. "We have big plans to ravage you as a group *after* the party!"

My tummy flip flops inside of me, and my vagina and clit high-five each other. My hips start working it to the rhythm of the music, and Torrez gives me an appreciative growl. I spot Tok and Marn talking with a few of Knox's dads. I just catch Trace asking Tok if he is team Edward or Team Jacob as Torrez and I pass by, and I lose it.

I shout out, "Team Jacob," and then throw my head back and howl. Once again all the shifters and a good number of the casters join me, and I point to the rising howls in the air as proof that Knox's dad's love for sparkly vampires is misplaced.

He points at me and gives an outraged laugh. "How can you still claim Team Jacob when you have a lamia for a mate also?" he questions.

I look over at Siah and give him a wink. "My lamia could kick your Edward's ass any day of the week," I challenge playfully.

Trace gasps and presses his palm to his chest like he's clutching his pearls in indignant shock. "Sumo!" he demands, and I laugh even harder.

"If you think I'm letting my mate cover that gorgeous dress and body up with a sumo suit, you're crazier than

Edward Cullen was for leaving Bella," Knox scolds his dad as he sweeps in and rescues me.

"My hero," I coo to him as both he and Torrez pull me closer to the dance floor.

"That fool probably has those suits in the trunk of his car. Just wait, somebody's going to be sumo-ing by the end of the night," Knox declares, and I laugh hard because he's probably right.

"Ooooh, let's make Elder Cleary sumo someone," I announce, and Valen fist bumps me.

"Vinna!" Mave calls out to me. I look around and find her holding up a shot glass. "Moonshine!" she shouts out, and I chuckle and make my fingers an *X*.

"Oh hell no! I learned my lesson last time," I shout back, and she laughs.

"Here's to my future harem," she toasts, and when she goes to bring the shot glass to her lips, Pebble comes out of nowhere and plucks it from her hand. He downs the shot and then throws Mave over his shoulder. She laughs and looks up from his back.

"This is not the last you've seen of me," she declares like some B movie villain.

Pebble slaps her ass and carries her out of view. I laugh and shake my head and continue to move toward the dance floor, ready to get my grind on. I spot Aydin's big ass moving through the crowd, and I shout for him to come join us. He has a phone in his hand and a serious look on his face that instantly makes me pause. Our eyes connect, and I see relief and...guilt?

Why do I see guilt?

"What's wrong?" I ask him as he and Evrin make their way over to us.

"Shit, I'm sorry, Vinna, but I just got a call from an Alpha Vorenno. He heads a large pack over in Montana, and he's had several females go missing in the last couple months," Aydin tells us, shouting over the loud music and the partying going on all around us.

"He just had another female go missing, and he's called us to see if we can help figure out what's going on," Aydin finishes, and shock surges through me.

"He called us...as in Sentinel us?" I ask, needing to wrap my mind around what he's saying.

"Yes," Evrin shouts out so he can be heard over all the noise.

"I'm really sorry, Vinna, I know this is all of your big night, but he sounded desperate. This will be the fifth female that's gone missing from his pack. He's not getting any cooperation from the other packs, and his relationship with the casters in the area is not good," Aydin tells me.

I turn to the guys, excitement and shock on my face. "Holy shit, we have a job, guys."

They all beam back at me, the same surprised excitement written all over their faces.

I pat Aydin's shoulder. "Don't be sorry, someone is asking us for help; that's a good fucking thing," I reassure him.

"Well, fuck. Okay then. Let's go," I announce, and we start to move away from the dance floor.

I spot my dads and wave them over to us.

"I have the plane on standby and ready to go when you are. I also have clothes ready in the SUVs. Your Tok and Marn brought a ton more of that Narwagh armor you guys like, so I have kits with all of your clothes in all of your vehicles. I'll stock up the plane too when we head out," Evrin tells us.

"You guys are the best," I tell them, and we all pick up the pace and move in the direction Aydin leads us.

"Okay, Aydin, fill us in on what we need to know," Sabin orders.

"The most recent female taken was a ward of the Alpha. I'm not clear on all the details, but his raising this female is what created an issue between him and the local casters. All the other females taken were all in their mid-twenties, all dark hair, all disappeared in the middle of the night. Alpha Vorenno had the last two females under guard when they disappeared, and they can't find any trace of how it happened. No scent of magic or other shifters," Aydin explains.

"Any bodies show up?" Valen asks.

"No, but the third female who was taken, trackers found a lot of her blood about twenty miles away. They have no idea what it means, and scenes like that haven't been discovered for any of the others," Evrin tells us.

"Shit. This sounds like a fucking doozy of a case," Torrez observes, and I nod.

"It is, that's why they're calling you," Aydin states, his eyes radiating his faith in us.

Nerves and excitement flash through me.

Our first job.

Our dream of taking cases and helping just became a reality.

What we're walking into is daunting, but I've never felt surer that this is what we were made for. I take a deep breath and put my game face on.

Let's fucking do this.

The End

AUTHOR'S NOTE

If you're like, I need more!!! You can't just leave some open ended questions like that!!! Fear not, I got you. The next series in the Sentinel World is the Shadowed Wings series and it starts with The Hidden. You'll find answers, new characters, and some beloved old ones between the pages of these next books.

I'm working on the third Sentinel World Series now. I'm hoping it will be out in spring of 2023.

Love you!!! Thank you for trusting me, and for reading, reviewing, and for all of the support!!! Tackle hugs!!!

Come hang with me on Instagram, my Facebook Reader Group, TikTok, BookBub, my Facebook page, or my website for updates on this series and more.

ALSO BY IVY ASHER

The Sentinel World

THE LOST SENTINEL

The Lost and the Chosen

Awakened and Betrayed

The Marked and the Broken

Found and Forged

SHADOWED WINGS

The Hidden

The Avowed

The Reclamation

MORE IN THE SENTINEL WORLD COMING SOON.

Paranormal Romance

Rabid

HELLGATE GUARDIAN SERIES

Grave Mistakes

Grave Consequences

Grave Decisions

Grave Signs

THE OSSEOUS CHRONICLES

The Bone Witch

The Blood Witch

The Bound Witch

Fantasy Romance

Order of Scorpions

Shifter Romantic Comedy Standalone

Conveniently Convicted

Dystopian Romantic Comedy Standalone

April's Fools

IVY ASHER

Ivy Asher is addicted to chai, swearing, and laughing a lot—but not in a creepy, laughing alone kind of way. She loves the snow, books, and her family of two humans, and three fur-babies. She has worlds and characters just floating around in her head, and she's lucky enough to be surrounded by amazing people who support that kind of crazy.

Join Ivy Asher's Reader Group and follow her on Instagram, TikTok, and BookBub for updates on your favorite series and upcoming releases!!!

facebook.com/IvyAsherBooks

instagram.com/ivy.asher

amazon.com/author/ivyasher

tiktok.com/@ivy.asher

bookbub.com/profile/ivy-asher